PRAISE FOR HILARY DARTT

"It was very hilarious, had loads of funny accidents and still had a way of being sincere and romantic … I also liked how much it was based around friendship, which added a nice, fresh take on a romance story. This is easily a five-star read."

NATURAL BRI BLOG

"Hilarious, truthful, and a little tear jerking. I think we all know someone that resembles Delaney and the girls. Great read."

BECKY PONSTEIN

"This book was a heart breaker but full of spirit. I loved it. I loved how the relationships evolved, fell apart, and came back stronger than ever. Pass me a vodka cranberry, please, and a box of tissue."

AMANDA THOMAS

ALSO BY HILARY DARTT

The Intervention Series

The Marriage Intervention

The Motherhood Intervention

The Garden Club Series

Jasmine's Pact

Studying Sequoia

Just Holly

The Seedling Homestead Series

The Composition of Order

The Architecture of Vision

The Structure of Perfection

THE DATING INTERVENTION

BOOK ONE IN THE INTERVENTION SERIES

HILARY DARTT

For my family.

CHAPTER ONE

EIGHT YEARS AGO

IT WAS time for Delaney Collins, doctor of veterinary medicine, to rethink her life.

She was just getting started, really. She was one year into her career as a veterinarian and the job—which she'd considered a calling for years—had seemed perfect. Until now.

The phone call she'd just received confirmed what she'd suspected all along: she was a fraud. She couldn't handle a serious situation, wasn't cut out for it. Pressing her lips together as hard as she could, in an effort not to cry, she placed the phone's handset in the receiver. Then, she took off her doctor's coat—the one she'd had embroidered with her name one year ago to the day. She crumpled it up, threw it in the trash, and walked out of the building.

Yes, she had patient appointments lined up. One of the other vets was on vacation and Delaney was covering for her. But this was a defining moment, one where Delaney realized that despite a four-year postgraduate degree, she wasn't cut out to work in a field that put someone's life in her hands.

As she got into her car, the tears flowing freely from her eyes and streaming down her face now, she replayed the events leading up to this epiphany. It started three days ago, when the Desert Veterinary Clinic's receptionist, Barb Dennis, paged Delaney over the intercom, her smoke-infused voice carrying a touch of humor.

"Doctor Collins, your favorite patient is in exam room five."

Delaney saved the chart she was working on and picked up the phone, dialing the front desk.

When Barb picked up, Delaney said, "Howie and Max?"

"I gave them to you—"

"Again."

"Again," Barb confirmed, "because you're the only one who's nice enough to give Max a full exam, every single time Howie brings him in."

"He's sweet."

"He spent the past five minutes talking to me about the new crosswalk signal at Central and Third," Barb said.

"There's a new crosswalk signal?"

"Apparently. One that begins the countdown before an old man and his old dog can make it halfway across the street."

"Huh," Delaney said. "What'd he bring Max in for, today?"

"Depression."

"All right," Delaney said. "I'll go in now."

"Hey, didn't you double major in psychology?" Barb said before Delaney hung up.

"Yeah," Delaney said. "But not dog psychology."

Human psychology told Delaney Howie was lonely. An eighty-four-year-old retired high school teacher, he'd spent most of his life surrounded by people. But he was slowing down, and couldn't get out as often as he used to. Max was an English Bulldog whose age in dog years most definitely exceeded Howie's. The pair of them were in at least once a week, and because she was the newbie, the other vets at the clinic let her handle Howie's increasingly frequent appointments. Delaney didn't mind. Probably because she was the newbie, she found them charming. She enjoyed hearing Howie's stories about his days teaching English, how he'd made his students sing jingles at the start of every period, and how he'd put on weekly competitions to encourage them to learn Latin roots.

And because she was the newbie, she completely missed the fact that there really *was* something wrong with Max this time. That's when Dr. Collins made a terrible mistake, one from which she could never recover, professionally or personally. If that mistake had affected Max, and Max alone, she could have gotten past it.

But, two days after that appointment, it spread. Three days after that appointment—significantly, on the anniversary of her signing hiring papers at Desert Veterinary Clinic—she received the phone call that proved she wasn't capable of something this serious. And she quit.

She went back to the cozy safety of her small hometown, promising herself she'd never get a life-and-death job again, and furthermore, that she'd never tell anyone—not even her best friends—what she'd done.

CHAPTER TWO

PRESENT DAY

THE MOMENTS where life seems perfect (or at least, perfectly mediocre) usually signify things are about to go awry. Maybe even Very Awry. Like an opalescent bubble, the illusion can burst in an instant.

Delaney Collins had just arrived at that realization for the second time. At thirty-four, just when her life should be taking shape, it had instead come to an abrupt halt.

"Fail-proof! It was supposed to be fail-proof!"

Delaney shook the last few drops of her Guinness into her mouth. She set the empty bottle down with more force than she meant to and flinched, although she figured no one else in Rowdy's Saloon noticed. The laughter, the cheering and the twinkling colored lights directly contrasted and probably amplified Delaney's sour mood, and they served as decent camouflage for her outburst.

"Nothing's fail-proof," said her best friends Summer Gray and Josie Garcia.

Summer shrugged one shoulder and added, "Except abstinence."

"Which Summer has obviously not been practicing," Josie said.

Summer elbowed Josie, amusement making her nose crinkle. "Funny. Four kids is a nice, even number."

The girls, assembled at Rowdy's for their weekly Happy Hour meeting, sat around their usual high-top table. Josie traced the rim of her glass with a fingertip and narrowed her eyes at Delaney.

"Seriously, though. Nothing's fail-proof. Especially when it comes to dating. Did you really think *any* dating system could be fail-proof?"

"I need another beer."

Delaney looked around Rowdy's for the server but he was busy passing out flaming shots to a group of sales sharks in loose ties. She put her head on the table and sighed.

"How could this have happened?"

She didn't realize she'd spoken out loud until Josie answered. "We've known you for twenty years, Dee," she said. "And I have to say, since you ditched veterinary medicine and moved back to Juniper, things just haven't been the same."

Delaney sat up, and Josie covered Delaney's hand with her own. "I mean, I never would have said this nine years ago when you were at the University of Arizona kicking ass with that crazy class load, or when you graduated and were kicking ass as a veterinarian, but today, my sister, it's no real surprise you've just been dumped by three–count 'em: *uno, dos, tres*–guys in two days."

Oh, that.

Not that Summer and Josie even knew why she'd stopped working as a veterinarian and come back to Juniper. But still. If her life was so obviously on the wrong track, why hadn't they said something before now?

With growing embarrassment, Delaney looked first at Summer, then at Josie.

"Wait. Are you saying it's me?" She didn't wait for a response. "You are, aren't you?"

Summer and Josie exchanged a look. Summer's attention snapped to the ice cubes floating in her glass. Josie stared at a spot on the table.

The answer rolled through Delaney's awareness like lava.

Finally, Summer spoke. "Delaney Collins," she said in what Delaney always referred to as her Mom voice. "You know it's you."

"You know that as your honorary sisters, we're bound to be honest with you. And you're the common denominator," Josie said. Her voice sounded cheerful, but her smile was sad.

Delaney was half-joking when she asked, "What does that mean again, Mrs. Garcia?" but Josie's answer stung.

"It means you're the one thing all three of your boyfriends have in common," Josie said.

"They're not my boyfriends," Delaney said.

"They're just guys I'm dating," Summer and Josie said in unison, their tone mocking.

Delaney flinched. She could hear herself saying these same words over and over during the past several months. Years, maybe.

"It's semantics," Josie said. "You know what we mean. It's not that there's anything wrong with *you*, exactly, it's—"

"Can we talk about something else?" Delaney said. She hated the defensiveness in her own voice and tried to soften it. "Summer? Any good yoga classes lately? Josie? Have you been shoe shopping?"

"You're not getting out of this conversation," Summer said. "What Josie's trying to say is that you always choose the wrong guys. To be honest, I'm not even sure I know what your system is. Was. Whatever. What is it?"

"It's an informal system."

"Are you talking to us or the table?" Josie asked.

"The table. You guys are bitches."

The girls laughed, which broke the tension enough that Delaney responded.

"It's a system that allows me to select between three and five men, each of whom fulfill a different need. I.E. a sex god, a philosopher and an adventure hound."

Summer rolled her eyes and Delaney continued. "This system ensures I have a constant flow of social engagements and, more importantly, at least two backup men if something, you know, fails to work out with one of the men."

Summer nodded. "So tell us what happened, exactly. How'd you end up single for the first time in years?"

"Hasn't she always been single?" Josie said.

"Josie! Seriously!" Delaney felt herself spluttering.

Is it true? Delaney dug into her memory. Yes, she was always dating someone … but no, she was never truly *with* a man. A tiny voice piped up inside her head: *Maybe you do have issues!* She silenced it. Who were Summer and Josie to have such strong opinions on her dating life? They'd both been off the dating scene for years.

"Well, you have," Josie said. "When is the last time you were in a committed relationship you actually cared about?"

"And speaking of that," Summer said, "have you ever really thought about the future? I mean, do you plan to just keep dating several men at once, perpetually? And working at a bar?"

She looked around Rowdy's, and then locked her eyes on Delaney's. "It's about time you put that big brain to use again. You didn't do a double major for nothing."

"Yeah," Josie said. "Who gets degrees in psychology and veterinary medicine? At the same time? You have a gift, sister." She tapped the side of her head with her pointer finger."

"You do," Summer said. "And the pets of Juniper need you. Surely, there's an open veterinary position somewhere in town."

Instead of answering, Delaney picked up her Guinness bottle again. Still empty. Her last real relationship had been a long time ago. At the time, she thought they were committed to each other and she thought of nothing other than their future. That turned out to be a complete waste of energy. Not to mention the heartache involved. And veterinary medicine? She couldn't do it. Ever again. Forget about the big brain and the expensive degree. She wasn't cut out for it. Her stomach swirled at the thought.

"Yep, your beer's still empty," Josie said. "Hey, you work here. Go get another one so we can finish this conversation. You can't even remember your last actual relationship, can you?"

"Josie," Summer said. "Of course she can remember. It was that guy, what was his name? The one who always wore his hat slightly off-kilter and didn't tie his shoes. Tom? Travis? Tyler?"

"Oh yeah," Josie said. "But does that even count? He totally cheated on her."

"Of course it counts," Summer said. "I mean, he put a ring on her finger, didn't he?"

Yes. Tucker (not Tom, Travis or Tyler) had cheated on Delaney. Heart in a scramble, mortified beyond belief, Delaney had decided then that she'd never again put all her dating eggs into one faulty man basket. Even a man basket who somehow managed to swing a two-carat diamond ring. Because he bought one for his other fiancée, too, even while Delaney was selecting tiger lilies and oysters for their upcoming wedding. And he ended up marrying that Other Girl, while Delaney spent what should have been her own wedding day in mourning. Now, five years later, she still felt the sting. And while her friends meant well, their dismissal of her heartbreak as insignificant hurt her feelings.

"Which, may I remind you ladies," she said, holding up her pointer finger, "is exactly why I created this fail-proof system."

"Right," Josie said, relentless. "But it failed. Why don't you tell us about that?"

Delaney propped her chin on her hand, hoping the casual pose did something to conceal the depression that had started to sneak in. "Mark—"

"Steamy Mark Cortez?"

"Yes. Steamy Mark Cortez. He's totally changed. Which I don't want to talk about. Obviously."

"Obviously," her friends said.

"Changed, like, swore off sex? Or changed, like, morphed into The Beast or something?"

"Summer. He changed, like, he wants to get married."

For the briefest of moments, Delaney's best friends sat in stunned silence.

"Whoa, crickets," Delaney said. "Did you not think anyone would ever want to marry me?"

"It's not that." Summer said. "You're better than a strawberry shake."

Delaney grinned, remembering the moment they'd come up with the little compliment. It happened in seventh grade, when Delaney gave her crush, an eighth-grader named Joe Jansen, a note asking if he wanted to go out with her. A week passed, and Joe Jansen had yet to respond. To be fair, Joe, the all-star athlete with a razor-edge crew cut, and Delaney, with her frizzy hair and forty-pound backpack, didn't quite fit into the same category. Dejected, Delaney pouted all day Friday. To cheer her up, Summer suggested the three of them go out for milkshakes. While they sat around the table at the ice cream shop, Delaney wondered aloud what was wrong with her, and Summer responded, "Nothing's wrong with you. You're better than a strawberry shake."

The three of them had used that phrase as a pick-me-up hundreds of times since.

"It's not that," Summer said again. "It's just that we can't believe you let him believe that was possible."

What is wrong with my friends? Delaney plowed on. "Zachary is philosophically superior. Which you probably already knew. He's always spouting off about some stupid paper or another and–"

"—and Xander?" Summer said.

Delaney put her forehead down on the table. "Sexually unsatisfied. And I need to be more honest with myself."

"Are you *kidding*?" Josie threw her hands up in mock exasperation, but her eyes twinkled with mischief and something else. "*Dios mío!* He said you need to be *honest* with yourself?!"

"I can't tell if you're joking or not," Delaney said, pouting into her empty bottle.

Joe Jansen had finally answered Delaney's note the following Monday, telling their entire pre-algebra class she was a dumb dumb dork for writing it in the first place. He'd written *NO WAY* in response to her, *Would you like to go to the movies with me?* and waved the note around for the whole class to see.

More than ready to think about something else, Delaney pointed to a black and white photo on the wall. In it, a cowboy, arm stretched above his head, rode a bull whose feet hung high above the ground in a twisting jump.

"That's Mark," she said. Then, pointing to a placid donkey standing in the background, she said, "That's Xander. It's no wonder we broke up."

She looked up just in time to see Josie nod at Summer, who nodded back and took a deep breath.

"Delaney," she said. "We have a … proposal for you to consider."

"Well, it's not up for consideration, exactly," Josie said. "It's more like a requirement for your love life."

"You've *talked* about this!" Delaney said. "You guys have been discussing my love life!"

"Of course we have," Summer said, placing a hand over Delaney's on the table.

"And not just your love life," Josie said. "Your whole life."

Summer added, "We've been discussing each other's lives, love or otherwise, since we were what? Fourteen?"

"That's true," Josie said. "Since we started calling ourselves the Milkshake Sisters. Remember when you guys made me that little quiz to help me decide whether I should kiss Elijah Parker behind our seventh grade homeroom?"

"Minus one point for the pimple on his nose. Add one for his cute smile," Josie said.

"He sealed the deal when he offered to carry your lunch to the cafeteria," Summer said.

"Three points," Delaney said. "Pushed him right into the 'definitely should kiss him' category."

"Ah, those were the days," Josie said.

"Anyway, Delaney," Summer said, anxious to return to the subject at hand, "your love life is like our love life."

Delaney looked at Summer and raised her eyebrows. Both Summer and Josie were married and Summer had a handful of kids. More than a handful. Their love lives were as much like Delaney's as a Fairmont is like a Motel 6.

"Well, okay," Summer said. "It's not. Not exactly. But that's what we want to talk about."

Josie cleared her throat. "We want to try an experiment."

"An experiment?" Delaney repeated.

"Yes," Summer said, drawing out the word.

Josie inhaled deeply.

"Um, okay," Delaney said. Was she actually feeling nervous? After the conversation they'd just had, it was no surprise. "What is it?"

"For the next six weeks," Josie said, her dark eyes boring into Delaney's, "you relinquish control of your dating life. Summer and I make all the decisions. You make none."

"Wait. What? I make none of the decisions?"

"Well, you can decide what to eat for breakfast."

CHAPTER THREE

It happened on Tuesday. The morning after Mark Monday. Delaney marched down the freshly salted sidewalk, relief and disappointment wielding swords at each other in her mind as angry tears blurred what should have been a picturesque snow-covered downtown Juniper.

Not twelve minutes earlier, she'd been cocooned in satin sheets and post-coital steam in Mark Cortez's apartment.

"Oh, Delaney," Mark said.

His caramel skin still warm from sex, he stretched his lithe, supple body alongside Delaney's and ran a hand up her side to her shoulder. They'd woken up to the bright silence of snow. It was undoubtedly the last storm of the season, and through the window, the world sparkled.

The perfect setting for romance. Or, at least, great sex.

It was the sort of morning Delaney loved, the kind where she could lounge around for several hours before allowing responsibilities of the unpleasant kind to sneak in. In fact, eleven a.m. had just ticked by, which meant Mark still had time to make coffee and bring it to her in bed before showering. They'd just sneaked in one more round of luxurious lovemaking. Her two favorite things: coffee and sex with Mark. Beyond blissful, she thought.

"Hmmm," Delaney responded, her eyes closed.

"You're delicious."

She chuckled.

"Look at me," he said.

She turned over, forced her eyes open and was surprised by the intensity of his expression.

"Wow. You've never looked so serious in the whole seven months we've been together," she murmured, although the warm and fuzzy sleepiness was quickly replaced by something she vaguely recognized as alarm.

"Yes," he said slowly. "Well, this is a serious topic. And for serious topics, I need a serious face."

Alarm gave way to panic, which set in with a swiftness that reminded Delaney of an avalanche—massive chunks of snow thundering down a mountainside. Her heart pumped adrenaline-spiked blood through her body. Her fingers tingled. She braced herself for disaster.

"Oh," she managed. "Coffee? We haven't even had coffee, yet."

"I need to ask you something," he said.

Her eyes flickered down to his bare chest, his muscular stomach.

He can't do this. We agreed it wasn't going to be serious. Is he really about to do this? She wondered if he had a ring stashed somewhere. She hadn't felt it on the bed any time during the past nine hours, since she arrived breathless with anticipation just after two a.m., having received Mark's mouthwatering text.

I am waiting for you.

At the time, the message shot a surge of heat right down to her center. Her carnal side looked forward to Monday nights more than any other night of the week. She almost always stopped by Mark's house on her way home from work for a session (or two) of healthy ravishing.

But this? Had he planned to pop the question all along? If she'd known, she probably would have skipped last night. She had to get out. Delaney scrambled to her hands and knees, looking for her underwear.

"It's on the blue chair," Mark said, pointing to the side chair, which sat at least fifteen feet away in the living area of his studio apartment. Ah. There it was. She shivered, remembering what he'd done last night as he peeled it off and flung it aside.

"Just settle. I want to ask you something."

She put her hands over her face.

"Hear me out, Delaney," he said. "Sit still."

"Fine." She sat down on her knees. "What is it?"

"Don't you think it's time we both moved on?"

The sound of a record screeching to a halt.

Moved on? Does he mean move on together or apart?

If it was even possible, her heart started to pound harder. Black swirls danced before her eyes. They often joked about how Mark misused American expressions. Was this one of those times? Or did he really want to break up?

"Move on?" she choked.

"Yes. Move on. Go our different directions. Stop seeing each other."

Wow. He was definitely using *those* expressions correctly. This was so far from what she'd expected. Relief made a brief appearance, but indignation quickly yanked it offstage to step into the spotlight.

"So… let me get this straight. You let me come over, have sex with you, lay in bed naked with you … and you planned all along to break it off with me?"

"Don't lift your voice."

She leapt off the bed and stalked over to the blue chair. The shiny hardwood floor felt cold on the soles of her feet.

"Have you been planning this?" She finally untangled her panties and put them on, wobbling madly from one foot to the other.

"No. Delaney. It's just that I–"

"You what? You wanted to knock boots one more time before you broke it off?" She found her shirt under the bed.

"I didn't plan this, Delaney."

"You just told me I was delicious." She pulled her shirt roughly over her bare breasts.

"You *are* delicious," he insisted. "So much so."

"But you want to stop seeing me." Her voice cracked.

Mark flopped onto his back, rubbed his hands over his face. Delaney took in the soft hair on his chest, his chiseled abs, his hipbones. The way the silky cream-colored sheets made his dark skin look so tan and smooth. She remembered the first time she saw him, last summer when he came into Rowdy's after the first festival of the year on the courthouse square. He stood at at the bar, staring at a photo of horses drinking from a river, looking very much like he belonged in an advertisement for a couples' resort. Or a phone sex hotline. At the same moment Delaney realized she was staring, he looked up and caught her. He grinned, walked over to her, and said, "I was just wishing for a beautiful woman to explain to me this art."

Now, even though they were on the verge of being over, Delaney wished she could have sex with him just one more time. Feel his broad, warm hands on her skin, his mouth on her neck…

"Delaney, do you want to hear my question? I wanted to ask you something. Remember?"

Reluctantly, she pulled herself out of the daydream. Realizing she'd frozen in place, one leg in her jeans and one leg still bare and planted on the floor, she gave herself a little shake and continued getting dressed. What was wrong with her, daydreaming about sex with someone who was trying to break up with her? What was wrong with him, trying to break up with her while she was still naked in his bed?

"You just asked me a question."

"That wasn't *the* question."

"Right. Ask me your question. Ask me *the* question."

"Are you ready to settle down?"

She stopped flouncing, pulled up her pants. He'd caught her off guard.

"What kind of question is *that*?"

Of course she wasn't. Settling down ultimately meant heartbreak, she knew that. Which is why she wasn't interested in settling down.

Shit. If I could guarantee myself that I'd never get my heart broken, I'd settle down right now. But I can't.

"Delaney. When we first started dating, it was you who wanted to keep things light. You didn't want to get serious. You've said that over and over since we've been together. I get it, I do. But I'm almost forty, Delaney. It's time for me to find someone to marry. Someone who will have my children. Someone as delicious as you who also wants to be with me. Forever."

He was right, of course. She *was* delicious. And she wasn't ready to settle down.

"Besides," he continued. "I saw your face when I first said I wanted to ask you a question. You should have seen it." He rubbed a hand over his mouth. "You were totally freaking."

She buttoned her jeans and sat on the edge of the bed. When she'd arrived at Mark's the night before, she'd thought the storm clouds outside had made the room, with its cheerful fireplace, cozy. But that fire had died hours ago and now, it just felt gloomy.

"Why today, Mark? Why did you text me, seduce me, as always, let me stay over, and then break up with me?"

"I enjoy you, Delaney. I enjoy our time together, our conversation, our delicious—what did you call it—knocking shoes. I enjoy all of it very much. But last night and this morning, lying here with you, I started thinking, I could do this forever. Every night. Every day. With you. But you can't do it with me. You're not ready. It's time for me to move on. I don't want to change you. But I know you can't be with me. And so, I must let you free."

Twelve minutes had passed since that conversation. Delaney had put on her shoes and coat, kissed Mark good-bye and was now walking down the sidewalk. And when she thought of how Mark had told her not to lift her voice this morning, she burst into tears, a full-on ugly cry, right there on the side of the road. She would miss him. His glittering honey-colored eyes, his lean muscular body, his quick, witty sense of humor. Out of all the guys she had dated recently, Mark had been her favorite. If some weird game show or end-of-the-world disaster scenario forced her to choose a man to be with exclusively, it would be him.

But he was right, she thought as she watched her breath turn to steam. She wasn't ready to settle down, not really.

This is the whole reason you designed your fail-proof dating system—so you'd always have a backup. Look at it this way: You can now begin the hunt for another sex machine. Won't that be fun?

The thought provided enough comfort that she was able to tamp down the sobs and continue walking, although a stray tear or two escaped every couple of minutes.

It's not like you'll be alone. Suck it up, Collins. You've always sworn crying over a guy was lame. Unless it was because he was so good in bed he made you weep.

She shook her head. She still had two more options. It was not quite noon, which meant it was early enough to salvage the day.

DELANEY FOUND Zachary while she was trawling a post-poetry-reading crowd for a philosophical, sensitive man to add to her dating roster. This morning, he answered on the first ring.

"Del! How are you?"

Yikes. I never noticed how high-pitched his voice is. Nothing like Mark's.

"I'm great! Are you hungry? I was just calling to see if you wanted to grab some lunch."

"Uh…yeah. Okay. Sure, let's grab some lunch. I need some fuel."

Had she imagined it, or did a slight hesitation precede his "yeah"? She was probably still sensitive from Mark's breakup, that was all. Zachary adored her.

"I'll pick you up," she said.

During the five-minute, three-block stroll from Mark's apartment to Zachary's tiny cottage, Delaney smoothed her short blond hair into a ponytail, put on lip gloss and powder, and prayed that her cheeks weren't still aglow from sex with Mark. Even if they were, she could attribute it to the cold. Despite it being almost noon, icicles still hung from the eaves of the little downtown shops. People walked the side-walks bundled up in puffy jackets, scarves and hats, their rosy noses just peeking out. She remembered she wasn't wearing a bra, and hoped Zachary wouldn't notice. She poked herself in the side of the nose when she put on her mascara, and spent the rest of the walk licking her finger, rubbing her nose and hoping she'd gotten it all off.

It wasn't that she'd told Zachary or Mark (or Xander, either) that they were exclusive. But it wasn't like they knew about each other. It had worked this way for months now. She always had options, always had something going … all her needs were met. And until this morning, she'd thought all theirs were, too. Why tinker with a good thing?

Zachary opened his front door. His smile didn't quite reach his eyes. *You're just being paranoid. He always smiles like that.*

"Hey," he said, reaching out and squeezing her shoulder.

"Hey," she responded. "You know, if you're too busy for lunch, we can just skip it. I can grab something from The Sand Witch."

"Nah, it's okay. I've got to eat, anyway, right?"

As Delaney attempted to quell the sense of foreboding growing in her stomach, Zachary shut and locked the front door, and they walked companionably toward the downtown square, side-by-side but not touching.

Instead of focusing on Zachary's cool reception, Delaney thought about the town of Juniper as they walked. The quaint little city had always been home. Nestled into northern Arizona's pine-covered mountains, it was cozy and absolutely imperfect for a single woman in her thirties.

Its turn-of-the-century downtown plaza featured perfectly manicured lawns, a bubbling fountain, and huge shade trees bordering all four sides. Boutiques, galleries, and restaurants lined the square, bringing tourists and locals into town year-round. Delaney loved everything about it. She loved that she could walk from her house to the square in less than ten minutes. She loved that she could shop for perfect, unique gifts, interesting books, and fun outfits without driving across town. She loved that she almost always saw a familiar face and that the people in her favorite shops knew her by name.

She inhaled the clean scent of the snow, smiling to herself.

"It snowed?" Zachary asked.

"Obviously," she said. It was almost noon, and he was so wrapped up in whatever he needed fuel for, he hadn't even noticed?

"What are you working on?" she asked, softening her tone.

"Oh, it's a new paper about John Dewey."

"Who's that?"

"He was a philosopher. One of the developers of pragmatism. Where should we go?"

"What will best nourish your huge brain?"

He chuckled.

"The Sand Witch sounds fine."

Delaney later thought she should have noticed Zachary's strange behavior. He barely spoke during their walk to the deli, ordered a plain turkey on rye rather than his usual Italian sub, and ate only half of it while Delaney wolfed down her veggie sandwich. For once, they ate in relative silence.

"So, no new opinion on gun control?" Delaney said, wiping the avocado off her fingers with the thin brown deli napkins.

"Not today," Zachary said.

"What about taxes?"

He didn't answer.

"You look tired, Zachary. I think you're working too hard."

"It's not that. Delaney–"

She held up a finger.

"You don't have to explain. You're allowed to have a biorhythm. This is just a low-energy day, right? I'll walk you home, drop you off and leave you to your herbal tea and philosophy paper. I just expected a zinger with you today after I saw yesterday's story on the news about the tax increases. But it's totally fine."

Zachary's thin chest rose and then fell. His light blue eyes, practically invisible through the layer of grease on his glasses, didn't meet hers.

"Delaney," he started again.

Oh, shit. Shit, shit, shit. You have to be kidding me.

Blake, the brawny owner of the deli, had stopped moving around in the kitchen. He stood behind the counter, drying blue plastic cups. He took off his chef's hat with a meaty hand and used the dishtowel to wipe the sweat off his head. Delaney wondered first if he'd keep using that towel to dry cups, and then she wondered if he was eavesdropping. She closed her eyes.

"Delaney," Zachary said again, "you know I really enjoy our conversations, right? I really enjoy our time together. But the thing is, I need to close this chapter of my life. I'm going for my tenure at the college, and I need to focus on my work. It's very important."

"And I'm *not* important?" she whisper-yelled, opening her eyes to glare at him.

Blake resumed his cup-drying. Sure enough, he continued using the towel he'd used to wipe his head. Delaney made a mental note to order bottled drinks from now on.

"Of course you are, Del. But that's exactly why you deserve someone who can devote more time and energy to you. More spirit."

"Of course you'd say something like that," she said.

Hating herself for the bitterness in her voice, she stood up, almost knocking over the tiny table, covered in its green and white checkered cloth. She threw her greasy, balled-up napkin onto her greasy paper plate.

"Forget my offer to walk you home," she said, infusing her voice with as much coldness as she could. She pulled her coat off the back of the chair, which tipped over. She scrambled to pick it up.

Just as she shoved through the glass door, making the bells jingle wildly, Zachary caught up with her.

"You're a free spirit, Del. You deserve to fly."

The door shut behind them.

"I admit, that's a good sound byte," she said. "But what is it, really? Why don't you want to be with me?"

Zachary looked down. Either he was looking at his feet, or he'd discovered a new bug species, Delaney wasn't sure. She just knew he wasn't looking at her.

"Del, when we first met, you were a breath of fresh air."

"King of clichés today," she muttered, struggling to get her coat on, annoyed that Zachary wasn't helping her. He'd never been big on manners, though. That was one of the things she'd so loved about Mark. Her eyes burned with the threat of tears.

"You were so fun, so full of life. Your eyes! They're so green. They just sparkle with mirth. I loved arguing with you, debating with you, just being around your ... energy."

Sparkle with mirth? How lame is that? "But?"

"But you're exhausting. I can't keep up with you. I was telling the truth, before, when I said I need to focus on my work. I really do. If you weren't so ... argumentative, so ... challenging, I could do both. But you drain me."

Ouch.

For the briefest of moments, Delaney felt like crying—again. Zachary was dumping her. *He* was dumping *her*! This was very depressing.

Am I really draining?

CHAPTER FOUR

SHE SHOULD HAVE SEEN IT COMING. BUT WHAT WOULD SHE HAVE DONE? Avoided Xander completely? Beaten him to the punch? She wouldn't have done either, she knew. Especially because she hadn't yet replenished her back-ups after Mark and Zachary ended things. And so it probably all would have played out the same way. In the end, she would still have ended up alone and lonely, the dating system she'd designed as fail-proof having failed. Completely.

After leaving The Zachary Scene, she called Xander to see if he wanted to go rock climbing or kayaking. No answer. That should have been her first clue, since he almost always picked up, but she persisted.

Finally, after she worked out, called Xander, showered, called Xander and ate a container of leftover cashew chicken from Red Lantern, she tried him again.

He finally answered.

"Hey," Delaney said. "You sound tired."

"What's up?"

"Oh. Okay," Delaney said, suddenly feeling awkward. She got off the couch and went to the kitchen to finish cleaning up the cartons from her lunch. "Well, I was calling to see if you wanted to go climbing out at the dells today, maybe after I drop Summer's kids off?"

"I can't today."

"Oh. Okay. Big plans on your day off?"

"We need to talk."

Dread, which had appeared at the murky bottom of her consciousness at the start of this phone call, came clawing its way to the surface. Delaney stopped cleaning and plopped down on the ottoman.

Maybe I should just hang up now. Pretend I lost the connection.

"Seriously?"

"Uh. Yeah, Delaney. Seriously. We need to talk."

She closed her eyes. Swallowed. Put a hand over her mouth to stifle a groan.

"Okay. Lay it on me."

She flopped onto her back so her head hung off one end of the ottoman and her legs off the other.

"When we're together, we have so much fun. You know? I love the climbing, the kayaking, the camping. Hell, I love the grocery shopping. Everything with you is an adventure."

That doesn't sound so bad.

"So …" she said.

"So," he repeated. "Everything is an adventure. Except the sex. I know you're with me, here. We like, barely ever have sex."

It was true. She just wasn't that attracted to him. Tall, thin, bordering on gangly, Xander probably weighed a buck fifty soaking wet and carrying a dumbbell or two. A large nose, small jaw, and perpetually grimy fingernails made him look like a caricature of himself.

"I mean," he continued, "can you remember the last time we did it?"

She thought back. "Oh! Yeah, I can. It was that time we went to the hot springs and you attacked me under that waterfall down the path."

"Do you remember when we went there? It was the weekend after Labor Day. We waited the extra weekend so we wouldn't have to deal with the crowds."

"Labor Day," she repeated in a wooden-sounding voice, calculating the time that had passed since then.

"Five months. A man can't go that long on a regular basis."

"I could do better," she lied, grimacing even as she said it.

"No, you couldn't. And neither could I. I think we both know we're more like brother and sister than we are like lovers."

She never considered that Xander felt the same way she did. She always figured he just wasn't that sexual, and that was only when she thought about it. Mark had sated her needs at least once every week. Maybe that was why she hadn't even considered Xander's needs.

"Could we still hang out? As friends?"

"No. We can't. I'm seeing someone else."

"Why didn't you say so?"

"You know I really like you. But I think it's time you started being honest with yourself."

What was this, The Delaney Life Review?

"Honest with myself?"

"Yeah. You don't want to be with me any more than you want to go to the dentist every six months. And I know I'm not the only thing in your life you feel that way about. Honesty, Delaney. It's the new black."

Time marches on, Delaney thought. Dejected or not, it was Carpool Tuesday. She'd just picked Summer's three oldest kids up from school.

It seemed only natural that after being dumped (not just by one guy, but by three in the span of a few hours), Delaney hit every red light during this trip. Here she was, for the first time in months with absolutely no romantic prospects, and the Universe was playing cruel jokes on her.

Her mantra, "It's a new beginning," wasn't helping at all.

Now she sat at the intersection of Highway 23 and Pinecone Street, waiting. Again.

The loud squeal of tires pierced Delaney's thoughts, and instinct had her looking in the rearview mirror. A huge black pickup truck came barreling toward the back of the van. She knew right away that the driver wouldn't be able to stop in time, and she squeezed the steering wheel, bracing herself for impact, mentally flicking through images of ice patches she'd seen all over town since leaving the school parking lot.

Nope. There is definitely no way he can stop in time. Oh, shit. He's really going to hit us.

She had nowhere to go. Neither did the truck. Squeezing her eyes shut didn't help, but at the last second she lifted her foot off the brake pedal. The truck slammed into the back of the van, and the impact sent the van lurching into the intersection. Delaney glanced to her left at oncoming traffic, and then gunned it, accelerating forward to avoid being T-boned.

"Well, that's a first for Carpool Tuesday," she muttered, concentrating on breathing deeply to slow her heart rate.

"Aunt Dee?" Summer's daughter, Sarah, squeaked from the back seat.

"Are you guys okay?" Delaney said.

"What just happened? Did someone hit us?"

"Sarah, we're fine, honey."

"Does our car still work?"

"Yes, Luke. The car still works."

Delaney looked for a place to pull over. The only option was a driveway about twenty-five yards up the road.

"You don't look fine, Aunt Dee."

"I'm fine. I was just surprised, that's all. Are you guys fine?"

"Mom's gonna kill you," Nate said.

"Well, you know I'm not your real aunt, right? So she can't actually kill me. It's against the rules to kill your best friends."

Delaney pulled the van into the driveway of Porky's Barbecue, parked, and turned off the engine. As she dug around in the glove compartment for the insurance card, her hands shook so badly it was a minute before she was able to get through the Legos and Lincoln Logs to the small slip of paper.

"Wow! That was awesome! Did someone just, like, hit us?"

"Yeah, someone rear-ended us. Stay in the car. It's freezing and I don't want you getting run over. I'm going to check the back, make sure there aren't any dents or anything."

"Luke, that is so *not* awesome," Sarah said as Delaney opened the door.

She stuck her head back in. "Quit bickering, you two. Luke, it's definitely not awesome. Your mom's going to be upset if something happened to the van."

"What about us? What if something happened to us?" Nate said.

"Oh, Nate. You're fine. It was nothing more than a bump." She infused her voice with a forced cheer she hoped would cover the shakiness of her nerves recovering. "Like bumper cars."

She shut the door. Out in the crisp, fresh air, she took another deep breath, willing her hands to stop shaking. It really had been a little bump, she thought as she walked around the back of the van. In fact, the bumper looked perfect, as if nothing had happened.

But still.

Delaney stood, hands on hips, watching the line of traffic move forward once the light at Pinecone Street turned green. The black pickup truck wasn't slowing down to turn in behind her as she'd assumed it would. In fact, it was speeding up. It whizzed by and the driver didn't even spare her a glance. Disgusted, she shook her head and climbed back in the van.

The kids pelted her with questions: "Is there a dent?" "Do we get a new car?" and "Is our car broken?" But she tuned them out, quickly dialing Summer.

"Hey, Summer," Delaney said when she answered. "We're okay, but some jerk rear-ended us at Twenty-Three and Pinecone. Some asshole in a pickup truck. And he just drove off."

"Shit," Summer said. "Watch your language. Are the kids okay? Are you?"

"Yeah. We're all fine. The van is fine. Now I see why Derek insisted on you buying this monstrosity. Not even a scratch. Anyway, we were stopped at the red light and he was trying to stop when he hit us. It's icy, you know? Not a huge impact."

"Thank goodness. Asshole. Did you call the police?"

"No. Should I?"

"Of course! Delaney, that's a hit and run! It's illegal. Call them, and call me back. Do you want me to come over there?"

"I have your car."

"Right. Okay, call the police and call me back," Summer repeated.

"Okay. Oh…"

"What? Are you okay?"

"Yeah. Someone just pulled up. It's a guy. He's getting out. And oh – he is *very* good-looking. Very. Call you back."

Dirty, scuffed brown cowboy boots, dusty ripped jeans, and a light blue t-shirt. *So yummy.*

"Hey," the man said.

Delaney couldn't stop herself from taking inventory: eyes the color of cobalt made contact with hers, and light stubble accentuated the planes of his face. He looked Greek, she thought, like Adonis. Longish, curly hair, full lips. He'd parked in the row behind Summer's van, and now bent down to inspect the bumper. Could this be the first man to fill an empty slot on her dating roster?

"I saw what happened." He straightened up. "Are you okay?"

"Oh yeah," she drawled. "I mean, it's fine. We're fine. I checked the car, it's fine."

You're fine.

"Are you sure you're okay?"

He squinted, leaned forward to look into her eyes. She nodded mani-acally, all the while wondering what he'd look like as a bare-chested marble statue.

"It's a big van. Full-size. And size *does* matter."*Oh, my God. Shut up, Delaney. Shut up. Snap out of it. This isn't like you. You're acting like a twelve-year-old girl. You're acting like the twelve-year-old you.*

The man chuckled.

"Have you called the police?"

"Nope. Nope, I need to do that. Thanks for reminding me."

"Uh, I think I'll wait with you. I got the guy's license plate number."

He handed her a green sticky note, and she noticed his tidy writing and his sexy worker's hands and muscled forearms. Unconsciously, she wiped her mouth and dragged her eyes back to the sticky note. The letters and numbers lined up perfectly. Delaney turned her back to him while she dialed the police, gave the report to a dispatcher.

When she turned around, she saw that he had turned away to make his own phone call, and she studied the fit of his jeans. Snug over a tight rear end and a strong-looking set of legs. When he shrugged, she watched the muscles in his back ripple. She didn't notice he'd hung up until he was walking toward her.

"Uh, I should check on the kids," she said as her face grew hot.

He followed her. For once, the kids sat quietly in their seats. Three pairs of bright blue eyes framed by thick black lashes blinked back at her.

"Are these all *your* kids?" the stranger asked.

She twittered, high and nervous.

"No! I mean, they're great kids but no! I don't have any kids. Not married. See?"

She held out her left hand, wiggled her fingers. Thought, *Oh, my God. What am I* doing?

"These are my friend's kids. Summer. It's Carpool Tuesday. They get out of school a couple hours early, and her baby's still napping. So I pick them up for her. Sarah, Luke, Nate. Say hi, guys."

"Hi," they chorused.

"What's your name?" Nate wanted to know.

"Jake," the stranger answered. He smiled for the first time since he'd pulled up, and Delaney almost swooned. She'd always wondered what swooning really was, and how it happened. Now she knew.

His teeth were square and white and slightly crooked. Lines deepened around his eyes and she thought she detected a dimple on his left cheek.

"Delaney," she said, sticking her arm straight out to shake hands. "Delaney Collins."

"Jake Rhoades," he said.

She held onto this hand for a little too long. Long enough to notice it felt as good as it looked: calloused and sturdy. Fortunately, a police cruiser pulled into the parking lot before she had a chance to rip his shirt off. She and Jake Rhoades filled out accident reports. The police officer, a stocky fellow who'd probably been on the force as long as Delaney had been alive, checked the van for damage.

"Good job getting the plate number," he said to Jake. "I'll run this guy and see if we can't find his address. Sure you're okay, ma'am? Ma'am?"

It took a ton of effort, but Delaney tore herself from her fantasy world, in which she had to brush Jake's manly hands off her bare skin and pull away from him and his warm, full lips so she could answer. She wiped her own mouth (again) with the back of her hand.

"Oh. Uh, yes. We're fine. Really. Thank you."

After the police officer had driven away, Jake motioned to Porky's.

"I'm gonna grab a sandwich. Want to join me?"

Hell, yes!

"No, thanks. I can't. I have to get the kids home. I'm sure Summer's worried about them."

But how could she get him to give her his number? She couldn't just give him hers. It was against her rules to make the first move. But he was so dreamy. And he obviously had a good heart. And those hands! She was tempted to break her own rules, just this once.

"Okay, then. Just for future reference, Porky makes a mean house sauce. Try it on a pulled pork sandwich sometime."

"Thanks for the tip. And thanks again for stopping. Really. That was really nice of you."

"Anytime," he said.

If he'd been wearing a cowboy hat, he'd have tipped it as he strolled across the parking lot to the front door of Porky's. Heart aflutter, Delaney climbed into the van. She put the air conditioner on full-blast and drove back to Summer's, sweating, even though the mercury barely reached thirty degrees outside.

Hanging out with the kids provided a temporary distraction, but Delaney plunged back into dejection as soon as she left Summer's house.

She went home, poured a healthy glass of pinot noir and immersed herself in a hot, steamy bath. Sulking, she analyzed the situation, being as honest with herself as she could.

Xander would be proud. She snorted at that thought and sunk down into the water.

Losing Mark really hurt. She hated herself for feeling a sense of loss over him. She dashed another tear away from the corner of her eye. Losing Zachary was more of a hit to her ego. She hated herself for knowing she wouldn't actually miss him. Same with Xander. She could take him or leave him.

A sob escaped her mouth and echoed in the bathroom.

For the briefest of moments, she wondered if the break-ups had something to do with her, and whether all of this tied in with her lack of a real career. Not that she'd be going back to a real career anytime soon.

Nothing like a little wine to get your mind off that track.

After a couple of healthy gulps and a refill (so what if she brought the bottle into the bathroom?), she forced herself to stop looking back. The timing was a coincidence, nothing more. Maybe her dating system wasn't as genius as she thought. Because despite having set everything up to prevent heartbreak, she was heartbroken.

It's time to look forward, Collins.

Then there was Jake Rhoades the Dreamy.

Why hadn't she just given him her number? Now she'd probably never get the chance to find out if he tasted as delectable as he looked.

For the first time, she experienced something completely unfamiliar: regret.

CHAPTER FIVE

ALMOST TWO FULL DAYS HAD PASSED SINCE THE BREAK-UP FIASCO AND NOW Delaney blinked, bringing herself back to the present. It was Thursday and she was still at Rowdy's, having just received a lecture (however well-intentioned it was) about how she was a dating failure. And possibly, a failure at life.

The dim interior of the bar felt claustrophobic. Summer must have noticed Delaney replaying Tuesday's film reel in her mind. She moved her wine glass off to one side and put her elbows on the table. Then she started to speak, a little too loudly for Delaney's comfort.

"Delaney," she began. "Let's be honest." (*There's that word again.*) "Your dating life has been fun. Right?"

Josie nodded vigorously.

"Yeess," Delaney said. "But where is this going?"

"It's time for a change, my sister," Summer said. "Your decisions aren't really serving you any more, are they?"

"What do you mean?" She took a deep breath to brace herself for the answer. It couldn't be too bad, right? The girls meant well. They were her best friends—her Milkshake Sisters (they'd done an official Blood Sisters ceremony when they were thirteen).

"Well, it's what we were saying before," Summer said. "Who has three semi-serious relationships, all at the same time, without any of the guys knowing there's someone else? I mean, after age twenty?"

Delaney thought this over for a minute. "Just because not many people do it doesn't mean there's anything wrong with it. Not many people become brain surgeons."

"Okay, let's move on," Summer said, narrowing her eyes. "I'm not even going to consider that as a point in this discussion. I mean, have you even thought about your future?"

"Of course I have."

"Don't be so defensive," Josie said. "What Summer means is, have you thought about, you know, whether you ever want to settle down, with one guy or a real job. Or do you want this 'fail-proof' system to carry on while you work as a bartender in perpetuity?"

I tried to settle down and we all saw how well that worked out, in romance and in my career.

As it always did when she thought about her short stint as a veterinarian, Delaney's brain flashed her an image of Max the bulldog, his white muzzle and deep brown eyes. She couldn't even bear to think of Howie.

It hurt to think about all of this, so Delaney turned to humor: "Yeah, of course I've thought about it. I'm going to be that crazy cat lady bartender. For perpetuity. Yeah, I might have a booty call every now and then, but…"

Summer shook her head. "So," she said. "Back to the experiment."

Then, as if she were admiring a brightly lit marquee, Summer put her hands up, palms out, and with a sweeping gesture announced, "We call it The Dating Intervention."

Delaney opened her mouth to answer, but Josie cut her off. "Just hear us out. Look, we've already done some research."

She climbed down off her bar stool, remaining completely steady in her super-high heels, then rummaged around in her bag. She pulled out her tablet and turned it so all three of them could see the screen. When Josie opened the Internet browser, Delaney saw a page whose heading read, Grant Application, but Josie closed it before she had a chance to ask about it.

"Welcome to FindLove.com," Josie said. "I've already done a quick search for local men in our age range looking for casual dates. The results aren't bad, really."

She opened a window and tapped on a photo to enlarge it. "*Guapo*, no?"

"Well, I wouldn't say handsome," Delaney said.

Online dating? What's wrong with meeting guys at bars? Aren't guys with online profiles usually creepy?

But her friends forged ahead. They leaned over the tablet, lips pursed in concentration.

"Oh, definitely not him," Summer said. "Too much hair gel, for sure."

"What's wrong with hair gel?" Delaney asked.

"See? This is exactly what we're worried about, Dee. Too much hair gel on a guy over thirty means he's a prima donna. It means he doesn't like his mother. It means he drives a nice car but wears holey underwear. It means he doesn't want children."

"You get all this from hair gel?"

"Oh yeah."

"Ooh, look at this guy," Josie said. "Very good-looking."

"Get the details," Summer said.

Josie tapped the tablet's screen.

"Damn. He's a consultant. Code for unemployed."

"Seriously, you guys? Code for unemployed? How do you even *know*? I've met plenty of nice consultants."

"Again. Another example of why we're doing this for you," Summer said. "You've demonstrated previously–and you're demonstrating now–that you don't have an instinct for this stuff. Next."

Apparently, Delaney had a lot to learn. During the ten minutes Summer and Josie spent scrolling through photos and profiles, Delaney realized that according to their standards for men, she was off. Not just slightly off, but way off.

Suddenly, Summer sat up straight, held up a finger and produced a pen from her purse, after setting a toy car, a length of rope and a dusty rock on the table. "We need a formal agreement, I think."

Delaney Collins hereby agrees to relinquish control of her dating life to Summer Gray and Josefina Garcia, she wrote on a bar napkin. She drew a line underneath, then handed Delaney the pen and pointed to the line.

"Sign, please."

"Do I have to?"

"Yes," Summer and Josie said at the same time.

Delaney tried to act like this didn't hurt, but it did. She knew they loved her, but still… it was hard to identify the feeling. Probably it was mostly embarrassment, she decided, and she'd have to let that go. She took a deep breath.

And she signed. Once the ceremony was complete, Josie pulled her tablet close and began typing furiously on the touchscreen.

"First step: get you set up for online dating."

"Don't make that face, Dee," Summer said. "Lots of people meet their mates online these days. Haven't you seen those commercials?"

"Let's set up her profile," Summer said. "Then we can actually talk to these guys on her behalf."

They don't even trust me to talk to guys online. What do they think of me?

Josie signaled to Benjamin, who hurried over.

"Benji, could you get Delaney another beer, please? She's gonna need it."

"Sure thing!"

Delaney noticed that the sales sharks were leaving Rowdy's now, walking out single file. Upon closer inspection, she realized these guys looked like babies, with their smooth faces, trendy haircuts, and white teeth. When had she gotten so old? It hit her: she was thirty-four going on cat lady.

"Let's see. Delaney, we'll use your email address. What do you want for a password?"

"I don't know. Make something up."

"Okay," Josie said. "It's going to be bigpenis, all lower case, all one word."

"Fine," Delaney said. "I can't believe you still use that password."

"It has a good security rating. Okay, here we go." Josie sipped her drink. "Occupation."

Josie looked nervously at Summer.

"That's something else we wanted to talk to you about, Delaney," Summer said.

Delaney groaned. Benjamin plunked her fresh beer down on the table and she picked it up and chugged it.

"You need a new job. It's time to grow up. Bartending – I know it makes you a lot of money, especially on weekends, but it's not serving you well."

"Summer." Delaney put the beer bottle down on the table. "I don't even know what that means, 'it's not serving me well.' It's a job. I kick ass at it. I enjoy it. I make good money. Probably more money than Josie makes as a teacher. It's serving me just fine."

"She means emotionally," Josie said. "She means you're not stretching yourself. You have so much potential, Dee, you're so smart. And you always said bartending was a good way to get through vet school – but now you've been out of vet school for almost a decade and you were an actual vet for only a fraction of that time. You quit your first job eight years ago, Dee. Which we thought was very mysterious. We always thought you'd go back to it, but you're just—well, *stuck*. It's time to do something that really forces you to use your brain. I mean, if it's not veterinary medicine, maybe it's psychology. Plus, this is where ninety percent of your dating pool comes from." She swept her arm, nodded in the direction of the bar. "You always end up meeting bar guys."

It was true. All of it. She'd chosen to become a veterinarian because she loved animals. She wanted to heal them, help their owners feel peace of mind. But then she'd actually become a veterinarian, and had failed at it. She'd done the exact opposite of giving Max's owner peace of mind, which forced her into deciding, eight years ago, that veterinary medicine wasn't for her. Or, rather, that she wasn't for veterinary medicine. She'd never told the girls the story behind why she quit, but reliving that dark moment put her into panic mode, every time. Even now, her heart was racing. She took a deep breath to slow it down. Then she switched mental tracks: yes, she loved meeting bar guys. She loved hearing their stories, being the one to help them through difficult times. She'd pursued her degree in psychology because she was a natural at helping people identify and resolve the emotional causes of their struggles. Tending bar was almost like being a psychologist. Only, she didn't get paid as well.

Suddenly, a hard realization dawned: Delaney had emotional issues. What she'd gone through with Howie and Max had caused her to quit veterinary medicine … and the only way to resolve her feelings around those issues was probably to go back to that career.

Summer plowed ahead, interrupting Delaney's thoughts.

"Case in point," Summer said. "Tom, wasn't it? He came in every night for a month. You thought he was so cute. So … what did you say? So *charming*. What kind of guy spends every single night of his life in a bar? You flirted with him, he flirted with you. You went home with him and he had swords all over his wall."

"And metal signs talking about boobs," Josie added.

"But what about that other guy, Javier?" Delaney said.

Summer rolled her eyes.

"You just thought he was sexy because he spoke Italian," Josie said. "But remember he had a weird foot fetish? He wanted to lick your feet or something?"

"He wanted me to rub my feet on his –"

"Exactly," Summer said, holding up a hand to stop Delaney. "Exactly."

Josie entered Delaney's height, weight, schooling, hobbies. The crowd at the bar went up in shouts and swear words, and Delaney's eyes flicked to the TV screen to see what had happened in the basketball game.

"Okay, we're almost done. It's time to set the rules."

"Rules?"

"Yes," Summer and Josie said together. "Rules."

"Did you guys practice this or something? You keep saying everything at the same time. I hear you in stereo."

Summer ignored her. "Of course, there's the job thing."

There was that punch to the gut again.

"And you're going to learn how to cook. You can't eat takeout forever, babe. But let's talk about the dating. First of all, you make no decisions on your own. We select the people you'll date, we set up the dates and we decide who you can date again. No more of these dead-end, going-nowhere 'relationships' that start out as one-night stands and turn into one-year stands."

"Enough with the air quotes," Delaney said.

"And," Josie chimed in as if Delaney hadn't spoken, "No sex. With anyone. At all."

Oh. My. God. There is absolutely no way this is happening.

"You've got to be kidding me. I'll implode from sexual frustration," Delaney whined.

"We'll lift the ban when we decide you're ready," Josie said. "But even then, no going home with anyone."

Delaney took a breath to speak, but Summer cut her off.

"Who said you have to have sex at home?" Summer said sweetly. "Sarah was conceived at the drive-in. And Luke was conceived not fifteen feet from where we sit now."

She pointed at the bathroom.

"I had no idea," Delaney said wondrously.

"Oh, yeah," Summer said. "In fact – never mind. Let's finish this up."

Delaney held up her index finger. "This doesn't seem fair."

"No decisions. We make them all."

Josie added, "Besides, rushing into sex in a relationship is like wearing beer goggles everywhere you go. It makes everybody look better than they really are."

"Fine."

"Your drink limit: two."

"Josie, seriously? Three?"

"Two."

"And you have to stop being so critical. Give these good guys a chance."

"It's totally weird," Summer said, almost to herself. "You love the losers but you tear the regular guys apart. You should psychoanalyze your tendency to do that, Dee." Again, before Delaney could defend herself, Summer went on, "One or both of us will be available by text at all times to answer your questions and direct you in your actions. You'll have a schedule."

"Really? A schedule."

"Really. Josie has created a rubric, which you will fill out after each date. We will use this rubric to determine whether you see a guy again. Or whether you sleep with him. Did you bring that, Josie?"

"I have it on my computer. I'll email it to you," she said.

"By next week, we hope to have several dates set up – we'll tell you about them during Happy Hour."

"Also by next week," Josie said, "we want you to report back to us about your job hunt. You should have created a resume and a cover letter and you should have applied for at least four veterinary positions. And you also should have signed up for a cooking class at Country Kitchen."

"By next week?"

"Yep."

Delaney's heart was back at it, pounding so hard her hand twitched as she gripped her beer bottle. She couldn't go back to being a vet. She just couldn't. And especially not by next week.

"All the cooking classes are at night. And I work at night."

"Not for long. Tomorrow, when you go in to work, you need to give your two weeks' notice."

"But what if I don't find a job in the next two weeks?"

"You will. Put it out to the Universe."

Josie chuckled at Delaney's exasperated expression. "It works, Dee. Summer has me converted. I'm a believer. Remember that time my microwave broke and I needed a new one? I put it out to the Universe and voilà! I found one on that yard sale website the very next day. Five bucks."

"Serendipity," Delaney said.

"Exactly. Thanks to the Universe."

"Okay," Delaney said, reluctance drawing the word out. "But just in case. What if I don't have a new job lined up? I'll be homeless. You guys'll have me out on the street?"

"You have savings. We'll reassess after one week."

"You can always move in with me," Summer said. "And my four children."

Desperate to change the direction of conversation, Delaney said, "I *can* cook."

"What's in your fridge right now?" Summer asked.

"Let me guess," Josie said. "Jelly, moldy bell peppers and old butter."

"And a couple of takeout boxes," Summer said.

"Just because I don't cook, doesn't mean I can't."

"Invite us over for dinner," Josie said.

"Over to my *house*?"

"Yes."

"You need to start taking care of yourself," Summer said. "Eating all that processed, salty food can't be good for you. You're not in college anymore."

Delaney dropped her head to her forearm, which rested on the table. "Do I have no say in this?"

"Yes, you have no say," Josie said.

"No say whatsoever," Summer said. "Just trust us. You're going to be happier than ever. And you're going to thank us."

"Yeah," Josie said. "You're going to worship us."

"I need another drink," Delaney muttered.

"Did I hear somebody say she needed another drink?"

"Benjamin. Impeccable timing, as always. Yes, please."

He nodded, his black cowboy hat exaggerating the movement. Within a moment he brought, with a great deal of fanfare, a vodka cranberry for Josie, a glass of chardonnay for Summer and a Guinness for Delaney.

"Cheers to honesty and a change of subject," Delaney said. "Let Happy Hour commence."

"I never got to tell you, Summer. Tuesday after that asshole rear-ended us, when that guy pulled up with the license plate number? Jake Rhoades. Absolutely gorgeous. Rugged, tall, looked great in his jeans."

"You didn't get his number, though, because you don't get guys' numbers, right?" Josie said.

"It's for the best," Summer cut in, without waiting for Delaney's answer. "We're starting fresh."

Delaney studied the tabletop again. Her best friends in the world thought she was a loser and maybe they were right. She was halfway through her fourth decade, working at a bar, neglecting her veterinary degree and dating greasy-haired leftovers. When she thought about it this way, she agreed that she needed a change. Just thinking about it was exhausting.

Delaney changed the subject, again. "What's new with you guys, anyway? How's your week been?"

"So…" Josie said. "Our principal is leaving."

"No! Scott Smith is leaving?! Whatever could be important enough to draw him away from Juniper Elementary School?" Delaney asked, genuinely shocked. "Hasn't it been his dream to be principal there since he was in the fifth grade?"

Josie giggled. "It has, yes. He talks about it at every single staff meeting, as you know. But I guess he got this new Director of Curriculum position at the district. So he'll be moving on."

"What does this mean for you? You can finally stop wearing those stupid polo shirts? And nylons?" Delaney said.

Josie shuddered. "Both of those are pretty bad. But actually, I was thinking about applying for his position."

Summer raised her glass. "Cheers! I think you'd be great!"

"But I thought you loved working with the kids," Delaney said.

"I do," Josie answered. "And I'd miss them, for sure. But at the same time, if I could make the school even better, inspire the teachers even more, imagine how many kids I could reach. Right now, I help maybe twenty-five kids a year. But as principal, I could help hundreds."

"I hadn't considered that," Delaney said. "That sounds great, actually. I'm really happy for you. What do you have to do?"

"Oh, you know, the usual. I already have my administrator's degree, so I just have to apply and then interview and stuff. There'll be a panel, I think. So you see, Dee? We'll be going through the job transition together."

Josie picked up a bar napkin and began shredding it into little pieces, which she put in a tidy pile off to one side. It looked like a miniature Matterhorn.

"Are you nervous, Josie?" Delaney asked. She looked at Summer. "She's nervous!"

Summer put a hand over Josie's.

"You'll be great. What does Paul think of all this?"

"Oh, you know. Whatever I want to do. He's about as interested in it as he would be if I took up knitting or checkers."

"Yikes," Summer said. "How are things going in the Garcia-Comstock household these days?"

"They're going okay," Josie said. "It's just that Paul is, like, married to his job. Ever since he took that undercover detective position. He works horrible hours, he's never home and when he *is* home, he's sleeping or watching TV."

"Yikes," Delaney said.

"I know. But it's all new to him," Josie said. "I'm sure he'll throttle back a little, return to reality, once he gets used to it. Anyway."

She shrugged and took a sudden deep interest in a tiny smudge on her glass.

"Ooh, we can practice the interview questions with you!" Delaney said. "I love doing that stuff. I did that with a customer the other night. He came in because he was nervous about a job interview the next day. So I gave him a beer on the house and ran through some questions. It was really fun!"

Finished shredding her napkin, Josie starting making patterns out of the torn-up pieces. "Perfect. Well, I'll keep you guys posted."

"What about you, Summer? What's going on in your world?"

"Well, I haven't really got anything. You know, it's wake up, feed the baby, feed kids, take kids to school, feed the baby, fold laundry, do dishes, feed the baby, work, pick up kids, feed the baby, make dinner, bathe kids, feed the baby, put everyone to bed. And then fall into an exhausted heap in my own bed, only to be woken ten times per night remembering stuff I forgot to do, remembering stuff I don't want to forget to do, feed the baby and then get up and do it all over again the next day. And I'm lucky if I ever speak to my husband, much less have sex with him."

In a display of said exhaustion, she put her arms on the table and put her forehead on them. Her long blonde hair, pulled into a messy pony-tail, fanned out and tangled with Josie's shredded-napkin designs.

"Wow," Josie said. "This is coming out of left field. I've never heard you talk like this." She paused. "And to think, this is what I have to look forward to when I finally convince Paul to have kids."

"Yeah," Summer said from under her hair. "You're a newlywed now, but you just wait. You think you're happy now. Wait 'til you're carting four kids around and ironing your husband's work clothes. That's paradise, my sisters."

"Wow, Summer," Delaney said, catching Josie's eye. "Sarcasm just doesn't look good on you. What's going on with you? I thought you loved being a mom."

"Bad day, I guess," Summer said. "I have to go to the bathroom."

She pushed her still-full glass of wine to the middle of the table, slid off her stool and walked over to the bathroom, all without looking at them.

"Geez," Delaney said in a loud whisper. "What's wrong with her? She never has a bad day."

"No idea," Josie said. "But you know how she gets moody some-times. Remember that time freshman year when we thought she was mad at us for, like, a week, but it was really just that she'd started her period and didn't want us to know? So she was avoiding us?"

Delaney smirked. "Yeah. How could I forget? Well, let's hope it's something like that."

"Or let's hope it's not," Josie said.

THAT NIGHT, Delaney thought about the first time she'd met Howie

White. He charmed her instantly. It was her second day at the Desert Veterinary Clinic, and the other vets rolled their eyes when Barb announced he was there.

"Give him to Doctor Collins," one of them said, and Delaney braced herself for a high-maintenance client. But as soon as she walked in, Howie, spry as a twenty-something, sprang up to shake her hand. His eyes, a startling light blue, met Delaney's, and she felt like they'd known each other for years.

He was so dapper Delaney assumed he was on his way to some kind of event, but as she got to know him she realized he always dressed to impress, wearing a vest or a tie, or both, and a hat, which he removed and set on the seat next to him.

Howie explained that his bulldog, Max, was vomiting continuously, and as if to prove it, the dog threw up on the floor, making a *yak* sound and leaving a bright yellow puddle on the floor.

While Delaney examined him, Howie talked and talked. He talked about his chess club and his former students, who still wrote to him to let him know what they were up to. He talked about his children, who were grown and lived all over the country: North Dakota, California, and Wyoming.

"I'm just so proud of them," he said. "They're all doing great things. My son is an air traffic controller, my daughter's an English teacher—chip off the old block, you know—and my youngest, a daughter, is a professional ballerina. A real-life ballerina. Can you believe that, Doctor Collins?"

"They sound great," Delaney told him. "They really do. I can see why you're proud."

"Just wish I got to see them more, is all. They're so busy, what with their own kids and all. But I've got Max, here."

"Speaking of Max," Delaney said. "I have good news. I don't think it's anything serious. How many times do you feed him each day?"

"Oh, just once," Howie said. "My wife, Shirley, she always said he was overweight. Said we should cut back, you know?"

Delaney nodded. "He's a healthy weight now, so you must have done something right. But I think you should feed him twice a day. Just cut the serving size in half."

"I may not have been a math teacher, but I understand the basics," he said.

At first, Delaney worried that she'd offended him, but then he laughed out loud.

"Oh, I'm just giving you a hard time," he said. "Shirley always said my straight face would get me in trouble one day."

Delaney couldn't help but notice Howie was talking about Shirley in the past tense, and she wasn't sure whether Shirley had left or died. Whatever the answer to that question, she could tell Howie was lonely and needed someone to talk to.

So a week later, when he brought Max in for an itchy ear, Delaney was happy to see them.

CHAPTER SIX

Friday night at Rowdy's: Delaney's favorite. No, tending bar didn't put to use all her years in college or vet school. Memorizing orders, mixing drinks, sliding glasses down the shiny wooden bar … none of it had anything to do with the skeletal structure of a dog or the anatomy of a horse.

But it also never put her in the position to try to save someone's life —and fail. Plus, she seriously rocked it. And she got to wear her psychology hat. It was *fun*.

And, a teeny voice whispered from somewhere in the depths of her subconscious, *it's comfortable*. The psychology major inside of her could hear that loud and clear.

"I need a six-pack of Coors for the six-pack of hunks who just took table fifteen," said Ivy Simone, Delaney's spunky co-worker, as she slid behind the bar to join her. "And can you mix me a couple of house specials for the ladies at seven?"

"Sure thing," Delaney answered.

The hunks were obviously out-of-towners – and here for women. Wearing name-brand jeans and t-shirts with brand new cowboy hats and stiff boots, they reeked of cologne and emanated pheromones. The ladies at table seven were regular Happy Hour visitors and entrenched in deep conversation. Mary and Carrie – work-from-home employees of the same online company who met up weekly for live face time.

"What about the couple at table two?"

"They're not sure yet." Ivy opened the beers, placed them on a tray.

"I can't tell if they're five minutes from breaking up or five minutes from running to the bathroom to have hot, sweaty sex."

Delaney scooped ice into glasses and used a stealthy sideways glance to check them out. "I'd say the latter."

The man leaned in close to the woman and was running a finger up her arm. Ivy shrugged. Delaney set the two house specials – Cactus Coolers with prickly pear juice and vodka – on the tray with the beers and Ivy hefted it and sashayed off to make her delivery.

It was nearly eight and Rowdy's was just heating up. Delaney felt the first beats of the rhythm of a good night. The way she saw it, she thought as she handed two Budweisers to a dirt-caked man in construction boots, there was nothing better than this: an upscale cowboy bar in the middle of this cowboy town. It attracted a huge following of regulars, plus college kids and visitors – all big drinkers. Delaney was always busy, moving, meeting new people, and making great tips.

"You're quiet tonight," Ivy said. "Two glasses of red, please. You were right. They're going to get wine-drunk and go have hot sex."

Delaney shrugged and slid a couple of shots across the bar to two college guys who'd just come in, and then poured the wine.

"Just tired," she said.

The truth was, she'd been deep in thought for the past twenty-four hours, since Happy Hour with Summer and Josie.

Deep in thought about Jake Rhoades – what did he do on Friday nights, why hadn't she ever seen him at Rowdy's, and why hadn't she asked for his number before this nonsense with Summer and Josie? – and deep in thought about The Dating Intervention.

Dread had clung, sticky like honey, since she'd walked into Rowdy's at six. Dread about the rules the girls had imposed, dread about all the time she was going to spend with herself during the next six weeks and dread about quitting this job.

She'd done a lot of soul-searching during that time. Making a real effort to be objective, she examined her life from the girls' point of view.

She was thirty-four, eternally single (even when she was dating at least three guys at a time) and working at a bar. She ate takeout, alone (or with her cat) every night. The most she did in the kitchen was brew coffee, throw together a PB and J, or microwave restaurant leftovers. Meanwhile, two college degrees gathered dust on the shelf.

A couple of girls came in and ordered vodka tonics. Delaney squeezed a bit of lime juice into each, slid them across the bar and watched as the girls walked onto the dance floor, drinks in hand.

Ivy had become a good friend, but she was only twenty-two and she'd probably leave town as soon as she finished earning her teacher certification. Benjamin – who always delivered their drinks during Happy Hour – was barely twenty-one. This was his college job. And it was true that the men she met at Rowdy's weren't that great. Wasn't it time to face the facts?

Mark Cortez. Steamy, dreamy, totally sexy. They'd met when he'd come into Rowdy's and asked her to explain the horse photo to him. After the initial flirtation, he spent that entire evening staring sadly into his whiskey on the rocks. He'd been depressed and clingy, lifting a hand every time she passed his spot at the bar. She'd slept with him that very night, reveling in his hunger for her, all while her intuition screamed at her that he was too needy. She'd ignored it because she liked being needed. Now she realized he'd just been lonely. Yes, he was a passionate lover. And he said he'd like to marry her. But she suspected it wasn't *her* he wanted. It was the idea of someone to be with. Chemistry had kept them together for several months, but that was it. He'd grown to care about her, but she never felt like he was all that *interested*. She'd felt the same way: the sex was great, the company was good, but they rarely had conversations any deeper than small talk. Didn't they both deserve more than that?

Zachary. Brainy and adorable in his wire-rimmed glasses. He was the perfect match to her middle school self. They met during his first – and last – visit to Rowdy's. He brought his brother, Eli, into the bar when Eli came from California to watch Zachary's first poetry reading. Zachary kept telling Delaney Rowdy's wasn't his type of hangout. She'd been inspired to convince him it could be. To prove intellectuals could work at country western bars, she engaged in a deep, if halting, conversation every time she returned to their table to deliver their pineapple juice and Malibu rum (and what man drinks that girly stuff, anyway?). Finally, he'd asked her to come home with him, challenged her to a game of chess. And again, her intuition whispered that he wasn't quite right for her. It told her, in a bossy voice, that she was sticking around only because she liked the challenge of proving she was up to his level. And she suspected he stuck around because he felt intellectually superior. Not a good foundation for a long-lasting, healthy relationship.

Finally, Xander walked in alone one night, in the mood for a cold one after a long day of kayaking. She was attracted to his adventurous side and quick wit.

"Want an adventure?" she asked coyly and he followed her back to the storeroom where they had a quickie.

That was one of about five times they'd had sex during the six months they adventure-dated. They never talked about much of anything, but enjoyed rock climbing, kayaking and hiking together. It was fun, but there was no passion.

Summer and Josie were right. She needed a big change. In fact, she needed a few big changes. If nothing else, this intervention would be an experience. What could it hurt?

Then Jake Rhodes walked into Rowdy's.

The setting sun outlined his unmistakably divine muscular figure in the doorway. Delaney's mouth dropped open. Her breathing hitched. Her heart stopped. At least for a brief second. Was this the Universe's doing? Maybe Summer and Josie were right about serendipity.

"Thank you, Universe," she whispered as he walked in.

She wished as hard as she could for dating autonomy. If it were up to her, she'd be running him down this very minute, dragging him to the back room, stripping off his clothes and having her way with him. She pictured herself raking her fingers through his hair, wrapping her legs around his waist and riding him, fast and hard.

Jake's eyes focused on her from the moment he walked through the door until he was standing in front of her. By the time he strode up, she was practically panting and could taste coppery adrenaline at the back of her throat.

"Delaney Collins," he said. He looked at her as if he knew exactly what she was thinking.

She thought she might drool when he leaned his elbows on the bar, showing off his sculpted, tan forearms and his rugged hands.

"A cold beer," she said, dragging her eyes up to meet his. "Rolling Rock."

"That'll do it. How'd you know?"

"It's my specialty," she said.

"You're good, Delaney Collins," he drawled.

"I am."

She set the beer in front of him and noticed with a great amount of relief that Ivy was taking his friends' orders, which meant she could focus on Jake.

"Jake Rhoades. What are you doing at Rowdy's?"

"Oh, you know. The usual. Hanging out, having a beer."

"I've never seen you in here before, have I?"

"A few times. My buddies are in from Nevada and they wanted to see a real cowboy bar. So I brought them here, saw you at the bar and came right up."

"Oh, that's nice."

That's nice? That's all you can think of? No wonder Summer and Josie want to take over your love life!

"How long are they here?"

"Just through the weekend. How long are you here?"

"Just through closing."

She saw his eyes flick down to her mouth and back up to her eyes. She pictured herself leaning into him, taking his face in her hands and kissing him like crazy across the bar. A surge of heat ran down her body and settled deep in her belly.

"Well, it's good to see you, Delaney. Real good."

Drinks in hand, Jake Rhoades and his friends walked away to find a table. Benjamin served them for the rest of the night.

Why didn't I ask for his number? she thought wildly when she saw them walking out the door just before one a.m. *Why?*

Oh. Right. She'd surrendered control of all matters of her love life to Summer and Josie. If they didn't come up with something as downright mouthwatering as Jake Rhoades, they were in trouble.

And so was she.

CHAPTER SEVEN

When the alarm buzzed at seven a.m. Delaney shut it off and pulled the covers up to her chin. Her cat, Pixie, dove off the bed and slinked under the dresser. She glared out at Delaney, blinking her big green eyes.

"Don't hate me, Pix. I haven't been awake this early on a Saturday in I don't know how long. I want to hide, too. But it's a big day. Or something. I'm writing a resume. And we're having people over for dinner."

Delaney rubbed her hands over her face, then dragged herself out of bed and to the kitchen where she set the coffee to brew while she showered.

Last night after work, motivation and enthusiasm – and maybe a little two a.m. craziness – had her setting out her black suit. Now, it hung ominously from the frame of her closet door, the nine-year-old ghost of her one and only job-hunting experience.

As she stepped under the shower's steaming spray, she thought about that dismal time in her life.

Fresh out of college and full of ambition, confidence and swagger at having finished two degrees in three years, Delaney Collins, twenty-one, had moved from Tucson to Phoenix to look for a young person's job in the big city. What else was there to do? Summer would soon give birth to her second child, Josie was student teaching at Juniper Elementary and jobs were scarce in Juniper – especially jobs in biology, which she'd originally chosen because a newspaper article said it was an "up-and-coming" industry.

The suit was an investment, she told herself then. Looking professional would help her launch a stellar career. Needless to say, it didn't pay off. She went to interview after interview wearing that damn suit, sometimes with a white shirt underneath, sometimes a red one, sometimes purple.

From her hair to her earrings, her shoes to her handbag, Delaney tried every combination she could think of to maximize the appearance of professionalism and hire-ability.

But nothing panned out, she thought now as she scrubbed her hair. She applied at a biotechnical company, an environmental testing firm, a commercial corn farm.

With every, "I'm sorry, we're just not hiring right now," Delaney felt her confidence shrivel just a little more.

Thinking about it now, all these years later, still caused a sick, nauseated feeling to roll into her stomach. Present-day Delaney pitied Delaney of the past for trying so hard only to achieve lackluster results.

What was wrong with her? Why didn't anyone want her? Was she destined to be jobless forever?

She dreaded running into the people who turned her down. She saw the corn farmer in the movie theater parking lot and ducked down behind a big truck to hide from him. Unfortunately, the truck belonged to him, and he came around the driver's side to see her crouched there.

"Uh, just found this penny!" she said to him, straightening up. "My lucky day."

Her fiancé, Tucker, was decreasingly sympathetic. At first, he bought her a tub of ice cream or a candy bar for every rejection. But after a dozen dessert nights, where they "celebrated every failure as a stepping stone to the perfect job," Tucker became disinterested. He stopped buying treats, and then he stopped coming over. Delaney told herself he'd come back around when she wasn't so depressing.

Then things got worse (if that was even possible).

Letting the hot water from the shower beat down on her scalp, Delaney closed her eyes as she remembered what happened next.

Delaney discovered Tucker had a handful of other girlfriends on the side, one of whom he'd proposed to. Now that she was thinking about it, she remembered a little voice in her head warning her something was going on in the weeks leading up to their breakup—something besides her being bad company due to the failed job hunt. Of course, she ignored that little voice because she didn't want it to be right.

One evening, they went hiking on one of Phoenix's most popular mountain trails and when they reached the peak, they stopped to take a picture.

The sunset looks so beautiful, she thought at the time. *Maybe we can use this photo for our Save the Date cards.*

Her body still flooded with the heat of embarrassment and anger at the memory. Tucker pulled out his cell phone, supposedly to check the time. Then he took his camera out of his pocket. They posed, arms around each other's waists, turning their backs to the city below, spread out like a blanket in the sparkling twilight. Romantic. Picturesque. He held the camera out in front of them. Just before he snapped the picture, his phone made a sound. Tucker jumped, startled.

He put the camera in his pocket and took his phone out.

"Just gotta check the time," he said.

Didn't you just do that? Delaney thought. She remained quiet, but peered over his shoulder. Before he could hide the screen, Delaney read the entire text, which was from someone named Mandy: *Hey honey, what do you want to do for dinner?*

Delaney caught the guilty look on Tucker's face before he cleared his throat and put the phone away.

"Smile," he said then, squeezing her waist.

A million thoughts clicked into place as Tucker pressed the camera's button.

He can never meet up with you on Saturdays.

He won't help choose the wedding location or date.

He's been going to the bathroom every time his phone makes a noise.

He's suddenly very in-demand, with "meetings" five times a week.

Infuriated, Delaney couldn't quite wait until the shutter opened and closed before starting to shriek at him, demanding to know who Mandy was and why he was having dinner with her when he was supposed to be going to a special banquet for his dad's company. A late spring breeze, which would typically feel warm and relaxing but now only agitated her, picked up Delaney's hair and sent it flying around her face. The camera captured everything: Delaney's wild hair and her evil, madwoman expression as she yelled at Tucker.

When she finished, Tucker, always so matter-of-fact, said, "You've got to understand. It's like having a second-string quarterback. You've always got to have a backup. I mean, what if something goes wrong?"

Staring into her eyes, imploring her to comprehend, he'd put his hands on her shoulders and continued, "You're my first string, Delaney."

She refused to speak to him all the way down the mountain and all the way home. As soon as she was alone in her house, she burst into tears. She took Tucker's two-carat sparkler off her finger with the intention of flushing it down the toilet, but she couldn't quite bring herself to drop it in the bowl.

Instead, she spent the entire evening on the couch, twirling the ring around, watching it twinkle through her tears. She felt betrayed, of course. Tucker made her believe he truly cared about her. He braided her hair when it was windy. He painted her toenails. He held her hand at the sweetest times, like when they were waiting in line to buy movie tickets or when they walked to their table at a restaurant.

All along, he'd likely been doing those same things with someone else. How could he? More than betrayed, though, she felt stupid. She actually took his affection at face value.

Once he gave her the ring, she started planning a wedding. A *wedding*, for goodness' sake. Of course, he gave her full control, telling her to choose the venue, the flowers, the silverware.

And she did. They would celebrate their lifelong commitment under a quaint gazebo surrounded by a lush rose garden in downtown Juniper. She would hold a bouquet of red roses, and they'd feast on his favorites, rosemary salmon and oysters.

And the silverware. It was beautiful, with swirly designs on the handles.

For weeks, she imagined the feeling of standing in that gazebo, the scent of roses surrounding her as she looked into the eyes of the man she planned to spend the rest of her life with. The garden would be shady and cool. Summer would dab at her eyes with a tissue and Josie would try to pretend she wasn't emotional. Delaney's parents would sit in the front row, beaming.

How could she have been so stupid? Why hadn't she paid attention to all the signs?

The day after The Discovery, Delaney had to face the impossible task of telling her parents and her friends the wedding was off. Her mom called the photographer, the florist and the caterer.

In her traumatized state, Delaney decided Tucker had shown uncharacteristic wisdom. She promised her bruised ego that from then on, she would implement a back-up system of her own.

Even now, years later, the memory was painful enough that Delaney scrubbed her skin raw.

Fiancé-less, jobless and licking her wounds, Delaney applied for and was accepted to the school of veterinary medicine at her alma mater, the University of Arizona. Bartending and tutoring paid her way through vet school, and immediately upon graduating, she got a job at Desert Veterinary Clinic in Phoenix.

It all worked out so seamlessly that she'd assumed it was fate or destiny. Everything was exactly as it should be.

Tell that to Howie's family, said a mean little voice in the back of her mind.

After things went so wrong there, Delaney moved back to her parents' house in Juniper. It was within walking distance of downtown and she spent more time than necessary at Rowdy's (and argued with Summer and Josie that seven evenings per week was, in fact, necessary). One evening, the owner, Bill, approached her.

"Miss Delaney," he said, "You spend enough time here, you might as well get up behind that bar and make some tips. Consider tonight a trial run."

Tending bar was supposed to be temporary. That's what she told herself, anyway. She sold Tucker's ring and remained at Rowdy's to support herself and eventually buy a house, both of which seemed like markers of success in the traditional sense.

Now, she'd been out of a vet job for a couple of years (okay, more than a couple) and she was still at Rowdy's. Not that she minded. Not really.

Honesty, Delaney.

Okay, she did mind.

What kind of a loser spends tens of thousands of dollars on vet school and then ends up working at a bar, perpetually single, for the rest of her thirties?

Exhausted after reliving what was inarguably the most miserable time of her life, through this new lens of honesty, Delaney got out of the shower and dried off. Pixie, recovered from her shock at the sound of the alarm, wandered casually into the bathroom and perched on the edge of the bathtub. She batted at the drops coming out of the faucet, then licked the moisture off her paw.

Delaney's inner debate lasted no more than half a second: instead of slipping into the suit, she pulled on some sweat pants. She didn't need to wear a suit to research online. In fact, she thought, she didn't need this stupid suit at all. It was ugly when she bought it, with its pleats and big plastic buttons. And it was ugly now – and out of style, more than likely. She yanked the suit down, balled it up and carried it over to the trashcan, which she slammed shut on top of it.

"There," she said to the cat. "That's better."

A few minutes later, coffee poured and a bagel toasted, she sat down at the computer to search local job listings. The job hunt had changed significantly in the past ten years. She really could research and apply without leaving her house. Which meant everyone else could, too. How on Earth was she supposed to stand out from everybody else?

Pixie jumped onto Delaney's lap and curled up. For a few moments, Delaney browsed the job listings in and around Juniper. Veterinary assistant, landscaper, laboratory technician ... then she realized the search was premature, since she couldn't apply to any of them without a resume. Fortunately, the website had tons of resources dedicated to helping her create one.

Instead of listing your jobs and education, list your accomplishments, one page suggested. *For example, 'Landed a $400,000 marketing contract,' or 'Completed a $100,000 project under budget.'*

"Ha!" Delaney said to the computer. "Mixed four hundred thousand drinks in one night after the annual rodeo dance."

She picked up the phone. This wasn't looking good, but Summer would know what to do.

"You're never up this early," Summer said when she finally answered. "Everything okay?" Before Delaney could respond, Summer yelled, "Luke! Put that sword down and get a shirt on! Then find some clean underwear." She spoke into the phone again. "Sorry. Getting ready to go to the Farmer's Market."

"It's okay. I shouldn't have bothered you this early. Want to call me back?"

"I'll call you back after I load the kids in the car, but is everything okay?"

"Yeah. It's just this job hunt thing."

There was a beat of silence, and then Summer said, "It's a job hunt, Delaney. Not brain surgery."

Before Delaney could answer, or comment on Summer's uncharacteristically harsh tone of voice, Summer said, "Sorry. I'm sorry. It's just—you're sitting on the computer right now, aren't you? Hold on." Again, she spoke loudly, away from the phone: "Sarah. You have three minutes to finish your hair." She returned. "Sorry. Every morning, Dee. She's not even a pre-teen yet and she has to style her hair every single morning. No ponytails for this girl."

"Are *you* okay?" Delaney said. "You're acting weird."

"I'm fine," Summer said. "Just overwhelmed, I guess."

"Is she too old for a sticker chart?" Delaney asked.

"Ha. Yes. Was I like that?"

"No. You are a free spirit," Delaney said. "I can't remember a time when your style was anything other than long, beautiful blond hair parted down the middle. Or the famous ponytail."

"Anyway, we got off track," Summer said. "Monday morning, you need to put on something professional and go pound the pavement. Go to some places, ask if they're hiring, pick up an application."

Just the thought of walking into a veterinary clinic again—the smells, the sounds, the memories—made Delaney's hands clammy. She could picture herself right back inside the Desert Veterinary Clinic, her world titling when she received that phone call.

She took a deep breath. "If they were hiring, wouldn't they post it on this website?"

"No, not always. Hold on."

Summer covered the mouthpiece of her phone, and Delaney heard muffled shouting.

"Sorry. Now Luke is walking around in a shirt, socks and shoes – nothing else – claiming he's going to town naked from the waist down. We have to load the car in three minutes."

Delaney couldn't imagine having to wrangle all those kids, every single day. She could barely get herself ready in the morning. Just thinking about getting four kids ready made her want to commit to life-long abstinence. *Well, not really.*

"Don't you have a suit?" Summer's voice cut into her thoughts. "You bought that suit when you were job hunting before, right?"

"It's ten years old. It's ugly. And it's in the garbage."

"Oh. You could wear pants and a nice sweater. Spend today working on your resume. And buy some nice paper to print it on. I gotta go. I don't think Luke has any clean underwear, actually. He might really be going commando today."

Crap. Delaney didn't have a suit, she didn't have a resume and she didn't have a printer.

"I guess it's time to go shopping," she said.

Her phone chirped. It was a text from Summer.

A suit in the garbage is not an excuse to go shopping. Don't procrastinate. Work on your resume.

"How did she *know*?"

IT WAS HER FIRST TRANSGRESSION, Delaney thought, but it probably wouldn't be her last. She was supposed to follow all directions issued by Summer and Josie. But if they wanted her to find a new job, she needed a suit. If they wanted her to print a resume, she needed a printer. Yes, she admitted to herself, she could have spent the morning working on her resume on the computer and gone shopping afterwards. But what fun was that? A little retail therapy never hurt anyone. Josie would definitely agree.

Manic. It was the only word to describe the shopping trip.

Delaney started at Juniper's only department store, where Candi, a gray-haired, pink-lipsticked older woman who dotted the *i* on her name tag with a heart, helped her choose a new suit. Gray with white pinstripes.

"You know, honey, this is almost exactly like the suit I bought when I started my first job, as the receptionist at a bowling alley. It was 1976."

Great. Perfect.

They moved on to shoes after that (Candi pressed for bright pink patent leather heels but Delaney chose black). Candi decided the outfit wouldn't be complete without a string of pearls.

"Good luck with your interviews, honey," Candi said as Delaney took her bag. "I can just see the potential inside of you! Let me give you a hug!"

Surprisingly touched by the gesture, Delaney felt tears spring to her eyes as she inhaled Candi's floral perfume and hugged her back.

Now, iced tea in hand, she headed to the office supply store. *Why stop at a printer and resume paper? I need to be prepared.*

If she was going to get a job, she had to let the Universe know she really wanted one. She had to act like a professional. She had to feel like a professional. She had to *be* a professional. At least, that's what Summer would say. She filled her basket with everything she thought she'd need for the job hunt: bright yellow paper clips in fun shapes, a new pencil holder for her desk, colorful stacking file holders and new pens.

Fully stocked for resume writing and job hunting, Delaney headed to the grocery store. She spent a long time perusing the frozen foods aisle in search of something that would look homemade for tonight's dinner but she came up empty. The girls would know if she faked it.

Lemon chicken. She could make that, no problem. She'd show Summer and Josie she knew how to cook. It had been a while, but she managed to find the chicken, breadcrumbs, lemons and butter in a half-hour. She grabbed some asparagus for a side dish and started feeling a bit smug. What else? Mashed potatoes. The kids would love mashed potatoes.

Several times throughout the day, she found her mind wandering to Max and Howie. Whenever it did, she distracted herself by glancing over her shoulder to look for any sign of Jake Rhoades, his light blue t-shirt or his muscled legs in those jeans. She hoped desperately that she'd get another chance to see him. As she finally headed home, she couldn't shake a vague feeling of disappointment that she hadn't.

She spent the rest of the afternoon getting everything set up and when she was done, she stood back to admire her work.

"Looks good, right, Pix?"

The cat, obviously onto Delaney's real goal – procrastination – stalked out of the room, her tail swishing behind her. Just after four, a knock sounded at her door.

"Let's see what you bought today," Josie shouted from the other side. "Summer tells me you went shopping."

Delaney rolled her eyes and opened the door. Josie's eyes widened when she saw Delaney's desk.

"I needed a few things."

"Oh my God, you redecorated your entire office area. This does not look like job hunting."

"Retail therapy?" When Josie only shook her head, Delaney quickly added, "I have to be prepared. I need a good environment from which to job hunt."

"Congratulations. Great job. But I don't think anyone in town is hiring a professional procrastinator."

"But look at it. It's beautiful!"

Josie took in the matching purple stacking files, pencil cup and lamp. She rubbed the petals of a silk flower between her fingers.

"You're supposed to be following our rules, Dee. Doing what we say. Summer and I want what's best for you. Your office space *does* look very nice. The flowers are lovely, although they aren't going to help you actually get a new job. Now, let's see your new suit, which might actually help you get a new job."

"It's about atmosphere," Delaney said. "It makes me more productive."

Josie tapped her fingers on the desk and Delaney went off to her bedroom, muttering, "*Be* the professional." While she changed into her suit, she could hear Josie speaking in rapid-fire Spanish to Pixie.

"Pixie says she's peeved," Josie reported when Delaney came back out. "But that is a nice suit. We both like it, don't we, Pix?"

"Is it okay?"

"Yes. It's good. Very professional. Your assignment for tonight is to write your resume and print off some copies."

"I work tonight. After I feed you."

"Should have done it today then, huh? Instead of shopping."

"You know, you could do it for me tonight. While Paul's working."

"That's true. But instead, I'm going to watch something horribly cheesy on TV while I appl—while I grade papers."

"You guys are slave drivers."

"You bet your ass."

"What are you talking about, 'apply,' by the way?"

"What are *you* talking about?"

"I saw something on your tablet when you were signing me up for FindLove.com. An application. And don't say anything about me being nosy. If taking over my life isn't nosy, I don't know what is."

"Touché," Josie said. "I'm applying for a grant."

"I saw the heading," Delaney said. "What's it for?"

"A community center. But I probably won't get it. I'll tell you more if I do. I've got to go—one of my students has a concert at his church, and I told him I'd go."

Delaney closed the door behind Josie and wondered if Josie wasn't as nervous about this grant as Delaney was about her job hunt. She'd have to remember to ask her.

SO, maybe the lemon chicken was a little more complicated than Delaney remembered. Pulling it out of the oven to serve it, she noticed it looked more like something she'd scoop out of Pixie's litter box. Maybe it just needed to sit for a while. She put the baking dish on the counter. Nervous now, she checked the potatoes. She remembered her mom telling her something about the potato falling easily off the fork … she had to shake it a little, but the potato did fall off eventually, landing back in the steaming pot with a plop and splashing her arm with boiling water. She drained the potatoes and began to mash them with a fork.

"Don't you have a masher?" Josie asked from the dining room table, where she was grading a social studies quiz.

"No. I meant to buy one today," Delaney lied, "but they didn't have any at the store."

"Mmm. Okay."

"What do you mean?"

"Sorry," Josie said. "I'm distracted. This kid, Joshua, whose concert I went to this afternoon, is so smart! He's so smart. But he always fails these quizzes. I just don't know how to help him. He needs more guidance, but both is parents work after school. That's what this community center is about. Anyway. I think I have two mashers at home. I'll give you one."

The door flew open before Delaney could respond, and Summer and her kids paraded in. First Sarah, carrying a big library book in front of her, then Nate, dragging his full-to-bursting backpack on the floor behind him, then Luke, with a sword in each hand. Finally, Summer walked in, holding hands with a toddling Hannah.

"We're all hungry, Aunt Dee," Nate said. "Mom says your cooking had better be good, because she doesn't want to take us out to eat after this."

"Nate!" Sarah said. "You weren't supposed to tell her!"

"Yeah, jerk," Luke said. "You're supposed to say it's delicious, no matter what. Remember?"

Summer shrugged apologetically at Delaney.

Great. Everybody's expecting this to be terrible.

Fortunately, she didn't disappoint. The chicken was mushy, as she'd anticipated when she took it out of the oven. The asparagus was overdone, limp and squishy and falling apart in strings. The potatoes were lumpy and bland.

"Aunt Dee, is this your first time cooking, like, ever?" Sarah wanted to know.

"It's my first time in a long time. I wanted to show your mom and Aunt J that I can cook. It's not great, but it's edible, right?"

"I hear crickets chirping," Nate said.

"Summer? Josie? What do you guys think?"

"Well ..." Summer said slowly. "Josie?"

"*Ay*, Summer. It's bad, Dee. I mean, yes, it's edible. But—well, sorry."

Delaney grimaced. "So I need those cooking lessons, huh?"

"Yes," chorused her guests. "You do."

"All right, all right. Sign me up."

Because Delaney cooked and Josie had to get home to her cheesy TV and more paper-grading, Summer volunteered to do dishes if Delaney would sword fight with the boys and watch Hannah.

They'd all eaten it, Delaney thought as she used her broom to ward off the sword-wielding boys, but she'd barely been able to choke it down, herself. Before tonight, she'd expected to feel triumphant when everyone finished eating. Now, she just felt embarrassed.

Summer and Josie were right. Just like the rest of her life, her cooking skills needed a serious boost.

CHAPTER EIGHT

"A RUM AND COKE," THE BUSINESS EXEC TOLD DELANEY AS HE SLID UP TO the bar. "Actually, might as well make it two."

He'd walked into Rowdy's a few minutes before, wearing dejection like a wet sock, uncomfortable and sticky. Tie untied and dangling limply, collar unbuttoned, head down, he tucked his long legs into the space between his stool and the bar. Delaney's intuition cringed and brought Jake Rhoades to the forefront of her mind. She wondered what he was up to tonight. Was he relaxing on his couch with a Rolling Rock? Or playing pool over at Fast Jack's?

She dropped a couple of ice cubes into a short glass and poured Mister "Make it Two" his first rum and Coke. Messy hair, a stain on his shirt and elbows on the bar: she pegged him not only as a man who'd been wronged, but also as an all-nighter.

"He's so your type, Delaney," Ivy whispered conspiratorially, wiggling her eyebrows. "He's going to hit on you. Wait and see."

THAT is my type?

"You think so?" Delaney said.

"Oh, yeah. Turn on that Big Delaney Charm, and he's going to turn into a quivering puddle of desire."

"Or a quivering puddle of rum and Coke. He asked me to pour him two at once and he just finished his second."

The man signaled for another, and Delaney delivered it. This time, she leaned her elbows on the bar and looked into his eyes.

"Rough day?" she said.

He chuckled. "The roughest."

"Want to talk about it?"

The words tumbled out of her mouth before she could stop them. Was this what her friends were talking about? It was her natural tendency to offer a listening ear.

"I was working on a project. With a team. Remember doing group work in school? It's just like that. You've always got that kid who's messing around, doodling in the textbook while everyone else slaves away. Right?"

Delaney nodded, and he continued. "So anyway, this project was due today. And the textbook doodler, he was supposed to run these reports to include as an appendix. Only, he didn't do it. I texted him this morning to check, and he said he'd forgotten. 'Shit, man, I'm so sorry.' So I spent all morning running these reports so we'd have them to include in the project. All this while textbook doodler apparently overslept, picked up a gourmet coffee, and breezed in just before we were due to present it."

"And how did that make you feel?" Delaney said.

"Angry, man."

"What else?"

"It made me feel taken advantage of."

The conversation went on like this, and before Delaney knew it, an hour had passed. Because Delaney had a certain amount of introspection, she was willing to admit the conversation had passed the threshold of a typical bartender-customer conversation. And it took quite a bit of effort to keep her voice neutral as she kept Mister "Make it Two" saturated with rum and Coke all night. Her intuition whispered that this wasn't quite normal, that maybe the girls were right.

But Big Delaney Charm came naturally, and it plowed down intuition like it was a dry cornstalk in mid-winter. By the time midnight ticked by, she lost count of the number of times she had to stop herself from making a witty, clever, or otherwise flirtatious comment to a man who really was turning into a puddle before her eyes.

"SHE'S EYEING THAT FLOPPY-HAIRED, pinstriped, red-eyed slob," Summer murmured to Josie.

The two of them sat in the back corner of Rowdy's. When they'd first slid onto the tall stools, Benjamin had rushed over, but the greeting died on his lips when they shook their heads frantically and waved him off. He shrugged, then bumbled over to a table where two couples sat, a chessboard set up between them.

"Do you think he'll tell her we're here?" Josie said.

"Doubt it. He grew up with a bunch of sisters. We're wearing disguises. He'll catch the drift." Summer adjusted the visor of her hat.

"He recognized us right away. Don't you think Delaney will see us, too?" To keep busy, Josie began braiding the long blonde wig she'd insisted on wearing.

"No. She's locked in on that flop."

"Why does she do this, Summer? Why?"

"I'm thinking that's a rhetorical question," Summer said. "But remember in junior high, when we met her? You were the sizzlin' hot Latin lover type—"

"And you," Josie said, "were the beautiful beach babe blonde."

Summer nodded. "And Delaney—well, Delaney was always the nerdy best friend. The confidant. Guys loved her."

"Like a sister," Josie said.

"Right," Summer said. "So you get the double whammy. One, she almost can't resist a good sob story. She didn't get a degree in psychology for nothin.' Two, she's lured in as soon as a guy seems to *like* her like her."

For a few moments, Summer and Josie watched Delaney. Her movements were efficient as she mixed drinks, handed out beers, took orders, carried on a conversation with the dud at the bar who downed rum and Cokes like he'd rather be swimming in them.

"She's totally in her element," Summer said.

Delaney cracked a joke to a college kid who ordered a six-pack of beers and the friends who were crowded behind him jeered and elbowed him.

"I know," Josie said. "She's really good. Why doesn't that confidence translate to the rest of her life?"

"I'm telling you. You're onto something. It's that whole I-like-you-as-a-friend thing from junior high. When the pressure's off, like when she's flirting with a college kid in whom she has no interest, she's fine. But when the pressure's on—" Summer swiped a hand across her throat.

Benjamin came back to the table, plunked a vodka cranberry and glass of white on the table.

"Thanks, Benji," Josie said. "Do us a favor and don't tell Delaney we're here, okay?"

"Glasses, hats, a wig, for crying out loud? Frantic waving? I got it," he said. "My lips are sealed."

He started to walk away, then suddenly spun around and came back, leaning over their table.

"You guys might as well be holding up fluorescent We Heart

Delaney signs, though. She looks over here once and she's going to spot you."

This time when he walked away, he was shaking his head.

"We've got to stop her," Josie said.

"You don't just want to see how this plays out?"

Delaney had stopped in front of the longhaired, rubber-jointed man. Again. Now she was bending down, elbows on the bar, eyes level with his.

"She's looking very sympathetic," Summer said. "Look at her nodding. Look at her eyebrows."

"She's already breaking our rules. If we don't stop her now, when do we?"

"We agreed we were coming here only to establish a baseline, Josie. Remember?"

Summer sipped her wine, picked up her napkin and began folding it into a crane.

"Fine."

At Josie's use of Delaney's new go-to answer, the girls dissolved into giggles. When they saw Benjamin look sharply at them from across the room, they slapped their hands over their mouths, becoming even more hysterical.

SURE ENOUGH, after an hour and two more rum and Cokes, Mister "Make it Two," also known as David, spilled his guts and told Delaney what was *really* on his mind.

"... and my girlfriend moved to Costa Rica with this surfer guy who looks like Fabio. Right before I was going to propose."

His pale gray eyes shone with emotion, his tie lay in a coil on the bar and Delaney almost had to wipe a tear off her own face after listening to his story. She wanted to soothe him. So what if that meant unbuttoning his shirt the rest of the way and peeling off those silky black, pinstriped pants?

She sent a text to Summer and Josie: *Super cute guy at bar tonight. Can I flirt my way into getting his number?*

Within a second, she received texts back from both of them: *No. Absolutely not.*

She wrote back: *Why? He's cute. And he's a doctor.*

UNDER ATTACK from a fresh wave of giggles, Josie and Summer took turns wiping their eyes with Josie's bar napkin.

"'Super cute?' She has to be kidding us," Josie said. "Now we know what her standards are. Haven't you always wondered, when she talks about those really hot guys she sees here all the time?"

"Now we know," Summer said, nodding so hard her sunglasses fell off her face and clattered onto the table.

"Come on, Summer. We have to do something. He is so *not* cute. He is so *not* a doctor. And I can guarantee he is *so* not good for her."

"What the hell. You're right."

SUMMER RESPONDED to Delaney's text right away: *He's at the bar telling you a sob story, right?*

Delaney didn't answer. How did Summer know?

She was going to employ her mommy senses during The Dating Intervention and Delaney didn't like it one bit. It was an unfair advantage. David requested another drink and Delaney mixed it.

"You're real cute, Diana," he slurred.

"It's Delaney," she said. "And you're not so bad, yourself."

Her phone chirped.

Josie: *Stop talking to him, Dee. Remember, we make the rules.*

Delaney didn't respond.

"So, David. What are you doing after this?"

Her phone chirped again.

Summer: *Step away from the drunk guy. Hair gel, remember?*

And again.

Josie: *He's wearing cheap shoes. He's not a doctor. My guess: he's in vacuum sales. He probably did a demonstration right before this and is drinking away his depression right now. He sucks for a living, Dee. And he hates his mother.*

Delaney scanned the bar's seating area. Were they here? They had to be. She'd noticed the cheap shoes, the hair gel, David's general pathetic nature. But sometimes pathetic fueled her need to nurture, despite the voice in her head telling her to back off. She was sucked in.

That's when she spotted two girls at the back of the room, wearing ball caps pulled low.

"I'll be right back," she said to Ivy.

Would Josie and Summer show up at Rowdy's to babysit her? No, they wouldn't do that. Would they? She walked to the back of the bar, trying to play it cool. This whole Dating Intervention thing was a terrible idea. No, Mark, Zachary and Xander hadn't been perfect. But they'd been *okay*. And they were out of the picture now, anyway. She was starting with a clean slate.

She stalked right up to the table where the girls were sitting, stuck her face two inches from a pair of mirrored sunglasses and felt completely foolish. These girls weren't Summer and Josie. They were just a couple of friends out on the town for a couple of drinks – and they looked very surprised to be approached in this manner.

"Sorry," Delaney muttered. "Get you a drink?"

Mouths hanging open like little goldfish, they simply shook their heads. She walked back to her spot behind the bar with less confidence, then poured David a straight Coke and plunked it down in front of him.

"This one's on the house," she said. "And after you're done, I'm taking you home."

CLOSING TIME. Ivy flicked on the lights and the few stragglers who hadn't already wobbled into taxis swayed their way out of the bar. Delaney swept the floor, wiped the tables and cleared glasses and bottles. David, for his part, remained on his stool, head pillowed on his arms. He'd snored a couple of times and Delaney wouldn't be surprised to see drool on his sleeve.

Her phone chirped. Another text. It was Summer again. What was she doing up at two a.m.?

Don't take him home, Dee. Fight your instincts. This is a moment. Choose to be the new you.

Delaney rolled her eyes. Summer had said something the other night about every choice being an opportunity to move one step closer to being your new self. You could choose to act like your old self and remain stagnant, she said, or you could choose to act like your new self and move forward. She probably threw in something about the Universe, too.

Delaney put away unused glasses and dumped the lime wedges in the trash. She glanced at the top of David's head. He had thinning hair, which revealed a big dark mole on his scalp. Up close and in the light, he wasn't quite as cute as she originally thought.

"Maybe you're onto something, girls," she muttered.

"Should I call him a cab?" Ivy said, coming up behind Delaney.

Even though Delaney knew that was the best idea, she said, "Nah. I've got him."

Ivy raised an eyebrow at Delaney and said, "Are you sure? I mean, he's a puddle."

Delaney shrugged at her, and Ivy said, "Whatever. Glad it's you and not me. I'm heading home."

She hung her apron on a hook behind the bar, grabbed her purse, and walked out the back door.

David woke with a start and Delaney noticed that he had drooled all over his arm, just as she expected.

"Was I asleep?" he mumbled.

"I think so. Want me to call you a cab?"

He straightened up, looked at his watch, noticed the drool spot on his arm, tried in vain to brush it off.

"I thought you were taking me home. That's why I'm still here."

What was it about guys like David that drew her in?

"Oh, that's right," she said, infusing her voice with cheerfulness she didn't feel. "I did say that, didn't I?"

"Well, you don't have to," he pouted.

"Of course I don't," she said. "But I'd really like to. Let's go."

From the other end of the bar, Ivy wiggled her eyebrows.

The walk home was quiet and very cold. David's conversational skills seemed to have dried up as he started to sober up. Although it was only seven minutes from Rowdy's to Delaney's front door, her face was numb by the time they got there. Anxiety, which had taken shape as a tiny black stone when David had woken up with drool on his arm, had developed into a full-blown boulder as they walked. She felt like she'd carried it all the way home and now her arms were so heavy she could barely get her keys out of her pocket as they rounded the corner of Oak Street.

But apparently, she didn't need her keys. As they approached her house, she noticed the lights were on and someone was standing in the living room, a silhouette in the big picture window.

CHAPTER NINE

DELANEY SLOWED TO A STOP WHEN THEY APPROACHED HER HOUSE. SHE knew she had turned off the lights when she left for work. This could mean one thing and one thing only. Delaney took a deep breath in an attempt to quell the panic rising in her stomach.

"Uh, David," she said quietly, "you're going to have to go home."

"What? Why?"

The orange-tinted light from the street lamp cast ugly shadows under his eyes and his breath puffed out in a foul-smelling cloud.

"I have a visitor," Delaney said.

"You don't have a roommate?"

"Nope. Not a roommate. I'll call you a cab."

"Will I see you again?"

"Probably not."

As she dialed the cab company they habitually used to send people home from Rowdy's, she couldn't help feeling like a teenager who'd been caught sneaking out of the house, or coming home way after curfew. She was scared and she wasn't afraid to admit it, she thought as she gave the taxi dispatcher her address.

"See you," she said to David.

Steeling herself, she walked up the path and into her front door, leaving David pale, shivering and fidgeting with his tie in the cold.

"I told you not to bring him home," Summer said in a deadly calm voice. Delaney imagined this was the scariest mommy voice she had – the one the kids really listened to. It didn't come out to remind the kids to put on their shoes or pick up their toys. No, it was reserved for critical situations, like when Luke came after Nate with a butter knife.

Delaney sat on the couch, biting her lip and examining her fingernails. Summer stood over her, hands on her slim hips, face twisted into a combination of concern and anger.

Oh, yeah. She's definitely pulling out all the mommy stops.

Even as Delaney waited in fear, she noticed the dark circles under Summer's eyes, the wisps of hair escaped from her bun. She looked exhausted. Delaney felt guilty. Not only had she failed The Dating Intervention less than forty-eight hours after its inception, but she was also the cause of her best friend being awake at two in the morning when she had to get up again at six with the kids.

"I know you did," Delaney said. "But he seemed really nice. And I— wait! It's kind of weird that you're in my house at two a.m."

Butterflies swirled madly in her stomach. Why was she *nervous*? This was ridiculous.

"Number one," Summer said, "'He seemed nice'? Did you *see* that guy? And number two, I knew we'd have a rocky start. You don't like being told what to do. Josie told me how, after you shopped Saturday, you spent the rest of the day decorating. Not job hunting."

"Well, I need a good atmosphere. You know. To *feel* like a professional. To *be* a professional. I could hear your voice in my head while I was buying the decorations. I needed a printer to print out resumes. And a suit," she said weakly, because she was now losing steam. "For interviews."

"Did you actually write your resume or print it?" Summer said. "No. I know you didn't. But let's not get sidetracked. We're here tonight because you brought home that … that … weasel! After I specifically told you not to!"

Delaney winced. She wanted to shrivel up right there on her living room couch.

"What was your inner voice saying to you in that moment, Dee?"

"He was nice."

"Tell me that's not what your inner voice was saying. Please."

"Okay. It wasn't. It was saying, 'This guy's a loser. What are you doing?' That's what it was saying."

Summer nodded. "Thought so. So why were you ignoring it?"

"I don't know. He liked me. He said I was charming."

"He did, did he?"

Delaney felt her resolve slipping.

"Sure, he was nice," Summer said. "You were mixing him free drinks." She was pacing back and forth across the living room now, her long skirt swirling around her legs. "You told him you were going to take him home. Because you liked that he thought you were charming and sexy. It's Psychology one-oh-one. You wanted to spend the whole night feeling sexy. Well, guess what? You wouldn't have felt very sexy when you woke up next to David Steadman tomorrow morning. Do you know who he is? He's the scumbag who got fired from the hospital because he was groping all the nurses. Don't you remember me telling you about that? The big hype at Derek's work a couple months ago?"

"You didn't know that until you saw him. And I wouldn't have known it tomorrow morning."

"Oh, you would have, after you heard all his one-liners. He's famous for them." She stopped pacing and stood facing Delaney. "Anyway. That's not the point. The point is, David Steadman is a type. The wrong type. And he's a prime example of the type you always pick for yourself. He's down here –" she held her hand, palm down, an inch off the floor, "and you're up here." She stretched her arm above her head.

"You accuse me of being judgmental and over-critical, but you guys find something wrong with every guy I date. Who's over-critical?"

"You're only critical of guys who'd actually be good for you." Summer shook her head. "If there's a nice guy, normal, with a decent job, who doesn't live with his mom, you find a sprig of ear hair or a splotch of eczema unbearable. Or the crescent-shaped mole on his cheek. I mean, really! This is exhausting. I thought I had a few more years before I had to parent a teenager, but look, I get practice now."

Apparently, this thought put Summer into hysterics, because she flopped down on the couch next to Delaney, laughing, her eyes leaking tears.

"That's mean, Summer."

"Face the facts, Dee. Now, I'm going home and to bed before I strangle you."

For the briefest flash of a moment after watching Summer flounce down the walkway to her car (why hadn't she noticed it when she walked up?), Delaney felt indignant. The facts? Delaney hadn't been a teenager for a decade and a half, at least. It wasn't even possible that she was acting like one now.

The realization didn't dawn on her until she had to fight off the temptation to turn off the porch light before Summer got in the car.

Delaney did behave like a teenager. Yes, she broke the rules. Yes, she tried to avoid being found out. And yes, she felt self-righteous and then completely guilty when Summer put her on the spot. But it was more than that. She loved psycho-analyzing other people, but rarely did she turn the lens on herself. Like a teenager, she craved male attention, even when it came from someone who was absolutely not a good match for her. Like a teenager, she went farther than she really wanted to, just to keep that attention flowing. And like a teenager, she had some growing up to do.

She brushed her teeth, changed into her pajamas, and climbed into bed. As Pixie curled up beside her, she let the tears fall. They slipped from the corners of her eyes down onto her pillow, one after another. She didn't cry out of anger at Summer and Josie, or out of sadness for herself. She cried because she knew they were right. She needed to make a change. The trouble was, although she had a vague image of where she needed to end up, she had absolutely no idea how to get there.

CHAPTER TEN

Weekly Happy Hour was starting to feel like a weekly examination.

"Yes. We were here Monday night, spying on Delaney," Summer said to Benjamin, popping a green olive into her mouth. "Yes, we're acting like the mothers of a teenage daughter. The crazy mothers of a teenager daughter. A crazy teenage daughter. And yes, we're proud of it."

Josie nodded, a demented smile plastered on her face.

"When she started mopping up," Summer said, "I hightailed it to her house. I thought that would give her one more out. She could say something like, 'Oh, my roommate must have waited up for me,' or 'My boyfriend's here.'"

"But no," Delaney butted in. "I said, 'There's a stalker in my living room.'"

At that moment, Ivy sidled up to the table. "You're talking about the other night, right? You didn't take him home, did you?"

"Oh, she tried," Summer said. Her voice had become a squeal. "But I stopped her."

"Thank goodness for your friends," Ivy said.

Someone at another table signaled to her, and she walked over to take the order.

"He was a slug, Dee," Benjamin said, nodding. "Soggy, floppy, dejected. You could do better. I'll get you ladies your drinks."

"Does anyone besides me notice that I'm being picked on?" Delaney said as Benjamin walked away.

Neither of the girls responded. Instead, Josie raised her glass and said, "You're a true friend, Summer. You had to get up at six with the kids and you were at Delaney's 'til two-thirty."

"She needs us," Summer said.

"Not to change the subject," Delaney cut in, "but did anyone notice that Summer is eating green olives out of a bowl?"

Silence descended on the table while the women exchanged meaningful glances. Then Summer, having just swallowed another olive, burst into tears.

"I'm pregnant," she wailed, putting her forehead on the table.

Benjamin had returned with their drinks and after setting them down, did a celebratory dance.

"Congratulations, Summer! I'll exchange that wine for water!" He plucked her wine glass off the table and danced off. This made Summer cry even harder.

"What? That's great news!" Josie said. "Cheers, Summer! Cheers to Gray Baby Number Five!"

"Wait," Delaney said. "Why are you crying? I thought you wanted a fifth baby."

"I do," Summer said, at once insistent and miserable. "I do want a fifth baby. It's just that I hope this little guy or girl can't sense my—I don't know—my anxiety."

She took a tiny sip from the water glass Benjamin brought back. Josie dug a tissue out of her purse and handed it to Summer, even as she blotted her own eyes.

"What? Why do you have anxiety?" she asked.

"Derek lost his job," Summer said. "They're downsizing at the hospital. We just found out last night. He's being laid off in a month. So I'll be three months' pregnant, supporting our entire family. Our growing family, I might add. On a freelance graphic design income. Not the best start to a new life for this little peanut."

"He'll find another job," Josie said in a soothing voice. "He will. There's a nursing home or hospital on every block in this town. Or maybe he could be a school nurse."

"I hope so," Summer said. "And you're right, Josie. You always know how to put things in perspective. There are a lot of nursing positions in town. You always hear healthcare is a growing field. And I really am happy. About the baby. It's just that I'm scared, too."

"You'll be fine," Delaney said. "You always are. You're the best mommy I know. You'll make it work. And if all else fails, you could probably use the same techniques you used on me last night to shame someone into giving Derek a job."

Summer chuckled.

"It was the middle of the night. I was tired and cranky. I wanted to be asleep in my bed, not at your house on loser patrol," she said, then quickly added, "I didn't mean you. I meant that guy. Anyway, Hannah's pregnancy was so easy, I'd forgotten they're not all like that. The insomnia, the nausea, the bladder. I tried to go to bed at eight, like I usually do, but I couldn't sleep. So I hatched this plan to get a baseline for you. So we'd know what you were really up to. Once it was clear you'd be taking that guy home, I ran over to your house and sure enough…"

Delaney shrugged her shoulders.

"Don't think you're off the hook," Summer said. "We still have rules for you. And Josie made a flow chart."

With a wicked grin, Josie pulled a folder from her purse. She slid a piece of paper out and placed it on the table in front of Delaney.

The Dating Intervention

The Rules

1. Do not, under any circumstances, tell the men you're dating that your girlfriends are in charge.

2. Summer and Josie make all the major decisions. If you must make a decision, use the flow chart (Appendix 1). No exceptions.

3. Find a new job. A good job. A job that actually challenges you.

4. Withhold all criticism of all men we select for you. Period.

5. Do not access your online dating profile without one or both of us present.

6. Do not, under any circumstances, date anyone we haven't selected for you.

7. Adhere to the 2-drink limit (that's 2 drinks per date, not per hour).

8. No sex. At all. Really. We mean it.

9. Remember, we love you.

Summer, who'd been reading over Delaney's shoulder, took the paper, got a pen out of her purse and added:

10. Follow directions. Or risk being shamed by Summer. Publicly.

Delaney flipped to the second page, which was labeled "Appendix 1: Decision-Making Flow Chart."

The first question: "Are you attracted to him?" led to "Are you attracted to him because he's a loser?" for a "yes" answer and "Could you be?" for a "no." There were questions like, "Are you having fun so far?" and "Have you seen his bare feet?"

"Seriously? 'Have you seen his bare feet?' What does that have to do with anything?"

"It's an intimacy thing," her friends chorused.

"Now. Any questions?" Josie asked in a sweet voice that contrasted her lethal expression.

"What if I totally hate the guys you pick for me?"

"Would we do that to you?" Josie said.

Delaney may be better at psychoanalyzing other people than she was at psychoanalyzing herself, but she knew what she was really afraid of. "What if *they* hate *me*?"

"Ah, there's the real issue," Summer said.

"Just sign," Josie said, pointing at the bottom of the paper.

Delaney signed, and couldn't say why she felt like she was signing her life away. Selling her soul. She cleared her throat.

"Now. I have some rules of my own," she said. "And I used my brand new printer to print them out."

Summer and Josie exchanged a glance. Josie shrugged. Delaney pulled her own sheet of paper out of her purse, unfolded it and smoothed it on the table.

"Summer, you have to agree to start looking for gigs for your band."

When Summer started to interject, Delaney held up a hand. "I know what you're going to say. You need to help Derek find a job, you're going to have to take on more design clients to supplement the income, you're pregnant and will be in the bathroom or at the doctor all the time, you have to take the kids to school, et cetera. Copy that. But you know what you'd say to me?"

Josie joined Delaney, in a mocking tone: "If you want something, you have to take the steps to get it."

Despite herself, Summer smiled. Delaney pointed to the X she'd made on her paper.

"Fine," Summer said. She signed. "I'll do it. We can't expect you to do all the work."

"Josie," Delaney said. "You have to start exercising. You've been saying for months that you're overweight, you're tired of being over-weight, blah, blah, blah. I think your curves are sexy as hell. But frankly, I'm sick of hearing it. Hit the gym, sister."

"Ouch," Josie said.

"It's just because I love you," Delaney said. "And because I love you, I'll join the gym with you."

"Me too," Summer chimed in. "If I'm going to get up on a stage, I've got to be in shape. I can at least do a little cardio and some light weights."

"Deal?" Delaney asked.

Josie signed her paper.

"Deal," she said. "I need a week to get mentally prepared. And to get my wardrobe situated."

"Oh, of course," Summer said. "Josie Garcia the Fashionable must ensure she is properly outfitted. Don't you have any sweats?"

"I'm not showing up to the gym, or anywhere else, in *sweats*," Delaney said in a high-pitched voice with a Spanish accent.

"Don't mock me," Josie said, her tone playful. "Just give me a week. I've been so busy after work, with my new project. The one I was telling you guys about? The grant for the community center?"

When both Delaney and Summer opened their mouths to ask questions, Josie held up a hand. "I promise I'll tell you more when I know if I got it. Anyway, next Thursday, we'll meet at the gym instead of Rowdy's. Then we'll come over here to celebrate. I'll get a light beer or something. A skinny something-or-other."

"Fine," Delaney said.

"Now. Enough business," Josie said. "I can't take this personal development shit much longer. Who wants another drink before I kill you at pool?"

NERVES MADE Delaney five minutes early. She hated being early. She stopped outside The Sand Witch and squinted down at her watch. She found herself tapping a toe – a nervous habit she hated – so she took a deep breath and forced herself to sit on the edge of a planter box full of snapdragons. Four minutes. The girls had instructed her to show up two minutes early, which she found acceptable. She spent plenty of time showering and putting on the outfit Summer and Josie chose for her: a light green sweater to match her eyes and dark skinny jeans with boots. She spent more time than usual applying her makeup. But it still wasn't time to leave. After a few minutes of pacing the living room, anxiety won, forcing her to start walking.

The slightly warmer weather had brought people out into the sunlight and Delaney found herself looking into cars and shop windows for Jake Rhoades. Every time she saw a faded blue t-shirt, she felt a tiny spike of adrenaline. Then she reminded herself that it had been a few days since she'd seen him and he probably wasn't wearing that same shirt. And if he was, he probably smelled pretty ripe.

"Get a grip," she muttered to herself.

She caught a glimpse of her reflection in the deli's window, realized she was scowling and made a conscious effort to relax her facial muscles.

The Sand Witch's Friday afternoon crowd, packed into tiny tables and rickety chairs, gave her a bout of claustrophobia. Should she keep waiting outside? Should she go in and fight for a table? Josie's flow chart wouldn't work, yet. It applied only after she'd met the guy. Should she text Josie or Summer and ask what to do?

"They're probably parked across the street," she said aloud.

She spun around to check, but she didn't spot them or their cars. She resolved to stop talking to herself and stood back up to pace.

"He's very much looking forward to meeting you," Summer had said the night before, winking. "And he'll be wearing a white Stetson."

"Seriously? What does *that* say about a guy?"

"He's a real-life rancher, Dee. It says he has rough hands," Josie answered. "Which, I don't think I have to remind you, you like."

That was true, anyway. But a white Stetson? Summer and Josie selected the rancher first thing. He was tall, strapping, handsome and most importantly, responded right away when they'd messaged him about a date this weekend. Delaney couldn't decide whether a fast – no, immediate – response time was good or not. And a white Stetson?

A white Stetson. It was coming up the street now, on the head of a very tall, broad-shouldered cowboy. Instinct kicked in and Delaney ran through her mental checklist. Would she sleep with him? *Oh, yeah.* Would she like to look at him? *For sure.* Would she like to look at him naked? *More than likely.* The answers to the other questions – Would they be able to carry on a conversation? and Would he make her laugh? were yet to be determined.

"Delaney," he said.

It wasn't a question. He spoke with confidence, ease and a drawl. She liked it and apparently, so did her inner voice. So much so that she felt her face splitting into a natural smile, one she didn't have to force.

"Jesse," she answered. An embarrassed heat blossomed on her cheeks.

He put out his hand and she resisted examining it for callouses. She put hers out, too, and when he took it, grasping it rather than shaking it, she was pleased to find it was large, warm and yes, rough. One point for Jesse. Eye contact, she noted. Two points. Josie's rubric probably said something about that. His eyes were brown with flecks of green. Nice.

"Shall we?"

He motioned to the door and at her nod, opened it.

"Crowded, isn't it?" His whisper in her ear sent a shiver down to her core.

"Yeah. I noticed that when I walked up," she said. "Fridays are usually pretty busy."

"What do you say we grab our sandwiches to go and find a picnic spot?" he said.

"Great idea." *Romantic. Another point for Jesse.*

She noticed with interest that he opened the door, held it for her and took off his hat when he entered. He paid for her lunch, which made her slightly uncomfortable even though she liked it. But Josie had predicted this: Jesse, she'd said, grew up in a culture where manners were instilled at an early age. She saw it in her students every day.

"Good, old-fashioned manners, Dee," she'd said. "I can guarantee you, neither Zachary the Brilliant or Xander the Adventurous had them. But Mark Cortez the Steamy did and Jesse the Rancher will. You let him pay. You let him hold the door for you. You say thank you. Be a lady. He's not going to appreciate the feminist crap Zachary probably thrived on. Which was only because he's cheap and weak-minded."

At that, Summer had kicked Josie under the table. Josie had shrugged. "Someone's gotta say it."

Jesse the Rancher took Delaney's sandwich box so he could carry it for her, then rushed ahead of her to open the door with a foot. She thought the move was a tiny bit awkward. Then she remembered Rule Number Four – withhold criticism.

"Thank you," she said, as Josie had instructed her to do.

The Stetson (which he'd had to put back on to carry sandwiches and open the door) nodded.

"I know a place," Jesse said. "And it should be just warm enough. Would you mind holding our sandwiches? I have a blanket in the truck."

Although it was caked with mud – he probably lived miles out a dusty country road, Delaney thought – the truck seemed pretty nice. Jesse returned with a thick blanket he'd retrieved from the bed.

"Might be a little hairy, but it's better than nothin'," he said. "Ready?"

"Ready."

Spring Creek ran merrily through downtown, winding its way between buildings and under quaint bridges. It sang this afternoon, thanks to the recent storm, and sparkled, too, thanks to the sun. Jesse led the way to a little bank behind the music store and he spread the blanket, which, Delaney noticed, *was* hairy. Very hairy.

"Sorry 'bout that," Jesse said. "One of my mares was in labor the other night in the snow. Wouldn't come into the barn. So I kept her covered with this."

"It's fine," Delaney said. "Better than sitting in the mud."

When she'd worried about making small talk, Summer had told her to start by asking questions about him. How his day was going, what he had planned for the weekend, what happened during the spring in the ranching business, why he wore a white Stetson, even on trips into town. Okay, Summer hadn't said anything about that last one. Delaney reprimanded herself for being critical again. He was a perfectly nice guy. So what if he had dirt caked under his fingernails and was, at the moment, removing a huge wad of chewing tobacco from his lower lip? They sat side by side on the blanket, their feet pointing towards the creek and their backs against a warm granite boulder.

"How's your day going?" she asked, unwrapping her sandwich.

He nodded and she was relieved to read enthusiasm in the gesture. "Great," he said. "Great. We butchered a hog this morning – enough meat to get us through 'til fall. But I made a mess out of my boots."

Lifting his right foot, he angled his boot so she could see a swirl of blood on the heel.

"Got 'em mostly cleaned up, though. Messy business."

Why did I order ham and cheese? Delaney did her best to swallow the bite she'd taken. *Why couldn't I have ordered a veggie sandwich?*

"Ever been to a butcherin'?"

The man was oblivious. He might have good manners, but he had no regard for proper mealtime conversation. Delaney shook her head.

"Messy business," he repeated, then a third time, drawing out "messy": "Meeessssssy business."

He took another huge bite.

Desperate, Delaney blurted out, "Have you ever been on a hot air balloon?"

The Stetson bobbed.

"Long time ago. My parents took me and my older brother to celebrate our first hog sale with 4-H. You know, kids raise livestock and sell it. We'd each raised a pig – their names were Lucy and Ricky Ricardo. You know, like the 'I Love Lucy' show? Anyway, you ever done that? Raised a hog?"

Again, Delaney shook her head.

"I've seen 'I Love Lucy,' though," she said.

"So you get 'em when they're these itty bitty piglets. And you feed 'em, care for 'em, clean their pen for months. When you're a kid, it feels like forever. I got attached. Of course."

He chuckled then.

"I bawled my eyes out when it was time to sell Lucy. I knew somebody was going to butcher her, even though my big brother, James, he tried to tell me she was going to live at an amusement park for pigs. Come on, right? Anyway, I was so upset. Inconsolable. So after we sold them, my parents took us to the hot air balloon park just north of Phoenix, you know it?"

"Yep," Delaney said.

"It was fun. Real fun. But I was still heartbroken about Lucy."

"Do you think you'll let your kids raise livestock for 4-H?" she asked.

"Oh, yeah. For sure. I mean, I don't have any kids yet – you know that from my profile – but I think it's important for kids to be self-sufficient. To know exactly where their food comes from. To appreciate that a single hog can feed a whole family for months."

"Do you live with your whole family?"

"Yeah, well, we all live on the property, you know. It's big. Fifty acres. I have my own house, my brother has his own house and my parents have theirs. So we all have our space. But when we butcher, like this morning, we share. Share the work and share the meat."

He licked a glob of mayo off his thumb. Still queasy, Delaney took a deep breath as she wrapped the rest of her meal in the deli paper. *Can this man not stop talking about meat?* She didn't need Josie's rubric to know she didn't want to sit through another meal hearing about bloody boots and butchering.

Again, she tried for a subject change: "Do you and your brother get along well?"

"Oh, yeah. We do. We have a lot of fun. We're always playing practical jokes on each other. This morning, when we were butchering, he took the hog's ears and –"

"Wait," Delaney interrupted. "Wait. You can tell me this one later. I don't think I can stomach anymore."

Jesse guffawed, the sound as big as he was. He slapped his thigh, wiped his eyes, took a deep breath.

"I'm real sorry, Delaney. I should have thought about that."

He stopped talking about hogs then and dug into his sandwich, still chuckling.

THE GIRLS INSTRUCTED Delaney that her date could last no longer than three hours. So precisely at one minute after the three-hour mark, her phone chirped. Delaney was sitting in the square downtown, watching a couple of kids throw coins into the fountain. The little boy, who looked to be about two, was throwing a tantrum because he wanted to throw another coin. When his dad had said he didn't have any more, the little boy tried to climb into the fountain to get the one he'd just tossed.

So, how was it?

The text was from Summer and she'd copied Josie on it. Delaney replied to both of them: *Bloody.*

Summer: *What?*

Delaney: *All he talked about was butchering a hog.*

Josie: *But was he nice? Did he have good manners? He was probably nervous.*

Delaney: *Yes and yes. He didn't seem nervous. Just regular conversation in the life of a rancher, I think.*

Josie: *So what's the problem?*

Delaney: *Not very romantic.*

Summer: *Reality check: Life's not always romantic.*

Delaney: *I know it's not. Believe me. I know.*

Josie: *Did you fill out the rubric?*

Delaney: *I don't need to. I'm not sitting through another meal with Jesse the Rancher.*

Summer: *Josie, we knew she was going to be tough to tame.*

Delaney: *I can still see what you're texting, Summer.*

Josie: *We're up to it. This is a test of patience for both of us.*

Summer: *You have another date tonight, Dee. Are you ready?*

Delaney: *I need a new outfit. This one's covered in horse hair.*

CHAPTER ELEVEN

"WELL, DON'T YOU LOOK FANCY!"

Camille Collins' voice rang out through Umbrella Coffee, embarrassing Delaney and sending a rush of pleasure through her at the same time.

"Oh, mom," Delaney said. "It's just a regular outfit."

As she always did when she came into Umbrella Coffee, Delaney immediately felt calmer. The paintings on the walls showed rainy scenes, each of them including at least one umbrella. A rainbow of open umbrellas hung from the ceiling.

"Did you have a date? With which guy? Mark? Or was it that other – Zorro, is that it?"

Delaney had forgotten that she was going to have to explain the whole failed-fail-proof-dating-system situation to her mom, disappointing yet another of the important people in her life. Maybe she could avoid it. She made a big show of setting her purse on the empty chair next to her, checking her phone and then putting her phone away and zipping her purse before making eye contact again.

"So, how was the beach, Mom?"

"Oh, it was wonderful. Just wonderful. You know, a bit chilly, but not a bit of fog. Clear as – well, clear as a summer's day. Only, it's late winter."

They settled into a pair of cushy lounge chairs in the corner, Camille sipping an iced latte and Delaney, images of a bloody pig still fresh in her mind, able to stomach only a cup of tea.

"So tell me why you're looking so nice today."

"What, I can't look nice to meet my mother for coffee?"

"There's more to it. Although you're looking a bit green around the gills. Are you sick?"

"No, I'm fine. A little queasy, but otherwise fine."

"Wait. You're not pregnant, are you? Nausea can be the first sign of pregnancy."

Delaney waved a hand, dismissive. "No, Mom. But thanks for asking."

Camille shrugged one shoulder. "I ran into Summer at the market. She said you were on a date."

"Is there no privacy in this town? Yes, I was on a date. With a rancher. A hog rancher. Jesse."

"But what about the others?"

"What others?"

"Those other guys you've been seeing? Mark? Zorro?"

"Summer didn't tell you that, too?"

"Tell me what?" her mother said.

Delaney took her time answering. It was humiliating, really, and she'd already moved past it in her mind.

After a long silence, she finally said, "Okay. Long story short: all three of the guys I've been seeing dumped me last week."

"All in one go?"

"All in one go. Yep. Practically." Delaney threw up a hand. "So, my intrepid friends Summer and Josie have taken over my love life—and my regular life—as a result."

"Sorry to say this, honey, but it's about damn time."

"Come on, Mom." She paused, waiting for her mother to laugh or otherwise indicate that she was joking. When no indication followed, Delaney said, "Really?"

"Yeah, really."

"What is that even supposed to mean? I was doing fine."

This time, Camille waited to answer. She used her straw to stir her latte. She'd always been so pretty, Delaney thought, and age hadn't changed that. Fresh off a trip to the California coast, her mom looked happy and relaxed, her skin tan, her long gray hair pulled back in a messy bun. Her fingernails and toenails were painted a blinding shade of pink and the sandals she wore were better suited for walking on a wharf than they were for end-of-winter Juniper.

Despite the carefree outfit, though, her green eyes were intense when she finally looked into Delaney's.

"You were doing fine, yes. *Fine*. But isn't it about time you were doing better than fine? I mean, you've always got something going, which is good. You're good with men. But – and I know you're going to hate hearing this, just like I would have before I met your dad – it's about time to stop messing around, Delaney. You aren't getting any younger. Have you thought about your future? I mean, long-term?"

Delaney took a sip of her tea to stop herself from blurting out something retaliatory. *How long have they all been thinking this? And it's not just Summer and Josie. It's my mother, too.*

"How come you never said anything about any of this?"

"It's your life, Delaney. I knew you'd settle down sooner or later. Probably later." She shrugged. "But eventually. And, I agree with them that it's time for you to get a new, more serious job. Bartending isn't an actual career. At least, not here in Juniper."

Delaney cringed as she realized there was another big fear lurking in her mind: the fear that she'd have to explain to Summer, Josie, and her mom what stopped her from pursuing a career in veterinary medicine.

Camille set her cup down on the table. "I mean, one of these days, aren't you going to want a husband, kids, a dog? I mean, that's what I always assumed you wanted, after watching you play house when you were little. And if you don't start evolving now, you're going to be stuck spending time with guys like David … what was it? Steadbaker? Oh, Steadman, that was it. Or, are you?"

Nope, nothing was sacred. Nothing. Summer had spilled the beans about David Steadman too.

"I know you love Dad," Delaney said, "but you guys got married when you were like, twenty. I just don't want to miss out on all the fun you're supposed to have once you're an adult."

"Oh, I think you've gotten plenty of fun in, sweetheart. For the past several years, you've been dating two or three men at the same time, consistently. You've tasted all the flavors. It's time to pick your favorite."

"Wow."

"You're so worried about missing out on the fun that you're actually missing out on creating a real life for yourself. You know, I never got to do the things you're doing. I didn't go to college, or have my own place, or hang out with my friends for Happy Hour every week. But I don't regret one minute of it. What I did have and still do, is a *home*. Your dad is my home. And that's something special. Don't miss out on the important stuff because you're so worried about missing out on the rest of it, honey. That's all I'm saying."

"But –"

"Don't 'but,' me. You know I've always told you to follow your heart. And I think, deep down, you want for yourself what your friends want for you: a steady relationship with a great guy, a good job that actually challenges you. But you're afraid to go after something that's actually important to you. Take a good, hard look at what you really want and then ask yourself why you haven't pursued it. It's time for a reality check." Camille paused and picked her purse up off the floor. "I gotta get going, honey. I've got to get to the store. I promised your father a roast for dinner tonight and it needs to go in the oven early."

"You didn't even tell me about your trip."

Her mother's eyes went dreamy. "Sweetheart, it's the beach. What is there to tell? Gorgeous sunsets, drinks on the porch every night, an ocean view from the bedroom. Lots of hot sex with your father –"

"Stop there. I think I get the picture."

Smiling, Camille stood, stretched and picked up her cup.

"Honey, Summer and Josie care about you. They have a good idea of what's right for you. Trust them. Give this a chance. Follow The Rules."

AFTER DELANEY LEFT UMBRELLA COFFEE, she pondered what Camille had said: *You're afraid to go after something that's actually important to you. Take a good, hard look at what you really want and then ask yourself why you haven't pursued it.*

Camille's observation was dead-on. Delaney wanted a great job and a great man, but the truth was that she was afraid to pursue either one of those things. The man issue was easier to address—she'd had her heart broken by that snake of a guy, Tucker. His rejection wasn't personal. It wasn't about her. And with Summer and Josie's help, she could overcome her fear of being rejected again.

But the job issue was far more serious.

Again, she thought of Howie and Max, and replayed one of their appointments in her mind.

This time, Howie brought Max in for a sore on his stomach. As Delaney examined Max, Howie told her how his wife, Shirley, had died a few months before.

"Her heart just stopped beating," Howie said. "She died in her sleep. I'm glad she went peacefully, but I miss her so much. Every single day."

Then, Howie surprised her by asking questions rather than telling her about the library remodel or the new sculpture installation at the park.

"Doctor Collins, do you have anyone special? A sweetheart? A young man who's earned your favor? Or, I'm a modern guy. A young lady?"

Delaney laughed, then. "No, Howie, I don't have anyone. I go for men, by the way. I was engaged, but that ended badly."

"Did you end it, or did he?"

"He did."

"Well, I'll tell you what, young lady. That stupid jerk is missing out. He obviously wasn't smart enough for you, anyway. You make sure that when you find love, it's real. You hear me?"

Delaney was—surprisingly— touched by the ferocity with which Howie delivered this advice, and she gave his shoulders a quick squeeze before she sent him on his way with a tube of antibiotic ointment for Max's sore, which they determined was a cut that had gotten infected.

Howie had been right all those years ago, Delaney thought now. She turned her car into her driveway and put it in park. But she didn't deserve Howie's good advice, or his friendship.

SEE? I can follow The Rules.

A couple of hours after her coffee with her mom, Delaney pulled on the soft blue sweater and clean jeans the girls had instructed her to wear on the second date. *Right down to the nighttime makeup.* Black eyeliner, smudged. Black mascara. Sparkly eye shadow. Lip gloss.

Tonight's feature: a kindergarten teacher.

"A male kindergarten teacher?" Delaney whined when Summer went through the roster. "Isn't that a little weird?"

"You're being critical already," Josie pointed out. "There are plenty of nice, normal kindergarten teachers out there, who happen to be male. It's a noble profession and it means he likes kids. It also means he works nice hours. He won't be gone day and night like my husband is. Trust me."

"Fine."

"Don't say, 'fine,' like it's your choice," Summer said. "This is our next pick for you."

"Fine."

According to the girls, Craig Densmore had suggested Delaney meet him at Mama's, Juniper's only upscale Italian restaurant. He was waiting (and twiddling his thumbs) outside when Delaney arrived two minutes early.

Exactly as advertised, she thought: his longish brown hair curled over the back of his sweater's turtleneck and his big brown eyes were warm when she approached him.

"You must be Delaney," he said. "I'm Craig. Craig Densmore. But I also answer to Mr. Densmore, or Mr. D."

"Can I stick with Craig?"

They shook hands. He pumped hers maniacally. She felt their palms stick together.

"Yeah." His voice sounded hoarse. He cleared his throat. "Sorry. I'm a bit nervous."

The admission softened her.

"Have you been waiting long?" she asked.

"Ah, no. Less than an hour."

"An hour? Am I late?"

"What? No! No, not at all. *I* just didn't want to be late." He wiped his clammy hands on his khakis.

"Oh. Okay." Poor guy. Delaney resolved to give him a fair chance.

As Jesse had, Craig opened the door for Delaney. She made a mental note to put that on the rubric.

The dinner conversation was relatively pleasant, she thought, as the server brought them their check. Boring, but pleasant. They discussed jobs, home ownership, hobbies … the usual. He'd become a teacher in part because he was an avid mountain biker and wanted weekends and summers off. He enjoyed kids, but his real passion was photography, which he did on the side. Mountain biking provided him lots of photography opportunities, as long as he didn't wipe out and mangle his camera. Teaching provided good benefits and regular pay and he liked it just fine. This made him slightly less weird, in Delaney's opinion. At least he had normal hobbies and an adventurous side. It could be promising.

He ordered lamb. She winced as she watched him chew the delicate meat of the baby sheep, but remembered to stop mentally criticizing him and focused on her own food: spicy spaghetti.

Craig took her up on her offer to split the bill. She couldn't decide whether she was relieved or disappointed.

"How about some mini golf?" Craig asked as they signed their credit card receipts.

"Mini golf? Isn't it a little chilly for that?"

"They just opened this new indoor course," he said. "Over where the roller rink used to be."

"Oh. Um, sure. It's been years since I played, but it sounds fun. Let me use the restroom real quick."

In the bathroom, still life paintings of bright red flowers hung on bright yellow walls, making the bathroom look dingy even though Delaney couldn't see any actual dirt. The grout on the floor was absolutely black, though and the toilet and sink looked grimy. She took out her phone, hung her purse on the hook on the back of the door and stood in the middle of the room, trying not to touch anything. She texted the girls: *He wants to mini golf.*

Summer: *So go.*

Josie: *Have fun.*

Delaney: *Seriously? Isn't it for kids?*

Summer: *He wants to spend more time with you. Quit being a snob.*

Josie: *Is he nice?*

Delaney: *Yes.*

Summer: *Is he talking about butchering?*

Delaney: *No.*

Josie: *Has he tried to have sex with you?*

Delaney: *No.*

Summer: *Has he talked about sex?*

Delaney: *No.*

Josie: *Is he creepy?*

Delaney: *No.*

Summer: *Has he asked you to look at his feet?*

Delaney: *No.*

Josie: *Haha*

Delaney: *Haha. Ha.*

Summer: *Are you having fun?*

Delaney: *So-so.*

Josie: *Go golfing.*

Summer: *But no holes-in-one, ok? Hahaha.*

Delaney: *Fine. I'll go.*

Summer: *There she goes with the fine again.*

Josie: *Seriously, Dee. Stop with the fine.*

Summer: *Have fun.*

Josie: *"Fine guys. If you're going to make me."*

Delaney: *Shut up, Josie.*

ORBIT GOLF WAS PACKED. Teenagers, determined to do well without actually looking like they were trying, milled around in the black light, their teeth glowing every time they spoke. Delaney and Craig stood in the doorway for a few seconds, admiring the fluorescent planets, moons and aliens painted on the walls. The course, which was outlined in multi-colored fluorescent duct tape, looked more complicated than Delaney had expected. She immediately noticed a tiny bridge on Hole Twelve and a tight left turn on Hole Seven.

"This looks cool," she admitted.

"You're goin' down," Craig said. "C'mon. Let's get some balls."

He hurried off. She thought she heard a nervous chuckle. Was he chuckling about getting balls, or chuckling with excitement about golfing?

Delaney wanted to shrivel up and hide under the counter when Craig said to the greasy-haired teenage employee, "I've already got two balls but I need two more."

In a stage whisper, he added, "Can't play golf with the two I have."

Is he for real? She and the kid behind the counter exchanged a quick glance. The kid grabbed a couple of balls and set them down in front of Craig.

Give him the benefit of the doubt, Delaney reminded herself. She grabbed the blue ball, hoping to prevent him from making jokes about blue balls. "Shall we?"

When they arrived at the first hole and had to wait for a group of kids to finish their turn, Craig stuck his golf club out in front of himself and said, "Check out my club, Delaney. It's a powerhouse."

She turned away to dissuade him from making further jokes, but he didn't stop there.

"Want to hold my ball?" he asked, holding his glowing red golf ball out in his palm, twirling it suggestively.

"I've got mine, thanks."

"Ah, you're just a one-ball kind of girl, huh?"

When someone made a wild putt, Craig shouted, "Ball on the loose! You'd better learn now, you young guns! Get your balls under control, fellas!"

Every time he made a joke, he turned to Delaney, eyebrows raised, waiting for feedback.

It reminded her of Summer's kids. Luke and Nate were always interrupting Summer's conversations to say, "Watch, Mom!" They'd ninja-jump off the couch, or spin around a dozen times, or do some fancy somersault, then turn to her, eyebrows raised, waiting for her to cheer.

That was cute. But Craig Densmore wasn't a little boy. At one point when he looked at her after pantomiming poking a slow golfer with his club, she shook her head.

"Whatsa matter? My club making you nervous?" He wagged the golf club back and forth in front of his body and came towards her. It took a gargantuan effort for Delaney not to roll her eyes.

By the time they reached the ninth hole, Delaney wished she could find somewhere to hide. She was more than grateful the building was dark so no one would recognize her. What about one of those fake moon rocks? Could she climb under it?

On another fabricated restroom break, Delaney texted the girls: *I need an exit strategy. ASAP.*

Summer: *Why?*

Josie: *Not the kindergarten teacher! I had high hopes!*

Delaney: *I was fine with the mini golf, until he started the endless club and balls jokes. Kill me now.*

Summer: *Are you for real?*

Delaney: *Is HE for real?*

Josie: *His profile didn't say anything about liking body humor. I swear. He's probably nervous.*

Summer: *Are his armpits sweating?*

Delaney: *Oh, I'm sorry. I didn't get a good look at his freakin' armpits, Summer. Geez.*

Summer: *Just trying to get a sense for whether he's nervous. Geez, yourself.*

Josie: *This is what we're talking about. You give up too easy. Get out of the bathroom, suck it up and finish the date.*

Summer: *What hole are you on?*

Delaney: *I think he's probably on 11 by now.*

Josie: *You can make it through 2 more.*

Delaney: *Josie, a golf course has 18 holes.*

Josie: *Oh. Right. Well, you can make it through 7 more.*

Josie: *Then just say you're tired. He'll get the hint. But I still think you give up too easy. If he wants a second date, he's getting it.*

Delaney: *Fine.*

Summer: *Haha, she said fine!*

Josie: *"Fine, you guys. Fine."*

Delaney: *I'm calling an emergency meeting for tomorrow. My handy dandy schedule says you're both free at 4. We'll meet at Summer's. That way you can go get the kids at 5. See you then.*

In a huff, she shoved her phone into her purse, threw the stall door open and stalked out of the bathroom and back to Hole Twelve, where Craig, tongue poked out between his teeth, was pouring all his concentration into getting his ball around the tight corner and over the small bridge. Once he'd completed the hole successfully, he turned and looked at her as if he wanted her to cheer for him.

He really is cute, with those puppy dog eyes. Maybe he is just nervous. Maybe I should cut him some slack.

She tried to get a good look at his armpits but it was dark and he was wearing a sweater. While they waited for the group ahead of them to finish Hole Thirteen, Craig looked earnestly into her eyes.

"Look, Delaney. I'm really sorry. About all the potty humor and everything. I obviously spend way too much time with five- and six-year-olds. I'm just nervous. It's been a while since I dated. Can we start over?"

Holes Thirteen through Eighteen went smoothly enough. Craig was subdued. A couple of times, she thought she saw him smirk, as if he'd thought of a really good joke but abstained from actually saying it. Although she was grateful for the respite, she found him pretty boring when he was this quiet. *Is there no happy medium?*

Sure, dinner conversation had stayed above the belt, but it hadn't given her much to think about. Despite having started over, she decided before they said goodnight that she wouldn't be seeing any more of Craig Densmore.

She didn't need a rubric to tell her that.

CHAPTER TWELVE

"Thank you all for coming. As you know, we're gathered here today to create an emergency exit strategy for Yours Truly."

Delaney and Josie stood in Summer's bright, cluttered kitchen, where Summer chopped onions, tossing them into a Dutch oven on the stove and Josie leaned against the counter, scanning her copy of "101 Tips for the Best Interview Ever."

"You don't need an exit strategy," Josie muttered without looking up from her book. "You need a try-to-like-someone-normal-for-once strategy."

"You weren't *there*!" Delaney said. "Was she, Hannah?"

From her high chair, Summer's one-year-old squealed and clapped her hands, then extended her arms to be lifted. Delaney took her out of the chair, wiped the smears of sweet potato off her face and hands, and kissed her cheek before settling her on one hip.

"You didn't see the way Craig Densmore was behaving," Delaney said. "You would have been mortified. I need to be able to make *some* of the decisions." She tossed Hannah high into the air, making her squeal.

"You can," Summer said casually. She shrugged a shoulder and stirred the beans and meat she'd added to her Dutch oven. "You did. Don't do that thing you do where you act like you don't have a choice. That's exactly how you've turned bartending into a permanent career."

Despite the objections that ran through her mind--objections about her making bartending a permanent career because at least she couldn't kill anybody—Delaney Delaney didn't respond, and Summer went on, "You made choices last night. Like what to order for dinner. What to say during conversation. When to go to the bathroom and text us like a crazy person."

She ticked these off on her fingers. Hannah copied her.

"You wouldn't have enjoyed that date, either," Delaney said. She could hear the poutiness in her own voice.

Instead of responding, Summer asked, "How was dinner?"

"It was fine." When Summer and Josie exchanged a look, Delaney switched gears. "Pleasant, even. I would say pleasant. We had a nice conversation. But the balls and club … it was too much. You would have thought so, too. Both of you."

Josie shrugged. "Maybe."

Delaney glared at her.

"Fine," Josie said. "I would have thought so, too." She marked her place and snapped the book closed. Then, still holding it against her body, she crossed her arms in front of her chest and gave Delaney the stink eye.

"But we wouldn't have hightailed it out of there," she said. She leaned against the counter again, her compact figure accentuated by a fitted black suit. "Look, Dee, I get it. He made weird jokes. Middle school jokes from the sound of it, and we all know how much you hated middle school."

"We weren't all gorgeous at fourteen like you were," Delaney muttered. "I was zitty, thick around the middle, and I had a huge metal mouth. And I had to endure fat jokes, acne jokes and brace-face jokes from the very same guys who made those balls and club jokes while they scampered after you, offering to carry your backpack. All night I was waiting for Craig Densmore to ask me if I had my own postal code. Remember that joke? 'You're so fat you have your own postal code.'"

"I get it. I do. I mean, I was pretty good-looking in middle school, I'll give you that." Josie winked. "If I were going to think about your motivations, I would say that you push guys away because you're afraid they're going to reject you. I know, that's practically what you just said, yourself. But you're not in middle school now. This is the real world and you've turned into a gorgeous, capable woman. Long-term commitment is about loving someone despite, and sometimes even because of, their faults. Not that my marriage is perfect. All I'm saying is, I get where you're coming from. But you need to give guys a chance."

"*We* get it, Dee," Summer chimed in. "Remember, Josie, we're unified."

Josie nodded, and Summer continued, "We do get it. But you've got to stick some of these things out, honey." She put the lid on the Dutch oven and started emptying the dishwasher. Did the woman ever stop?

"Right," Josie said. "*We* get it. Anyway. I have to get home to study for my interview. So let's plan the exit strategy. But you have to get our permission to use it."

"Do you hear this, Hannah? I have to get their permission to use an exit strategy, even if a juvenile kindergarten teacher is thrusting his mini golf club at me."

"Do you hear this, Hannah?" Josie said in a sing-songy voice. "We have to beg our best friend of almost twenty years to find a guy who's actually good for her. *Dios mío.*"

Hannah giggled.

"All right. Let's do this," Josie said. "But let me ask you something, Delaney. Did he give you a sob story? Was he super-depressed and needy?"

"No, he was perfectly normal." She closed her eyes against the onslaught she knew was coming, then opened them when Josie yelled, "Ha!"

She jabbed a finger at Delaney, her expression triumphant.

"You just can't handle not having a fixer-upper. That's all there is to it. You can't handle dating a normal guy. And you can't give anybody half a chance. Unless he's in ultimate peril. Near death, near suicide, or near insane."

"I can! I swear! It's just –"

"Now, now, girls," Summer's mommy voice cut through. "Let's stay on task. I have to leave in twenty-five to pick up the kids."

"Fine," Delaney huffed.

Delaney set Hannah on the floor. She buzzed off to the living room, where banging sounds commenced.

"Exit strategy, huh?" Josie said. "If it's really bad, just tell the guy you have a yeast infection and it's really itchy. It's bugging you and you need to get home."

"Josefina. I can't say that."

"Why not?" Summer asked. She handed Delaney a stack of plates, which Delaney put away in the cupboard.

"That's your only option," Josie said.

"What?"

Hannah returned with a pretend vacuum and industriously vacuumed the kitchen floor.

"There's your exit strategy," Summer said, now loading dirty dishes. "If you want to end a date early, you have to tell him you have a yeast infection."

"Itchy!" Hannah said.

"Oh. My. God. You guys can't be serious."

To busy herself, Delaney started scrubbing pots and pans from the massive mountain of hand wash dishes in the sink.

Josie, still smug, looked at her watch. "I gotta go. Love you girls."

She leaned down to kiss Hannah, whisper something sweetly in Spanish–which Delaney suspected was a diatribe about the exit strategy–and then she stalked out, her high heels sounding very important on the hardwood floor.

"Geez," Delaney said.

"You've got to start sticking things out, Dee," Summer said. "You can't jump ship at the earliest opportunity."

"Do I do that?"

"Oh, yeah. You do. Only on important stuff."

"Give me an example."

"Don't make me do this."

"Come on. An example," Delaney said. Her arms were starting to burn from scrubbing so hard. "You're throwing around some pretty hefty accusations, here, Summer."

Hannah pushed the vacuum up against Delaney's toes, then dropped it. Her tiny hand skimmed the countertop until it landed on a rogue bean. She put it in her mouth, her face contorted and she spit it out.

"Your job hunt. Post-college. You applied to what? Four jobs?"

"Three," Delaney corrected her, in a near-whisper. "Three. But they were three really good ones."

"Were they?" Summer said.

When Delaney didn't answer, she went on. "Here's the thing. You didn't even try for jobs you thought were great. You researched the heck out of them, yes. But you applied only for the select few that were mediocre: crap pay, crap location, crap job duties. Your job hunt lasted a mere two weeks before you threw in the towel. Then you went back to school, which was just an extension—an expensive one—of your procrastination. And after a year—a year! It's like a blip on the radar of your whole life!—of working as a vet, took up residence at Rowdy's and pulled on your permanent uniform of a black t-shirt and tight jeans. Which suits you," she added as an aside. "But look. Sometimes you have to be willing to give things time. Even if they don't seem perfect right away."

Delaney was tempted to tell Summer then, about what had happened with Howie and Max. How, on the way to exam room five that day, she'd seen a very hot pet owner in exam room three and made what was supposed to be a quick detour. How that detour turned into a longer stop because she decided to spend a little time with the muscular surfer-guy firefighter who'd brought in his adorable new puppy for a routine exam and immunizations. How they'd gotten to talking, found things they had in common—the University of Arizona and a penchant for cinnamon lattes at the school's student union—and kept right on talking while Howie watched Max, his beloved canine companion, collapse.

And that was only the beginning of that story. Delaney couldn't bear to think about the middle or the end. So she tried stalling.

"So you're saying –"

Summer held up a hand like Delaney had seen her do when one of the kids interrupted a lecture.

Why am I constantly undergoing the same treatment as Summer's kids?

"I'm saying, when it comes to dating, every time you find a great catch, you fixate on the small stuff that makes him seem gross or unworthy somehow. On the other hand, you consider fixer-uppers 'perfect.' My guesses about the reason why aren't important right now. But if you find a perfectly normal, reasonable guy, you won't even give him the time of day. And your job. Don't even get me started on that."

"But last night –"

The hand went up again.

"I hear you, sister. I live in a world of balls and club jokes. I have two boys in elementary school, remember? And their father loves revisiting that time in his life. But you said dinner was pleasant. You don't *have* to see Craig the Kindergarten Teacher again. Although Josie and I agree you should give him another try. In general, you need to be willing to give people a chance. Not people on the edge of a mental cliff. Normal, happy people."

Summer kissed her on the cheek, hoisted Hannah onto her hip. "Now get out of here. I have to go get the kids."

Delaney walked out of Summer's house, picking her way through the plastic swords and discarded pajamas strewn on the floor. Just as she got to the front door, nudging a remote control monster truck out of the way with her foot, Summer called, "Oh, and Dee? We know this online dating stuff is hard. We know you need an alternative."

"Thank goodness," Delaney muttered.

"So we signed you up for a speed dating event this week. I almost forgot to tell you. Let me check the details again and I'll email them to you."

Without answering, Delaney tried to sneak out the front door as if she hadn't heard her.

"I know you heard me," Summer yelled before she made it outside. "And have fun at cooking class! Don't be late!"

COUNTRY KITCHEN, Juniper's lone specialty cooking boutique, sat across the street and down the block from Rowdy's. Delaney often window shopped there as she walked to work, impressed (but mostly overwhelmed) by the tools and gadgets displayed in the picture window.

The storeowners, a retired couple from Phoenix, ran a bed and breakfast for years and brought their expertise to Juniper. High-end utensils, cookware and accessories lined the shelves. Classes took place in the actual kitchen, which sat at the back of the store.

Delaney grimaced when she realized people walking by could see the kitchen from the sidewalk. She wasn't ready to go in, just yet.

"As long as I don't cut off a finger or something," she muttered to herself.

"I know what you mean. You're here for How to Boil Water, right?"

Delighted, Delaney turned to face the woman who stood next to her. Short, wild, curly hair the color of honey framed an oval face and horn-rimmed glasses framed bright blue eyes.

"Beth," the woman said, smiling and extending a hand.

"Delaney."

"My mom's making me take this class," Beth said. "She thinks it'll help me get a decent guy."

"My best friends. Ditto."

They grinned at each other.

"Shall we?"

A bell over the door jangled when they walked in, making Delaney feel conspicuous. The hardwood floor, which was probably original to the 1930s-era building, creaked as they walked back to the kitchen. Free-standing islands (half countertop and half stovetop) were placed in two rows, three deep.

A couple already stood behind the middle island on the right, so Delaney and Beth took the other middle island. Long counters lined the two side walls. A huge refrigerator and more counters, topped with baskets of onions and potatoes, occupied the back wall. Open cabinets beneath the counters held mixing bowls, baking dishes and serving dishes. Whisks, spoons, spatulas and other implements Delaney didn't even recognize hung from pegs on the walls.

An older woman wearing a white apron and daisy-pattern head wrap approached them. Her skin was the color of chocolate and her dark eyes held a mix of warmth and humor.

"I'm Wendy, your instructor," she said. After introductions, she said, "Write your names on your aprons. You get to take them home with you at the end of the class. We'll get started in a few moments."

Wendy walked over to greet another pair of women who had come in. Delaney and Beth wrote their names on their aprons.

"Now what?" Beth asked. "Should we get some wine, or something?"

She motioned to a wine rack above the refrigerator.

"We should. Definitely. But I think it might be for cooking."

"So, your best friends are worried about the state of your love life, huh?" Beth asked as she tied her apron on.

"Yeah. Well, it's more like they just don't like the guys I choose. They say I always look for fixer-uppers and it's symbolic of how I run my entire life. They want me to get a new job, learn how to cook and get a decent boyfriend."

"Ouch. Is it all true?"

"Yep," Delaney said, trying on the acceptance. She wouldn't say it felt good, but it definitely beat the rose-colored glasses of avoidance. "What about you?"

"Pretty much the same. I just went through a divorce, actually. My mom told me it's because I was selfish and ate takeout all the time."

"But you read between the lines, right?"

"Right. I sucked at marriage. I suck at cooking. I'm not sure how my cooking skills relate to my marriage skills, but we'll see. I figure it couldn't hurt. Right before he left, I decided to mend things. We'd been growing apart for a while and I knew it was my fault. So I cooked him what was supposed to be this big, fancy steak dinner. Only I overcooked the steak, undercooked the baked potatoes and wilted the crap out of the green beans. Don't even ask me how dessert turned out."

"Ugh. I know. To prove I could cook, I offered to make lemon chicken for my friends the other night. One of them, Summer, has four kids, so I cooked for them, too. They ate it, but I have a sneaking suspicion she bribed them. Told them that if they ate my dinner she'd take them out to eat, after."

Delaney felt herself relaxing. Maybe this could be fun. Aside from the couple across from them, a pair of men, another pair of women and two other couples had come in. Once everyone had put on their aprons, Wendy stepped to the front of the kitchen area.

"Good evening, everyone," she said. "Welcome. I know this class is called, How to Boil Water, but I think it's safe to assume everyone here already knows how to do that, right?"

Everyone chuckled. One of the gay guys elbowed the other, who shrugged.

"You already know this is a four-session class. During the first two sessions, we'll cook entrees. During the third session, we'll work on side dishes. And during the final session, we'll put some salads together. At the end of the course, you'll each receive a cookbook containing all the recipes we work on, as well as several variations on each recipe. If you want desserts, you've got to take How to Bake a Cake or Feed Your Sweet Tooth. Okay? Tonight, we're starting with a simple spaghetti recipe."

A low murmur ran through the student body.

"Spaghetti? I can do spaghetti-os," Beth said.

"Now, students," Wendy said, interrupting the chatter, "don't worry if it sounds complicated. We're taking it step by step. I'd like one partner to go get a yellow onion and a package of Italian sausage from the back and one to get a pot" (she held one up as an example), "fill it with water and start it heating on your stovetop. Once you've done that, grab a saucepan" (this, too, she held up).

"I'll get the meat," Beth said. "Just can't resist a good sausage."

Delaney snickered and walked over to the side cupboard to retrieve pot. She set it to boil, then grabbed a saucepan and returned to her post. Beth came back with the sausage and the onion.

"You'll find olive oil in your cabinet, under your counter," Wendy said, "and measuring spoons. Measure out a tablespoon of olive oil, put it in the saucepan and put the meat in. Then we'll chop. Grab a zucchini and a bell pepper from the fridge."

Wendy continued speaking as the students scurried to the fridge. Someone handed Delaney her vegetables. "Always work with sharp knives. I'll demonstrate the onion chopping and then once we get that in the pan, we'll add the sausage and then do the garlic bell peppers and zucchini. Ready?"

Side by side, Delaney and Beth chopped their vegetables. Delaney found the rhythmic tapping of her knife on the wooden countertop oddly soothing. Why hadn't she done more cooking before this? She remembered thinking it was so weird when Josie would call and say she was cooking, drinking wine and listening to music. Now she could see just a glimmer of the appeal.

"That looks very nice, Delaney," Beth said. "Very nice."

"Why, thank you, Beth," Delaney said. "As does yours."

The truth was, neither set of vegetables looked particularly pretty. The pieces were irregular and oddly shaped. But they were chopped and added to the pan with tomato sauce, stewed tomatoes and plenty of seasoning.

"I never have this much stuff in my kitchen at once," Delaney said to Beth, who nodded.

"Don't worry, ladies," Wendy said. "I'll also be giving you a list of items to stock your kitchen with so you can always make yourself something to eat. No more bare cupboards, no more bare tables."

The setup was perfect, Delaney thought. Wendy glided around the room, reminding each pair to add their seasonings, put their pasta in the water, drain their pasta, or stir the sauce.

"Can I just bring you home with me?" Delaney asked as she passed by on her final walk-through. A few of the other students chuckled.

"I'm sure I'd love that, Delaney," Wendy said, "but after I'm done with you here, you won't need me. I promise."

The finished product steamed from colorful bowls, sending off scents of spicy sausage, tangy tomatoes and sweet peppers. Delaney's mouth watered.

"Wow," Beth said. "This is the first time I've ever actually wanted to eat something I cooked!"

"You have an uncanny knack for echoing my sentiments."

Returning home after the three-hour class, Delaney felt exhausted. Who knew cooking could be so much fun and so tiring, all at the same time? Her legs were sore, her neck was sore and her stomach was full. The house seemed so still, so quiet, so … *lonely* after an evening spent in a busy, bustling kitchen packed with people stirring up savory scents, together.

Was that the difference between a house and a home? Not just the cooking, of course. Anybody could cook. But the having someone to cook with, to eat with? Cooking together, with the intent of filling your bellies, of nourishing your bodies, of falling into bed to sleep together … that was a home.

Maybe Summer and Josie were onto something, she thought. Of the three of them, Delaney was the only one who came home to an empty house every night. A house that smelled like vanilla-scented candles or berry-scented lotion or maybe microwave popcorn.

But it never held the rich smell of a dish she'd put her time, energy and thought into. And, although she hated to admit it, she thought, wrinkling her nose, love. You could put love into cooking. Delaney never prepared food for anyone – not even herself. And after tonight, she realized maybe she was worth it.

CHAPTER THIRTEEN

When Delaney originally volunteered to pick Summer's kids up from school each Tuesday, Summer gave her strict instructions about what they could listen to on the radio. She started with a list (a long one) of unacceptables—and this was just in regard to music: "No rap, no foul language, no sex music, no hard rock, nothing about guns or prostitutes."

When Delaney tapped her foot impatiently, waiting for Summer to hand over the keys, checking her watch because she was afraid of being late on the inaugural Carpool Tuesday, Summer finally said, "Oh! I have an idea!"

After a good three minutes' worth of rummaging around on the floor of the van's passenger side, she came up with a CD.

"Just play this," she'd said. "It'll make things simpler."

Within a minute of playing the cheerful, high-pitched, repetitive kids' music, though, Delaney could feel her ears starting to bleed. The CD mysteriously disappeared. Since then Delaney had allowed the kids to take turns choosing the radio station on the ten-minute drive home. If she heard bad language or sex talk, she switched the channel.

Today, because it was Sarah's turn to choose, Delaney put in her mental earplugs. Sarah always chose the easy listening station. Always. And belted out every song. So today, by the time Sarah's voice broke through the barrier, she was shouting:

"Aunt Dee! Aunt Dee, can you hear me?"

Delaney turned down the cheesy love songs and said with exaggerated sweetness, "Yes, Sarah?"

"I've been trying to get your attention for, like, six minutes!"

"Since the school dismissal bell rang only four minutes ago, I sincerely doubt it. But sorry. I was tuning out your sappy romance music. Let's start over."

"Okay." Sarah rolled her eyes. "Aunt Dee?"

"Yes, Sarah?"

"Remember that guy who helped us after the car accident last week?"

Boy, do I.

"Yep," Delaney said.

"Well, he was really handsome, wasn't he?"

Boy, was he.

"Yeah. I thought so."

"Are we going to see him again?" Sarah said.

"Probably. It's a small town."

"Is he going to be your boyfriend?"

"I don't even know him, Sarah. What if he's not even nice?"

"Well, he's handsome, isn't he? And he did stop to help us after the accident. And he didn't even know us. Only a *nice* stranger would do that."

Delaney nodded at Sarah's sound reasoning. "Good points," she said. "All of them. Well, we'll see, I guess."

"We'll see," Sarah said.

THE WHEELCHAIR ACCESS stall in the Juniper Public Library's bathroom barely fit all three of them, but Delaney, Summer and Josie crowded in anyway, trying at once to be quiet and lay the ground rules for the next phase of The Dating Intervention.

"I've always wanted to do this!" Summer squealed.

"You've always wanted to do what?" Delaney said. "Strip down your best friend and tape a wire to her boobs, before eavesdropping on her pathetic conversations with pathetic men?"

Josie, who was busy taping a wire up Delaney's torso and between her breasts, chuckled.

"No! Speed-dating!" Summer said.

That morning, Delaney had received an email from Summer, marked urgent. It was a forward, an advertisement about a speed-dating event that night. "Mid-week for Mid-Life," the ad proclaimed in hot pink and purple letters.

"I'm not mid-life," Delaney snapped when Summer answered her phone just a second after the email landed in Delaney's inbox. "And the public library is not the most romantic spot for speed dating."

"Who cares? It'll be fun," Summer said.

So here they were, a half-hour from starting time, stuffed into a bathroom stall and wiring Delaney up so the girls could listen to her exchanges and advise her, or, in other words, boss her around, about what to say. Josie had borrowed the wire from Paul, who said he'd arrest all three of them if they broke it.

"Paul says this thing can be wonky, but if we tape it right, it should hold. See? The microphone can come off the wire right here. I'll just add a little tape…"

"Remember to keep your hair over your right ear, Dee," Summer said. "Don't do that thing you always do, where you tuck your hair behind your ear."

"It's a trick I picked up from you sophomore year, Josie. Remember? You used to do that all the time to make the guys hot."

"It worked, too," Summer said. "But neither of us could ever get the hang of it."

"No, we couldn't," Delaney said. "But I still do it."

"You guys kill me," Josie said. "Just don't touch your hair. And don't bite your lip."

"Okay. All right. I only do that because you told me you read about it in a magazine or something."

"When we were *freshmen*," Josie said, laughing. "I can't believe you're still holding onto that."

"Can I go now?"

Together, the girls emerged from the bathroom stall. A woman on her way into the stall next to them looked like she didn't know whether to hide or turn tail and exit as quickly as possible. Summer and Josie linked their arms through Delaney's and propelled her over to the mirror.

"You look great," Josie said.

"Just have fun," Summer said.

"And be yourself," Josie added.

"What? Mid-life?"

"We'll be right there with you," Summer said, patting Delaney's arm.

As Delaney left them, she called back over her shoulder, "Enjoy living vicariously through me, ladies. Only chance you're getting."

Two-person tables decked out in yellow tablecloths ran along the room's edges, forcing the participants of the Mid-Week for Mid-Life to crowd into the center. Uncomfortable, Delaney approached the knot of people looking for a friendly face. The woman from the bathroom came in, made eye contact with Delaney and immediately changed her course of direction.

"You look nervous." A man spoke from behind her and Delaney thought, *That's a crappy pick-up line.* Just a breath later, she wondered if she really did look nervous and if so, whether nervous was ugly. Then she thought maybe this guy wasn't even trying to pick her up. Maybe he was just being kind because he thought she looked nervous. She sighed.

"Nice voice," Summer said cheerfully in her right ear.

He did have a nice voice. But he suffered from a geek complex: a scraggly comb-over, a closer-than-necessary shave (he had nicked his chin and forgotten to remove the tiny fleck of toilet paper) and a sweater vest. A bulbous red nose overhung a thick mouth. His lower lip protruded in a manner Delaney thought was quite unfortunate. Actually, he reminded Delaney of her junior high self.

"It's my first time," she said.

Oh, geez. Her voice was high, breathy, and yes, nervous. She heard Josie giggle in her ear.

"Oh, I'm an old pro," the man said. Then, holding out his hand, he said, "Karl."

"Elizabeth," Delaney said.

"Elizabeth!" Josie shrieked.

Delaney's hand flew to her ear and she winced.

"Are you okay?" Karl said.

"Yeah, fine. I'm fine."

"Your name tag says Delaney."

"Yeah. That's my name."

"I thought your name was Elizabeth."

Shit.

"She forgot about the name tag," she heard Josie whisper to Summer. They giggled. Delaney sighed.

"It is. It's Elizabeth Delaney."

Karl raised his bushy eyebrows. "Oh. So is this your first speed-dating event, ever, or just your first time at Mid-Week?"

Delaney could tell the girls were trying to muffle their laughter, but she could hear it just the same.

"What? Oh. Sorry. First for both."

"It's fun, actually. You get to meet some interesting people."

"Yeah. I can imagine. So how does it work?"

As Karl explained the drill (women sit nearest the wall, men sit nearest the center of the room, moderator rings a bell every three minutes and men shift to the next table), Delaney looked at the motley group who'd shown up. Were they all very desperate? They looked very desperate, she concluded, taking in the women's too-bright lipstick and the men's too-stiff posture. She scolded herself for judging them.

I'm here, too, aren't I?

"Well, thanks for explaining," she said. "Looks like we're about to get started."

A schoolmarmish woman in a knee-length skirt, tight vest and puffy-sleeved shirt approached a podium and held up her bell. Delaney walked toward one of the corner tables near the window.

"Don't sit by the window!" Josie shouted into her ear.

Again, Delaney was surprised at her friends' psychic-like ability. She did an about-face and chose a chair near the door, instead. Once the women were seated, the men filed into their positions.

"Hi, Karl," Delaney said as he sat down across from her.

"Ooh, it's the nice voice guy!" Summer squealed.

The moderator rang the bell, shouted, "Three minutes, Mid-lifers!" and stepped off the podium. The noise level in the room rose immediately as the very desperate Mid-Lifers started rattling off questions in a rapid-fire attempt to get to know one another. On one hand, Delaney could see the appeal. She'd get through a bunch of men in one sitting. But on the other hand, this whole process felt ridiculous. How much could you really learn about someone in three minutes? And were people in such dire dating circumstances that they couldn't go out and meet people in a real setting?

"You can take notes," Karl said, motioning to the notepad and pencil on the table.

"What kinds of things do you write?"

"Well, most men write things I won't say out loud," he said, "but I usually write down a comment that struck me. Like for you, I'll write that it was your first time speed-dating."

"For him, write that he has a nice voice," Josie prompted through the earpiece.

Delaney pictured her friends, perched side by side on a toilet seat, huddled in a tiny stall, listening intently to everything she said. It was all she could do to avoid rolling her eyes.

"What'll you write for me?" Karl asked.

"I'll write that you were the first friendly face I saw," Delaney answered. "And that you were very helpful."

"Awww," she heard Summer say.

"And then, if you want to see someone again, you put a checkmark next to his name," Karl said, watching her pad carefully.

With that, she busily began scribbling notes. *Mental note: Kill Summer and Josie.*

"So what do you do, Delaney?"

"I'm a bartender at Rowdy's, but I'm looking for a different job. How about you?"

"What kind of job are you looking for?"

"A veterinary position. I graduated from vet school a few years ago."

"Don't tell him how long ago that was," Josie barked.

Delaney nodded, but froze when she realized she was nodding at Josie. She switched gears and asked, "What about you, what do you do?"

"Oh, vet school," Karl breathed, sitting back and crossing his legs. "Must be interesting. How'd you like that?"

"I liked it okay," Delaney said. She tried again. "What about you? What do you do?"

"Answer the damn question," Josie shouted.

Delaney flinched.

"So how'd you come to work at Rowdy's?"

On her notepad, Delaney wrote, *Won't talk about himself at all. It's a no-go.*

Out loud, she said, "Isn't it uncomfortable to cross your legs? I thought men always sat with their legs spread."

The bell rang.

"Well, see ya," Karl said.

"Yeeeeah, probably not," Summer said into the earpiece.

"Guys, shut up!" Delaney said under her breath. "You're supposed to be coaching me!"

"Well, hello, gorgeous!"

A slick, plastic-looking man slid into the seat across from Delaney and she immediately noticed his perfectly straight, bright-to-the-point-of-glowing white teeth. His hair resembled a helmet, shiny and hard, mounding up over his skull in a perfect sphere.

"Wait. Don't tell me. Hair gel," Summer said. "Lots of it."

"Delaney, huh?" he squinted at her name tag. "I'm Patrick."

"Nice to meet you."

"First time, huh?" He winked.

"Yeah. How could you tell?"

"You said 'nice to meet you.' Usually people don't waste time on the pleasantries since we have only three minutes to chat. But it's sweet. It's nice to meet you, too, Delaney."

She felt oddly charmed.

"He is sweet," Summer said. "Ask him how his day's going."

"How's your day going?" Delaney asked.

"It's all right," Patrick answered. His dark eyebrows drew together.

"Busy, you know? I deliver furniture and damned if the crappy economy's not stopping folks around here from buying furniture!"

He slapped his hand on his leg and giggled wildly. Furniture buying and delivering was a funny business, apparently.

"Ask him if he has a big penis," Josie said.

"Do you have a big –" Delaney began, before stopping herself. "A big truck? Do you have a big truck?"

"Oh, yeah. I have a big truck. It's huge."

The bell rang.

Josie's voice piped up in Delaney's ear: "What'd you write down for that one?"

The rest of the evening proved relatively painful, Delaney thought as she collected her notes and deposited her name tag. After Karl and Patrick, she'd met ten others, including Joey the plastic surgeon (surely he could find dates elsewhere?), Nicholas the car salesman (who Summer declared a definite narcissist) and Eric the pastor ("Even pastors need some love, Josefina," Summer said when Josie scoffed at his profession).

She heard grown men, single men looking for women, say things like, "But I don't need a job. Screw 'em. That's what welfare's for, right?" and "Yeah, I live with my mom, but things are different nowadays. Haven't you heard of the boomerang generation?"

Meanwhile, Josie said things like, "Do you smell something? This guy's voice is so high, he must have terrible gas," and "I don't know why, but his story about being in an outhouse when it got knocked over made me want to eat chili cheese fries."

"Well that was a resounding disaster," Delaney said as the girls came out of the bathroom to meet her.

"Yeah, but it was fun," Summer said.

"Your next date will be better," Josie said. "I promise."

"I hope so. If not, you guys are fired."

"Oh, honey," Summer said. "It's not gonna be that easy."

THE CALL NEVER CAME. Delaney had expected the puffy-sleeved moderator from Mid-Week for Mid-Lifers to provide her with a list of all the men who were interested in her. She was surprised and slightly offended, not to mention disappointed and feeling rejected, even though she hadn't thought any of the men were a good match, either.

She steeled herself for the next date, another man the girls found on FindLove.com.

"Uh, I'm in consulting," Mitchell Evans, Esq. said.

All the din in the crowded restaurant – silverware clinking, conversation humming, piano music tinkling – ground to a halt in Delaney's mind. She remembered Josie (or was it Summer?) saying "consultant" was code for unemployed. He definitely hadn't listed "unemployed" on his FindLove.com profile and the girls certainly wouldn't have chosen him if he'd listed "consultant." She was puzzled … she was almost positive they'd said he was a lawyer. But maybe she was getting him mixed up with someone else.

"What about you?" he said, his tone implying he'd already asked her once. Maybe even twice.

"Me? Oh. Uh, right. I have to use the ladies' room. I'll be right back."

She texted the girls: *He's a consultant!*

Josie: *Hahaha!*

Delaney: *What do I do?*

Josie: *Back to the table, sister. Suck it up.*

Delaney: *But he's unemployed!*

Josie: *And you're a bartender.*

Delaney: *I need a second opinion. Where's Summer?*

Summer: *She's barfing her brains out.*

Delaney: *Oh, I'm sorry, Summer. I forgot. Late first trimester. Gets you every time. You can ignore this, then.*

Summer: *Oh, I'm not ignoring it. Back to the table, sister. Suck it up.*

Delaney: *Fine.*

She'd always liked The Blue Fish, Delaney thought as she walked back through the dining room. Hand-painted Mexican tiles on the tabletops and pottery in festive colors on wooden shelves along the brick walls made for a cheerful atmosphere. And she would enjoy it tonight, she promised herself. She had to.

"Sorry about that," she said as she sat back down across from Mitchell.

"It's okay. You were saying you…"

"I tend bar at Rowdy's. But I'm looking for a new job."

Mitchell threw his head back and chortled.

"I wait tables at Eddie's. I, too, am looking for a new job."

Relief flowed through Delaney, even as she scoured her memory for images of Mitchell at Eddie's when she'd gone there with Craig ball-and-club Densmore.

"Really?" she said.

"Really."

"But your profile says you're a –"

"A lawyer, I know. I am, technically. But I'm taking a break right now.

It's false advertising, right? But the thing is, it's as hard to find a woman as it is find a job in this town."

"Don't I know it!"

"Well, now that that's out of the way," he said, "let's eat."

Over a huge plate of nachos, they eyeballed the other patrons at The Blue Fish, guessing what they'd order.

"Name her drink," Mitchell said, pointing a tortilla chip at a woman who was wearing a navy suit with a red scarf.

"White wine. Something sweet, though. Riesling, I think."

"And to eat, Pollo Fundido. No finger food for that lady."

"Him."

"Overalls, dirty boots, dirty fingernails? Corona. With lime and a Cuervo sidecar."

"Fish tacos."

"Those two, in the corner."

"Sharing fajitas."

"And Margaritas. See her brand new, pink cowboy boots? Going for a theme night."

When their server, a tall, thin woman with a huge nose, an even bigger chin and bright blue fingernails, came to offer them dessert, they simultaneously said, "Flan, please!"

Finally! A normal person! Someone I have something in common with.

"So, what do you want to do after this?" Mitchell asked. "We could go bowling."

"I can't. I have a two-drink limit. I can't bowl on a two-drink limit."

"What? A two-drink limit? What's up with that?"

"Oh. Well, first date, two drinks," Delaney stammered, realizing she'd almost let it slip about The Dating Intervention. Rule Number One, she reminded herself. *Absolutely no revealing my friends are in charge.*

"You can't bowl on two drinks or less?" Mitchell said.

"Absolutely not. How about a walk?"

"I have an idea. You game?"

THE STARS GLINTED, winking down at Delaney and Mitchell as they lay on their backs, staring at the sky. Now that the sun had slipped behind the mountains, the spring air felt chilly and damp.

When they left The Blue Fish, Mitchell grabbed Delaney's hand and practically jogged to his Altima. She had to climb in from the driver's side because the passenger door was permanently locked, but she didn't let it bother her. She considered it a mark of character.

"You're gonna love this," he promised as the car choked to life.

They'd driven out Governor's Highway, rising high above downtown on the serpentine road until its lights were tiny specks in the rearview mirror. For a split second, Delaney worried Mitchell might be a serial killer, taking her to a desolate mountaintop hideaway to strangle her and hide her body in a shallow grave. But finally, he pulled up to the city's water tower. He got out, offered his hand and pulled her over the center console to climb out his door.

He led her to the narrow ladder that wound its way up the side of the tower. She went up first, he followed her and they spread out the blanket he'd brought.

"This is perfect," she said.

One-and-a-half-hours flew by while they talked shop, swapping horror stories about their customers.

"One woman sent her food back so many times," Mitchell said, "I finally dumped her sixth plate into her lap."

"You didn't!"

"I did."

"Love it! One guy ordered a beer, drank half of it, then told me it tasted like crap and ordered another. Four times! But I was finally onto him, so on the last one, I dumped a bunch of hot sauce into it and his eyeballs just about popped out of his head!"

Hysterical now, they wiped tears from their eyes.

"This has been really fun," Delaney said, as much to herself as to Mitchell. "Really fun."

CHAPTER FOURTEEN

Muscles Gym, a glossy black pyramid that rose out of the concrete like a submarine coming out of the ocean, stood glinting in the background. As always, Delaney arrived two minutes early, Josie a minute after that. They waited on Summer, who texted, as always, that she was running five minutes late. Which really meant ten.

"We talked about everything," Delaney told Josie. "It was awesome."

"Did you fill out the rubric?" Josie said. She was leaning against her car with her arms crossed, staring at the gym. Delaney got the feeling she wasn't really listening, but she answered anyway, her voice a borderline squeal: "I did!"

"Good," Josie said. "We'll go over it at Happy Hour after this."

"Why aren't you acting more excited? I thought you'd be happy for me."

"Sorry, Dee. I am excited. Really. It's just – oh, Summer's here. Let's go."

"Sorry, ladies. Couldn't stop retching over the toilet. Ten times worse because Luke and Nate can't pee inside the actual bowl." She held up an empty paper bag. "Let's do this. Nice new workout duds, Josie. But you know we're not working out today, right? We're just signing up. Right?"

Josie made a sound, something between a grunt and a chuckle. Still, she stared straight ahead.

"What's up, Josie?" Delaney said. "I thought you were going to say something like, 'I know, it's hot, right? And I got it for sixty percent off.'"

"I did, actually. I got it for sixty percent off."

"So why are you so gloomy?"

"It can wait. Let's get this done."

Less than an hour later, they'd received a tour of the gym, including locker rooms, the cardio room, the free weight area and the classrooms. There was also a studio, which featured a huge tire and a bunch of brightly colored exercise balls, about a hundred mats, a pull-up bar and a punching bag. Delaney found the last room rather intimidating, Summer said it was all she could do to keep from throwing up. But Josie punched the punching bag a few times, increasingly harder, before Delaney and Summer reminded her they were just having a tour.

"I don't know if going to the gym during The Dating Intervention is a good idea," Delaney said as they walked down the street to Rowdy's after signing their membership contracts and receiving their swipe cards. "I mean, it's just full of good-looking, sweaty men. Full of 'em."

"You'll get over it," Josie said.

Benjamin turned to wave as they entered.

"So dish on why you're being so subdued, Josie," Summer said.

"Don't you want to hear about Delaney's date with the esquire guy?"

"Yes," Summer answered. "But first, I want to hear what's got you so quiet on a Thursday. Need I remind you this is *Happy* Hour Thursday?"

Benjamin brought their drinks. Josie snatched hers up before it even had a chance to leave a ring. Then she took a long breath and finally made eye contact.

"Remember that horrible woman, Blair Upton?"

"The one who eats small children and kittens for lunch?"

Shuddering at the memory, Delaney took a long swig of her beer.

"Yes. The very same woman. The one who practically started a riot when we both applied for the lead third-grade teacher position a couple years ago."

"She was so intense you just stepped down, right?" Summer asked. She opened a packet of saltine crackers.

"Right. Crazy hag announced today she is also going to apply for the principal's position."

"Great," Delaney said. "I'm buying you an extra drink tonight."

"She was ruthless," Summer said. "Remember how she started that rumor that you were dating a high school senior?"

"How could I forget?"

"We'll help you, Josie. We'll help you kick ass on the interview and everything. Not to worry. We'll call it," Delaney paused for effect, then spread her hands out in front of her just as Summer had, "The Interview Intervention."

"Thanks," Josie managed. "Really, it does mean a lot. But I'm so nervous. I could stand her getting the position over me, if she was a decent educator. But she's not. Plus, I'm afraid of what she's going to say and do this time, before we get to that point in the application process. Remember that kid I told you guys about?"

"The one who you've been so worried about?" Delaney said.

"Yeah," Josie said. "He's been coming to school without a lunch. Every day."

"Can't he get a school lunch?" Summer said.

"He can," Josie said. "But he doesn't have money on his account. And his family doesn't qualify for the free lunch program. So he's just not eating at school. He's a mess by the afternoon, you know? Can't pay attention, acting out, you name it. I can't blame him. He's starving! To make it worse, he's not the only kid in this situation. And everything just seems worse because Paul, who is supposed to be my main confidant, doesn't seem to care. I'm sure he does, but he's so wrapped up in which drug dealer is doing which deal that I never have a chance to talk to him about my stuff."

"Oh, honey," Summer said. "This will pass. Have you tried talking to him about it?"

"Not really," Josie said. "I honestly rarely see him these days."

"Maybe you should schedule a time to talk to him," Delaney said.

"I should," Josie said. "And I will. But meanwhile, I'm worried about the principal position and these poor kids."

"We'll take care of it," Summer said through a mouthful of saltine crackers. "I'm in full mama bear mode right now. Nobody messes with me and mine. I could just pack an extra lunch for him every day."

"Oh, Summer," Josie said.

In an unexpected turn of events, her eyes filled with tears.

"You don't have to do that. Thank you, though. I actually started bringing him lunches. And I do feel better," Josie said. "Thanks, you guys. Now that that's settled, let's hear about your date, Dee."

Delaney went into full detail about the date, from Mitchell being a waiter to the water tower stargazing and the shared customer-related horror stories.

"It was just so much *fun*," she gushed. "And we're in the same place, you know?"

She noticed Josie and Summer share some unspoken thought and she knew exactly what it was. Mitchell's profile had said he was a lawyer. And that's what they wanted for Delaney: someone who was moving forward in his career. Someone who had a real job. A serious job. A marriageable job. She didn't let it dampen her spirits. She'd enjoyed herself. She had withheld her initial judgment, per their request. Now they could live with the consequences. They could withhold *their* judgment.

"Just remember," Summer said. "You have another date tonight."

"I know, I know," Delaney said. "I'm keeping an open mind, I promise."

Then, anxious to get out of the spotlight, she asked, "How's Derek's job hunt going?"

"Oh, you know. It's going. I don't really want to talk about it. It raises my stress levels. If I'm not careful, this baby will come out of my womb a complete stress monster."

"Are you sure?"

"Okay," she answered. "I'm not sure. But I'm going to need crackers. I'd kill for a glass of wine."

"Chocolate?" Josie said. "I have chocolate."

She reached into her purse and pulled out a white paper bag from The Sweet Tooth, the candy store on the square, then handed out pieces of fudge. "All right, then, Summer. Dish."

"You guys know I've always loved Derek's free spirit. Right?"

"Right," Josie and Delaney said.

"There's a but," Josie said.

Summer nodded. "But right now his free spirit is killing me. I thought he'd be in a rush to get a new job, but he's just waiting for the Universe to bring him something. The good news is that he's been a huge help with the kids since I haven't been feeling well. He's a great husband. I mean, he cooks, does dishes and he's a great lover. I'm just freaking out. Especially with another baby on the way. And the worst part of it is, I feel like the baby can sense my stress."

Her face crumpled as she began to cry. She covered her eyes with one hand and used the other to wipe her nose with a bar napkin.

"Oh, Summer. Don't cry," Delaney said. "Please don't cry. The baby's fine. He senses that his mama loves him."

In an obvious attempt to break the tension, Josie said, "Ooh, Dee, are you laying down your official gender hypothesis?"

She slipped off her stool to hug Summer, and Delaney answered, "No, not at this time."

"Although you've been right about all the other four," Summer said. "I don't know if I can handle another boy, though."

"Sure you can, *amiga*. You can handle anything," Josie said, running a hand over Summer's hair. "Anything. How can we help?"

Summer just shook her head. "You're already doing it," she said. "Dwelling on it isn't going to change anything. Let's talk about what Delaney should wear on tonight's date."

Josie kissed Summer's temple and sat down again.

"You know what you should wear, Dee?" Summer said. "That green dress. You know, the one with the sleeves."

"Those bell sleeve things?" Josie said. "She always ends up dipping those in her dinner. Remember that time, at Hot Diggity Dog?"

"Oh, the time she got mustard all over those sleeves and then they trailed all over her brand new skinny jeans?" Summer said.

"Right," Josie said. "So don't wear that. Wear that black sweater you got at Suzie's and that green scarf."

Delany nodded. "Copy that. Black sweater. Green scarf."

"I gotta go," Josie said. "Papers to grade, interviews to practice for."

She tossed back the last drink of her vodka cranberry, put her glass down on the table, gave them each a fierce hug and walked out, her black hair flowing behind her.

"Well, I'd better get going, too," Summer said. "You need time to get ready for your date. Look, Dee, I know you liked Mitchell, but I want you to keep an open mind for tonight. You'll give him a chance, right?"

"Of course," Delaney lied. "What does this guy look like?"

"He's like the mystery guy," Summer said, her voice like a voiceover for a spooky movie. "He didn't have a picture posted, but we liked the sound of him. This is the woodworker, remember?"

"An artist?"

"Stop sneering," Summer said. "I'm an artist, remember? Besides, it means he's good with his hands. You ought to like that."

Delaney rolled her eyes. "What's his name, again?"

"Sebastian."

"Right. Sebastian. Wasn't that the name of the little red lobster guy on *The Little Mermaid*?"

"Knock it off." Summer stood up, brushed the cracker crumbs off her shirt and skirt and gave Delaney a kiss on the cheek. "Love you. Be good and follow the rules."

"Okay, mama bear. Love you."

———

AS DELANEY WOUND the silky green scarf around her neck, she thought again about Jake Rhoades. She should really put it out to the Universe that she wanted to see him again. That's what Summer would suggest. Why hadn't she thought of it before? Pixie, who'd been curled up at the foot of the bed, stood up, stretched and yawned.

"Bored of watching me think about Jake Rhoades?" Delaney asked.

In answer, the cat hopped off the bed and walked out of the room, her tail high.

"You know, Pixie, you'd like him, too," she called after her.

She thought back to her date with Mitchell. She'd really enjoyed the easy conversation, the water tower, the sexual tension. Laying there next to him, she wanted more than anything to lightly trail a finger down his stomach, or press herself against him. She could tell he wanted it, too. She couldn't really discern whether that resulted from The Rules, which forbade her from kissing on the first date, or from good, old-fashioned chemistry. Normally, she'd kiss away on the first date. On any date. She'd kiss even if she and a guy had specified they *weren't* on a date.

Was that a crime?

So why was she still holding a flame for Jake Rhoades? She didn't know. But if Summer was right, a little shout out to the Universe couldn't hurt. Pixie wandered back in just as Delaney flopped down on her bed.

"I'm not really sure how to do this, Pix," she murmured.

The cat hopped onto the bed, too and curled up at Delaney's waist.

"Hey, Universe," Delaney said quietly. "I'd sure like to see Jake Rhoades again. I promise that this time, I won't squander my opportunity."

Nothing happened. No flash of lightning, rattle of windows or rush of wind. Delaney sat up and shrugged. Pixie, irked at having her cuddle disturbed, glared at her.

"I guess we'll see what happens."

Sebastian the Mysterious had said he wanted to try the newest restaurant downtown, a piano bar that served pizza. According to Josie, he'd be wearing a black button-down shirt and jeans.

The girls had a good chuckle at this.

"Perfect," Josie had said. "You guys wear matching uniforms."

CHAPTER FIFTEEN

IT COULDN'T BE. WAS THIS SOME COSMIC JOKE? AS SHE ROUNDED THE corner of Main Street and Grove, she saw him. Jake Rhoades. She'd recognize the fit of those jeans anywhere. He was waiting outside the piano bar, looking insanely tasty. He turned at the sound of her boots on the sidewalk, and smiled.

Delaney stopped dead. A rambunctious coil of snakes took up residence in her stomach.

Why, oh why, she wondered, *do I have to run into Jake Rhoades here, now, when I'm about to go on a date with someone else? Thanks, Universe, but I could have waited until tomorrow.* After a pause in her thinking, she smiled back. *At least I look presentable.*

Trying for discreet, she straightened her sweater. And she made herself keep walking toward him.

"Hey," she said, hoping for casual. "You're the Good Samaritan who stopped when I got rear-ended at Highway Twenty-Three and Pinecone."

Her insides turned to hot liquid when their eyes met.

"You're the woman with the kids," he said.

"They're not mine," she said, and he chimed in with her, "Great kids. But not mine."

She giggled nervously, fidgeted with her scarf, forced her hands to come to rest at her sides.

"I was hoping I'd see you again," he said. "That is, after the quick encounter at Rowdy's where you shoved my drink in my hand and all but shouted at me to leave."

"You were? And I did that?"

"Sure. You turned me down when I invited you to eat at Porky's. Three kids and pulled pork. The height of romance. I thought I couldn't go wrong. But you turned me down cold."

"I had to get the kids home."

"I've heard that one before. And then at Rowdy's, you didn't want anything to do with me."

"I was working! It was busy! Trust me, I'd much rather have had a drink with you than stay behind that bar."

"Really?"

"Yeah. Really."

For the briefest moment, they stood there, grinning at each other. Delaney shook herself when she remembered why she was here.

"Well, I'm meeting someone, so ..."

"Online dating, huh?"

She hadn't expected this. Her face flushed before she had a chance to pretend it wasn't true.

"How'd you know?"

"Sebastian," he said, offering his hand.

"What?" she blurted out, before she had the chance to come up with something more civilized. Then she noticed the black shirt. "I'm meeting *you*? I'm meeting you! But you said your name was Jake. Jake Rhoades."

Oh, God. Why did I blurt out his entire name? Like a mantra. Like the very same mantra I've been repeating over and over in my head for the past ten days.

He dropped his hand. She felt a mixture of delight (warmth throughout her upper body) and nerves (sweaty armpits. Thank goodness for the black sweater).

"You remembered, huh?"

She hoped the excitement she felt inside wasn't showing on her face. It might make her come across as desperate. "I've been thinking this whole time that your name was Jake."

'I've been thinking this whole time'?! Come on, Delaney!

"So you've been thinking about me?" He pulled open the door to the restaurant, gestured for her to go in ahead of him.

Oh, yeah. You should see what I've been thinking. Also, one point for opening that door.

"Well, yeah. I mean, you were like a hero to the kids that day."

"And to you, too, right?"

She shook her head, rolled her eyes. The hostess asked, "Two?" before leading them to a corner window table that looked out over Main Street. Dusk was just settling in, throwing a dusty pink light over everything.

"So who are you, really?" Delaney asked.

She took a moment to take in the scenery: wood paneling, landscape paintings of vineyards, still life paintings of cheese and crackers. She unrolled her linen napkin, draped it carefully across her lap and arranged her silverware on the table, stopping to remind herself Josie had said she was absolutely not to make napkin figurines on a first date.

"Sebastian Jacob Rhoades. I go by Jake in real life, but it's such a small town, I put Sebastian on my dating profile so no one knows who I am. Would you have accepted my invite if you knew it was me?"

"Is that why you don't put a picture on your profile? Or is it so you can hightail it if you show up somewhere and the woman doesn't look like you expected her to?"

"Yep. Yep to both. And because the only picture I have is one my sister took of me when I was rock climbing. It's not a very good view, you know?"

"Guess it depends on where she was standing."

He chuckled, then leaned forward, his eyes still smiling but his face serious. "So would you?"

"Would I have come on the date if I knew it was you? Yes."

He sat back. The server set down water glasses and then gargantuan, bowl-like wine glasses.

"Would you like to try a sample?" she asked. "We just got in a new red from a local winery. It's a cabernet grown, harvested and made right here in Arizona."

"Sure," Jake and Delaney said simultaneously.

They ordered full glasses to go with their meat lovers' pizza. Dark had fallen and the quaint little street lamps flickered on.

"So can I call you Jake, then?"

Delaney served him a melting slice of pizza, resisted the urge to lick the grease off her fingers and then served herself. *Mental note: Thank Josie for nixing the green dress ... I definitely would have gotten the sleeves oily.*

"Of course. Did they ever catch the guy who hit you?"

"Nope. He was out of Phoenix. But my friend Summer—the owner of that rockin' van—is all forgiving about it. 'All's well that ends well,' she says. The kids are fine, the van is fine. No harm, no foul, I guess."

"Well, I'm glad it turned out all right. And I'm glad you didn't turn me down for this date like you did when I invited you to Porky's."

Again, she found herself entertained. "Wow. You're really holding onto that. I told you, I had to get the kids home. I was disappointed I didn't get your number."

"Why didn't you ask for it?"

She was learning quickly that something about Jake made her want to be very honest. Was it too honest?

"I don't do that."

He laughed. "You don't do that?"

"No."

The pianist, a petite old woman with cotton for hair and arthritic looking knuckles, sat down and began to play. The melody drifted softly through the restaurant, reminding Delaney of an old-fashioned lounge.

"How do you ever go out with people?" Before she could answer, he asked, "Is this your first date, like, ever?"

"No, it's –"

"Oh, you have *rules*, right? I've heard about girls like you. In fact, I've dated girls like you. My favorites, though, are the girls who don't have any rules."

When she blanched, his serious expression transformed into a smile. "Just kidding. There was one girl, kind of the one who got away, I guess, who had a bunch of rules. Brittany."

Delaney was mortified to see that Jake looked nostalgic. Sad and a little dreamy.

"What happened with her?" *This is like a car accident. I don't want to know but I can't help asking.*

Jake shrugged. "It was weird. She just kind of disappeared. I figured I broke one of her rules, and that was that."

Unsure of what to say, Delaney didn't answer. Jake took a sip of wine, then shook his head just a little.

"So why are you dating online, then?" he asked. "Surely that's against your rules."

Should she tell him? Should she say it's because she was too lame to figure out dating on her own and this was her friends' way of reining her in, of screening her dates before she chose toxic men? *Nah.*

First of all, telling him really was against the rules and she had promised the girls she'd try harder to follow them. Plus, it was a bit too much information for a first date, probably. She'd leave that for later.

"Oh, you know. Just a change of pace, I guess."

"Well, I'll tell you what, Delaney Collins. When I met you outside of Porky's, I thought, here's a girl I've got to get to know. But I shut down. I was nervous as hell. Which, by the way, never happens."

Delaney wondered if Jake could see the glow of happiness radiating out of her heart. Then she wondered if he'd think that analogy was as lame as it sounded.

Jake continued, "Then I saw you at Rowdy's. But the nerves kicked in again. All my friends were there. It's a man thing. I couldn't ask for your number. So when I saw your picture on that profile, I was pleased. Actually, I was ecstatic. I thought, here's my chance. So I'm going to go all out, here. Prepare to be wooed."

CHAPTER SIXTEEN

"'Prepare to be wooed?' He actually said that? I think I'm in love!" Summer said.

An overcast sky made everything look bright and surreal, especially the black pyramid that was Muscles Gym.

Summer wrapped a hair tie around the end of her braid and said, "Okay, I'm ready to go."

Josie released a huge sigh.

"Whoa," Delaney said. "Sounds like you've got some tension to pound out, Josie."

Josie rubbed at the crease between her eyebrows. "I've just got a lot on my mind, that's all."

"Why don't you tell us about it?" Summer said.

For the second time in as many days, Josie's eyes filled up, and Summer hugged her. "I'm sorry," Josie said. "Today I saw that snot, Blair Upton, flirting with Scott Smith. Which means they're probably sleeping together. I mean, it's shameless. She's a teacher and he's the principal. He's flirting right back. In public. It's ridiculous. You should see it."

"But he's leaving. What good will it do her to flirt with him?" Delaney asked.

"Oh, I can guarantee you she's not stopping at flirting," Josie said. "And he's on the hiring committee for the principal position. Of course."

"Let's start walking," Summer said. "You need to hit the treadmill. Or something."

Josie nodded. "I mean, I've already started thinking about all the awesome stuff I can do as principal, and I'm afraid Blair Upton is going to sneak right in and steal the position out from under me. I'm made for this position. You know?"

"What awesome stuff?" Delaney said, hoping to shift the mood.

It worked: Josie's eyes went dreamy. "I just keep thinking about my community center. An after-school program where kids can come and eat snacks and get help with homework and stuff. Where they can have a, you know, positive influence and supervision for a few hours each day."

"I love that idea," Delaney and Summer said at the same time.

"Yeah," Josie said, her expression turning dark again. "Me, too. But I won't get to do it if Blair Upton sleeps her way to the principal position."

She yanked the door open and gestured for the girls to go in.

"Couldn't you still do it as a teacher?" Summer said.

Josie shrugged. "I want to do it as a principal.".

"Want us to beat her up?" Delaney said.

Josie's laugh came out short and harsh. "Yes, please."

They arrived at the free weights. Each of them took a set off the rack.

"So can I message Jake Rhoades today? Set up another date?" Delaney said.

"Oh, no, sister," Summer said. "You're not messaging anybody. We do that. What about Mitchell?"

"True," Josie said. "During the Mitchell and Jake-slash-Sebastian dates, we barely heard from you. Except, 'Guys! You won't believe this! It's the hot car accident guy!'" Josie said.

"Right," Summer said. "So that means they were successful. I think you need to go out with both of them again. But no kissing, no sex."

"So do I contact them? Or wait for them to contact me?"

Delaney, unsure of what to do with her weights, mimicked Josie's position and began doing bicep curls, too.

"I checked your profile right before I got here," Summer said. "Mitchell already sent you a message. And Sebastian, or Jake, hasn't. I think that's enough on the bicep curls, Josie."

"He's probably testing me," Delaney said. "I told him I don't get guys' numbers. So he probably wants me to make the next move."

"Do you want to?" Josie asked. She put her weights away and grabbed a lighter set for tricep extensions.

"Hell, yeah, I want to."

"Okay," Josie said. "I'll log into your profile and write him a note."

"What will it say?"

"Probably something like, 'Hey, big guy, I enjoyed our time in the backseat of your big truck. Wanna do it again?'"

"Shut up, Josie," Delaney said. "There was no backseat. No truck, either. Say something good."

"I will."

An hour later, sweaty and red-faced from their cardio workouts, the girls gathered in the gym's foyer.

"First gym day: success," Summer said.

"My legs are going to fall off," Josie said. "I walked for an hour and I feel like I'm going to die. But it did improve my mood."

"Thank goodness for that," Delaney said.

"I failed to mention, too, that I got a call from a parent today," Josie said. "A dad. His kid, who was a straight-A student, started failing all his math quizzes about a month ago. I'd called the dad to see what was up. He returned my call today and told me that he lost his job two months ago, and they were evicted from their apartment last month. They've been couch surfing, mostly, but now they've got a spot in the homeless shelter. He's looking for a job, but you know, it's stressful. Anyway, it just underlines the need for some kind of resource. If that kid could get his studying done after school, in a great environment, he could thrive again. You know? And then Blair and Scott—ugh. I'll stop. I'm sorry."

"Group hug?" Summer said.

Josie nodded and held her arms open.

THE STUDENTS in Country Kitchen's How to Boil Water class bustled around the back of the store, taking out their aprons, setting up their dishes and perusing the evening's menu. Delaney and Beth, done with their prep work, stood behind their island.

"So, the day after our last class, my mom calls, wanting to know if my new cooking skills have landed me a new guy," Beth said.

"Well, have they?"

Beth snorted. "I don't think I'm going to put 'How to Boil Water Graduate' on my FindLove.com profile, thank you very much."

"I know. Seriously. I'm putting it on mine, though."

"You're on FindLove.com?"

Delaney cringed. "Yeah. Why? Should I not be?"

"It's not that, it's just that you seem so outgoing and friendly. I wouldn't think you'd need online dating. You're probably great in person."

"My best friends again." Delaney shrugged. "I'm *too* good in person.

Too approachable. Losers just love me. So my friends, Summer and Josie, they're screening everybody on my profile."

"You're letting them?"

"I hate to say it, but they're doing better for me than I am for myself."

At that moment, Delaney glanced up at the storefront window and saw Jake Rhoades on the sidewalk, staring at her with an intensity that bordered on scary, but mostly just made her want to strip him down right there where he stood.

Beth followed her gaze and said, "Ooh. Who is *that*? He looks like he wants to eat you up. Right now."

"Ahhh," Delaney sighed, "Jake Rhoades. Jake Rhoades the Dreamy. A FindLove.com find."

"No!"

"Yes. Yes, indeed."

As they stared at each other, Delaney felt a slow, sexy smile spreading across her face. She also heard a tiny voice wondering if he'd ever looked at The-One-Who-Got-Away Brittany like that. Shaking it off, she gave Jake a little wave. He smiled, then, sudden and bright, before waving and going on his way.

"Let's begin," Wendy said then, and the moment was gone.

That evening during class, Delaney worked through the roasted chicken and grilled steak, pretending she was cooking for Jake.

"Would you like some rosemary on your chicken?" she'd ask. He'd respond, "Of course, sugar lips."

They'd sip cold white wine from sparkling wine glasses and she'd feed him a taste of the chicken, which he'd nibble sensually from the tips of her fingers.

"You're burning the steak," Beth said, nudging Delaney with her elbow and popping the bubble of fantasy she'd been living in.

"Oops."

"Thinking about The Dreamy, huh?"

"You caught me."

DELANEY DIDN'T TELL the girls about her first official job interview. She didn't want them to be disappointed if she didn't get the job.

If she were being honest with herself (*haha*), she had another reason for keeping it a secret: she wasn't convinced she wanted a veterinary job. As she pulled into the parking lot of the Mountain Top Veterinary Clinic, a tiny stone building with generous windows in front, her memory flashed on various images from the day that had ended her career in the first place: the heart monitor showing a flat line, Max's lifeless body, limp on the operating table. Howie's tear-stained face. Not being able to save animals was part of being a veterinarian. But what happened when your mistakes caused even worse destruction?

Palms sweating on the steering wheel and breath coming way too fast, Delaney forced herself not to give in to this panic attack.

She'd arrived exactly two minutes early and opted for the cat entrance, figuring it improved her suit's chances of remaining fur-free. Naturally, as soon as she walked in, a huge, white, fluffy dog made a beeline for Delaney, its whole body trembling with joy. Its owner chuckled like a proud parent would, wearing an *isn't-he-cute?* expression. It was all Delaney could do to keep from rolling her eyes. Within seconds, her pants were covered in wiry white fur.

"Sorry," the dog's owner said indulgently. "She just loves people."

Delaney bit her tongue, literally, and was glad she did. Just then, a door behind the counter opened.

"I assume you're Ms. Collins?"

Dr. Alexander Mott, a stern-faced, gray-haired man in jeans, a plaid flannel shirt and a white doctor's coat, looked over his glasses at Delaney, who was madly trying to brush the hair off her pants.

"Uh, yes. I am," she said. "Dr. Mott?"

"Right this way."

Discomfited, she scooted around the counter and followed him back to his office. Why had she worn a suit? What on *Earth* had made her think wearing a suit (a brand new suit) to an interview for a veterinary position was a good idea? She should have known better. Shoving the thought out of her mind, she took in her surroundings. Cluttered. The shelves were packed with pamphlets, binders and books, and paper covered every horizontal surface. *He needs a professional organizer more than he needs another vet.*

"You can sit here," Dr. Mott said, scooping a stack of papers off a rickety-looking office chair.

She sat.

"So, your resume shows you've been unemployed for the past several years since—uh, since a year after you finished vet school."

Wow. Cutting right to the chase.

"Actually, I've been working, but I didn't think it was relevant to this position, so I didn't put it on my resume."

Again, Dr. Mott looked over his glasses at her, his steely gray eyes piercing hers.

"What have you been doing, exactly?"

"I tend bar at Rowdy's. Not exactly animal-related." Her armpits tingled.

"Hm. I see. A word of advice, Ms. Collins?"

Delaney doubted he was really asking her permission, so she nodded, simultaneously cringing.

"Never leave a spot on your resume blank if you actually have something to put there. It makes you look like you can't get or keep a job. Bartending is not, shall we say, the most pertinent experience, I realize. But at least your long-term employment proves you have staying power."

Delaney nodded, too dumbstruck to respond in any other way.

"So you worked as a vet for a year, then?" Dr. Mott said.

"Yes. I—"

"Eight years ago. And that is all the veterinary experience you have?"

That could have gone better. Delaney replayed the interview in her mind as she drove the short distance home just fifteen minutes later. After the first set of scorching questions, Delaney asked Dr. Mott why he even called her for an interview. He responded that she'd been the only applicant. Finding vets in Juniper was difficult, he said.

Then he told her he simply couldn't hire someone who'd been tending bar for the past eight years. He hadn't actually said that. He'd said he couldn't hire someone with such limited in-clinic experience after vet school. She wanted to explain, to tell him what had happened with Max and Howie, but she couldn't bring herself to share the story. It would probably sound like an excuse and it would definitely ensure she never got hired.

The moment she got home, Delaney took off her suit and replaced it a clean pair of jeans and a nice top. After seeing Dr. Mott in his jeans and flannel shirt, she was pretty sure her fancy suit shouted, "I'm desperate."

She didn't have to call Summer or Josie to know what they'd say. Summer would say, "You learn something every time, Dee," and Josie would say, "Suck it up and go to the next one. Somebody's gotta hire you."

For the past few days, she'd spent every spare moment at her computer, scouring the job ads, polishing her resume and applying for open positions. She was surprised at the number of veterinary clinics in Juniper, and even more surprised at how many were hiring.

In an hour, she'd be rolling up at another interview, at a big box pet store on the opposite side of town. In a renewed effort to be proactive and prepared, she had printed out fifty copies of her resume just this morning. At the time, she thought leaving the past several years blank was a stroke of genius. More like a colossal mistake, she now realized, in more ways than one. She sat down at her desk, adjusted her resume to reflect her time at Rowdy's and printed out a single copy.

Absolute mayhem greeted her when she arrived at the big box store. The clinic was at the back, in a tiny room whose walls were lined with what seemed like hundreds of kennels.

What is it with vets and flannel shirts? A hulking woman with a huge mop of greasy blond hair approached her. The dogs along the back wall yipped and whined. One of them, a tiny terrier with a bandage over one eye, scratched incessantly at the gate on its kennel.

The woman put out a massive hand. "Dr. Rosen," she said. "Pleased to meet you."

"Likewise," Delaney said. "Delaney Collins."

Scratch scratch scratch scratch. Yip.

"So … you've spent the past few years working at a bar?"

"Yeah. Rowdy's. On Main."

"I know it. Met my husband there, actually. Great place. You'll see my boots on the wall. Top right. 'Met my future husband.' I left the bar barefoot that night." She whooped. "What a hoot!"

Suddenly seeming to remember why they were there, she said, "But you've worked in the field for a year?"

"Right," Delaney said, trying for charming.

"Look, you seem nice. But we're swamped here, as you can see. I'm really looking for someone with more experience, someone who can handle this workload, get through the patients fast." She slammed a fist on the table. "Hit the ground running! I don't have the time to bring you up to speed."

Delaney had to admit she wasn't disappointed she hadn't gotten that particular job. Just the thought of walking into that din every single day gave her the beginnings of a migraine. At the same time, she was disappointed. It stung to think she didn't look like a good prospect. Summer would say something now about the right position falling into her lap at precisely the right time.

Someone will hire me, she reminded herself in the confident tone of voice she imagined Josie would use. *Someone has to.*

ALL THE VETS at the Desert Veterinary Clinic thought of Howie as a bumbling old guy who had lost awareness of what the people around him thought or said.

But that wasn't the case at all.

One day, he said to Delaney, "You know, I know all the other vets think I'm just a hypochondriac, that I bring Max in for silly reasons. But you always give me the time of day, Doctor Collins. You're a good person. You understand. You understand that Max is all I have. And you're a good vet. You're thorough and kind and patient, even if you do think I'm overreacting."

"I'm so glad you feel that way, Howie," Delaney said. "I *do* understand. And I want you to know that I'll always be thorough when you and Max come in. But I think it's time we take this to the next level. I'm giving you my personal cell phone number so you can call me with questions. You've paid a small fortune in vet bills for problems I think could be handled with a quick phone call."

"My peace of mind is worth it," he said. Still, he took the business card she offered, and turned it over to read her cell phone number on the back.

"I appreciate it, Doctor Collins." He looked up at her and smiled. "All of it."

Would he have said that if he knew how things would end? Would he have felt the same way about her?

CHAPTER SEVENTEEN

Rowdy's dim lights and loud music provided a welcome respite from the job search.

"Well, at least you've had two interviews," Josie said as Delaney pouted into her drink. "Give me an interview tip."

"Don't wear dark pants to a veterinary clinic."

"Shit. You did that? Do Summer and I need to take over your job hunt, too?"

Josie stirred her vodka cranberry.

"Can we talk about something else?" Delaney said. She could hear the edgy tone in her voice and tried to lighten it. "My cooking class is super fun. How about that? I've cooked spaghetti, pork loin, roasted chicken and steak."

"Wow. You just quadrupled your cooking repertoire," Josie said, winking at Delaney.

"Geez, Josie," Summer said.

"What?! It's true!"

Summer rolled her eyes, then turned toward Delaney. "That's great, Dee. Isn't it fun? Enjoy it now, before you have kids and it becomes a form of slavery."

"Speaking of kids, did you ever find out why Nate punched that kid at school?" Delaney asked.

"Yeah. For the past week, every time they play kickball at recess, the little asshole pegs Nate in the face with the ball. On purpose."

"So he deserved it." Josie said.

Delaney winced. The kid did deserve it. She wondered how mad

Summer was going to be when she found out Delaney had encouraged Nate to punch the little bully right in the kisser. Charlie Wilkes was the kind of fourth-grader who turned into a Joe Jansen, Delaney's eighth-grade crush, shaming dorky girls by publicly rejecting their invitations to the movies.

"I guess." Summer shrugged. "I mean, I asked him if he talked to him first and he said he did, but the kid kept throwing the ball at him. He talked to a teacher on the playground, but she didn't see it happen, I guess. So she said she couldn't do anything. I can't really blame him, but I don't want him going around punching people."

Covering her mouth with her hand, Delaney looked down at the table.

"Delaney, why do you look so guilty?"

"Who, me?" She took a drink of her beer.

"Yeah. You."

"No reason."

"Is there something you want to tell me about my son?"

"Cat that ate the canary," Josie said, under her breath.

Delaney looked from Summer to Josie, and back to Summer. It was now or never. "Okay. All right. I told him to punch the kid. Last time I picked them up. He was upset, practically crying. I asked him if he used his words! I swear! He said he did! He said the yard duties didn't do anything about it because they didn't see it. So I told him, 'The next time that horrible boy throws the ball at your face, you punch him right in his nasty little mouth.'"

"Seriously?" Josie asked. She was smiling broadly but glanced quickly at Summer to gauge her reaction.

"Yeah. Seriously." Although Delaney heard the indignation in her own voice, she could feel embarrassment on its heels. She cringed.

"Fine," Summer said. "You were right. Damn kid deserved a good punch in the face."

Delaney shrugged, hoped the relief didn't come through in her voice. "That's what I thought."

Then she quickly changed the subject. "So Josie. How's Blair?"

"Uppity bitch," Josie said, waving a hand dismissively. "Actually, she's been out sick the past couple of days. I highly suspect someone put a hunk of rat poison in her coffee. It may have been me."

"Was it?" Delaney asked, but before Josie had a chance to answer, Summer held up a finger.

"Great news," she said. Her eyes were alight with excitement and her voice was breathy.

"Another girl?" Josie said.

"Won't know for a couple more months. Actually, it's not kid-related. Believe it or not," she added when they feigned shock.

Benjamin plunked her water on the table. Summer muttered a distracted, "Thanks," as she continued to dig through her huge purse. Finally, smiling, she announced, "Here it is! The Sweets' first official CD!"

Delaney and Josie squealed, leapt off their stools and ran around the table to hug Summer. The men at the next table, stuffy types in expensive suits, drinking expensive beer, went quiet and stared at the women, who were now wrapped in a group hug.

"Sorry," Delaney said as they climbed back into their barstools. She giggled.

"A copy for each of you," Summer said.

"You designed the cover, right?" Delaney asked.

"Naturally," Summer said.

A rushed conversation followed, Delaney and Josie demanding to know how Summer got this all done in secret and Summer explaining how one of the band members had tutored the recording studio manager's daughter in exchange for a recording session. She wanted to keep it a secret, Summer said, because she wanted to see the looks on her best friends' faces when she handed them the finished product.

"Phew!" she said when she finished. "That was just as thrilling as I'd hoped. You know, I think I was meant to be a rock star. I had so much fun recording that CD. You guys have to promise to give me feedback once you listen to it."

Delaney smiled at Summer's faraway expression.

That faraway look transformed into one of focus, and Delaney braced herself. "Now," Summer said, "let's talk about our other pet project. Dee, you have a couple – actually, three – more date requests on your profile. Josie and I have talked, and we agree that you should chat with two of them, but not go on dates with any new guys, just yet. We want to explore Mitchell and Jake, first."

"Do I have to chat with them? Isn't that just leading them on?"

Summer took a long drink of her water and Josie answered. "No, not really. Online dating is all about getting to know people without taking the risk of actually going on a date. This will just keep your options open. No cybersex."

"I admit, I'm feeling a little … dry."

"A dry spell is a good thing," Summer said. "You don't end up knocked up."

"And when you get married, he's going to want it all the time," Josie said.

"Only at the beginning," Summer muttered.

"You say that like it's a bad thing, Josie," Delaney said.

"It's not. It's just a fact."

"Ah, those were the days," Summer said.

"Hey, at least you guys get to do it," Delaney said. "I'm about ready to burst. Especially after Jake Rhoades The Dreamy incinerated my panties during cooking class last night."

She shivered remembering the way he looked, standing there on the sidewalk.

"You both need to work out more," Summer said. "You know, scientific studies have proven exercise reduces stress."

"I worked out with you guys," Josie said.

"That was one time," Summer and Delaney said.

"Maybe we need to make *you* our pet project," Delaney said.

Instead of answering, Josie dragged out her tablet and signed into Delaney's FindLove.com account. Summer shoved her bar napkin across the table to Delaney, who read the note she'd scribbled on it: *We need to get Josie drunk and take her dancing. That always works.*

Delaney nodded, crumpled the napkin in her hand and shoved it into her pocket as she stood up.

"I need to use the restroom," she announced.

"Are you going to go text us about ourselves?" Josie asked without looking up from the tablet. Summer giggled.

Benjamin was at the register between the bar and the bathroom, which put him in the perfect spot for Delaney to pay him a quick visit.

"Make Josie's next one a double, would you, please?" she asked sweetly.

"Sure thing, Dee," he said, and his black cowboy hat bobbed. "How's your sister?"

"She's good, thanks. Excited to graduate in a couple of months. Applying to college. You know, the usual. Doesn't want to end up bartending 'til she's thirty. Oops. Sorry, Dee. I wasn't referring to you."

But it was true. Delaney Collins, professional bartender, apparently couldn't get a real job to save her life. She really had gotten stuck working at Rowdy's 'til she was thirty (a few years past that, but who was counting?). When she came out of the restroom, she said to Benjamin, "You know, I'm going to switch to vodka cran, like Josie. Make mine a double, too."

It was a good thing The Teeter Totter wasn't their normal hangout, Delaney thought. She carried their drinks to the booth they'd snagged in the back of the sweltering bar. It was dark, loud and sweaty. Multicolored lights flashed continuously. If those things weren't enough to put a person into overwhelm, the place was constantly packed with college kids celebrating the weekend, starting Thursday night and finishing strong Sunday night. As it went in college, the girls wore tight, ripped jeans with swatches of fabric for tops and the guys ogled them unapologetically. If Delaney and her friends met here every week, they'd probably die from overstimulation. The regulars were just starting to flow in and Delaney could feel the hormones radiating off them.

"Ready to dance, Josie?"

"Oh, yeah."

Throbbing music pulsed down deep into Delaney's bones. She drained her drink.

"Let's do this."

The three of them, hands linked, made their way to the dance floor. They weaved through the mass of gyrating bodies until they reached the center and threw their arms in the air.

It wasn't until the next morning, when the ping of Delaney's phone broke through the sleepy fog and hammered at her piercing headache that Delaney realized she'd had too much to drink.

Way too much to drink.

CHAPTER EIGHTEEN

The Friday morning light scorched Delaney's dry eyes. Her phone chirped again, the sound so loud she cringed. What time was it? She had no idea, but she knew it was earlier than her usual wake-up time. Lying on her back, she read her new messages.

Summer: *What were you up to last night?*

Josie: *We've been on your FindLove profile.*

Uh oh. Delaney rolled over and propped herself up on her elbows. She responded: *What are you talking about?*

Summer: *Log on.*

Josie: *Why can't you just follow directions?*

Summer: *Are we not being clear? Do you understand that you're not supposed to do anything without our permission? That includes going onto your profile and berating people, seducing people, and winking at people. Or nudging them. Or whatever it's called.*

What had she done? The clock on her nightstand showed it was eleven, quite a bit later than she'd thought. Delaney staggered, nearly tripping over Pixie. The coffeepot had turned itself off a while ago, so she heated a cup of coffee in the microwave and turned on her computer.

"Shit," she muttered when she saw all the activity on her Find-Love.com profile page.

It all came back to her: she'd given Jesse the Rancher a piece of her mind about the bloody hog talk during lunch. She'd laid into the Craig the Kindergarten Teacher about the club and balls jokes. Mitchell, the waiter, had heard all about how romantic she thought it was that he'd taken her up to the water tower. And the message she'd written to Jake … she read only the first few words ("You are so dreamy!") before clicking out of it. She was mortified to see that none of them had responded. She considered writing fresh messages, notes of apology.

But as the coffee started to hit her veins, she remembered she had an interview at noon.

"Shit," she muttered again. "Shit."

She quickly texted the girls: *I have an interview at noon. Talk later. Remember, you love me. Wasn't that Rule 8?*

No response.

At exactly noon, Delaney swung her car into the parking lot of the Double R Veterinary Clinic. The tires screeched as she turned into a spot, and she jumped out even as she was putting it in park. The heel of her boot snapped off as she slammed her door.

"Great."

Should she try to make it look like both her boots still had heels? Or should she limp in? She tried the former first, and thought she did a pretty good job, until the receptionist asked, "Are you okay?"

"My heel broke off." She held it up as if to explain, then shrugged. Then she wondered why she hadn't left it in the car. She stuck it in her purse. She and the receptionist grimaced at each other and the girl looked sympathetic. Glancing at the clock behind the receptionist's head, Delaney noticed it was a minute after noon.

"Oh, you're fine," the girl said. "Delaney, right? Doctor Rick's running a bit behind. She'll just be a minute."

Instead of the usual pet prescription posters showing bloodsucking parasites and dogs' internal organs, paintings of horses warmed the waiting room walls. Instinct would have had Delaney strolling around the room, scoping things out, but the broken heel made her plant herself on the wooden bench.

Because she had time, she did a quick check: her dark jeans were clean, her sweater was buttoned, and her hair (still wet and in a bun) seemed to be in place.

The door behind the receptionist's desk opened and a tall, slender woman with a long blond braid and hazel eyes poked her head out.

"Ms. Collins? Sorry I'm late. Come on back. Mind if I eat while we talk?"

Delaney walked behind Dr. Rick, doing her best to minimize the limping. They sat at a small dining table in the break room. Doctor Rick pulled a salad and a root beer out of the mini fridge. Delaney saw, with some disdain, that her resume sat on the table, too. The "current employment" section was highlighted.

Shit.

"So, you're working over at Rowdy's, huh?"

"Yes."

Why did she have to start with that?

Delaney was tempted to add something like, "But it's only temporary," or, "I did finish vet school," but for once, she waited for the next question.

"What do I order? What's my signature drink?" Doctor Rick asked, her mouth full of salad.

Delaney glanced around the room. More horse paintings, sturdy wooden furniture, everything neat and tidy. She checked the doctor's shoes. Expensive, but well-worn boots.

"Newcastle. On tap if they have it. Otherwise, in a bottle with a cold glass."

"You're good."

"Yeah. I am. It's sort of like a specialty."

Doctor Rick wiped her mouth with a napkin.

"Why aren't you a vet?"

"I don't know," Delaney said, even though she did know. But she wasn't going to admit the truth to this stranger, who was obviously a professional.

"Okay. Well, Ms. Collins, I'll give you a call."

IT WAS WORSE than she'd anticipated. Not only were Josie and Summer not speaking to her (or texting with her, or anything else), but Delaney had also effectively ended things (not nicely) with Jesse the Rancher and Craig the Kindergarten teacher, and made a fool of herself with both Mitchell and Jake.

She wanted to feel hopeful about the job interview with Dr. Rick. Instead, she felt the now-familiar sense of dread in her stomach. She sat in front of the computer, her alternately scathing and desperate words black on the screen like a fly on a clean window. She could see them but try as she might, she couldn't get them to disappear.

Jesse had been so nice, so well-mannered. Why did she have to say anything at all to him? She could have just let it go. But no. She'd ranted: *especially while I was eating a ham (also known as pig) sandwich and trying to avert my eyes from the drops of fresh pig blood on your boots. Have a little sensitivity!* Apparently, she tried to soften the blow by complimenting his manners: *Thank you for showing me that great manners still exist, but I'm afraid I won't be able to see you again. I'm not cut out to be a rancher's wife.* As if he'd even want to see *her* again.

Her comments to Craig had been even more scathing. Obviously she told him he acted juvenile, *like a sixth grader who just discovered what his parts are for and can't wait to use them,* and she wasn't interested in spending any more time with his balls and club, period. *It doesn't make it ` any better that you apologized and said you were nervous. I was nervous too. Nervous that I'd run into someone I know, and they'd think I was actually enjoying your stupid sense of humor.*

To Mitchell, she'd written, *maybe on our next date we can spend a little longer on top of the water tower. ;)*

Naturally, in the long, flowery, poetic message to Jake, she told him, *From the moment I first saw you, I wanted to take off your shirt and run my hands over the muscles in your back while kissing you passionately.*

"Oh, God," she moaned. "Who talks like that?"

Reading through her outgoing messages was bad enough. It would only get worse when she read their responses. Knowing she had to face the fire at some point, she bolstered herself and started with Craig. She didn't want to see him again, anyway.

It's fine. You're an uptight, prissy, washed up bartender, and I'm sure I can find someone who appreciates me just the way I am.

Says who? Delaney thought, even as the first part of his message burned and she was tempted to text Summer, Josie, and her mom to ask if they thought she was uptight and prissy, too.

Jesse's message: *I'm sorry for having offended you, Miss Delaney. I should have known it was bad manners to discuss a butcher on a first date. But you're right – I don't think we're quite right for each other. I wish you luck.*

That wasn't so bad. In fact, he was so imperturbable that she felt even worse about last night's message.

Mitchell hadn't responded at all. Delaney felt foolish. He was thinking one of two things, if she had to guess: one, that she was an insane, horny, forward hussy, or two, that he was getting in her pants the next time they saw each other. Or both. That was always a possibility.

Then there was Jake. She saw the first two words of his message: *Wow, Delaney,* but couldn't bring herself to open it right away. Out of all of them, he had the most potential. It would be just like her to go and mess it up before they even got started.

Her finger hovered over the button of her mouse for a long moment before she finally clicked.

Well, since we didn't quite get to that, Jake wrote in response to her smut, *I'm hoping we can go there the next time, although I didn't originally peg you as a girl who'd get down and dirty on the first couple of dates. I'm excited to hear that I may have been wrong about you. From the first moment I saw you, I wanted to ... oh, never mind. I'll just show you. Did I see you coming out of the Teeter Totter last night?*

"Shit. Shit, shit, shit."

She couldn't decide whether to be over-the-top excited about Jake's response, or put off by his excitement over her being a girl who'd get down and dirty on the first couple of dates. *Don't lie to yourself, Collins. You're excited. Really excited.*

Should she respond to any of them? Probably not. Best to let sleeping dogs lie.

Her cell phone pinged.

Summer: *How'd your interview go?*

Delaney: *Good. I got it.*

Summer: *You got the job?*

Delaney: *No, I got the message that I should stay off the computer. The vet said she'll call me.*

Summer: *Good. I'll tell Josie. Now do us all a favor and stay off the damn computer.*

That was it. Not sure what to do with herself, she decided to mope for a while. She sat on the couch and picked up a magazine. Pixie wandered in, jumped onto her lap.

"At least *you* still love me," Delaney said.

The cat meowed, jumped down.

"Or you're just hungry."

As she fed Pixie, she thought about Summer and Josie. She hated that they were mad at her, and for a moment she tried to rationalize her behavior. But then, a tiny voice from somewhere in the far recesses of her reasonable mind whispered that she was only rationalizing because she felt guilty for being so mean to Jesse and Craig, and stupid for drooling all over Mitchell and Jake. She told it to shut up.

***

SATURDAY AFTERNOON, Delaney received a text from Summer:

You have a date tonight with Mitchell. He's intrigued by your offer to spend more time on the water tower. Meet him at Rowdy's at 7.

Before she could answer, Josie chimed in: *Rules, schmules. Do whatever you want.*

You guys, I'm sorry!

No answer.

Just after seven, Rowdy's was still relatively tranquil. A group of younger guys played pool, and another couple occupied the tall table in the corner.

"You're quiet tonight," Mitchell said to Delaney. They sat at a table in the back and Delaney was grateful for the darkness.

"I know. Just tired."

"Up late last night, huh?"

His eyes crinkled and the hint of a smile played around his lips. She felt embarrassed.

"I went dancing with my friends. Summer and Josie? I mentioned them last time, I think. We've been best friends since junior high. Anyway. Josie needed a little cheering up, so we went dancing. That always does the trick."

"I think you got a little cheering up, too, judging by that message."

"Don't remind me."

"Hey, you called in sick and you show up to drink?" Benjamin said as he approached the table.

"I didn't call in sick. I took a mental health day. I seem to recall a certain Benjamin Walker doing that a few months ago after his dog died. You showed up here that night, too. And I practically had to pour you into a bucket to get you in the back of that taxi."

"True." He switched gears. "The usual, then?"

"Just water, thanks," Delaney said.

"Hair of the dog," Benjamin said in a sing-songy voice.

Delaney declined the offer again, so Benjamin shrugged and turned to Mitchell, who ordered a Bud Light.

They sat quietly for a couple of minutes, while the jukebox blared out something about pickup trucks. Mostly, Delaney stared into her water glass, noticing the tiny black flecks in her ice cubes. She wondered whether Summer and Josie were still mad at her.

Why, oh why, did she go home last night and make the infantile decision to get on the computer? It was like drunk dialing, except the messages were right there, fully visible. Illuminated, even. At first, she'd felt somewhat piqued when she discovered Summer and Josie were angry at her. But now her resolve weakened. Maybe they had a point. She couldn't make good choices on her own. But why?

"Look, Mitchell, I've got to go."

"What? We just got here."

"Can I take a rain check? I'm just not feeling like myself."

Delaney stepped out into the evening air, and a definite springtime chill skidded across her skin. Her ears buzzed from the loud music that had been playing over the speakers at Rowdy's. Mitchell had been understanding, she thought. He'd sensed something was wrong from the moment they sat down. At this very moment he was probably thinking she was a crazy, moody woman.

Maybe she was. She was also mortified. Pausing in front of one of the downtown art galleries, Delaney wondered when she'd grow up enough to buy a real oil painting as a living room centerpiece, or a blown-glass vase to put in the dining room. Something permanent.

At some point, she had to stop decorating with "eclectic clearance" from all over Juniper.

Then it hit her: was "eclectic clearance" the story of her love life? The girls were right. Most of the men she dated were cast-offs of some kind. She took them all in, used them to add color and flavor to her collection. The parallel was too much to bear, so she moved on to the next shop.

The shelves inside the Paws-n-Whiskers window offered up human-like treats for four-legged companions. The mini donuts, cupcakes and cookies looked good enough to eat, Delaney thought. A colorful display of dog strollers sat inside the picture window, waiting to be wheeled onto the sidewalk as soon as the store opened the next day. At the rate Delaney was going, she was going to need one of those strollers. She pictured herself forty years from now, still single, wheeling her cats (lots of them) around the downtown square in a stroller.

"Oh, my God," she said aloud. A feeling of doom settled over her as she imagined eating frozen TV meals alone on the couch at age sixty, seventy and eighty. She was destined to be alone and lonely forever.

Festive music tumbled out the open door of Eddie's Pizzeria. The big windows cast warm, inviting light on the sidewalk. Delaney didn't want to spend too long standing there, but a hearty – and familiar – laugh grabbed her attention.

Jake Rhoades sat at a two-person table right in the middle of the restaurant. As Delaney passed, he looked up. Although she put her head down and picked up her pace, it took her just a split second too long. He spotted her. She pretended not to see him.

Just as she passed the open door and smelled the spice of tomato sauce with a healthy dose of garlic, Jake stepped out.

"Delaney. I've been hoping to talk to you."

CHAPTER NINETEEN

WAS IT POSSIBLE TO SINK INTO THE SIDEWALK AND DISAPPEAR? THE LAST time Jake had heard from her was when she'd written him that lewd message on FindLove.com. Delaney closed her eyes, willing the ground to swallow her up. *It'd probably choke on me.* She opened her eyes. Jake was right in front of her now, his hand on her arm. The scents of cheese and fresh-baked pizza crust followed him out and enveloped her in a warm cloud.

"Hey," she said, blinking rapidly to keep herself from crying.

"What are you doing?" he asked.

"I'll give you three guesses."

"Okay. I like this game. First guess. You're heading back to the Teeter Totter."

She rolled her eyes, but her mind hastily tried to remember whether she'd glimpsed him last night when she was coming out of the Teeter Totter. He said something in his FriendZoo message. She didn't have time to ask, though, because he plowed ahead.

"Okay, sorry," he said. "Second guess. You're going to meet someone for a drink."

She scowled.

He grimaced.

"Hmm, that one's no good. You're probably taking tonight off, right?"

"Isn't your date waiting on you?" she said.

"What? Oh. My brother? Nah. He's used to me running into women everywhere we go. He's fine. Only kidding," he added quickly.

"Besides," he leaned back to look in the door of Eddie's, "I think he has a thing for our server. He's probably been waiting for me to leave so he can ask for her number. So. What are you doing?"

"I'm walking home."

"Can I join you? Maybe you'll cook for me. I saw you at Country Kitchen and wondered what you'd look like standing in my kitchen with a glass of wine and a thick steak. Maybe an apron with nothing underneath. Some music."

So that's what he was thinking while he stood there. She shivered.

"Listen, Jake. That message last night – I didn't mean it. I mean, I meant it, but I wouldn't have said it if the girls and I hadn't gone out."

"So you're telling me you're not inviting me home to ravish me?" he said.

"I didn't even invite you. And how did you know I was at The Teeter Totter?"

"Do you want to? Invite me, I mean?"

She didn't answer, and started walking instead.

"Wait." He grabbed her arm. "Wait right here."

Jake pulled his wallet out of his pocket, slid out a twenty and ran it in to his brother, who turned around to gawk at Delaney as Jake rejoined her outside, falling into step with her.

"So, what's eating at you?" he said.

"It's that obvious, huh?"

"You don't look a thing like the Delaney Collins I had dinner with the other night. Or the one I saw coming out of the Teeter Totter last night. Or the one I met outside of Porky's."

"Do I have to tell you?"

"Nope." He shrugged and put his hands in his pockets.

They walked a block, past another art gallery, the hat shop, a kids boutique. As they came to the corner of Main Street and State Avenue, Jake folded his hand around hers. The gesture was romantic and surprisingly comforting.

"Are you wooing me right now?" she asked, smiling up at him despite her bad mood.

They stepped off the curb in unison.

"Maybe," he said.

"It's been a long time since someone held my hand."

"How does it feel?" he said.

"Nice," she said.

"So, how are you? I mean, besides whatever's eating at you."

"Good," she said. "I had a good job interview yesterday. Spent the day shopping for essentials."

"What job?"

They stopped at the next intersection to let several cars turn in front of them. The lawn on the downtown square was packed for the first time in months. Delaney watched a couple of kids kicking a soccer ball around in the fading light.

"It's for a vet, Doctor Kathryn Rick. She just opened a new position. It went okay. She said she'd call me."

"That's great. Want to do a few laps before you go home?"

Delaney shrugged, and Jake led her along the edge of the square. A pair of teenagers had spread a blanket on the grass and were making out feverishly. The girl had pulled the boy's shirt up in back, and was clawing at his skin.

"That's what you're going to do to me, right?" Jake squeezed Delaney's hand. She blushed and was grateful for the dark. He said, "I thought you liked tending bar at Rowdy's."

"I do," she said. "I'm not sure if I told you the last time, but I promised my friends I'd get a new job."

There. That wasn't saying too much, was it?

"Why do they want you to do that?"

"I'm thirty-four, with a doctor of veterinary medicine degree, commensurate loans and a love life I just realized I should have entitled 'eclectic clearance' a long time ago."

When he chuckled, she said, "Pretty clever, right? But seriously, I know they're right. They're just more honest with me than I am with myself."

"That's how it goes, I guess," he said. "But you want to be a vet, right? I mean, that's why you went to vet school and everything?"

They rounded the corner of the square. An old man walked by with his old dog. Of course, Delaney instantly thought of Howie and Max. Her throat closed up.

"Yeah. I love animals," she said. "I've wanted to be a vet ever since I was ten. We had this dog, Leia."

"Star Wars?"

"Of course. Anyway, she was a Boston Terrier. The best dog in the world. We'd had her since I was a baby. I grew up hanging out with her, taking her for walks, reading to her. She slept at the foot of my bed, every night, on her own little blanket. She was my dog, you know? Once when I got the chicken pox, she sat on the couch with me for three entire days, her head on my lap. So, when I was ten, she got sick. Really sick. Cancer. My parents took her to the vet, but I guess there was nothing they could do. It had already spread throughout her body."

Delaney was surprised at the force with which the memory hit her.

She swallowed, hard, and continued. "My mom came home from the vet without Leia. They'd put her to sleep. I didn't even get to say good-bye."

Now she was near tears. Again. "God, I loved that dog," she said. "Anyway, I resolved to become a vet. So I could help other people's pets."

Jake took his hand out of hers, and put his arm around her shoulder. He pulled her close and kissed the side of her head. Talking about herself and having someone listen, understand, was like a balm. She inhaled the scent of his skin, soapy with a bit of pizza sauce. They'd made a full lap of the downtown square's lawn.

"So why'd it take you so long to finally look for a job as a vet?"

"I didn't," Delaney said. "I worked for a year right out of vet school."

This was a road she didn't go down with anyone, ever. But for some reason, she found herself wanting to open up to Jake.

"What happened?"

Delaney took a deep breath. "This isn't something I share with every-one. In fact, I've never shared it with *anyone*."

"I feel special."

"You are special," Delaney said. "And also, I guess I'm just tired of hiding from what happened. Ever since, I've been running from it, you know? I quit veterinary medicine, my passion, because I couldn't deal with it. But I think I'm ready now."

Jake gave her hand a squeeze. "So what happened?"

Suddenly, Delaney was back at the Desert Veterinary Clinic, in exam room three, flirting with that good-looking guy—a firefighter in a tank top that showed off his weightlifter's physique. They were chatting about the puppy as it gnawed on one of the guy's thumbs. It was a chocolate lab with beautiful blue eyes. Delaney crouched down to pet it, and was enjoying puppy kisses on her face when the door flew open and Barb, the receptionist, rushed in, her face pale and her eyes wide.

"It's Max," she said.

The present-day Delaney felt all the nerves of that day, as if she were experiencing the moment again. Her mouth went dry, her stomach churned, and her palms became so sweaty she extricated her hand from Jake's and wiped it on her jeans. Maybe she wasn't ready to share the whole story. But she could share part of it.

"There was this old dog. Max. An English bulldog. And an old man. Howie. Kind of like that pair we just saw a few minutes ago. Howie's wife had died a few years before, and all he had was this damned dog—his words. I mean, the stupid dog was almost twenty years old. When his wife first brought it home, the man hated it. It was constantly growling at him, piddling on the floor, you name it. Of course, he grew to tolerate the dog. It would sidle up to him on the couch and curl up against his leg. And he'd let it. So when Howie's wife died, he turned to Max. They were inseparable. He had children but they were grown, had kids of their own, and they were so busy. So he spent all this time with Max. Gardening, going for walks. He even brought him to these outdoor chess tournaments. Max became a mascot."

A sob escaped Delaney, and she forced herself to laugh, to lighten the mood.

"I'm getting off track, here. Anyway. Howie would bring Max into the clinic at least once a week. It seemed like he almost imagined ailments and really just wanted company, you know? Or maybe he did it because he was so afraid of losing the only friend he had left. Well, I was the newbie at the clinic, so I was usually the one assigned to see them. We'd always spend a few minutes talking, and then I'd reassure Howie that Max was fine, and they'd leave."

Delaney took a deep breath and Jake gave her shoulder a squeeze. "On the day in question, Howie brought Max in for depression. I, of course, thought it was nothing other than an excuse to bring him in. So I dilly dallied. On my way to exam room five, I spotted a guy with a puppy in exam room three. I mean, who doesn't love puppies?"

It felt physically impossible for Delaney to continue, but she forced the next words out.

"Of course, I was chatting him up. The guy, not the puppy. And getting puppy kisses. And poor Howie was in there with Max ..."

"You couldn't have known," Jake said. "He brought that dog in every week."

"I know," Delaney said.

"And the dog was, what, like twenty years old?"

"Yeah. But still. I was in the next room, having a great old time, and Max collapsed. Howie started yelling. I can still hear his voice, the panic in it. He was so scared, Jake. And I was just taking my time."

"I'm sure he didn't blame you," Jake said. "He probably didn't even know you weren't with another appointment."

"He knew I wasn't there. And worse, I know I was just shooting the breeze, you know? By the time I got in there, he was laying on the floor with Max, sobbing. I don't know if I can ever forgive myself."

They'd reached the fountain, and Delaney stopped walking. She turned to face the water, and put her hands on the railing. If she had a penny, she'd toss it in and wish for forgiveness.

"I understand," Jake said.

He wrapped an arm around Delaney's shoulders and she leaned into him. Sure, he could understand the dog dying. But that was just Act Two of this tragic story. There was still an Act Three, and even though she wanted to tell someone, to get it off her chest, she couldn't bring herself to do it.

Instead, she said, "Thanks, Jake. I appreciate it."

Jake put his hands on Delaney's shoulders and turned her to face him. He bent down so their eyes were level and he said, "It's not your fault, Delaney. Dogs die. It's part of the circle of life."

Delaney nodded. "I know you're right. I've just always felt so—so guilty, you know? I felt so stupid. Like I let a cute guy and a cute puppy come before the well-being of this dog—this dog I'd come to love."

"I get it," Jake said again. "But I'm pretty sure a few moments didn't make a difference in that particular situation. Besides, how many pets will you save? I mean, you've got to save at least one every month over the course of a career, right? Probably more."

She chuckled. The knot that had formed in her stomach loosened. "True."

Jake took her hand and they started walking again.

"Wow," Delaney said. "I can't believe how good it felt to share that story. I haven't told that to anyone."

"Never?" Jake said.

"Never," Delaney said. "I feel a million times lighter."

"Glad I could help," Jake said. "Now. I want to show you something."

He led her down an alley between an art gallery and the Polar Cap ice cream shop.

"This isn't what I had in mind," she said.

"Trust me," he said. "When we get to that, you're not going to care where we are, so advanced are my wooing skills."

She laughed, the sound echoing off the high brick walls on either side of them. At the back of one of the galleries she'd walked past earlier, Jake entered a code on a keypad next to a scuffed, dented metal door. He pushed the door open, gestured for Delaney to go in and flicked on the lights.

"This is spooky," she said, looking around.

In the half-light, the subjects of the paintings looked ghostly, and the sculptures cast weird shadows on the walls.

"Here."

One more set of lights flicked on. Jake took her hand again and led her over to the front corner of the gallery. The window overlooked Main Street and the square.

"So remember I told you I do woodworking? Well, here it is."

He motioned to a low, shining table that looked at once like a tree trunk straight from the forest and a fine piece of furniture manufactured from scratch. The surface was sleek and smooth and showed off the rings of what must have been a humongous tree. On the pedestal, dark bark swirled upward from the tops of the roots, elegant and sturdy.

"It's beautiful," she said. "Can I touch it?"

"I see my wooing is paying off. Yeah, go ahead. Touch it all you want to."

Delaney ran a hand over the tabletop. The glossy surface felt as smooth as it looked.

"I love it."

"Here's another one." He motioned to a taller, narrower table. It was a bit rougher, Delaney thought, but it still gleamed.

"You really should quit that day job," she said. "This stuff is great."

"I was twelve," he said. "A little older than you were when Leia died. But I remember this moment. It's so clear. Anyway, one night at dinner, my dad – he was a miner – started talking about his painting. Whenever he'd start talking, my brother and sisters and I would listen, just enthralled. Because he never did anything aside from working and coming home. But when he talked about painting, his eyes just lit up. So I remember this particular night, he came home and he was telling us about the sunrise that day. He'd seen it at the camp, just before he'd gone into the mine. If only he could paint it, he was saying. He'd never seen anything so beautiful. And my mom, she just shut him down. She said, 'Skip, if you could paint anything to save your own life, we wouldn't be sitting around this table eating dry bread and drinking dehydrated milk. Now quit your daydreamin.' Kids, finish your dinner.' I remember, I just put my head down, shoveled my stew into my mouth, mopped my bowl up with my dry bread and left the table. I felt so bad for my dad. I knew then I wanted to always do something that brought me joy, even if I was terrible at it. And to marry a nice woman."

"But you're not terrible at this," Delaney said, motioning to the tree trunk table. "It's amazing."

"Thanks," he said.

"And doing this full-time probably beats the pants off professional fishing."

"Well, it's a tough call. But the fishing pays the bills, for sure."

They stood in silence for a few beats, then Jake said, "I want to open my own gallery."

"That's great!" Delaney said. "You should."

"I don't know why I'm compelled to tell you, but I am. Maybe hearing about you taking that leap, applying for a vet job. You inspired me."

"*I* inspired you?" she said.

"Don't gawk at me like that. You did! You're finally doing something you feel like you're meant to do. It's inspiring."

"Tell me that when I actually get a job."

"We'll have to do this again," Jake said as they approached Delaney's house twenty minutes later.

"What, run into each other downtown and spend the evening sneaking around dark buildings?"

"Exactly."

"This is it," Delaney said, slowing to a stop.

Jake took both of Delaney's hands in his.

"That was really nice," he said. "Can I call you?"

Delaney panicked. She wasn't supposed to give people her number – Summer and Josie had said not to. But this was different, wasn't it?

"Let's just message each other on FindLove," she stammered.

"What? I spill the contents of my heart at your feet and you won't even give me your number? Fine. Okay. I'm sending you a message right now." He dropped her hands, fished his phone out of his back pocket and spent a few seconds typing.

"There," he said. "Read it when you get inside."

Then, he took her face in his hands and kissed her, long and deep. Without another word, he walked away.

Hundreds of thoughts, without beginnings or ends, swirled through Delaney's mind as she watched him go. That single kiss, warm and firm and absolutely breathtaking, had reduced her to a quivering mess.

Jake didn't look back.

Still trembling, Delaney let herself in and turned on her computer to read the message he'd just sent.

And THAT is what I've been wanting to do since the first time I saw you.

For the second time in as many weeks, she wondered if she'd swoon.

CHAPTER TWENTY

Delaney's phone rang first thing Monday morning. She recognized the number on caller ID and answered it right away.

"Ms. Collins. It's Janie from Doctor Rick's office."

Delaney could tell from the tone of Janie's voice she wasn't getting hired. After experiencing a quick stab of disappointment, Delaney wondered whether it would be lame to hang up now and then show up at Doctor Rick's office in scrubs and a lab coat. Probably.

"Hi, Janie."

"Hi. Look. Doctor Rick really liked you. But the reason she's hiring right now is because she needs a massive amount of help. And she said she doesn't have the time to bring you up to speed. She needs someone with more experience."

Delaney nodded, then remembered they were on the phone. She cleared her throat.

"I understand."

When they hung up, Delaney burst into tears. Not only had she failed yet another job interview, but she also had managed to make both of her best friends so angry at her that they weren't speaking to her except as necessary.

What was wrong with her? Why couldn't she just get her life organized? Why wasn't she capable of making one single thing go right?

Although she had started her morning full of hope, drinking coffee, showering and getting dressed before seven a.m., the crushing disappointment had her changing back into pajamas and climbing into bed again.

She tried to fall asleep. But images of her own eighty-year-old hands, with gnarled knuckles and age spots, filling drinks for Rowdy's customers as her sagging breasts dragged on the bar, kept her awake. Yes, she'd be an octogenarian cat lady working at Rowdy's.

Doctor Rick had liked her. Delaney thought she'd nailed the interview. She'd known which drink Doctor Rick would order. Didn't that count for something? No, she'd never actually let a boil on an angry horse. But she *had* been a damned good bartender for seven years. How fast did seven years turn into twenty-seven? Fifty-seven?

It looked like Delaney Collins was going to find out.

She knew she should get out of bed, find that sense of purpose with which she had woken up this morning and start looking for more jobs. Instead, Delaney lay there all morning, staring at the ceiling.

As a child, she'd liked finding shapes – usually animals or unicorns or airplanes that would whisk her somewhere tropical – in the drywall texture on the ceiling. But today, the splotches looked like nothing more than splotches: shapeless, irregular blobs.

Just like my life.

A hot tear ran down the side of her face and onto her pillow.

CHAPTER TWENTY-ONE

The glaring silence wore on her. Only a few days had passed since Delaney last heard from Summer and Josie, but it felt like weeks. Every time she thought about it, she felt a lead weight drop into her stomach. How long would they give her the silent treatment?

Yes, she'd made a mistake. She should not have logged onto Find-Love.com after imbibing. And she should not have written those comments, however honest they were. But, in her own defense, since that night, she'd resisted the sometimes-strong urge to sign on and chat with good-looking men, who, according to Josie, were actually average-looking men with glamorized profile pictures.

Delaney's phone chirped as she put on her makeup. Her heart practically leapt with joy when she saw the text was from Josie. Dozens of tiny thoughts flitted through her mind before she actually read the message: maybe it was an *I-forgive-you* text, or maybe Josie had forgotten about the whole incident and was inviting Delaney out for coffee, or maybe …

Mitchell wants to know if you're out of your funk and want to go on a date with him.

"That's it?" Delaney said to Pixie. "No 'Hello, how are you,' or 'I have really missed you'?"

Pixie blinked and looked away.

Delaney responded, *What do you guys think I should do?*

Whatever you want, of course, Josie texted. Then she sent a smiling devil emoji.

Delaney clicked her compact closed. "These women are infuriating."

She texted Josie: *Fine. Set it up and send me the details.*

Josie: *Fine.*

A while later, as she was getting in her car, her phone chirped again. It was Josie: *Dinner at the pizza place at 7. You have time to go home and change out of your job hunting outfit. I figured you didn't want to be covered in animal hair on a date.*

Delaney's mood lifted slightly. At least Josie had considered that she'd need time to change into clean clothes.

"So you do still love me," she said. She texted back, *Thanks, Josie.*

Delaney resumed her job search with renewed purpose. She put on her new interview uniform: jeans and a button-up blouse, and a facial expression she hoped looked more confident than she felt, and she started knocking on doors.

The same response, in a few different versions, met her everywhere: "You don't have any recent experience?" or "You've worked at a bar for the past decade?" or "You've never treated a festering bite wound?"

Sometimes it was just a look – an exasperated *I'm-too-busy-to-talk-to-someone-who-works-as-a-bartender* look, accompanied by an irritated exhale and a quick, "Look, Ms. – what was it? I'm sorry. I'm just not hiring."

How long will this go on? Delaney wondered as she drove home. Halfway there, she realized her face was still frozen in that lame, confident expression. She rubbed a hand over it and let it relax into a frown.

EDDIE, the owner of Eddie's Pizzeria, had declared the official arrival of spring by setting up the patio between the front of his building and the sidewalk. Two- and four-person tables crowded cheerfully together, decked out with flowers in vases.

As Delaney approached, she couldn't help but notice that Mitchell seemed a little dim compared to all the joviality on the patio. Not only was he wearing a somber black shirt, but his complexion looked a bit pasty. The bags under his eyes were big enough to hold the load of groceries Summer bought each week for her family of six. And it wasn't rare for that load to require two shopping carts. A feeling she couldn't quite identify pricked the back of her mind. Was it annoyance? Anxiety? Whatever it was, she didn't like it, and though she tried, she couldn't shake it.

"Everything okay?" she said as she sat down across from Mitchell.

"Of course," he said. "Why not?"

"You just look a little down."

Huge jug of wine in hand, a server approached the table and turned over two wineglasses.

"None for me, thanks," Mitchell said, covering his glass with his hand.

"For you, miss?"

"Sure, thanks."

"No wine, huh? I thought you loved wine and pizza. Didn't you say that?" Delaney said.

"Yeah. I usually do," Mitchell said.

"So, what's wrong?"

"The other night, when we met up, you inspired me. I thought I'd try for a new job, too. Why not? I'm a lawyer. I could make what I'm making now, times about thirty. So I gave my two weeks' notice, found some job listings, wrote up a resume and set up a couple of interviews. I was ecstatic."

The server returned with a basket of garlic bread. Delaney's mouth watered.

"Go ahead," Mitchell said, nodding at the breadsticks. Then he went on, "I realized I don't want to be an attorney."

"So what's wrong with that?" Delaney asked.

She'd taken a breadstick and now offered the basket to Mitchell. He closed his eyes and shook his head. Delaney hated it when people closed their eyes and shook their heads. Hated it. *Refrain from judgment*, she reminded herself.

"Well, then I thought about all the time and money I spent on law school. I thought about the long nights studying for the bar exam. I thought about how disappointed my parents will be when I don't actually use the education I got. And I started to hate myself."

"Do you think you're just nervous about the interview process and all that?" she said. "I've been really nervous about my interviews."

"Maybe." He picked up a piece of bread. "But I also can't imagine my life as a lawyer. Nine to five, wearing a tie, you know?"

"Yeah, I get it," Delaney said. "My mom reminded me the other day, though, that once I finally get married and have kids, I'm not going to want to be working all hours of the night. Nine to five is pretty good if you're a family man."

"At this point, I don't think I'm going to be a family man. I can't stand kids. I mean, they're dirty, they cry all the time and you have to pay for them to go to college – which they'll turn around and throw in your face by becoming a lifelong waiter."

Wow. I don't remember talking about this on top of the water tower.

Dinner arrived and they ate in relative quiet, speaking only once or twice to comment on the house specialty pesto pasta. So how they ended up back at Delaney's place after dinner, she didn't quite know.

"Well, I feel lots better," Mitchell said. "Would you hand me my glasses?"

Although the sex had fallen quite short of great (she'd managed to *almost* enjoy some of the encounter, but definitely not the part where Mitchell smacked her ass, hard, as he was finishing up), Delaney felt a strange lack of satisfaction. She wanted Mitchell out of her house so she could contemplate it, alone.

She handed him his glasses and pulled on her robe, hoping he'd get the hint and take off. But instead, he stretched luxuriously before propping his head on a hand. His pasty skin contrasted starkly with the patchy dark hair on his chest.

"That was nice," he said.

Surprisingly, Mitchell's sob story at Eddie's had not gotten Delaney's juices flowing. In fact, for once, she had wanted to call it a night after dinner. But he'd looked so pitiful when he asked if he could walk her home. She thought it was stupid now, but at the time she'd considered that bringing him home might erase that horrible feeling that had started growing at the base of her neck. Without Summer and Josie hovering via text, she had agreed to the escort as he finished his pizza Margherita.

She felt uncomfortable, like she wanted to unzip her skin and crawl away, leaving it empty and crumpled up on the bed next to Mitchell. She was uncomfortable with her decision, with Mitchell, with herself. She wondered why. For one (here she imagined Summer ticking the list off on her fingers), she couldn't completely ignore Mitchell's comment about not wanting a family. Two, she'd noticed during the conversation that he gave up so easily. Intimidation, on its own, had kept him from pursuing what he'd once considered a lifelong dream. Dreams change, she knew. But he hadn't even made it to – much less through – an interview. Third, the spark she'd noticed on their initial date wasn't there. She couldn't really say why. Fourth, he was a downer tonight, and she had a feeling this was the real Mitchell, the Mitchell without the first-date sheen. The worst part of it was that she suspected everything she was noticing about Mitchell was the same stuff she disliked about herself.

"Well, I've got to get to bed. Job-hunting tomorrow," she said.

"See? You nine-to-fivers miss out on all the fun."

But it worked. He got up, dressed and headed for the door.

"When will I see you again?"

He leaned in for a kiss and she leapt off the bed before it could even land on her cheek.

"Let me settle into this nine-to-five thing, and I'll let you know," she said.

CHAPTER TWENTY-TWO

This particular Happy Hour was going to require some preparation, Delaney decided Thursday evening. She filled her tub with hot water and scented bath salts and soaked for a half-hour while visualizing the confident Delaney she knew she'd need to be to face Summer and Josie.

Happy Hour itself had been a constant in Delaney's life for the past several years. It was more important than any other aspect of her schedule. So why did she feel so nervous? Wouldn't they just settle in, like they always did? If not, she had some ammo of her own, she thought as she selected sparkly blue earrings to match her bright blue top.

"Hey Dee," Benjamin greeted her as she walked into Rowdy's a half-hour later.

She didn't have to wait for her eyes to adjust to the dim lighting to see their usual table was empty. Feigning self-assurance, she sat down, hoping the girls wouldn't stand her up for the first time ever.

"How's it hangin', Benjamin?"

"Oh, you know. The same. There's a guy I want you to check out. He's coming in later."

"For me or for you?"

"For me." Benjamin adjusted his hat.

"You look sheepish," Delaney said. "I'm so intrigued."

"Me, too. I'll be right back with your drink."

The clock above the bar said it was two minutes after four. Josie came stalking in at the same time as Benjamin returned to the table with a tray.

"Hey, Benji," she said, then shifted her attention to Delaney. "Dee."

"Ouch," Delaney said, in an attempt to keep the mood light. "Still mad, huh?"

Josie remained standing, and put a hand on her hip. Delaney knew she was in trouble.

"'Mad' doesn't really cover it," Josie said. Delaney braced herself, but Josie's attitude took a surprising turn. She sat down across from Delaney and reached for her hand before speaking. "It's just that Summer and I want you to have a relationship with a regular, normal guy. And we feel like your own baggage is holding you back from doing that. You deserve it, Dee. You deserve a great relationship. You deserve a great life."

Her eyes were actually watering. She was starting to *cry*, Delaney realized. '

"That stupid Tucker guy duped you," Josie said. "But he was a jerk. Summer and I never liked him. And they're not all going to do that. I promise you, there's a wonderful guy out there for you."

Feeling uncomfortable in the spotlight, Delaney shifted in her chair and said, "How was your day?"

Josie sighed. "It was okay. I finally turned in my grant application. The deadline's tomorrow, so I'm actually early. I'm just so stressed, so afraid I won't get it. I just really want to help these kids. I think that's what's making me so emotional. You know, these parents work so hard. Some of them work overnights or two jobs or whatever, and they do it because they want more for their kids. They want their children to have a better life than they did. But they're not able to help their kids with homework, or talk to their kids about the social problems that come up."

"Why wouldn't you get the grant?"

"I don't know," Josie said. "Everything I want to do aligns with the purpose of the grant. Here, I'll show you." She pulled out her phone, tapped the screen a few times, and handed it to Delaney. "It will pay for a leased space and a salaried director for a center like I'm talking about."

"This is the application?" Delaney said.

"Yeah," Josie said. "It's, like, a thousand questions. But I filled it out. Sent it in. Just waiting to hear back."

"It sounds perfect," Delaney said.

"I think so. On another note, in her quest to snag the principal position right out from under me, the conniving Blair Upton has announced she's starting a sewing club at school. And a racquet club. Seriously? A sewing club? For elementary students?"

"What's this about a sewing club?" Summer asked, approaching the table. She tossed her purse on the spare chair and sat down.

"Blair Upton," Delaney said. "She plans to start a sewing club. Josie thinks it's just one more move in the scheme to rob Josie of the principal position."

"You know what?" Delaney said. "Screw her. She's an uppity bitch, anyway. We'll come up with something better."

"Oh, yeah? Like what? Our efforts at a dating club won't work, obviously."

Josie smiled a cool smile, and Delaney flinched.

"Okay," Summer said. "Let's get this out of the way. Dee, we are really upset with you. You're totally interfering with our attempts to help you find real love."

Before she had a chance to answer, Josie added, "We're doing this for you because you *need* it. You're in a bad pattern, and you need to break out of it. And you said, yourself, that you want to. Didn't she? Didn't she, Summer?"

"Well, it was implied, honestly. I guess we never asked her about it."

"I *do*! I do want it! I want to find real love. If I could bottle what I have with you two and somehow transpose it to my relationship with a guy, I'd be thrilled. But I can't."

"You don't have to," Josie said. "You have to stop mucking up our perfectly decent efforts. I feel like you're doing it on purpose, just to mess with us."

"Oh, Josie, I'm sure she isn't doing it just to mess with us. She just doesn't have the confidence to let something sail smoothly along."

"Well, why not?" Josie threw a hand in the air, then slapped her palm on the table for emphasis with each point: "She's gorgeous. She's nice. She's funny. She's smart. And she's a real-life veterinarian. Not to mention her wicked uncanny sense for getting a great read on a person."

Delaney wanted to say, "I'm not a real-life veterinarian," but she didn't.

"She doesn't think she's worthy of love from a decent, happy, successful guy," Summer said. "Even though everything you just said is true."

"But why not?" Josie looked at Delaney as if she were some kind of alien species. Then, before Delaney could answer and explain why she was undeserving of a great, happy life, Josie said, "I need another drink."

"Well, that went well, considering," Delaney said as Josie harrumphed off to the bar, too impatient to wait for Benjamin to return.

"We're not angry," Summer said. "And we want to do this for you. But we don't want you to mess up our hard work. It's like we're planting you this beautiful garden. We're working the soil, we're watering the tiny seeds and the plants are starting to grow. They're wonderful, some of them. Others are a little wilted, maybe, but some of them are even getting flowers. And we're so happy. And then here comes Delaney, stomping on the plants. Not just the wilted ones, but also the beautiful ones, which have so much potential. You're stomping on our plants, Dee." Tears filled Summer's eyes then and Delaney's mouth dropped open in surprise. Summer shrugged. "Sorry, it's the hormones."

By now, Josie had returned, still flushed.

"Oh, no," she said to Delaney. "How'd you make her cry?"

She set her glass on the table and hugged Summer before sitting back down.

"It's not hard to do these days," Summer said, dabbing at her eyes with the end of her skirt.

"I'm sorry for stomping on your plants," Delaney said quietly, near tears herself. "I'll do better. I can follow instructions. I'm really sorry. I'll let them grow."

After a moment of heavy silence, she asked, "Can we change the subject now?"

"Please," Josie said. "Let's."

"How's the exercise coming, Josie?" Summer asked.

"That's not the subject I was hoping for," Josie said. "It's not coming very well."

Although Delaney was tempted to ask if it had something to do with her gym wardrobe, or lack thereof, she decided to tread carefully.

"What's stopping you from going?"

"I don't know, really. I just haven't felt like going." Her voice came out muffled. "It's pointless. I don't even like working out."

"Start small," Delaney suggested. "Go to a class after work."

"Do you have your tablet?" Summer said. "Let's look at the schedule right now. Let's find a class we can all go to together."

Finding a class to agree on was much like finding a man to agree on. Delaney thought spin class would be too hard, Summer didn't think she was coordinated enough to do Zumba, and Josie refused to do anything that required a step. They finally settled on a yoga class Saturday morning, although Josie said she was sure someone would smell like body odor and patchouli.

Now it was Josie's turn to change the subject. "Did you hand out any CDs?" she asked Summer.

"I can tell you're thinking I didn't," Summer said. "But you're wrong. I handed out seven of them. Even left one here. Wouldn't it be a kick if we performed at Rowdy's?"

"Wow," Delaney said. "I can't wait to see you onstage!"

"At the rate I'm growing with this pregnancy, though, you won't be able to see my face past the belly," Summer said. "But I'm doing it, even if I have to perform while I'm in labor. I'm doing it!"

"That's the spirit," said Benjamin, who'd returned with another round of drinks. "He's here, Dee. Back corner, red t-shirt."

The girls all swiveled around to look.

"Ooh," they all said in unison. "Very yummy."

"You guys are so obvious!" Benjamin hissed.

"I think it's Ivy who's obvious," Delaney said. "She keeps sending him drinks, 'on the house.'"

"I know," Benjamin said. "I know. This is the third night he's been in here. Second night alone. I'm not sure if he's coming back for Ivy's signature Green Ivy drinks, or to see me. I'll be back."

They watched him walk over to the table.

"Ahh, young love," Josie said. "Speaking of young love, I just pulled up your FindLove profile and Sebastian-slash-Jake wants to know if you can go out tomorrow night."

"Of course I can. Right? Can't I?"

"He's pursuing you now," Josie said. "I think it's time to make him wait, just a little. Can we do next Wednesday? Push it back? We want him to think your social schedule is very busy."

"I'm confused. You say you want me to stick with a normal guy. Then a normal guy comes along and you want me to play hard to get."

"It's all part of the game, my sister," Summer said. "Josie's right. You can't be available every time he asks. You have to show interest, but also come across as having your own life. So he doesn't think he's taking on too much importance."

"So I'm just going to say, 'Sorry, I'm busy tomorrow, but I'd love to see you. How about Wednesday before my cooking class, instead? Short and sweet."

The word, "Fine," died on Delaney's lips as she remembered her renewed effort to follow instructions. Instead she said, "Thanks, Josie."

"Oh. He must be online right now. He just wrote back, 'Wednesday's good. Shall I pick you up at your place?'"

"Sure," Delaney said.

"No," Summer and Josie said in unison. Summer added, "We don't want him knowing where your house is, yet."

Delaney didn't mention that he'd walked her home that night she'd run into him outside Eddie's. She didn't mention the steamy kiss, either.

"I'll just tell him to meet at Eddie's," Josie said.

"No!" When both girls jumped with surprise, Delaney explained,

"It's just that I met Mitchell there… during my phase of disobedience. It'd be awkward to meet Jake there, too."

It was a lie—Mitchell, who was supposed to be a lawyer, worked there and she didn't want to run into him when she was with Jake—but the girls would never know.

"All right," Josie said.

"Hey, look at Benjamin! That's so cute!"

At the corner table, Benjamin had slid onto the barstool across from the good-looking guy in the red t-shirt. They leaned toward each other, talking intensely.

"I wonder what they're saying," Summer said.

Then, the moment ended as both men howled with amusement, tipping their heads back. Benjamin got off the stool and walked to the front of the bar, tapping the girls' table as he went.

"You know," Summer said, "I have an idea. I think we need a break from talking about The Dating Intervention, Josie's working out and my band stuff. What do you guys say we go to the spa this weekend? Pedicures, massages, whatever?"

"Oh, I could kill for a good pedicure," Josie said.

"Saturday?" Summer said. "After yoga?"

"It's a date," Delaney and Josie said.

"I'll make appointments at Hot Rocks," Delaney said. "This will be perfect, in case you guys find me a date with another guy who has a foot fetish."

"So, back to Sebastian-slash-Jake," Josie said. "How about the fountain on the square? And you guys can go from there?"

"Sure. Perfect."

Even as her mouth formed the words, though, Delaney's mind began to form another plan. Even as she yearned for her friends' approval, she craved autonomy. She craved Jake Rhoades, and she didn't want to wait until Wednesday to see him.

CHAPTER TWENTY-THREE

The Internet, as far as Delaney was concerned, was one of the best spy tools around. With a little work, you could find the dirt on just about anyone you wanted to. Jake Rhoades was no exception.

A quick search brought up tons of results. Most of them had to do with his furniture. A couple of the results showed that he was on the social networking site FriendZoo. She logged into her own account and searched for him there.

She was surprised when the profile picture loaded: it was definitely Jake Rhoades and he was flashing the same cocky smirk she'd thought about so often since she'd first seen it. The quick flutter in her stomach and the memory of his lips on hers made her shiver.

Then she saw the other pictures, loading under the heading, "Photos of Jake." Even though Delaney's rational mind knew these weren't images Jake had uploaded, jealousy hit her like a karate chop to the chest (she'd seen firsthand during one of Summer's boys' fights what that could do to a person).

In one picture, a beautiful blond girl smiled at the camera, her tan, toned arm around Jake's waist. In another, Jake kissed that same girl on the cheek.

Delaney's first instinct was to call Summer or Josie. But she squelched that even as her hand reached for her phone. She didn't want them to know she was cyber-stalking Jake. Her second instinct was to start cyberstalking Michael Kirk, the guy who had posted the photos in an album labeled, "Jenny's birthday party." With enough research she could probably discern when the photos were taken and who this girl was. This instinct was strong.

Fortunately, her third instinct—to get off FriendZoo before she spent all night there—kicked in.

First, though, she decided to send him a quick message: *Hey, Jake. I don't know what I was thinking earlier. I'll feel pretty rushed if we meet before cooking class Wednesday, but I can meet tomorrow after all. How about 6 pm at the fountain on the square?*

Before she could chicken out, she clicked Send. After all, she reasoned, an extra date would give her the chance to beat around the bush about that girl. Then, knowing every minute she remained signed in was another chance for her to do (or type) something stupid, she signed off and went to bed.

Just before she fell asleep, somewhere in the recesses of her fuzzy mind, it occurred to her to think about whether Jake would think she was cyber-stalking him. She hadn't sent him a friend request, but she'd obviously found his profile. Was that creepy?

By morning, she'd forgotten about those small questions of creepiness. He'd returned her message with a short and sweet, "Great! See you then," and all she could do as she floated through the rest of the day was think about six p.m.

EARLY SPRING TWILIGHT cast soft shadows on the downtown square. The fountain bubbled merrily and a couple of kids tossed shiny pennies into the water, watching them sink to the bottom before closing their eyes to wish.

Delaney strolled casually toward the fountain, her face alight with excitement. Summer and Josie crouched behind a nearby shrub, watching her.

"I can't believe she's doing this!" Josie growled.

"Shh. She'll hear you," Summer said. "We're only, like, four feet away from the fountain."

"I can't believe you caught her in the act," Josie whispered.

"I know. She has to know I pass by here every day on my way home from the kids' baseball practice."

"Your instincts were right on. She *does* look too good for a visit to Rowdy's or coffee with her mom. Good thing you called me. Where are the kids, anyway?"

"I ran them home, dumped them in the kitchen with Derek and a frozen pizza and left," Summer said.

"Oh! That has to be him," Josie said. "Jake-slash-Sebastian. Dreamy for sure. Here he comes."

"Wow. He really *is* sexy," Summer said. "Look at that bod. Wow."

"I can see why she didn't want to wait."

Jake spotted Delaney and his face lit up, too. He began walking a bit faster.

"I've never seen that look on Delaney's face," Josie said, wonder creeping into her voice. "She looks like she's been taken over by some love alien zombie thing."

"I know, really."

When they reached each other, Delaney lifted her arms for a hug, but Jake took her face in his hands and kissed her, hard and long, on the mouth.

"I'm getting all hot and bothered," Summer said.

When they finally broke apart, Jake said, "Hi," and Delaney breathed, "Hi, yourself."

"Shall we?" Jake asked. He held out his arm, Delaney linked hers through it and they sauntered away.

"Well, they are really sweet together," Josie said. "I hate to admit it."

Summer nodded and Josie said, "Should we follow them?"

"I don't know," Summer said. "Don't you think we should give her some privacy, Josie?"

After a long look from Josie, Summer said, "Nah. You're right. She agreed to this. She can live with the consequences."

Fortunately, Delaney was so wrapped up in Jake that it was easy for the girls to follow her, unseen. Delaney and Jake walked along Main Street for a few minutes, then stopped to look in the window of an art gallery. Summer and Josie ducked into the doorway of The Sweet Tooth, the old-fashioned candy shop where Summer indulged the kids on weekends with a piece of taffy or licorice.

A few seconds later, Jake and Delaney began walking again. Summer and Josie sneaked onto the sidewalk to follow.

"I think they're going to Umbrella," Josie said.

"For dinner?"

Sure enough, Jake opened the coffee shop's door for Delaney. He glanced behind them when she went in. Josie jumped behind a bush and Summer yanked her back out by the sleeve.

"He doesn't know us!" she said in a loud whisper. "He's never met us! It wouldn't have mattered if he saw us. He would have thought we were just two girls walking down the street. Now he's going to think we're creepy stalkers!"

"Shit. You're right."

But Jake didn't seem to have noticed. He went in behind Delaney. Summer and Josie leaned against the wall.

"Well, we can't go in there," Summer said. "There's no way to get in the door without her seeing us."

"True. What should we do?"

They stood in silence for a few moments, Josie tapping a foot and Summer tapping her index finger on her chin.

"Oh. I know," Summer said. "I can't believe I'm thinking of this. It's totally up your alley. Info-gathering. But I want to see what she does."

"Well, don't hold out on me."

"So we go on your tablet, log into FindLove.com and ask Mitchell out."

"Okay," Josie said. "I like where this is going. And then we text her, right? And we tell her she has a date with Mitchell. Her reaction will tell us how much she likes Jake and how much she likes Mitchell."

"Exactly," Summer said. "So, do we set the date to begin, like, right now? So she has to leave Jake? Or do we make it for tomorrow night, because we're nice and we see the sparks between her and Jake?"

"Second option. Tomorrow."

Josie sat down on the curb and pulled out her tablet. After a few minutes, she said, "Done."

Summer joined her on the curb to wait for Mitchell's response, but they both jumped to their feet and spun around when they heard the door to Umbrella open – and lurched into the entrance of the flower shop next door when they realized Jake and Delaney were coming back out to sit on the patio.

"Shit. Don't move, Summer."

Summer stifled a giggle and said, "Okay, Josie."

Josie elbowed her.

"Isn't this weather just beautiful?" they heard Delaney say. "It really feels like spring."

"It does," Jake agreed. "But you know we'll get one more good snow before spring really hits."

Josie shrugged at Summer. Summer shrugged at Josie.

Jake asked Delaney about her job hunt and she listed out all the disappointments she'd experienced.

"I can tell she's trying to keep it light," Summer said. "But she's really hurting."

Josie nodded. "Now I'm feeling a pang of guilt for not asking how her job hunt is going. We didn't bring her wine or anything."

"We were mad. Remember? You were the maddest."

"True," Josie said. "But she's taking this huge step and we're not even there for her."

"We'll be there for her now."

They listened as Delaney talked about her cooking class. She sounded animated. She used her hands. Suddenly, she became serious.

"Jake," she said, "I have a confession."

"Ooh. Sounds very intriguing," he said. "Let me guess. You don't really like pepperoni pizza or wine."

"Oh, no. It's nothing like that," Delaney said.

"Then I can guarantee it's not going to break my heart."

"I was online the other night," Delaney began.

Josie elbowed Summer, who put her hands up and shrugged her shoulders in an *I have no idea* gesture.

"Oh, wait a minute," Jake said, his eyes laughing but his expression serious. "These stories never end well."

"I don't know how to say this without sounding like a total stalker," Delaney said.

"You were cyber-stalking me?" Jake said. "I love this. Go on."

Josie's tablet dinged and distracted the girls from hearing the rest of the conversation.

"Oh, Mitchell's already responded. He can do tomorrow. I'll text her."

"Right now?" Summer said. "When she's on the verge of making a big confession?"

"Her reaction will tell us everything."

Delaney's phone chirped. She didn't quite hide a guilty expression as she pulled her phone out of her pocket. The conversation paused.

"Sorry," Delaney said to Jake. "I'm expecting a message."

"More like, 'I don't want my friends to know I'm with you,'" Summer whispered to Josie.

Delaney's face fell when she saw the message Josie had sent: *Mitchell wants to meet up tomorrow. Date at 6 p.m. Place TBD.*

"Priceless," Josie whispered. "She looks totally disappointed."

"And guilty," Summer said.

"Everything okay?" Jake asked.

"Yeah," Delaney answered. "Fine."

Her "fine," morose and pouty, had Summer and Josie practically hyperventilating with giggles.

"Well, I guess we know how she's feeling about Mitchell." Josie snickered. "She's not even texting back."

"Let's do this again tomorrow when she's with Mitchell," Summer said. "I like observing."

DELANEY HAD to drag herself out of a deep sleep to turn off the alarm Saturday morning.

"Weekend," she said to Pixie, who glared at her from the foot of the bed. Then she remembered.

"Yoga."

She was supposed to be meeting the girls for that eight a.m. class.

Finally, her senses cleared enough that she realized her alarm hadn't actually gone off. Instead, she'd received a text from Josie.

Josie: *No yoga. What was I thinking? I want to sleep in. Then hit the spa.*

As she was reading the text, Summer's reply popped up: *Sleeping in is overrated. You can still make it by 8, even if you shower and put on your makeup. See you then.*

Delaney had seen Summer's house at seven a.m. Hannah was in her high chair, alternately taking bites of egg or toast and throwing her food on the floor. The boys were running around with swords. Or guns. Or guns they were using as swords. Sarah, the oldest and most civilized, was probably baking something that required a huge amount of flour and would taste like bricks. Summer was, no doubt, wide awake and had been for at least an hour.

Josie: *Nope. I'm putting my phone on silent. Sweet dreams.*

Summer: *You're not very committed. You're letting yourself down.*

Delaney, for fun, added: *This isn't serving you, Josie.*

Josie: *Oh, shut up, Dee. You're in bed, still, too. See you later.*

Later that afternoon, feet freshly buffed and toenails lacquered in a spring shade of aqua, Delaney, Summer, and Josie sat in the soaking tub at Hot Rocks, drinking ice water with cucumber slices in it.

"You've got about five more minutes, Mama," Josie said to Summer. "We don't want you cooking that baby."

"I know," Summer said. "It just feels so nice."

"Mmmmm." Delaney sank down so the water came up just below her chin. "What are you doing after this, Josie?"

"I'm going to take my new toenails shopping for some new shoes. There's a new shoe store at the mall and I see some sandals in my future. You know, those peep-hole ones?"

"With three-inch heels, no doubt," Summer said. "How do you walk in those things?"

Josie stretched her legs dramatically so her toes came out of the water. "It hasn't always been easy, as you know."

Delaney giggled. "Yeah, Summer. Remember her first time?"

"Homecoming sophomore year," Summer said.

"Are you going to make me relive it? Again?"

"Oh, yeah," Delaney said. "Most definitely."

"So it's Homecoming night," Summer began, mimicking a movie voiceover. "Josie, of course, is on the Homecoming Court. She's found the perfect dress."

"Silver," Delaney said. "Silver with a low back."

"It shows off the curves of which she is so proud," Summer said.

"But," Delaney said, pausing for emphasis. "There's just one problem."

"The shoes," all three of them said, dissolving into giggles.

"So," Summer began, and Delaney went on, "She raids her mom's closet and finds the perfect pair. Perfect. Silver. With sequins."

"And three-inch heels," Summer said.

"It was traumatic enough the first time," Josie grumbled.

Delaney plowed ahead: "She looks hot. I mean, sizzling."

"She takes the arm of her counterpart, the sexy stud Chris Decoterro. She can feel his bicep through the sleeve of his collared shirt."

"And she's feeling really good," Delaney said. "I mean, she looks good, Chris looks good. He smells good. This is her moment."

Josie sank down lower in the spa, pretending to drown herself.

Summer went on, "In front of hundreds – no, thousands – of adoring fans, they walk up the steps to the stage."

"The announcers call their names," Delaney said. "'Presenting the Duke and Duchess of Juniper High, Josie Garcia and Chris Decoterro.'"

"The crowd goes wild."

"No, it doesn't," Josie said. "Polite applause follows."

Delaney said, "Can the crowd go wild? Just this once?"

"Sure," Summer said. "The crowd goes wild."

Josie shook her head. Delaney went on, "Then, just as she makes her way off the stage, thinking she's nailed it in that dress and those shoes, Josie twists her ankle. She grabs onto Chris Decoterro's arm to keep herself from falling, but he's not the stud she thought he was. They both go down. Hard. In front of thousands of adoring fans."

"And now the crowd goes wild," Josie muttered.

"I would have thought you'd swear off wearing heels after that," Delaney said.

"But no," Summer said. "It only made you more determined."

"That's right," Josie said. "And now we never have to revisit that horrible, traumatic night again."

Still smiling, Summer stood up.

"Time's up," she said. "I'm going to dry off."

As Delaney drove home a while later, relaxed and pliable from the pedicure and the soak, she realized why she was feeling so tranquil: she'd spent an entire afternoon with her friends, without once feeling like she was under the microscope.

"HER AURA IS DECIDEDLY DIFFERENT TODAY," Summer observed that evening as she and Josie watched Delaney approach The Sweet Tooth. "She's calmer."

"She also hasn't put as much work into herself today," Josie said. "She looks remarkably less ready to *meet* a man, if you know what I mean."

"Well, I should hope she's not ready to *meet* a man, Josie, if you know what I mean. She shouldn't be *meeting* any men right now."

"There you are," Delaney said to a man who looked quite a bit nerdier in person than he did in his FindLove.com profile picture.

Mitchell Evans, Esq. had thinning hair, pouchy eyes and a stooped hit-me-while-I'm-down posture.

"Yikes," Josie said.

"Yikes," Summer agreed.

"But it's no wonder he made the top two."

They'd staked out inside the candy shop, squatting behind a barrel of saltwater taffy near the door. From here, they could see Delaney and Mitchell through a crack between two posters in the window, and they could just make out the sounds of their voices.

"Before we go anywhere, Delaney," Mitchell said in a high-pitched voice, "I want to tell you I'm really sorry about the other night. It was too soon for me to go home with you. I'm really sorry."

"Ew," Summer said, making a face. "Sounds like they've already *met*, if you know what I mean."

"Why didn't she tell us?" Josie said.

"Of course she didn't tell us. She didn't want to face our questioning."

"She wouldn't have," Josie said. When Summer leveled a long look at her, she said, "Okay. She would. But still."

"And she likes Jake so much."

"You know, Summer," Josie said, a defensive edge creeping into her voice, "Delaney doesn't have the market on self-sabotage. We've all been there."

"Don't you dare use this as an excuse to sabotage your principal application."

"I won't! I'm not. I swear. I'm just saying."

"Hmm."

———

WHEN MITCHELL SUGGESTED he and Delaney go back to his place and order Chinese takeout, Delaney's tight smile showed a mixture of relief and annoyance.

"That sounds fine," she said.

Josie said, "She probably wants to go to his place so they can turn on the TV and she can ignore him." Summer nodded and said, "But going back to his place seems sleazy after their last *meeting*."

"Oh. I wasn't thinking," Mitchell said then, his pasty complexion coloring. "We don't have to. Let's just go to Red Lantern and eat there."

From their spot behind the saltwater taffy barrel, Summer whispered, "Good boy, Mitchell."

"We'd better hit it," Josie said.

When Delaney and Mitchell headed west, Summer and Josie headed east. Once they turned the corner to go north and then west again, they broke into a full run in order to beat Delaney and Mitchell to the restaurant. They were seated, red linen napkins on their laps, slightly breathless, when Delaney and Mitchell walked in.

Josie would later remark that Delaney's face when she saw them (stunned and then contorted into a terrible smile) was better than priceless, but at the moment, it was all she could do to stop her laughter from bubbling out. The whole thing was so absurd, really. But Summer's hard kick under the table reminded her to hold it together.

"Why, Delaney Collins!" Summer said, infusing her voice with surprise and a Southern lilt. "What are *you* doing here?"

Delaney, who'd stopped stone cold upon entering the dining room, gathered her composure just enough to say, "Eating. You?"

"Oh, just grabbing a bite," Josie said. "You know."

"Oh, I do know," Delaney said slowly. "I do."

"Who's your companion?" Summer asked.

"Oh." Delaney cleared her throat. "Mitchell. This is Mitchell."

"Oh, how lovely to meet you," Josie said.

"Yes, just lovely," Summer echoed. "I'm Summer. And this is Josefina."

The hostess, who'd watched the exchange with more patience than even Summer had, finally interrupted: "Would you like to sit here?"

She motioned to the table adjacent to Summer and Josie's.

"Oh, uh, sure," Mitchell stammered. The hostess started laying the menus on the table. She jumped a little when Delaney said they'd been hoping for something a little more private and romantic, but she recovered quickly, picked up their menus and began walking to a table on the other side of the dining room.

"No, it's fine," Mitchell insisted, following the hostess and taking the menus from her. "We'll eat here."

"Great," Delaney muttered.

Mitchell opened his menu while Delaney glared at Summer and Josie.

"I hear the cashew chicken is to die for," Summer said to Mitchell, leaning toward him.

"You know, I need to use the restroom," Delaney said. "Please excuse me."

As she walked away, Mitchell cleared his throat and said, "Allergic to nuts, actually."

———

SHE WAS STILL PACING the bathroom when Josie walked in.

"What are you *doing* here?" Delaney hissed.

"Just getting a bite," Josie said coolly. "The cashew chicken really is good."

"You're spying on me."

"You had *sex* with him?!" Josie said.

Delaney began pacing again. She'd known it the moment she'd invited him to come home with her. She'd known they would find out. They always did. And although she should have anticipated they'd stoop so low as to spy on her, she hadn't expected it. She felt stupid. She felt betrayed. And she felt angry.

"I chose to. I wanted to. I wanted sex. He was nice. Is that so bad? You didn't even go to *yoga*!"

"We're talking about you, not me, Delaney. Rule Number Eight. No sex."

"You know what? You say *everything* is Rule Number Eight! Three-drink limit, no logging onto FindLove.com, no sex. It's *all* Rule Number Eight to you!"

Josie shrugged. "We didn't say no kissing. No messing around. No going to third base. No having a decent orgasm. We said no sex. You don't even like this guy. We saw the way you lit up when you met Jake at the fountain yesterday —"

"What? You saw me at the fountain yesterday?"

Josie's face froze, mouth open, eyes wide. "Shit. I'm sending Summer in."

In a rare display of backing down, she ducked her head and scuttled out of the bathroom.

"You have to be kidding me," Delaney said to her reflection.

In the painting on the wall, a serene Chinese woman under a blooming cherry tree looked on. Delaney rolled her eyes just as Summer breezed in.

"Josie's sent me in to smooth things over."

"She realized the big guns were too much and sent in the professional mediator, huh?"

Summer nodded, shrugged. "Guilty. Anyway, we totally spied on you. Yesterday when I was driving home after Sarah and Nate's baseball practices, I saw you. You looked really nice, by the way. But you looked too nice. I knew what you were up to. So I called Josie, dropped off the kids and we came to watch you."

"You guys are crazy. Don't you have anything better to do?"

"Right now? Probably. But let's face it: *you need us.* You chose to go out to dinner with Mitchell Evans, Esquire, who hasn't smiled a genuine smile, not one single time, since he saw you. If you didn't notice that yourself, then you need us even more. So I'm sorry if you're mad about us spying on you. I know it's juvenile. But we're only doing it because of Rule Number Eight, Dee. We love you."

With that, she walked out of the bathroom.

At a loss, Delaney shrugged at the serene Chinese woman in the painting. "I have no idea how to fix this," she said. The Chinese woman just stared. "Why can't I be more like you?"

When she walked out of the bathroom, she wondered (not for the first time) why Chinese restaurants were always so quiet. Why didn't anybody put on some nice music? The people seated in the back room stared at her as she walked back to her table, muttering to herself.

Summer and Josie had vacated their table, and left their full glasses of water sweating on the paper placemats. Mitchell looked apologetic. Summer was right: he hadn't looked happy to see her all evening. He just looked like he was sorry he existed.

"Your friends left," he said, adding an awkward, "Stating the obvious, right?"

"Sorry, that was awkward," she said. "They mean well."

"It's okay. That's part of why I don't have friends. More work than they're worth."

They hadn't discussed that on top of the water tower, either. More work than they're worth? What was that supposed to mean? She felt her hackles rising.

"Well, I don't know about that," she said. "They're really great.

They're the first people I go to whenever anything happens. They encouraged me to get a new job, to stop sticking around in dead-end relationships, to want more for myself. Before I even realized I needed to."

"Sounds to me like they just wanted to change you."

A tiny flame of indignation caught hold in her stomach and started to grow, hot and bright. Summer and Josie just wanted Delaney to be the best version of herself. What did this Mitchell character know about their friendship? Her scathing retort died on her lips though, when a petite server in a red silk robe, black silk pants and red slipper-shoes delivered their food.

"I ordered for us," Mitchell said. "I hope it's okay ... you'd said you were hungry and I thought it'd be nice if the food came out sooner rather than later."

"That was thoughtful," Delaney said quietly.

They ate without speaking. She noticed how loudly Mitchell breathed through his nose when he chewed his food. She then noticed that he had quite a bit of nose hair. Actually, quite a bit of ear hair, too. By the time she'd gotten through the hot and spicy soup and a couple of bites of the cashew chicken, she was no longer hungry. She signaled for the bill, paid it and left Mitchell Evans, Esquire at the table with three full plates of food and an empty chair.

ONE EVENING, Howie came into the Desert Veterinary Clinic at the end of a particularly grueling day. He didn't make an appointment or call ahead; he just showed up at the front desk.

Delaney was beyond exhausted, having performed two planned surgeries and an additional emergency surgery just that afternoon. Someone's dog had eaten an entire rawhide bone and it had somehow made its way to the intestines, where it got stuck and created a bacterial infection. That had been a doozy, and she couldn't wait to get home and have a glass of wine.

Just at closing time, she staggered out of the back to see Howie standing there, his hat in his hands.

She wanted nothing more than to turn right around and head out to the parking lot, but he'd already seen her.

"Howie," she said, halfway to saying she just couldn't see him today. Only then did she really look at him, and when she did, she noticed the lines around his eyes. "Are you okay?"

His shoulders slumped.

"It's Shirley's birthday," he said. "My first one without her. I was wondering if you'd have dinner with me. Nothing fancy, just the place by the movie theater, where they sell chili cheese fries."

He shrugged, the movement almost apologetic.

"I tried to get my kids together, but they couldn't come out. They sent cards, and my daughter called, but I just didn't want to spend the evening alone."

Delaney paused before answering. She thought about the bottle of wine she had in the cabinet at home and the show she'd recorded to watch. She thought about taking off her shoes and propping her feet up on the coffee table.

And she looked at Howie again.

"I would like that, Howie. Let me just go back and change."

The relief that crossed his face almost brought Delaney to tears, and she wasn't sure whether it was because she felt sorry for him or because she felt sorry for herself, because she'd have to delay that wine.

But it turned out she didn't have to feel sorry for herself: Howie ordered her a glass of red to go with her chili cheese fries and said, "Looks like you've had a long day, too, Doctor Collins. Thank you so much for having dinner with me. Shirley would get such a kick out of this."

At one point, Howie said, "Shirley used to cook these big dinners. Lasagna. Meatloaf. Stuffed zucchini. A huge pot of chili, better than what we're eating now. Once the kids were grown, she always made too much. The two of us would eat on a single dish for days. A week, even. But oh, I loved her cooking."

Then, in an unusual turn of events, Howie turned the spotlight on Delaney.

"Do you cook, Doctor Collins?"

"Oh, no!" Delaney said, wiping her mouth and shaking her head. "Absolutely not."

"Well, my mama always said a woman should know how to cook. And a man should, too. She had me in the kitchen every week, stirring the pot, browning meat, whisking eggs."

"Not mine," Delaney said. "I think she was afraid I'd burn down the house."

"You ought to learn how to cook," he said lightly. "It's actually quite fun."

"Old dog, new tricks," she said.

He made a dismissive gesture with his hand. "You're hardly an old dog, Doc. Especially from where I'm sitting. So tell me. How did you decide on veterinary medicine?"

"To tell you the truth, I've always done better with animals than I have with people," Delaney said. "I loved animals as a kid. I was always begging my parents to go to the pet store and look at all the fish and hamsters and frogs and ferrets. My dog, Leia, died when I was about ten, and that sealed the deal for me. Any pets I could save, as a vet, would help other people avoid that loss. I know it sounds silly, but that's what really drove me. And then of course, as I became an adult, I realized it's a good career. The field is evolving and there are so many new ways to treat chronic pain, chronic disease. It's pretty cool."

"Well, I know the two cents of an old man doesn't mean much, but I think you're pretty darn good with people, Doctor Collins. Lord knows you're patient with me whenever I come in."

"Thank you, Howie. It means a lot to me. What about you? Why did you become a high school teacher?"

"Two reasons," Howie said. "I was better with kids than I was with adults." He chuckled. "And I always loved reading. The classics, poetry, new literature. I love the English language and all the stories. And I loved nothing more than sharing them with bright young minds."

"How long ago did you retire?"

"Oh, I worked right up until my seventy-fifth birthday. And then Shirley, she said, 'Howie, I'm laying down the law. You've got to retire. These are our golden years.' And she was right. So I retired and we traveled the world."

"That sounds wonderful."

"It was, Doctor Collins. It really was. It's wonderful to have a career at which you're really good, where you truly excel. And it's also wonderful to have a partner who truly understands you. Not many wives would have approved of their husbands working well into their seventies. But Shirley, she was special. You're special, too, Doctor Collins. You're a special girl. And, today, on what would have been Shirley's eighty-third birthday, I want to wish you all the happiness of a good life."

He held up his glass. "Cheers."

CHAPTER TWENTY-FOUR

"I, Delaney Collins, hereby officially apologize for breaking several of the rules of The Dating Intervention. I hereby agree to abide by all rules and regulations, henceforth."

Rowdy's was crowded tonight. As always, people came out of the woodwork when the weather warmed up. The back door was open and the patio, strung in colored lights, was packed with young people holding beers and cigarettes. Something honky tonk played on the jukebox.

"Wow. That was not what I was expecting to hear from you this evening," Josie said. "But I'm not sure we believe you, anyway. The last time we were here, you gave us a dramatic show of tears over stomping on our plants."

"We're sorry for spying on you, Dee," Summer said. "We are. It was an invasion of your privacy."

"Maybe a necessary one, but an invasion, nonetheless," Josie said.

"It was an invasion of my privacy," Delaney said. The apologies took the wind out of her sails, though, and she hung her head. "But you guys were right. I needed it. My first date with Mitchell was pretty good, really. But the next couple of times I saw him, I realized we had clicked that first time because he had so much in common with the old me. He doesn't want kids. He doesn't have or want friends. He told me you guys just wanted to change me."

"You know we don't, right?" Summer said, and Josie added, "We just want you to be really, really happy. And part of doing that is living up to your potential. Which you weren't doing."

"Yes," Delaney said. "I totally get it."

It was true: Delaney wasn't living up to her potential. She did want more for herself. She wanted a wonderful career and a wonderful partner. She wasn't okay with being a lifelong bartender who lived alone (with her cat) and couldn't cook. It was time for an evolution, a metamorphosis. It was time for Delaney Collins the worm—or was she a caterpillar?—to turn into a butterfly.

Summer's voice broke into Delaney's thoughts. "Okay, now that that's settled, I have some big news of my own. Drumroll, please!"

Delaney and Josie drummed their hands on the table until Summer held up a finger and announced, "The Sweets have a gig! Our first paid gig!"

Josie and Delaney looked at each other and then back at Summer, each grabbing one of her hands.

"Really?" Delaney said, her excitement for Summer overshadowing the residual tension from the Red Lantern incident.

"That's awesome news," Josie said. "Spill the details."

"So, it's next weekend, actually. The band that was supposed to play at The Blue next Saturday canceled. Just this morning. So Miz Blue herself, Lily Blue, called me and asked if we could get it together in time to play. I was thinking, we can't possibly, but of course, I told her to put us on the marquee. So The Sweets are playing at 8 p.m."

"We are so going to be there," Josie said. "Right, Dee?"

"Right," Delaney said. "I may even throw my bra at you."

"Perfect," Summer said.

Benjamin, who'd once again been snuggled up with the guy in the black t-shirt at the corner table, strode over. "Did I hear you say you're playing at Madame Blue's next Saturday night?"

"Yes! Will you bring your new beau?"

"Of course I will! That sounds great, Summer! Congratulations. Another round, on the house."

"Ooh, I'm so excited," Summer said. "And now that that's out of the way, let's get back to biz, Dee."

"Do we have to?"

A cheer went up at the bar. Delaney watched the shot-taking competition that was now in full swing. The contestants: a pretty blonde girl with a tiny waist and a lumberjack of a guy with tree stumps for legs. A crowd had gathered and two rows of empty shot glasses glistened from the bar. Delaney'd put her money on the girl. Girls who had the guts to enter a shot-taking contest usually won.

"We've come to a decision," Josie said.

Delaney looked to the ceiling. "God help me," she said.

"We think you'll like it," Summer said.

"I'm sure I will," Delaney said.

"We want you to see Jake," Summer said. Josie added, "Exclusively."

"Okay," Delaney said, nodding.

"Wait." Josie put a hand on her arm. "We thought you'd be more excited. Why aren't you more excited?"

"I am. It's good news. I really like him."

"But?" Summer said.

"There's no 'but.'"

"Oh, there is," Josie said. "We can tell."

"Are you sure it's time for me to settle down?"

"You're not settling down, Dee," Josie said.

"You're just seeing one guy, for now," Summer added. "You can always open up the playing field again later. We're not saying you have to marry him or anything."

"We saw a lot of potential there," Josie said. "We want you to focus your energy on this one."

"Okay," Delaney said.

At first, she couldn't really put a finger on her vague sense of unease. Of course, the girls nailed it right away.

"We know this makes you uncomfortable," Summer said.

"You're not used to having all your dating eggs in one man basket," Josie said.

"You're afraid that if it ends, no matter how, you'll be left without a backup," Summer added.

"And we get it," Josie said. "Drop that man basket and all your eggs are broken." She looked at Delaney, serious. "You have to trust us here."

"Yes. You have to put it out to the Universe that this is your guy. You're into him. You're enjoying him. And you don't need anyone else."

That was it, Delaney thought. They really did know her better than she knew herself.

"I hate when you guys are right," she said. "But you are. So I'll do it."

"Okay. So you have to tell him," Josie said. "You have to tell him you're not seeing anybody else."

Oh. Seeing him exclusively was one thing. Talking about it was a whole different matter.

"I do? What if he says he wants to keep dating other people?"

"I have a feeling he's not going to say that," Josie said. "But if he does, you move on. It's simple."

"Is it?"

"Yep," Summer said. "It is. There are lots of other fish in the sea."

At this, she gestured grandly around Rowdy's. It was true. The place was packed with good-looking, Wrangler-clad men in scuffed boots and work shirts. Plenty to choose from. If Jake didn't want to be exclusive, she could move on.

It was simple. Right?

"Right," Delaney said.

Another round of cheers from the bar as the lumberjack slid off this chair and onto the floor. His friends did their best to scoop him up and he suddenly came to, slurring, "I'm all right, give me another."

"See?" Josie said, sounding wicked. "Other fish in the sea."

AS DELANEY PREPARED for her third official date with Jake Saturday evening, she marveled at how much she enjoyed having something to look forward to in terms of the manhunt, especially since the job hunt situation felt so dire. If she weren't a slave to The Dating Intervention, she thought as she put on fresh mascara and lip gloss, she would invite Jake over for a pizza and a movie.

But pizza and a movie always included wine. And pizza, a movie and wine always led to the bedroom. Or the couch. Or the kitchen counter. Once, it had even led to the coat closet. Knowing this, her two best friends had banned her from inviting Jake Rhoades to anyplace within one hundred yards of her house.

So, she'd get out. Jake had asked her to meet him in front of the gallery where his furniture was on display. She arrived at five p.m., as instructed. He thundered up to the curb in an ancient Jeep.

He jumped out, jogged up to her and folded her in a long hug.

"Hey," he said.

"Hey."

"I have a surprise for you."

Within thirty seconds, she fell in love with the Jeep. It had everything: the old car smell, a good rumble and fresh air. She could feel the evening sun on her skin and the spring breeze in her hair.

"This is awesome," she said as he drove them out of town and toward Pine Mountain.

She watched in the side view mirror as the houses fell away below them.

"Here we are," Jake announced a few minutes later as they rolled to a stop at the Pine Mountain trailhead. "Hop out."

When she saw him pull a pizza, a picnic basket and a bottle of wine off the back seat, Delaney felt a rush of pleasure.

"There's a blanket, too," he said. "Would you mind grabbing it?"

Why did she always feel like swooning when she was in the company of Jake Rhoades?

The picnic spot was a good half-hour's hike uphill. Delaney was starving by the time they reached it. Jake took the blanket, spread it on the ground and set the picnic basket on it.

"What a view, huh?" he said.

They were perched on the Western side of the mountain, and the City of Juniper sat below them, tucked neatly into the valley. She could see the downtown square, the big trees just starting to leaf out and her own tiny house just a couple of blocks up from there.

"I bet you bring all the ladies up here," she said.

She'd meant it as a joke, but simultaneously remembered that Brittany-who-got-away character, the photos of the gorgeous blonde on FriendZoo *and* that she was supposed to tell him she wasn't seeing anyone else. She wished she hadn't brought it up. She clamped her lips together, hoping her joke hadn't brought fresh memories of Brittany or the blonde to his mind. They sat on the blanket and Jake opened the picnic basket.

"All the ladies," he said. "Yeah, I bring 'em all. Actually, this is where my parents used to bring my brothers and sisters and me when we were younger. I've never brought an actual *lady* up here."

Delaney was grateful he was so busy unloading plates, napkins, wine glasses and bottles of water that he couldn't see the relief on her face.

"How many siblings do you have?" she asked.

"Seven. Four sisters and three brothers."

He opened the wine, poured each of them a glass.

"No way," she said.

"Way. How about you?"

"One of each."

She took a couple of sips of the wine and felt it go immediately to her head.

"Pizza?" he said.

"Oh, yeah."

"So what was it like growing up with all those kids in the house?" Delaney said between bites.

"Crazy. It was crazy, and fun, and exciting. All those things. You know, people worry about giving their kids enough attention, but when we were growing up my parents always had time for us. It was so much fun. Even now, when we all get together, it's so much fun. I want a whole gaggle of kids."

What guy says that? Delaney wondered.

"You'd have to get a lot of pizzas," she said.

"True. We always had to get, like, four or five pizzas. When we were teenagers my parents started having pizza parties at home so we could make our own. We all liked different stuff, you know? For a while, when we still went to pizza parlors, my mom would be like, 'We'll get four large pizzas, please. One half cheese and half pepperoni. One half combo and half anchovy.' And then it would get complicated. 'The third one should have onions on the whole thing, but half of it should have bacon and sausage and the other half should have pineapple, ham and what was it, Honey? Oh, right, roasted garlic. Oh. We ordered one more, didn't we? Okay, the fourth one should have …' You get the picture."

Delaney imagined the chaos of a bunch of kids sitting around the table giving orders to their mom. "So do you all still see each other often?"

"Oh yeah. I mean, we're all over the place, but we see each other often, considering."

"Where do you fall in the birth order?"

"Second. I have an older sister and the rest are younger."

He refilled her wine glass. In the easy silence that followed, Delaney thought, *this would be a perfect time to tell him I'm not seeing anyone else.*

But she couldn't muster up the courage. Instead, she sipped her wine and listened to Jake's stories about Allie, his four-year-old niece, and their antics at family get-togethers. Because she was an adventurous tomboy, he employed her for all kinds of shenanigans, like putting a frog in her mom's water glass or starting an all-out water balloon fight in the middle of dinner.

The sun began to set, and the sky looked like a watercolor painting, huge swaths of wispy gray clouds on a backdrop of candy pink and fire orange. Streaks of sunlight shone through the clouds, sending out ethereal beams of light.

"This is beautiful," Delaney said. "I've always missed this time of day – for so long, I was behind the bar at Rowdy's during sunset. And when I wasn't working, I couldn't be bothered to actually step foot outside."

Jake chuckled. "It is beautiful, isn't it? Sometimes I wish I'd pursued painting instead of woodworking. But I'm terrible at it."

"How's that all coming? Your woodworking, I mean."

"It's coming," he said. "I found a gallery space I really like. Maybe I can show you next time."

Speaking of next time, this is the perfect opening to tell him I'm not seeing anyone else.

Instead, she said, "That'd be great."

"How's the job hunt going?" he asked.

Delaney cringed. "Not great."

She told him how she'd applied to or visited every single clinic in town, only to be turned down at every stop because of the nobody-will-hire-you-without-experience-but-you-can't-get-experience-until-some-one-hires-you malady.

"You know, I never thought about it like that," he said. "I'm sure you'll find something."

As he spoke, Delaney thought she saw a thought flicker through his mind. She wasn't sure what it was, but it made her uneasy. Probably he didn't want to date a long-term bartender. Someone with no prospects for a real future.

"It's getting pretty dark," he said then, sending her hopes plummeting. "I guess we should pack it up, so we don't kill ourselves getting back down the hill."

As they walked back to the Jeep, Delaney was surprised to realize that even though they hadn't kissed or hugged or even held hands, she felt closer to him than she had to anyone in a long time. And, even though a tinge of worry had started gnawing at the back of her mind, she felt something else she hadn't felt in a really long time: contentment.

CHAPTER TWENTY-FIVE

The crowd at Umbrella Coffee was unusually chatty today, Delaney noticed as she waited for her mom. She twirled the straw in her iced tea. The shop's buy one, get one deal made Wednesdays busy. But typically the people were quiet as they read, studied and worked on their laptops. Probably it was the weather, which had warmed to a balmy seventy-five. Delaney had trouble believing the forecast, which predicted another massive snowstorm in a couple of days.

"I ordered you a latte," Delaney said when her mom walked in.

"Thanks, honey," she said. "Sorry I'm late. I was at the travel agent's, booking a trip to Australia for our fortieth anniversary."

"Wow. Forty years," Delaney said. "And Australia. I didn't even know you were thinking of going there."

"I know. It's wild, isn't it?" Camille sipped her drink, sat back in her chair. "It's last minute. You know your dad, he got a wild hair and now we just *have* to do it."

Delaney experienced a quick flash of envy. Her parents operated in their own world. Completely satisfied with one another, they didn't need approval or feedback from anyone else. They were perfectly content to go about their lives together. And they'd done so for forty years. She couldn't even maintain a relationship for forty days.

"So how'd your last date go with that dreamy Jake guy?" Camille asked.

"You ran into Summer again, didn't you?"

"Yeah. So how'd it go?"

Delaney remained silent, but the look on her face gave her pleasure away..

"Say no more. It was great, wasn't it?"

"It was. He's great, Mom."

"You're all aglow."

"Am I?"

"You know," Camille said, "when I first met your dad, I was so smitten. He was so … different. He seemed shy, introverted. So much so that I didn't even know he was interested until one of his students came over and told me, 'Miss Wilcox, Mister Collins really likes you.'"

"I didn't know that."

"It was so cute. She was this precocious little thing, nine or ten, you know, fifth grade. Susie. I'd had her for first grade and I had her sister the year I met your dad. She had this awful haircut and teeth that were way too big for her face. Adorable. She had that very grown-up affect, you know. She says, 'I think you should go in and talk to him.' I thought, you know, he is really cute. I've just never heard him say more than a word or two. But the kids love him, the other teachers love him. Maybe there's something to this guy. He later told me that whenever Susie mentioned my name, he'd blush. Uncontrollably. Susie was mature for her age, so she picked up on the cues."

Camille shook her head.

"So, you know how it goes from there. I went to talk to him, asked him out and that was that. The rest, as they say, is history."

Delaney loved the story of her parents' courtship. Her dad was still quiet, a little eccentric, a little introverted. Pretty much the opposite of her mom. But when they were together, they made the perfect pair. Roger had the vision, the big ideas, the energy. And Camille had the systems, the practicality. She kept things grounded.

"And now, forty-something years later, you're going to Australia."

"That's right. Beaches, snorkeling, warm sun. It's perfect."

"What made you choose Australia?"

"Oh, you know. It's a whole different hemisphere. At certain points in your life, Delaney, you realize you have to turn everything upside down."

The next day, Delaney parked on the street in front of her house and jogged the short distance to Rowdy's for Happy Hour. Even as she rushed along, she noticed the bright pink blossoms on the cherry trees, the happy chirping of the little birds that had returned to Juniper for spring and the scent of newly-planted flowers in hanging pots on the street lamps. Smiling, she dashed into the bar.

"Sorry I'm late," she said to Josie and Summer, who were already sipping on their drinks. "This job hunting stuff is killing me! I've been sending resumes all day."

"It's no biggie, we ordered you a beer," Summer said.

Now that she was back on good terms with her two best friends, Delaney felt like her world was in balance. This week, Rowdy's cheerful, festive St. Patrick's Day decorations, a string of shiny green shamrocks behind the bar and green and white balloons floating near the ceiling, aligned with Delaney's enthusiasm.

"Cheers to Summer and The Sweets. Two more days 'til the first live gig!" Josie said.

"Cheers!" Delaney said.

"Cheers to that," Summer said. "Not quite the same, toasting with water, but still."

"So, are you ready?" Josie asked.

"I'm nervous," Summer said. "Really nervous."

"You guys will be great," Delaney and Josie said at the same time.

"And it'll be the first of many performances," Delaney said, "So get used to it! Stardom is just around the corner."

"True." She took a deep breath, inhaling through her nose and exhaling through her mouth. "Okay, I'm letting it go. Plus you guys will be there to support me. So, Josie, tomorrow's the deadline to turn in your principal application. You're in, right?"

Tomorrow, Josie would know who else was on the list of applicants. This meant they could start working on their plan of attack: which strengths they'd focus on, which accomplishments to play up and most importantly, which shoes to pair with her power suits for the long series of interviews to follow.

"Oh, yeah. I'm in. I was thinking about putting some ipecac syrup in Blair Upton's coffee today during morning recess, so she couldn't turn in the paperwork tomorrow. But I held back."

"She's got nothing on you," Summer said.

Delaney narrowed her eyes at Josie. "Have you been working out? I thought we agreed you were going to. For stress relief. You still seem really stressed."

Josie looked down at her vodka cranberry.

"Josie!" Delaney said. "You need to start working out. That is your *one* rule. I'm following your rules, so you have to follow mine, too."

"I know," Josie said. "It's just that I'm so stressed out with applying for the principal position, along with my regular lesson-planning and paper-grading, I can't see how adding one more thing to my to-do list is going to help."

"When you release all the tension through exercise," Summer said, "your mind is calmer and you're able to focus better on that long to-do list."

"Do we need to spy on you, Josie?" Delaney said. "Make sure you're going to the gym after school?"

"Oh, God, no. I'll start going. Tomorrow, I promise."

"I can go with you," Delaney said, and then, because she couldn't resist a little dig, she added, "Moral support, not spying."

"Okay, already, Dee. We get your point," Summer said.

For the next hour, they settled into their usual conversation topics. It was just like pre-Intervention times, Delaney thought.

Summer told the girls how Luke unrolled an entire roll of paper towels on the kitchen floor so he could make a telescope out of the cardboard cylinder. Delaney told them about a dog who'd peed in the front room of a vet's office where she applied that day, creating a vast puddle that required a massive number of paper towels to mop it up. And Josie told them the stomach flu was going around her school and one of her students barfed all over her floor. The janitor had used a mop and a truckload of paper towels to clean it up, but Josie was so busy trying not to gag that she hadn't watched.

When Summer stood up to pee for the fifth time at seven p.m., they decided to call it a night.

"I know my hormones are making me haywire," Summer said, stretching, "but I sure love you girls."

"We love you too," they said, embracing her.

"I'll see you tomorrow," Delaney said to Josie. "Five o'clock."

"Five o'clock," Josie said. "Sharp."

She was so lucky, she thought on the way home, to have two friends who she loved so much. She'd do anything for them. Anything.

CHAPTER TWENTY-SIX

Wednesday evening, Delaney didn't even look at her phone as she drove to the gym. If Josie attempted to text Summer and Delaney to slither out of their workout commitment again and didn't get a response from them, she would show up out of obligation.

In the gym parking lot, Josie leaned against her car, arms crossed.

Uh oh. This doesn't look good.

Delaney steeled herself and got out of the car.

"Hey," she said.

"Hey," Josie responded, without looking up or changing position. Delaney skipped the pleasantries and went straight to the meat of the matter.

"So … is it official?" Delaney said. "Are you an applicant for the principal position?"

"No. I didn't apply."

"I thought you said today was the deadline."

"It is," Josie said. Now, her shoulders slumped, just the tiniest bit.

"What? Why?"

"It's pointless. Blair Upton is going to get that position. I can't go through the whole application process just to see her victorious expression in a few weeks when they announce she's the new principal at Juniper Elementary."

"But who's to say she's going to get it?"

"She is. And Scott Smith. Who she's probably going to sleep with, if she isn't already."

"This is ridiculous," Delaney said, running a hand down Josie's arm.

"Number one, you want this position. You want to help more kids, and this is the perfect opportunity to do that. And number two, you're going to be great at it. Number three, you can't let Blair Upton control your life. You need to go back to work and get your application in."

When Josie didn't answer, Delaney said, "Did you do this just so you wouldn't have to work out?"

Josie rewarded her with a tiny half-smile, and said, "No. But I'm not applying. I'll just keep focusing on the community center. It's a different way to help more kids."

"Let's go in and change."

"Okay."

Josie picked up her gym bag and they walked across the parking lot, but Delaney found she couldn't let this one go.

"So when is the deadline to apply?" she asked.

"Today," Josie said.

"Right," Delaney said. "But I mean, what time?"

"Midnight."

"How do they know if you turn it in by midnight?" Delaney said. "Nobody's going to be at the office, are they?"

"It's electronic. You do it all online. It's the world we live in, Dee. Technology is remarkable."

"So you could still go home and apply."

"I'm not," Josie said. "Stop talking about it."

The locker room desperately needed a renovation. Cracked wooden benches stood on cracked white tile floors. Bright orange lockers, most of them covered with chipped and peeling paint, lined the walls.

"It stinks in here," Josie said.

"It's bad," Delaney agreed. "Stop changing the subject."

"I will, if you'll stop talking about the application."

"What about the application?" Summer asked from the doorway.

Thank goodness. Reinforcements.

"She didn't apply." Delaney recapped the situation.

"Josefina Garcia," Summer said. "You will apply for that position immediate— wait. Did you do this just so you wouldn't have to work out?"

"No! Geez, you guys!" Josie said.

"Fine," Summer said. "You will apply for that position right when we're done here. Number one, you really want it. Number two, you'll be great at it. Number three, you can't let Blair Upton control your life."

Delaney raised an eyebrow at Josie, but chose the high road and remained silent.

After moving her eyes from Delaney to Summer and back again,

Josie said, "I left my water bottle in the car. Be right back. You guys can get started."

"If you don't come back in three minutes, we *will* hunt you down," Summer said as Josie rushed out.

"We have to do something," Delaney said as she and Summer walked into the gym. "We can't let her back out of this one."

"You're right.."

In the free weight section, burly men in short shorts grunted as they curled twice their body weight.

"That is just unnatural," Delaney said. "Look at that guy's legs. They're, like, as big around as a wine barrel."

Summer wrinkled her nose. "I think that guy shaves his chest."

Delaney nodded toward a guy who was doing squats with a huge bar across his back. "But that guy's not bad to look at. Let's focus on him."

They lifted weights for a few seconds.

"I know!" Delaney said. "After this, I'll come over to your house and we can send in her application."

"But how will we get into it? It's all online, right? We don't have her password."

"You know she always uses bigpenis, all one word."

Delaney and Summer racked their weights and walked over to the first two treadmills in the cardio room. Summer nodded.

"Dial it up," Delaney said. "I'll meet you at your house after this."

"Perfect," Summer said.

By the time Josie returned, they were both wearing their headphones. Summer walked at her pregnancy-friendly pace and Delaney jogged. Neither of them acknowledged Josie when she stepped onto her own treadmill. They didn't want to give anything away.

After exactly thirty minutes, Josie made a big show of turning off her treadmill and stretching.

"That was so hard," she said when they gathered in the locker room after cooling down.

"It'll get easier," Delaney and Summer said at the same time.

"So you say. I'm out. Love you guys."

They waited for her to leave the room, even giving her a few extra seconds. Summer turned to Delaney. "Well, it was easier to get rid of her than I expected. I thought we were going to have to stand around trying not to act suspicious."

"I know. I just remembered I have cooking class. So I'll come over after and we can do her application on your computer."

"Sounds good," Summer said. "Bring me leftovers. Baby's hungry. My tummy's grumbling."

THE STUDENTS in the How to Boil Water class chattered, bustling around the kitchen as Delaney walked in, just a minute early.

"Change of plans," Beth announced. "We're doing a *dessert* tonight!"

"No wonder everyone's so excited," Delaney said. "What are we making?"

"Whatever it is, there's lots of chocolate," Beth said, pointing to a stack of chocolate cubes on the counter.

"My mouth is watering already."

"Mine, too," Beth said, and then, after a pause, she said, "So I have some exciting news. I finally have a date."

"FindLove.com?"

"Actually, no. Blind date." She winced. "My mom set it up. One of her co-workers has a son that's also single and they decided we should go on a date."

"Have you ever met the guy?" Delaney said.

"Nope. We're going for ice cream."

"What's his name?"

"Josh."

"Good name," Delaney said.

"I don't care what his name is," Beth said. "I just hope he has that smoldering, I-want-to-devour-you look *your* boyfriend had when he was standing outside the window licking you with his eyes. That's not every-thing, but it's a fine start."

Delaney flinched at Beth's cavalier use of the term "boyfriend," but before she could respond, Wendy clapped her hands.

"Time to begin," she said from the front of the kitchen area. "I decided to surprise you today with a sour cream chocolate cake recipe. It's a bit complicated, but I have confidence you can pull it together. It's my birthday and this is my favorite chocolate cake recipe. So don't mess it up."

She winked, and then began to demonstrate how to use a double broiler to melt the chocolate.

As Delaney filled the bottom pot and Beth unwrapped the chocolate squares and added them to the top pot, Beth asked, "So how is it going with Jake?"

"He's dreamy," Delaney said, setting the top pot inside of the bottom pot and turning on the burner. "Really dreamy. I know it's crazy, but I like him. Like, a lot. My friends are doing this thing, The Dating Intervention, and they want me to stop seeing other people. But I always feel like I need a backup, you know?"

"I totally know," Beth said. "I get it. But your friends are right – and let me just say it sounds like you have awesome friends. The thing is, if you're always looking for something else, you're putting the wrong message out there. Then of *course* it's not going to work out with Jake."

"Why is everyone saying this to me?" Delaney said.

"Maybe because it's true. I guess we should start mixing the dry ingredients. Grab that bowl."

An hour later, Beth said (through a mouthful of chocolate cake), "This is, like, the best cake, ever. So decadent."

"Agreed," Delaney said, wiping chocolate off her lips.

"What a wonderful birthday," Wendy said at the end of the session. "This is absolutely divine, everyone."

She'd spent a good ten minutes walking from island to island, tasting each pair's cake, closing her eyes in ecstasy every time she tasted a piece.

"Now package up the rest of this cake and take it home to share. If I take it all, I'll gain a good thirty pounds tonight."

Summer's kids would love the cake, and so would Summer, Delaney thought as she wrapped her half in plastic wrap.

"Save some of this for Josh," Delaney said to Beth, winking. "He'll fall in love with you instantly."

Beth nodded. "Great idea."

EVEN THOUGH SHE always left Summer's house exhausted from sensory overload, Delaney loved being there. Most of the time, chaos reigned. Usually it was happy chaos, but it was chaos nonetheless. Tonight was no different. When she walked in the front door, she was pelted with foam darts and cries of "Invader! Invader! Shoot 'er!"

Delaney screamed, grabbed her heart and fell to the floor where she lay flat on her back, motionless. Summer, immune to foam darts, chased after the boys, trying to wrestle them into pajamas, while Hannah squealed and climbed onto Delaney's stomach. Sarah sat on the couch, reading quietly amidst all the action.

"Hi Dee," Summer's husband Derek said as he scooped Hannah up and offered Delaney a hand. "Want a late dinner? We already ate, but there's plenty left."

"What'd you have?" She took his hand and he pulled her to standing.

"Spaghetti," he said.

"Who cooked it?"

"Sarah."

"Is it safe, Sarah?" Delaney said.

Sarah emerged from her book long enough to nod at Delaney.

"All right. I'll eat. I made dessert."

They sat down to the table a few minutes later, the kids descending like hungry vultures when they realized they were getting chocolate cake.

"Wait. *You* cooked dessert?" Nate said.

"Nathan." Summer said, the warning tone thick in her voice.

"Sorry, Aunt Dee. Why are you here?" Nate asked.

Summer rolled her eyes.

"Your mom and I are going to work on a project on the computer."

Derek looked at Summer, his eyebrows raised.

"We're applying for Josie's principal position," Summer said.

Derek shook his head.

"Are you amused or do you think we're crazy?" Summer said.

"Both," Derek said. "Definitely both. But mostly the latter."

"Why aren't you in bed?" Delaney asked the kids.

"Movie night!" they chorused.

"We just finished 'The Fox and the Hound,'" Summer said.

"You're going to be a principal?" Luke said.

"No, we're filling out Josie's application for her," Delaney said.

"Why can't she do it herself?" Nate wanted to know.

"She's scared," Summer answered.

"So we're helping her," Delaney said.

Sarah put in, "You mean, you're interfering in her life."

At this, Derek shrugged and nodded. So *that's* what he'd been thinking.

"You're already so cynical," Delaney said. "And at such a young age, too."

After dessert, someone (was it Nate?) assigned Delaney to dish duty, and as Derek cleared the table and brought her plates, she scraped them and loaded the dishwasher. Summer supervised baths and Derek started reading to the kids. As she did every time she came over, Delaney marveled at how smoothly the household ran. A sudden silence fell like a blanket when all four kids were washed, read to and in bed.

"All right," Summer said. "Let's do this."

In the Employment section of the school district's web site, Summer clicked on "Apply for Open Positions."

"Oh, this is so user friendly," Delaney said. "'Continue existing application.'"

Summer nodded. "Perfect."

Getting in was easy enough using Josie's school email address and, of course, bigpenis as a password.

"She's almost done," Summer said. "Look at this. Almost every section is filled in."

"Why didn't she just finish up?" Delaney said. "She kills me."

"I know."

Summer clicked through the online application. Window after window, section after section, Josie had filled out the application meticulously.

"She needs one more letter of reference," Delaney said.

"You write that," Summer said. "It'll sound more professional coming from a veterinarian than it will from a graphic designer and aspiring musician."

"But I'm not a practicing veterinarian. I'm a bartender. Besides, you have four kids and one more on the way. You know what you want when it comes to educating actual children."

"Okay, we'll write it together," Summer said.

They spent an hour writing the letter, then uploaded it to Josie's human resources file. "There's just one more thing," Summer said. "Her statement of purpose. It says, 'Please explain why you believe you're a good fit for this position. Include your professional reasons for being an educator as well as your personal reasons for applying for this job.'"

"Oh, geez. That's hard," Delaney said.

"Remember that story she told us once?" Summer said. "The story about her first teacher here in the States?"

"The one who basically taught her English when her family first moved here?"

"Yeah," Summer said. "Remember, the teacher was bilingual and taught the entire first semester in Spanish and English so Josie could learn?"

"Yes!" Delaney slapped her palm on the desk. "You're right! That's perfect."

"All right. Let's write it up and send it off."

"When are we going to tell her we applied for her?" Delaney asked after Summer pressed "Submit."

"We'll wait until they call her and tell her she's a finalist. If they don't, she'll never know we did it. No harm done."

Driving home that night, Delaney thought about what had just unfolded with Josie's application. Specifically, she thought about what she had said to Josie.

You want this position. You'll be great at it.

Josie hadn't applied because she was scared. Until recently, fear had kept Delaney from doing something she wanted to do. Something at which she had the potential to be great. Why was it so easy for her to push Josie past the fear, even though she struggled to get past it, herself?

CHAPTER TWENTY-SEVEN

The Blue was everything Rowdy's was not: sophisticated and classy, smooth and sleek. The patrons were mostly women, and the wine list miles long. Velvet cushions lined the booths and chairs carved with the utmost intricacy sat around low tables.

Summer, who had arrived an hour early, was adjusting her microphone when Delaney and Josie walked in. She glanced up as their shadows blocked the sunlight coming in the door, and squinted for a moment before waving.

"Isn't this great?" she said as they approached her.

"Stop bouncing, you're shaking the baby!" Josie said.

Summer rubbed her belly. "Oh, the baby's fine, I'm just so excited! I saved you a table right over here. Front row seating. I'm nervous. I wanted to be able to see your faces. I ordered your drinks already, too."

"You *are* nervous!" Delaney said. "You're talking a mile a minute."

"Eeee!"

"And you're squealing," Josie added. "Break a leg."

The girls embraced one more time before Summer returned to the stage and Josie and Delaney sat down at their table.

"So I'm bummed I didn't apply for that position," Josie said to Delaney. "I don't know why I chickened out. God only knows when another principal slot will open up. And probably not for a long time at the school where I work. I probably had an advantage for this one."

Delaney sipped her beer, took a deep breath, purposely making eye contact with Josie so she wouldn't suspect Delaney was keeping a secret. "You know, it'll work out for the best. It always does, right?"

"I guess so," Josie said. "But not if you chicken out at the last minute, every time."

People were starting to come into The Blue now. Sleek women whose curled hair, matched accessories and applied makeup made the place look even more stylish.

"You don't do it every time, Josie. You showed up at the gym earlier this week. Ran on the treadmill like you were being chased by a bobcat."

"Coyote," Josie said. "It was a coyote. I was visualizing."

"Hey, whatever works. Oh, look. They're starting. Now perk up. It's Summer's special day. You don't want her to look over here and see you sulking. She'd say everything happens for a reason. And you know it's true."

Delaney reached over to give Josie a quick squeeze around the shoulders and kissed her on the cheek.

"It'll all work out. Besides, maybe this means you'll have more time to work on the community center idea."

"I know. That's a good point. Did I tell you I'm a finalist for that grant?"

"No!" Delaney said. "You didn't tell me. But that's awesome."

Josie nodded. "Yeah. It *is* awesome. I should know within a few days."

"Maybe the community center is your new direction," Delaney said.

Josie nodded, sighed. "Yeah. Maybe. It's just that as the principal, I could do both. I could run the community center and I could create new programs that reach even more kids. You know?"

"I do know. I get it," Delaney said. "It will all work out. Now, that's enough moping. Here they go."

Summer beamed at them as her guitarist started to strum, and then she began to sing.

"Brilliant!" Josie and Delaney said when Summer came over to their table after several encore songs.

"It was perfect," Delaney said. "How'd it feel?"

"You guys, it was so great. It was so much fun. I want to do it all over again!"

Lily Blue, her silver-white hair in a beehive and her lips painted bright fuchsia, came billowing over. The tails of her periwinkle sweater trailed behind her and a cloud of cigarette smoke enveloped them all. She wrapped her arms around Summer, inhaled deeply and breathed out in a smoky voice, "Wonderful, my dear, just wonderful. I can't wait to have you back! Call me, honey. Next week. We'll set up another date for you to play."

As soon as she was out of earshot, Delaney and Josie hugged Summer, too.

"You're better than a strawberry shake," they said to her.

"Can we celebrate?!" Summer said.

"To The Teeter Totter?" Josie asked.

"To The Teeter Totter," Delaney and Summer chorused.

The sound of The Teeter Totter's throbbing music poured out onto the street, bringing with it a mix of good-looking young people wearing way too much cologne and too little clothing.

"Ready to hit it hard, girls?" Josie asked, turning to face them and wiggling her eyebrows like a lascivious teenage boy.

"*So* ready!" Summer said. "Let's do this."

They pushed through the crowd at the front door and headed for the bar.

"Is it seriously eighties night?" Summer asked, her voice rising several octaves with excitement. "It *is*!"

The girls in the crowd wore bright layered tops, leggings, lace-edged bobby socks and lace gloves. Fluorescent scrunchies held side ponytails in place, while bangs stood high, teased into colossal waves.

"Hey, Dee, I don't think I mentioned this earlier," Josie said, yelling over "Girls Just Wanna Have Fun" as it blared through the bar. "But you're limited to two drinks tonight."

She held up two fingers.

"What? Five? Okay."

Josie rolled her eyes, handed Delaney a beer and jerked her head toward the dance floor.

Eighties night was always popular at The Teeter Totter. The music was good, the outfits were better and the drinks were half-price. The girls joined the writhing mass of bodies and cheered when Michael Jackson's "Don't Stop 'Til You Get Enough" came on.

"This is awesome!" Summer yelled.

"Cheers to our resident rock star!" Josie said.

For the next half-hour, Delaney lost herself in the rhythm, the sea of swaying bodies, the heavy bass that vibrated through her body. When "Love Shack" came on, she glanced at Summer and Josie just in time to see comical looks of surprise cross their faces. Before she had a chance to figure out what they were looking at, she felt a body slide up against her from behind. A pair of arms encircled her waist.

She recognized those arms. Jake Rhoades was holding her. Holding her close. And dancing with her. Summer and Josie were smiling now, in that same lascivious teenage boy way Josie had earlier. Summer even gave her a double thumbs up. Delaney rolled her eyes, but giggled despite herself.

"Hi," Jake said into her ear.

"Hi," Delaney said back.

Fortunately, she thought, the blaring music prevented her from having to think of something clever to say as shivers cascaded down her entire body. Jake put his hands on her hips, then ran them up her sides to her rib cage, then spun her around and pulled her close. He smelled so good, like soap and spicy cologne that reminded her of the beach. And he felt *so* good. Warm and lean. He pressed his body against hers. She thrust her fingers into his hair and leaned her forehead against his. For once, his eyes weren't smiling. They held that same smoldering intensity they had when he'd stood outside Country Kitchen and looked at her through the window. Delaney felt her insides turn to hot, molten lava. Or cake batter. Was it wrong that she wanted nothing more than for him to take her, right there, or maybe up against the wall?

The song ended and the DJ switched gears. "Almost Paradise" blasted through The Teeter Totter, and Jake smiled.

"Slow dance?"

"Yeah," she breathed.

"This is nice," he said.

"Yeah," she said again.

"Your friends are watching us," he murmured. His breath on her ear made her shiver all over again. It was delicious.

"Of course they are," she said, closing her eyes. "They think you're dreamy."

"Do you?"

"You bet I do."

"Mmm," he said.

For several moments, they swayed together to the song. It seemed to Delaney as if all her senses were in overdrive. She could feel the fabric of his jeans through her silky skirt. She could feel the callouses on his hands through her cotton top. She could feel his heart beating against her ribs.

"You smell so good," she murmured.

"I put on cologne for you. Part of my wooing prowess."

"For me?"

"Yeah," he said.

"How'd you know you'd see me tonight?"

"I have my ways."

After what seemed like five seconds to Delaney, the song ended. *Everybody knows the DJ never plays two slow songs in a row.*

Summer and Josie had disappeared. Probably they'd left altogether. Delaney checked her phone. Sure enough, Summer had texted: *We headed home. Didn't want to ruin your romantic evening. Follow your heart. Even if it leads you to his place. ;)*

Delaney, anticipation now building from somewhere deep inside her, stuck her phone back in her little cross-body purse and looked up at Jake. Although another fast song, "We're Not Gonna Take It," started playing and the dance floor pulsated with its heavy beat. Jake stood perfectly still, staring at her. Again.

Why did that look strike fear into her heart at the same time as it made her quiver with desire?

Without speaking, Jake grabbed her hand and led her outside. Once they were on the quiet sidewalk, Delaney managed to breathe. "Where are we going?"

"Right here."

He pushed her back against the side of the building, put his hands on either side of her head and kissed her, hard. The urgency of it, the primal feeling of his tongue on hers, made her heart hammer. She hooked her thumbs into his belt loops and pulled his hips toward hers. He groaned, stopped kissing her and grabbed her hand again.

This time, he half-dragged her across the street, then turned left, stalked up a half-block and turned right down an alley between two buildings.

"This isn't exactly where I pictured your wooing skills coming to a head," Delaney said.

He stopped her again, pressed her against the brick wall and framed her face with his hands. Then, with a great deal more tenderness than he'd shown the last time, he kissed her. Her insides simmered.

They were on the move again. He pulled her up a set of narrow metal stairs to the second level, where he fished a set of keys out of his pocket and unlocked the door. It swung open, creaking , and he pulled her inside.

It was an apartment. A bachelor pad. Huge windows faced the street and she could tell without looking that they overlooked the storefronts on the other side, including The Teeter Totter. So that's how he'd seen her the night she'd written him that embarrassing message.

Comfortable-looking leather couches faced the windows and a huge flat-screen TV was mounted on one wall. A fireplace sat opposite that, under a mantle displaying a dozen photo frames. A soft, white rug covered most of the hardwood floor. To the left stood the kitchen, all straight lines in black, stainless steel and light wood. He'd even put a bowl of green apples on the counter.

Jake flipped on a single light in the entry and the streetlights did the rest. They cast a warm yellowish glow into the apartment.

Perfect mood lighting.

It was clean, but homey. Manly, but comfortable.

At least, that was her first impression, which she made in a millisecond, before Jake led her over to the couch, leaned back and pulled her down on top of him.

"Delaney Collins," he said, his mouth already against hers again. "You are interfering with my wooing skills."

"I'd say they're working pretty well, actually," she said.

He laid back, but didn't release her. "Usually I'm much more refined."

"So I bring out the barbarian in you?"

"Definitely."

Now he shifted, tucked her underneath him and slid his hands under her shirt. She practically exploded when she felt his rough palms on her stomach, his thumbs on her breasts. He kissed her neck and his stubble scraped gently over her collarbone.

"This skirt," he murmured, running his hands down her legs. "I could see every curve. I wanted to take you, right there on the dance floor."

Delaney smiled.

"Glad to hear it was mutual," she said, running her hands through his hair.

The skirt in question was now up around her hips, and Jake was doing something very amazing to her legs. It involved his lips and his tongue. She could feel his teasing breath just next to her panty line and her lower belly trembled.

Without warning, images of Summer and Josie appeared, twin angels hovering over her shoulder. She sighed in exasperation. Jake took it as a sign of passion and reached around to unhook her bra. She was positive he was a master at the one-handed flick, so she sat up quickly. Her head bumped his chin.

"You okay?"

"Yeah," she said. "Sorry. It's just that I need to tell you something."

"Uh oh," he said. "These conversations never end well."

He was smiling, unsure.

"It's nothing bad," she said. "It's just that I need to say it."

"Well, out with it, then. I was just getting momentum."

She imagined swatting the little angels that were Summer and Josie, floating near her shoulder, and blurted it out: "I'm not seeing anyone else."

Jake's body relaxed all at once. "I thought you were going to say you're married, or you don't like men, or you never want to talk to me again."

"Nope. Just that I'm not seeing anyone else. You know, before your wooing skills take control of the evening. Thought I'd throw it out there."

He leaned forward and kissed her. "Good to know. I really like you, Delaney. But you should also know that my first priority right now is getting my gallery set up. It's taking pretty much all of my time and energy right now. I'm not seeing anyone else, either, but I don't know if I can give you the devotion you deserve."

So, a mixed response. Delaney watched the smoke rise from the ashes of the passion that had just died out.

He really liked her, *but ...*

Was it Brittany again? Was her tiny, skinny, blond image running through Jake's mind right now?

She shrugged. "I understand. I know you've dreamt of this for a long time."

Jake reached out and tucked a piece of hair behind her ear.

"I have. And as I expected, it's taking up a ton of time and energy. So if you could just be patient with me..."

He trailed off.

"Of course," she said, hoping her tone didn't convey her disappointment. "Of course I can."

Jake stood up. "Want a drink?"

"Sure." Then remembering her two-drink limit, she quickly added, "Water, please."

While he was in the kitchen, Delaney smoothed her hair, pulled down her skirt and looked around. The view was pretty nice. She could see the entrance to The Teeter Totter and people still standing around the front door, smoking. He returned with a glass of water.

"So you saw me coming out of The Teeter Totter that night, huh?"

"Guilty. I was spying on you."

"Nice. Is that how you find ladies, spy on them as they come out of The Teeter Totter?"

"Slim pickins, I tell you what," he said. "But you want a lady, you should see the bartender at Rowdy's."

"Oh, really?" Delaney said. "I heard she gave her two weeks' notice."

CHAPTER TWENTY-EIGHT

Delaney knew before opening her eyes Sunday morning that it had snowed overnight. Contentment filled her when she saw the heavy quilt of soft, pure white snow frosting the ground outside her bedroom window. The clouds had already cleared off and the sun sparkled with such brilliance she had to squint. Mornings like these called for staying in bed, snuggling under the covers for hours. With coffee. And magazines. A man would make a great addition to the mix, she thought. She felt her skin tingle as she imagined what Jake's bare back and arms would look like against her pillows.

Although, it could be some time before she saw any part of his body in her bed. Last night's conversation left her feeling deflated. She'd definitely been getting the vibe that he liked her. Still, she couldn't help but think about his motives. But was he using his gallery as a ready-made excuse to spend less time with her? Or worse, an excuse to spend time with other people (i.e. Brittany) without her knowing? It could be a man's twist on the, "I can't go out tonight, I'm washing my hair," thing. Or, maybe she should take what he said at face value. He was obviously very driven, and maybe he was just being upfront with her. And she was a bartender. A retiring bartender with no employment prospects in sight. He was also obviously very good-looking. Which meant women were probably chasing him around town like bobcats chasing antelope.

She got out of bed, her mouth watering in anticipation of coffee.

"It's cold in here, Pix," she said to the cat, who had followed her into the kitchen and was now making figure eights between her calves. "Why am I wearing shorts?"

She lifted the coffee pot and began to pour before realizing it was empty.

"Power's out," she said. "No coffee."

The vision of sipping coffee in bed vanished.

The doorbell rang. Delaney jumped and Pixie bolted for her under-the-bed hiding spot. Delaney looked out the peephole. Jake peered back at her, holding up a white bakery bag and two cups of coffee in a carrier.

"Good morning," he said when she opened the door. His voice was still deep and scratchy from sleep. She felt a tug in her lower belly. "Figured your power'd be out, so I brought you coffee and breakfast."

She held up her empty coffee mug. "It is. I just discovered that, myself. I was so disappointed my coffee maker wouldn't turn on. So you came at exactly the right moment. Knight in shining armor, seriously."

From the other side of the door, he kissed her, long and slow and gentle.

"Mmm," she said. "That's the best breakfast I've had in a long time. Do come in."

"Wait 'til you taste this bagel. Incredible. It beats 'em all."

They sat at her little dining table. Jake wouldn't be here if he didn't like her, right? The power had gone out and one of his first thoughts was to bring her breakfast? Definitely a good sign.

"When I was little and I first started playing sports, no matter how excited I got, I never wanted to smile," Delaney said. "If I hit the ball in baseball, or scored a soccer goal, or made a basket, I'd look at my parents but I'd never smile. I think I didn't want anyone to know what a big deal it was to me. Anyway, my parents always took pictures of my face and showed it to me. I know that's what I look like right now. It's the trying-not-to-smile smile. Totally goofy, right?"

"Nah. It's not goofy at all. It's cute, actually. So are you saying my breakfast visit is a big deal to you?"

"Yeah. It is. It's totally sweet."

"That's me," Jake said. "And when we're done here, I have something to show you."

"I'm intrigued."

"You should be. When I was little, my parents loved snow days. They'd even take off work when school was canceled so they could take us sledding. To this day, I can't pass up a good snow day."

"Should I be scared?"

"No, but you should dress warmly. Lots of layers. I'll clean up. Get movin'."

Delaney's hopes of seeing Jake's bare back and arms in her bed had just risen exponentially, and now they plummeted again. Only slightly disappointed that he'd instructed her to put more clothes on instead of taking them off, she pulled her gloves, hat and snow boots out of the closet. As she added layers, she realized she was more relieved than disappointed. This was the first time in forever that a guy had planned a fun activity just to show her a good time … and not just between the sheets. Summer and Josie would be pleased, too. No sex for … what was it? A lifetime?

Forcing thoughts of prohibited activity out of her mind, Delaney added warm barrier after warm barrier to her now sensitive skin. When she walked outside and saw Jake's Jeep loaded up with a couple of big sleds, she was thrilled. A folded blanket sat on the passenger seat and a packet of foot warmers sat on top of it.

Snow-covered downtown Juniper looked so quaint and cheerful. Turn-of-the-century buildings, painted bright pastel colors, flanked the snowy streets and everything shone and sparkled in the sunlight. Delaney envisioned people driving horse-drawn sleds through town on snowy mornings. That was one thing she loved about Juniper: the second-story balconies overlooking the streets and the false-fronted buildings had barely changed since they were first built. Today's people walked down the concrete sidewalk instead of a boarded walkway, and they wore designer suits instead of chaps, but it still felt cozy, and life felt simple. Warm under her blanket, Delaney looked over at Jake.

If it wasn't romantic enough that he'd shown up at her door, saving her morning by bringing steaming coffee and food, he had also planned what promised to be a delightful outing. She couldn't remember the last time she went sledding. During the past couple of years, Summer had invited her to go when the kids had a snow day, but she'd always turned her down, in some misguided attempt to prove how much of an adult she was.

The idea of breathing the freezing air, careening down the slope of a giant hill past huge, fragrant trees, and rushing back to the top to do it again – all with Jake – sounded exhilarating.

"Warm enough?" Jake asked.

"Yep! Just right."

He rubbed her leg briskly and then pointed to Conifer Mountain, which boasted the highest peak in the Juniper area.

"Can you take it?" he said.

"Oh, yeah. I can take it. Can you?"

"Seeing that fierce look in your eye scares me a little," he said. "But I think I can knock you down a few pegs."

Finally, they reached Devil's Slide, a popular sledding spot where Delaney had come in high school. A few hardy souls (shouting, rowdy teenagers barreling down the hillside face-first) had already begun, and Jake and Delaney followed the trail their footprints left from the parking area to the top of the hill.

"Good thing we got up here early," Jake said. "I'll bet it's packed by eleven."

For the next hour, they flew, side by side, down the hill. They collected their sleds and raced back to the top, over and over. They raced sitting up, lying on their backs, flat on their stomachs, the snow spraying up around them each time they skidded to a stop. By the time several more families and groups of teenagers showed up to sled, snowboard and build snowmen, Delaney and Jake were exhausted.

"I'm gonna be sore tomorrow," she said as they loaded the sleds into the back of the Jeep.

"Worth it, though, right?"

"Every minute."

Jake wrapped his arms around her and she felt the now familiar surge of energy at the very center of her body as he kissed her.

He squeezed her hands, swatted her bottom and said, "Let's hit it. It's freezing out here."

As the Jeep wound its way back down the mountainside, Delaney admired Jake out of the corner of her eye. She wondered whether he noticed her taking in his chiseled features, his rough hands, the muscles in his thighs when he downshifted.

The yearning hit her hard and Delaney felt her entire body heat with desire, like a pan heating up on the stove.

Flashes of Jake's hands on her skin, his mouth on her body and his fingers in her hair when they got back to her house made the twenty-minute drive seem very short indeed.

They'd pull into the driveway and look at each other, the unspoken question hanging between them like a bubble. She'd ask, "Would you like to come in?" and he'd say, "Sure, for a minute."

Jake had proved himself a gentleman, so he'd let her walk in ahead of him. Then, he'd follow her in, shut the door behind them and quickly pull her close for a kiss. First, he'd run his hands down the sides of her body, then slowly circle her breasts with his thumbs before peeling her clothes off her. (Never mind that she was wearing her huge, bulky jacket. She'd do away with that, at some point. Maybe she should take it off now.) Unable to wait, he'd take her right there, standing up, in the entryway.

Forgetting herself, Delaney almost cried out.

A patch of black ice patch caused the Jeep to slide, just a bit, and the movement jerked her out of her daydream. Breathing fast, she put a hand to her chest.

"Sorry, didn't see that ice there," Jake said. "Are you okay?"

She nodded but didn't answer. Jake slowed down. A few minutes later, they pulled up in front of Delaney's bungalow. Jake left the engine idling and leaned toward her. Although the kiss was lingering and steamy, and left Delaney practically quivering, he didn't ask if he could come in. And something, probably the imagined looks of disapproval on Summer's and Josie's faces, stopped her from inviting him.

Thank you," she said, instead. "That was really great."

He gave her one more light kiss and hopped out of the driver's seat. He helped her down from the Jeep, walked her to the door and kissed her cheek.

And then he was gone.

Back on the solid ground of reality inside her house, Delaney made herself a nest on the couch with her favorite down blanket, a cup of hot chocolate and her cat. All she could think about was Jake Rhoades stripping off her clothes. No, ripping them off. When she couldn't even force herself to concentrate on the latest gossip magazine, she texted the girls: *When does the sex come in?*

Summer: *All good things in life are worth waiting for, Dee. It's too soon.*

Josie: *Hold your horses, sister. Have you even had The Talk with him?*

Delaney: *The exclusivity talk?*

Josie: *The very same, yes.*

Delaney: *Kind of.*

Summer: *Kind of? You need to REALLY have that talk before you have sex.*

Delaney: *I'm scared. Must I?*

Summer: *You must.*

Josie: *Well, what do you mean, kind of?*

Delaney: *I told him I wasn't seeing anyone else.*

Summer: *And?*

Delaney: *And he said he's not looking for anyone else but he's really busy with his art gallery and he doesn't have much time to date and stuff. He asked me to be patient.*

Josie: *Hmmm.*

Delaney: *I know.*

Summer: *No sex. Not until you're officially a couple. Officially.*

Josie: *She's right, Dee. Keep us posted. Now stop bugging me. I'm watching my show ... er, grading papers.*

CHAPTER TWENTY-NINE

MONDAY MORNING PASSED IN A BLUR OF COFFEE DRINKING, RESUME REFINING and job applying. Delaney inquired about jobs as far away as Phoenix and Flagstaff and in blink-and-you-miss-'em towns like Paulden and Belmont. So what if she had to commute? So what if she ended up spending most of her time in a town the size of her bathtub?

Still, a tiny part of her wondered if her lack of success on the job front was a message from the Universe: *You're not cut out to be a veterinarian. You had your chance.*

When her phone rang at five minutes after noon, Delaney's hopes shot through the roof. Was someone already responding to one of today's applications?

She answered the phone.

"Delaney. It's Doctor Rick. Kathryn Rick."

Doctor Rick... Newcastle in a cold glass. She had turned Delaney down, hadn't she? Lack of experience? Before Delaney could think of something halfway intelligent to say, Doctor Rick plowed ahead.

"I've reconsidered. I'd like to offer you the position. Can you start Wednesday?"

Delaney could barely contain her emotions and managed to hold it together until they hung up.

When they finally did, Delaney burst into tears, a multitude of feelings—relief, happiness, fear—causing her to heave out long sobs. She flung herself onto the couch and Pixie jumped up next to her, curious.

"It's a new beginning, Pixie. Now let's just hope I don't mess it up."

CARPOOL TUESDAY HAD TURNED into a weekly interrogation.

"You guys are destined for the CIA or something," Delaney told Summer's kids, glaring at them in the rearview mirror.

"Aunt Dee, I heard my mom talking to Auntie Josie last night. They were talking about you."

Nate had chosen the pop station today and the music pumped, vibrating the entire car. Delaney had to turn it down so she could hear Sarah, who held a book on her lap but whose gaze pierced Delaney's in the mirror.

"Oh yeah?"

"Yeah," Sarah said. "They were saying you're in love."

The traffic signal at Hidden Knoll turned red, giving Delaney a chance to turn around and return Sarah's look, face to face. She closed her book. *Uh oh.*

"They were, were they?" Delaney said.

"Yes. So. Are you?"

"Sarah, I don't know if you're old enough to talk about this."

"Light's green," Nate said. "She is, because she heard Mom on the phone, and Mom didn't tell her to go away. But don't change the subject, Aunt Dee. Are you in love, or not?"

"Nathan." Delaney turned around and pressed the accelerator. "You are definitely too young to discuss this with."

"Ooh, she called you Nathan," Luke said. "She's serious. Look, Aunt Dee, we're passing the scene of the first meeting. This is a magical spot for you. So are you? In love?"

Unfortunately, the traffic signal at Pinecone also turned red and Delaney was forced to stop at the *magical spot.*

"You know, I still haven't tried that Porky's place," she said. "Have you guys ever been there?"

They all shook their heads and Luke rolled his eyes. "You know Mom won't take us to a place like that. They don't have whole wheat buns. Stop changing the subject."

"Since when have you guys taken such an interest in my love life?" Delaney said.

"Since The Dating Intervention began," Sarah said.

The boys giggled.

"Green light," Nate said again. "We've never seen Mom so mad at you, for one thing. And also, she's been spending a lot of time with you guys. Don't you think we deserve to know why?"

"You should be an attorney, Nate."

"Hear it all the time," he said.

When Delaney didn't respond to Nate's line of questioning, Luke and Sarah pressed on: "So?" they said at the same time.

"Guys, it's not that simple," Delaney told them. "When you're my age, it's not like you're just all of a sudden in love, like you read about in Sleeping Beauty or whatever. It's complicated."

"What's so complicated?" Sarah said. "I think you're just *making* it complicated. I mean, you're both adults. You both have jobs. You glow when you're together—"

"Who said that?"

"Auntie Josie."

Delaney opened her mouth.

"Well, *do* you?" Luke asked before Delaney could respond.

"Maybe."

"Then you're in love," Sarah said knowingly. "Or, at least, in very deep like."

"So is he ... your boyfriend?" Nate asked, making the word "boyfriend" sing-songy.

"Fortunately for all of us, we're almost home," Delaney said. "Which means the inquisition is nearly over. I'll be dumping the lot of you on the doorstep and leaving immediately. Thank you for this lovely experience."

She turned the music back up, Sarah went back to reading her book and the boys started punching each other.

The questioning was over. For now.

CHAPTER THIRTY

"So this is your desk. Computer, file cabinet, office supplies,"
Doctor Rick said.

The thing was gargantuan – a huge corner desk with a hutch on one
side that nearly reached the ceiling. It was completely empty except for a
computer. Delaney wondered what she was going to put on all those
shelves. Doctor Rick's identical desk stood in the opposite corner, and
Delaney saw her shelves were stuffed with books like Veterinary
Anatomy, Veterinary Dentistry, Dog Psychology. All of Delaney's veterinary school textbooks were in storage, but she could probably dig them
out. She may need them for reference.

"I know, it's like a library, right?" Dr. Rick said. "Don't worry. You'll
ease into it as you go. Anyway, you saw the break room, right? You can
eat in there. I usually don't eat in the office because the bugs are hell
during the summer. I try to keep crumbs confined, you know? I think
that's it. Your first appointment's at nine. Janie will work with you until
then, getting you up to speed with how the office runs."

"Okay," Delaney said. "Uh, Doctor Rick?"

"Call me Kat."

"Okay, Doctor Kat?"

The vet laughed. "Yes?"

"Thanks for hiring me. Really. Thanks."

"Thank me this afternoon." She winked, took a drink of something
green in a clear travel cup and walked off.

Janie, a young, perky brunette with bright orange fingernails, tiny
freckles across the bridge of her nose, and huge brown eyes, was the

most organized person Delaney had ever met. Ruthless. She showed Delaney how to use the digital charts and where to file everything. Then she gave her a quick tour of the building.

"The last person Kathryn hired didn't work out," Janie loud-whispered as they walked through the surgery suite. "She's a sink-or-swim boss, and your predecessor barely knew the doggie paddle."

"She knows I only worked as a vet for a year, right?"

And she doesn't know why I stopped, right?

"Right." Janie touched Delaney's arm in what Delaney figured was supposed to be a reassuring gesture. "But she has a good feeling about you."

"Is that good?"

"You tell me."

"Yes!" Delaney said. Then, when she realized how eager she'd sounded, she added, "Of course it is."

Janie winked and handed her the file for her first patient. Delaney felt a flash of bone-crushing anxiety and hoped it didn't show on her face. As she walked down the hallway to her first appointment, she repeated a mantra:

You can do this.

You can do this.

You can do this.

Fortunately, the first three appointments were easy. A Persian cat with a bad case of hairballs, a Rottweiler with an ear fungus and a rat with cancer. Then it was lunchtime, and even though she hadn't brought anything to eat, she headed to the break room. Doctor Kat sat at the table, wolfing down a chorizo burrito.

"So what's your story, Doc Collins?"

"What do you mean?"

"I mean, why aren't you married with five kids under five by now, like all the other women your age in Juniper?"

"Are you?"

"No," Doctor Kat drawled. "But I'm not from around these parts." Caught off guard, Delaney wasn't sure how to answer. Doctor Kat switched gears. "Did you bring lunch?"

"I forgot."

Doctor Kat stood up, and Delaney noticed again how tall she was. Tall, broad-shouldered, cowboy-booted. The tip of her long braid just touched the waistband of her Wranglers. She took a knife out of a drawer, set her burrito on a paper towel on the counter and cut it in half.

"I need your help in surgery after this," she said, handing the burrito to Delaney. "Can't have you passing out from hunger. Or the sight of blood."

"Thanks."

"No problem. I'll take it out of your pay." She winked.

"So what's your story, Doctor Kat?"

"Mine? It's pretty simple. My husband's a professional team roper. We have acreage just outside of town, real pretty, with a house and a barn and a corral and all that. It was a whirlwind romance." She looked happy, reminiscent. "I run a thriving veterinary practice, which I can now expand, thanks to Doc Collins, here. So that's my story."

She crumpled up the foil she'd used as a plate and stood up again.

"Now, I could use your help. Ready to scrub in?"

It should have been a routine tooth extraction. The patient, a fifteen-year-old Lab mix with a gray muzzle and silky black fur, had stopped eating. When Doctor Kat examined him, she'd found that one of his molars was terribly rotten.

Turbo was calm and obedient as they prepped him for surgery. They got him sedated and onto the surgery table without incident and Doctor Kat started drilling into his tooth. Delaney worked the suctioning tool. Suddenly, the abscess exploded, splattering blood and pus all over Doctor Kat, her goggles, her jacket and every section of exposed skin. The suctioning tool, suddenly having a lot more liquid to suction, started making a strange noise—one that sounded exactly like Max the bulldog's wheezing right before he died. Delaney's body went into full panic mode: her hands and feet began to tingle, her vision went blurry around the edges and her stomach threatened to return the half-burrito she'd eaten only minutes before.

Everything went eerily quiet, then Doctor Kat yelled, "Fuck!"

Delaney continued to suction near the tooth, but the blurriness was closing in. She had an absurd vision of suctioning off Doctor Kat's goggles so she could see. The room titled.

"I might need to sit down," she said, even as the blood continued to pulse out of Turbo's mouth.

"Doc Collins, I need you to snap out of it. You're not sitting down. I didn't hire a woman with a weak constitution, did I?"

Now she spoke harshly, giving rapid-fire instructions: "Get the bleeding stopped, make sure this dog is stable and get ready to pack the hole I'm about to blow."

Delaney nodded. "Okay. Okay, I've got it."

When the abscess had burst, Doctor Kat's drill had slipped, slicing Turbo's gum wide open. Delaney packed gauze pads into his lower lip to stop the bleeding, then turned up the IV to get more fluids going. She changed her gloves, then carefully arranged the material she'd need to pack his gums once Doctor Kat extracted the tooth.

It was messy, but within a few minutes, the tooth was out, the hole was filled and Delaney was stitching up the gash in Turbo's gums.

"Well done, Doc Collins," Doctor Kat murmured as she typed the case summary into her computer. "I owe you a drink."

"I won't turn you down."

That evening, the doorbell rang as Delaney stepped out of the shower.

"That's Mom," she said to Pixie.

She'd done her best to scrub the memory of that wheezing, suctioning sound—and the spatter of Turbo's blood—out her mind, but she thought she could still hear and smell them.

"Perfect Plumeria body cream doesn't have anything on Turbo blood," she said to the cat as she wrapped the towel around her hair, threw on her robe and rushed to answer the door. "But Mom probably won't notice."

When she looked through the peephole, she was surprised to see a deliveryman peering back at her. He had his arms around a huge box and Delaney could just see his eyes over the top of it. She opened the door.

"Here ya go, Miss," he said, hefting the box toward her.

As she carried it to the dining room table, the doorbell rang again.

"Come in, Mom," she called.

"I brought you a coffee," Camille said as she breezed in. "To celebrate your first day. I want to hear all about it. Ooh, did you get a delivery? What is it?"

Delaney couldn't help but picture a pinball whizzing around a pinball machine.

"Thanks for the coffee. I did get a delivery, but I haven't opened it yet. Let me get dressed."

"Ooh, it's from the flower company," Delaney heard her mom say.

She reemerged a few minutes later, wearing jeans and a t-shirt. Camille came over to watch as Delaney opened the box. The rich scent of Tiger Lilies floated toward them. The bouquet was a gorgeous blend of the lilies, baby's breath, some fuzzy-looking greenery and white roses. She lifted it out of the box and set it on the table.

"Ooh," Camille breathed again. "Beautiful. Is there a card?"

"There is." She opened it: "To Delaney. To celebrate your first day as a veterinarian. Cheers to doing what you love. Jake."

"Oh." The flowers were from Jake Rhoades. The picturesque, the handsome, the rugged. The rock-star-sexy kisser. She melted into a chair and fanned herself with the tiny card. This was another definite sign he really liked her. A feeling of extreme happiness rose up in her torso like bubbles rising to the top of a glass of champagne.

"Honey, what's wrong?" Camille said. "You look faint."

"I think I need to sit down," she said. "This is the first time anyone has sent me flowers."

"You are sitting down," Camille said, her smile spreading across her face. Which one is Jake again?"

"Oh, Mom. This is a story you won't believe."

She launched into the story of Jake, starting with the car accident ("He was so dreamy, I just couldn't believe he'd stopped and helped me. And then he'd thought Summer's kids were mine.") and explaining the scene in the bar ("Of course I knew exactly what he'd order and I watched him all night … those jeans.").

"Then he was one of the guys Summer and Josie picked for me from FindLove.com! Can you believe it? I know Summer told you about one of our dates, but I haven't told you all the rest."

Finally, she told about their chance encounter, when she'd been walking down Main Street feeling sorry for herself and he'd come out of the pizzeria and cheered her up.

"To think, he's been in Juniper this whole time and I've never seen him. And then, within a matter of weeks, I see him everywhere!"

Camille listened, rapt, to the entire story. She sat perfectly still, but with the telling of each new detail, her eyes became more alight with excitement. Finally, when Delaney finished, she sat back, sipped her coffee and said with a calm that belied the energy radiating off of her, "Well, this is all very serendipitous."

"I know." Delaney said. "It is, right? But I don't want to get my hopes up."

"Delaney, I'm going to be honest, here."

Delaney took a deep breath. Any portion of any conversation that started out with those six words required some mental preparation.

"Okay," she said. She took a sip of her coffee.

"Remember how I said sometimes you have to turn things upside down?"

"Yes," Delaney said. "Like how you and Dad are going to Australia."

"Right," Camille said.

"And …"

"And you're so used to having a backup plan in place that you never really let yourself enjoy what you've got going. Enjoy this, Delaney. Just enjoy it."

THE SCENT and sting of freshly-cut onions filled the back room at Country Kitchen. Delaney's eyes watered as she continued chopping, and she swiped at her tears with the sleeve of her sweater. Today, Wendy planned to walk them through a simple cucumber, tomato and red onion salad, followed by ham and pesto roll-ups.

"Sorry you're crying," Beth said, handing Delaney a tissue.

"No, you're not," Delaney said. "This is why you didn't want to chop the onions. You don't want to ruin your mascara."

Beth continued slicing her cucumber and adding it to the bowl, making a show of being industrious. Delaney could see her hiding a smile.

"You're right. Josh, the guy whose mom teamed up with my mom to send us on a blind date? He invited me for drinks after this. So you're right. I want to look good."

"Second date, right?"

"Right."

Beth slid a tomato knife out of the block and began chopping the tomatoes while Delaney measured mayonnaise and vinegar for the dressing.

"So how was the blind date?"

"It was good, actually. Our moms might be onto something. He owns that auto shop, over on Beale Street? And he is really, really nice. We've read a lot of the same books and liked a lot of the same movies. We met for dinner and talked for hours. I didn't get home until after midnight."

"I remember when I was in high school, my friend Summer used to always say she was 'talking' to a guy until late into the night, but it really meant she was totally making out with him."

"We were talking, really," Beth said. "I swear!"

"Sure you were," Delaney said.

"Ready to toss?"

Beth carefully tossed the dressing into the salad. Delaney added salt and pepper.

"So how's it going with the delicious stalker who stared at you through the window?"

"He *is* delicious," Delaney said. "It's going good. I just want to jump his bones, but my friends are making me verify we're exclusive, first. I told him I'm not seeing anyone else. His response? He's super busy with opening his art gallery. So they want me to wait until it's official. Or whatever."

"It is a good idea, if you don't mind me saying so. I mean, I know I'm just your cooking class partner, but it seems like you're pretty smitten. Exclusivity decreases your chances of having your heart broken."

"See, I think it's the opposite. I mean, what if he never wants to be exclusive?"

"What if he does?"

"You sound just like Josie and Summer."

Beth shrugged, a gleam in her eye. "I think we're ready to eat."

Delaney was surprised to discover the salad was great. Who would have thought such a simple combination of veggies could produce something so mouthwatering?

"The roll-ups are a bit more complicated," Wendy said from the front of the classroom area. "Let's get everything cleaned up and then we'll prep."

As Delaney scraped the onion skin from the cutting board into the compost bin, she was startled by a voice in her ear.

"You should have the talk. Force him to give you a straight answer."

It was Myron, the glasses-wearing half of the gay couple who stood behind her during class. Delaney flinched.

"Why is everyone saying that?"

"Because it's true. Look, I know it's uncomfortable, but it's necessary." When she moved aside so he could scrape his own cutting board clean, he continued, "You don't want to be left wondering what he's going to do if he meets some other cutie patootie. Right?"

She shrugged. "Right."

As Wendy had promised, the ham and pesto roll-ups were only slightly more complicated than the cucumber salad. Together, Delaney and Beth rolled out pastry dough, then spread cheese and pesto onto it and topped those with slices of deli-style ham. They then rolled the dough up, sealed the seam and baked it.

"This. Is. So. Good."

"You should cook this for Jake when you invite him over for pre-sex dinner," Beth said.

Delaney closed her eyes in ecstasy.

"Seriously," Beth said. She swallowed a bite of the roll-up. "I mean, now that you can cook, you've got to invite him over. That's what I'm doing."

"You know," Delaney said, "we're definitely going to have to keep in touch. I can't be left wondering what happens between you and Josh. And I'm going to need your advice."

"You're right. You are going to need my advice. In fact, before we leave tonight, I want you to text Jake and invite him over for dinner this weekend."

"I don't have his number. But I'll message him tonight on FriendZoo or something. I guess this makes you an official, participating member of The Dating Intervention."

Beth winked.

Just as class ended, Delaney texted Summer and Josie to get the go-ahead on inviting Jake over.

A couple of hours later, she relaxed on her couch with Pixie and a cup of tea. Well, semi-relaxed, she thought. She hopped up every few minutes to check her computer for Jake's reply to her invite.

She knew Beth was right: having Jake over for dinner really did provide a good opportunity to strengthen their relationship. But what if she burned the food? What if she undercooked it? What if it tasted horrible? What if he said he wanted to keep his dating options open?

Beth, of course, had provided a simple answer when Delaney had rushed through these questions at the end of cooking class.

"Wine. Lots and lots of wine."

HOWIE WOULD BE EXCITED to know that Delaney was finally learning to cook.

The friendship between Delaney and Howie developed over the months that followed their dinner date on Shirley's birthday. When he and Max came into the Desert Veterinary Clinic, he brought Delaney simple recipes, hoping to spur her interest in cooking. Every so often, he'd call and leave a message with Barb, telling Delaney about a "TV program" she might be interested in watching. Usually it had to do with animals or cooking, and sometimes wine.

She kept some things on hand for Howie's visits, too: a magazine article about chess being good for the brain, a book comprising stories of students whose teachers changed their lives, a funny little statue of an English bulldog she found at a yard sale one Saturday morning.

But she never did cook any of his recipes. She tucked them into the front of a cookbook (a housewarming gift from her mom when she'd gotten her first apartment) and never looked at them again, preferring her Chinese takeout and to-go sub sandwiches.

CHAPTER THIRTY-ONE

Delaney entered Rowdy's Thursday night feeling like things were looking up. She'd been messaging with Jake all week, saying things like *Don't you have any pets? I'd love to examine them.* and *Happy Humpday.* Work was going smoothly.

She saw Benjamin right away, leaning over the table where his new beau sat. Their heads were close together and he winked at her when she raised her eyebrows at him.

Then she saw Josie. She was sitting at their normal table, her legs crossed and her chin propped on one hand, in a deceivingly relaxed posture. But her eyes were not relaxed. They narrowed on Delaney as she approached. Delaney knew that look: Josie had something to say. Something important. And she was trying not to tip Delaney off to what it was.

Only one explanation existed: Josie had found out about the application. Which meant she was a finalist for the principal position. Delaney felt a surge of excitement. She wanted to run to Josie, to hug her, to congratulate her. But she knew better.

Josie was going to kill them.

Where was Summer? Delaney didn't see her corpse on the ground, so she was probably late.

For a full second, Delaney debated, frozen mid-stride in the shaft of dusty sunlight coming through the door. Should she go sit with Josie? Should she back out the door and wait for Summer to show up so they could face her together? Summer probably wouldn't show up for at least five more minutes, and what was she supposed to do with herself until then? Wither under Josie's glare?

I survived the Carpool Tuesday Inquisition. I can survive this.

"It's now or never," she murmured.

Shoulders back, head held high, Delaney approached the table and slid onto her stool.

"Hey," she said, as casually as she could, although her heart raced.

"Hey."

"How's your day?"

"Fine."

"Mine's good." Delaney said. "Did a cataract surgery on a cat, had a couple of spays and a neuter. And a toenail trim on a Yorkie. You'd love that little guy. So cute."

Josie arched an eyebrow.

"Remember that time you waxed my eyebrows?" Delaney said. "Freshman year? And you promised they'd look awesome but you accidentally waxed off some of the skin? I walked around for four days with scabs on my eyelids."

A hint of amusement reached Josie's eyes, but her face remained immobile.

"Wait for Summer," Delaney said. The words tumbled out in a rush.

"Fine," Josie said.

They sat in relative silence for the next five minutes, which inched by like a snail in peanut butter. Delaney remembered her dad using that expression one morning when she'd taken too long to get dressed.

Finally, Summer walked in. She, too, paused in the doorway, before approaching the table with obvious caution, no doubt tipped off by the icy standoff at the table.

"Hey," she said.

Finally, Delaney was able to let some of her excitement out. "Josie's a finalist," she said.

"That's wonderful news!" Summer answered, relief lighting up her face even as she scooted her stool closer to Delaney's before climbing onto it.

Again, Delaney thought she saw a flicker of happiness in Josie's eyes, but her stony countenance remained unchanged.

"Wait. Isn't it?" Summer said.

"You guys," Josie said, her voice barely registering above a growl. "Why didn't you tell me?"

"Tell you what?" Summer said.

"Don't play dumb, Summer," Josie said.

"We wanted it for you," Delaney said. "We know how much you wanted it. We saw you chickening out."

"Chickening out?" Now it was a full-on growl.

"Oops. But you used that phrase at The Blue." When Josie only stared at Delaney, she shrugged. "Fine. Wrong word choice. But it's true."

Benjamin walked over with their drinks, placed them on the table and then slipped away, probably close to drowning in the tension. Josie drained her vodka cranberry in one gulp, then re-crossed her arms.

"We knew you weren't going to do it," Summer said, lifting her hands as if to surrender. "Despite how much you wanted to. We were just helping you."

"And our assumptions were only confirmed when we saw how much you'd already gotten done on the application. You were so close. We couldn't just stand by while you gave up."

"When did you do it?"

"That Friday it was due," Delaney said.

"How did you get into my account?"

"Bigpenis, all one word," Summer said.

"I have to start using a different password." Josie smacked herself in the forehead, then crossed her arms on the table and put her head down. "What did you put for that one essay question?"

"Oh, you know," Summer said. "A bunch of stuff about how awesome you are."

Josie sat back up. "You guys really put me on the spot," she said. "When Scott called and said I was a finalist, I was, like, spluttering. I didn't know what to say. I couldn't tell him I hadn't applied. And then I knew. I knew you guys had done it. You're so interfering!"

"Welcome to my world, Josie," Delaney said. "You guys were spying on me. Remember that?"

"I do remember that. It was for your own good. Because you suck at making decisions."

When Delaney and Summer stared at Josie, her shoulders slumped. "But what if I don't get it?" she said. "What if I'm a finalist but then I don't get it?"

"What if you do?" Summer said, her voice gentle. "What if you get it, because you're the perfect person for this job?"

"Well, good point," Josie said. "Now you guys have to help me get ready for my interview."

"Don't say it like it's a punishment," Delaney said. "We've been telling you all along we'd help you with your interview."

"Fine. I'm still mad, though."

"We did it from a place of love," Summer said.

"I know," Josie said. "But I'm still mad."

"Okay," Summer and Delaney said at the same time.

And now for a change of subject, Delaney thought. "I invited Jake over for dinner this weekend."

"You're cooking?" her friends chorused in what she hoped was mock shock.

"I'll have the fire department on standby," Josie said.

"Oh, Josie. She'll be fine." Summer turned her attention back to Delaney. "You'll be fine, Dee. Don't listen to her."

Josie's answering chuckle sounded good-natured, but Delaney detected a definite wicked gleam in her eyes.

"Beth, my cooking partner, says that should seal the deal. He'll want nothing more than to be with me and only me."

"Has she tasted your cooking?" Josie said.

"Shut up," Delaney and Summer said.

A huge group of real-life cowboys chose that very moment to saunter into Rowdy's, and the conversation was put on pause as the girls admired their Wranglers.

"That's right," Summer said. "The rodeo's in town next weekend. I guess these guys are here a week early to adjust to the elevation."

The rodeo came to town three times per year, once each during spring, summer and fall. Horsemen and women drove their big, shiny trucks into town, hauling horse trailers full of athletic, majestic horses and set up camp at the rodeo grounds. The town bustled with activity throughout the entire week, from daytime kids' sheep races to the evening rodeos and the nighttime rodeo dances on the high school football field. As a real-life cowboy establishment, Juniper thrived on these events.

"I wanted to take the kids," Summer said. "And speaking of that, I have a special surprise for you."

"What is it?"

"The Sweets are playing at the rodeo dance on Saturday night!"

"What? Why didn't you tell us before now?" Josie asked.

"Well, I don't know, to tell you the truth," Summer said. "It's a big crowd. A lot bigger than the one at The Blue."

"Oh, I love the rodeo dance," Delaney said.

"I know. You're going to love this. We've been practicing all these country songs. It's going to be so much fun."

"I am *so* there," Delaney said. "I can't wait."

"Hey, if you can talk Jake into going with us," Josie said, "you can have hot hay bale sex under the bleachers after you do a couple of slow dances with him."

"That was a long time ago," Delaney pouted. "And it was hot."

His name was Colby. He was tall and slim and wore his flannel shirt unbuttoned at the collar. He approached Delaney at the beginning of the rodeo dance the summer she turned twenty-one and they spent the entire evening together, hopping from the dance floor to the bar at the end of the stadium and back again, twirling, singing along to the music. That perfect evening culminated in sweaty sex on a hay bale under the bleachers. Of course, they never spoke again. Colby lived on a ranch in Montana and they didn't even exchange numbers.

"Yeah," she said. "I'd like to do that with Jake."

The visuals came unbidden into her mind: Jake taking her from behind as they stood against the posts under the bleachers, his hands grasping her hips and his mouth near her ear.

She shivered.

"Geez, Dee," Summer said. "Don't get carried away. We're sitting right here."

"Sorry."

CHAPTER THIRTY-TWO

WHY HAD SHE THOUGHT INVITING JAKE OVER FOR DINNER WOULD OR COULD be a good idea? How could this *possibly* turn out well?

Delaney wandered through the produce section of the grocery store, carefully examining apples as if her life depended on finding one of just the right shape, size, color and firmness. She actually knew she wasn't going to buy any apples, but as she had no idea what she was going to buy, examining the apples seemed like a good way to give the appearance that she knew what she was doing.

I should have planned a menu.

She strolled casually along in front of the shelves stacked with vegetables she couldn't even identify. Summer would know what to do. She was a mom. She had about a dozen go-to meals she cooked in a pinch. Delaney pulled out her phone: *What should I cook Jake for dinner tonight?*

Summer: *Didn't you learn roasted chicken?*

Delaney: *Yeah. But what if it comes out dry?*

Summer: *What if it doesn't? Download a recipe app on your phone and look up a good recipe. Or just use the one from class. Didn't you get a recipe book?*

Delaney: *Yeah.*

Summer: *Where is it?*

Delaney: *At home. I'm at the store.*

Summer: *Oh, for goodness' sake. Just get a whole chicken, celery, onions, salt, pepper, butter.*

Delaney: *I have salt and pepper, Summer.*

Summer: *Don't get snippy.*

Delaney: *I'm not.*

No response.

Delaney: *Okay. I am.*

Summer: *I'll come help you. Don't refrigerate the chicken.*

Delaney: *What? What about salmonella?*

Summer: *Trust me. Get stuff for a side dish. That cucumber salad?*

Delaney: *Fine.*

Summer: *And you need a starch. Grab a couple of potatoes.*

Delaney: *A whole bag?*

Summer: *No, you'll never use them and they'll grow eyes and you'll have an entire potato patch in your pantry.*

Delaney: *Fine.*

Summer and her four children descended on Delaney's house two hours later, armed with aprons, chef hats and a variety of cooking utensils including tongs, spatulas and a whisk.

"We're not going to need all that, are we?"

"Don't look so panicked," Summer said. "It was the easiest way for me to get the kids out of the house. I told them we were coming to help you cook and they had a blast collecting all their cooking stuff. Just don't let Nate put that whisk in your pot. God only knows where it's been. How long do we have?"

"He'll be here in an hour," Delaney said.

"Perfect."

Summer was like a sweet-voiced drill sergeant, directing the lot of them in every step of dinner preparation. Even tiny Hannah helped, washing the potatoes while standing on a chair at the counter. Sarah sliced cucumber, tomato and onion. Nate sprinkled salt and pepper on the chicken and Luke mixed the dressing for the salad.

"I'm in awe. Do you do this every night?"

"Oh, no," Summer said. "Not every night. But on weekends, when we have time. I love being in the kitchen with the kids. It's so much fun. As you know, it's never this quiet in my house. Look how busy they all are."

Within moments, the chicken was in the oven, the salad was made and the potatoes were boiling on the stove.

"Okay, can you handle mashing the potatoes and mixing in some butter, milk, salt and pepper?" Summer said.

Delaney rolled her eyes.

The kids lined up at the door, tallest to shortest. Nate held Hannah's hand and all four of them looked soberly up at Delaney.

"I hope I can handle the potatoes," Delaney said.

"Don't disappoint me," Summer said.

"I won't. They'll be delicious."

"That's not what I mean," Summer said, "and you know it."

"No funny business, Aunt Dee," Sarah said.

Without speaking, Delaney pointed to the door. Obediently, the kids – and Summer – filed out.

"Thank you!" Delaney called from the front door. "It's already smelling wonderful!"

Delaney heard the Jeep's engine rumble into her driveway a minute before Jake was due to arrive.

"Why am I so nervous?" she asked Pixie, who had jumped onto the windowsill to see who had come to visit. "It's just dinner. Oh, I should open the wine."

Her phone chirped.

Summer: *Good luck. Open the wine.*

It chirped again.

Josie: *You got this this. Don't sweat it. It'll go great.*

Delaney: *Thanks, guys. He just got here. I'll text you when it's over. xo*

Despite the words of encouragement, Delaney's hands shook as she fought with the wine opener before realizing the bottle had a screw-on lid. She took a deep breath to steady herself, then bobbled one of the wine glasses and nearly dropped it.

"Get yourself together," she muttered.

Jake knocked on the door. Delaney quickly poured the wine, left it on the counter and went to the door. When she opened it, Jake pulled a bouquet of bright yellow tulips from behind his back with a flourish.

All at once, most of Delaney's anxiety melted away. She thanked him and leaned forward to kiss him on the cheek.

"It's the least I could do, considering you're cooking me dinner," he said.

"Wait 'til you taste it. You might take the flowers back. They're so cheerful."

He chuckled and followed her to the kitchen.

"Wine?" she said.

"Sure."

"My cooking class partner, Beth, said I should give you a glass of wine before I feed you. To soften you up."

"Smart woman." His eyes locked with hers over the rim of his glass. "Cheers. To a delicious, home-cooked meal."

Delaney raised her glass and downed half the wine in one gulp. "Cheers."

"I can see why you fell in love with this place," Jake said, leaning against the counter after refilling her glass. "It's so light and airy, and cozy at the same time. And the hardwood floor's incredible. Is it original?"

"Yeah, it is. It's a little squeaky, but it has personality. My parents thought it was a terrible investment. A money pit, I think is what my dad said. But I love it."

"It's great."

"The chicken should be ready in about fifteen minutes," she said. "Summer said –"

She stopped herself, not sure if she wanted him to know Summer and her miniature Army had been here, helping with dinner.

"What did Summer say?"

"Summer said it might take a little longer to cook since it hadn't come all the way up to room temperature before we put it in the oven."

"We?" Jake said.

"Okay, I admit it," Delaney said. "I had help with this dinner. I was so afraid I'd ruin it, Summer brought her kids over and they helped me. It took six people to cook this meal. You'd better like it."

"Tell me more about your friends," he said.

For the next fifteen minutes, she shared the best Summer and Josie stories from their teenage years, from Josie sneaking them out of school in the trunk of her car junior year to Summer proposing to Derek right after graduation.

She expected black billows of smoke to greet her when she opened the oven, but on the contrary, she smelled the homey scent of roasted chicken. She could hear the drippings sizzling in the roasting pan, and was pleasantly surprised when she pulled it out and saw the bird's skin was a crispy, light brown.

"That looks perfect," Jake said.

"It does."

"You sound surprised," he said.

"I am."

He carved the perfectly-roasted chicken while she served the salad and mashed potatoes. Then they sat down at her dining table.

"Was that a huge sigh of relief?" he asked.

"It was," Delaney said. "Even though we haven't tasted any of the food, yet. Maybe I should rescind that sigh of relief until we've tasted everything. Go ahead."

Jake cut a piece of chicken and put it in his mouth. He chewed, staring into her eyes. He chewed. And chewed. Impatience took hold.

"Well?" she said.

He held up a finger. And chewed.

"The suspense is killing me!"

He swallowed. "It's good. Really good. Well done."

"Now I can breathe that sigh of relief."

"You deserve it. Cheers, again. To a perfectly cooked chicken."

As Jake cleaned his plate and she did the same, Delaney felt a tiny glimmer of pride taking shape in her chest. She'd done it. Sure, she had a little help (okay, more than a little) from Summer and the kids, but she'd taken the chicken out of the oven on time. She'd provided the salad recipe. And she had even mashed the potatoes. And someone other than her parents, Summer, or Josie was eating it. *Devouring* it.

Maybe it's because he was raised to be a gentleman, her inner critic whispered. *Maybe he actually hates it but his mom always told him he has to clean his plate.* But she knew better. She was tasting the food, too, and it was pretty good.

"So I imagine you'll have to report back to Summer and Josie after this, huh?" Jake said.

"Yeah. I imagine I will."

Although she tried to maintain an air of calm, inside, she felt jittery. She couldn't put her finger on exactly why until Jake licked his lips. She wanted him. But, she knew the timing wasn't right and she didn't want to mess things up. She had to wait until he'd confirmed they were an item. A couple. Boyfriend-girlfriend. Seeing each other. Something. Something official. Something besides, "I really like you but I'm super busy."

She'd put herself out there, hadn't she? And now she just had to wait. He knew what she wanted. And he must like her. The flowers, the sledding, the dinner…

Couldn't she just make a cootie catcher or pull out the Ouija board to find out if he wanted to go steady?

"I have to ask you something," she said.

"Shoot."

A long pause.

"Can I get your number?" she said.

"Geez. I thought you were going to ask me my deepest, darkest secret or something. Of course you can."

After they'd exchanged numbers, Jake said, suddenly, "I have a surprise for you. Wait here."

He walked out the front door and returned a moment later, holding a movie case in front of him.

"You're full of surprises," Delaney said.

"It's a specialty. This," he said, "is my all-time favorite movie. I couldn't let this relationship go on any longer without watching it with you. Youngblood."

Did he say relationship? "Is it a hockey movie?"

"'Is it a hockey movie?' Only the best hockey movie ever made!"

"Do you show this to all the ladies?" she said.

"Absolutely not. Only to those who invite me over for a lip-lickin' home-cooked meal."

So she *was* special to him. Or did all the ladies make him a home-cooked meal? He did seem to inspire strange domestic tendencies.

"Looking forward to it," she said. "I'll just clear the table."

"One more thing," he said, pulling something out of his back pocket. "Popcorn."

"I love popcorn." Delaney opened the pouch and put the bag in the microwave to pop while they cleaned up. She put the movie in the DVD player and they settled on the couch.

"I love this movie," Jake said as the previews played.

"I'm honored that you brought it for us to watch together," she said.

"You should be."

He put his arm around her shoulders and pulled her close. Even though she tried her best to pay attention to the plot, the characters and the scenery, Delaney was distracted by Jake's warmth, his soap-and-spice scent, the rise and fall of his chest.

Hockey games, hazing rituals and fights were enough to put her to sleep, but she held on. At one point, Pixie hopped onto the couch and plopped down on Delaney's lap. Jake stroked her, rubbing her neck. She purred.

I'd be purring right now, too.

The movie ended. Jake stretched.

"So? Did you like it?"

"I did," Delaney said. "It was really good."

"Good. I would love to stay longer, but I really should go. I've got to get up early tomorrow to work on … some stuff."

That sounds ambiguous, Delaney's inner voice whispered. She swatted the thought away. It was probably something to do with his gallery. *Probably. Most likely.*

"Thanks so much for coming over and eating my food." Delaney's cheer felt forced and she imagined she was grimacing at him. Jake didn't seem to notice. He kissed her and headed for the door.

"Thank you. It turned out great. I look forward to eating lots more of your cooking."

SURE, he'd kissed her goodnight. And it had been a warm, lingering kiss. Full of promise, she'd say, if she had to describe it. But promises just weren't doing it for Delaney Collins' libido. She felt needy, hungry. Starving.

Instead of running down the walkway after Jake, she sent the girls a text: *The evening is over. Went well. Food was perfect (thanks, Summer).*

Summer: *Did you guys make it official? And then do The Deed?*

Josie: *Don't hold out on us.*

Delaney: *Well, he said some really nice things. But no. He brought that movie, Youngblood? He said it's his favorite movie and I'm the first woman he's ever shown it to. Also he wants to eat more of my cooking.*

Summer: *Well, that's something.*

Josie: *I bet you're so horny right now. Haha.*

Delaney: *Haha. Ha. Well, it was a perfectly pleasant evening.*

Despite the fact that it had, indeed, been a perfectly pleasant evening, Delaney felt a little uneasy as she fell asleep. Questions floated through her mind like amorphous ghosts: What did Jake have to do tomorrow? Why hadn't he told her about it? Did he have another woman to see? A date? It felt like hours passed before she finally drifted off.

CHAPTER THIRTY-THREE

"PAGING DOC COLLINS," DOCTOR KAT CALLED FROM ACROSS THEIR SHARED office space.

Delaney shook her head to clear it and swung her chair around to face Doctor Kat, who sat in hers, long legs splayed out in front of her.

"Sorry. What'd you need?"

"I need my second-in-command to stop daydreaming. We have a surgery in five minutes."

Doctor Kat looked entertained, and Delaney struggled to keep her composure.

"I'm not daydreaming," she said.

"What's going on with you?"

"Nothing," Delaney said. "Just concentrating."

During her first few days at work, she'd remembered that she enjoyed surgery. The clean, sterile room, the precision of a clean cut, the ability to heal, quickly. Maybe she'd ask Doctor Kat if she could take the lead on one in a couple of weeks.

"So, you had a date last night?"

How'd she know?

"How'd you know?"

Without making eye contact, Doctor Kat turned her chair around to face her desk. "Who was it?"

Chuckling in bewilderment, Delaney shook her head and answered, "It was this guy. Jake."

"'This guy'? Sounds impressive."

"You're my boss. Do you want me to tell you he's really hot? I mean, mouthwatering? Because he is. I mean, seriously good-looking." '

Doctor Kat made a sound that was somewhere between a laugh and a harrumph.

"Going steady?"

"I'm not sure. I'd like to, but he's really busy. And stuff. Starting his own business." Delaney shook her head, adding, "The dating scene is brutal. I've been testing the waters."

"Anything good?"

"You should *see* some of what's out there. I don't know where these guys come from. But actually, it's funny. The hot guy I was just talking about? Jake? I met him a while back. He came to my rescue when someone rear-ended me on the highway, then drove off. Then I ran into him at Rowdy's. My mom calls it serendipitous that he also turned up as a match on FindLove.com." She could practically feel Doctor Kat raising an eyebrow. "Yes, I'm on FindLove.com. Don't ask. Anyway, our first date went pretty well, and then I ran into him again outside Eddie's."

She found she couldn't stop talking about Jake now that she'd started. "He looks like a Greek god. The nose, the profile, the lips. You know what I mean? Anyway, it's probably too good to be true."

"Maybe not." Dr. Kat stood up. "You never know. I actually thought that about my husband at first, so I hear you. But it's okay to go for something really great. In fact, if you don't go for it, you might regret it. So go all out, Doc Collins. Let's go scrub in."

JUST AFTER TEN, as Delaney grabbed a water from the break room, her phone chirped.

Jake: *Meet for lunch?*

Her heart scrambled up into her throat. She responded: *Sure. When/where?*

Jake: *Sand Witch? When are you open?*

Delaney: *12:15*

Jake: *Can't wait to see you.*

The hands on the office clock finally crawled their way upward to noon. Delaney parked a couple of blocks away from The Sand Witch and walked over, enjoying the warmth of the spring sun on her face. Her feelings of tranquility ended abruptly when she walked right into The Sand Witch's glass door as someone else walked out. The impact knocked her back a couple of steps and made her see stars.

"Delaney!" Jake's voice cut through the fog.

The couple coming out of the restaurant hadn't even noticed she was there, but, of course, Jake, who'd been waiting for her on the sidewalk, had seen everything. He rushed over to hold the door for her.

Mortifying.

"Are you okay?" he asked.

When she regained her balance and her vision, she couldn't tell if he was trying not to laugh, or just really happy to see her.

"I'm fine."

He guided Delaney in by her elbow.

"What happened?" he said.

"Distracted, I guess."

"I guess." Jake's eyes shone with merriment, but he managed to keep a straight face.

Just as they found a table after ordering, Jake's phone rang. He jumped about a mile, fumbled to put his sandwich down, nearly spilled his drink and then glanced nervously at Delaney before practically sprinting outside.

That old sense of unease crept into her stomach. From where she sat, she could see him, standing on the sidewalk, phone pressed to his ear, body rigid. She couldn't tell whether he was nervous or excited, but the muscles in his back and shoulders looked tense.

Finally, by the time she was about three-quarters of the way through her veggie sandwich, he ended the call, slipped his phone into his back pocket and turned around. He jogged back to their table and began scooping up his sandwich and drink.

"Sorry, Delaney. I've got to go."

He leaned down to give her a brief kiss on the cheek, and then hurried out of the restaurant, leaving her holding a soggy quarter of her sandwich. Suddenly the alfalfa sprouts didn't seem very appetizing.

I DON'T KNOW if I can ever have kids of my own. Carpool Tuesday is such hard work, and it lasts less than an hour each week.

After a five-minute argument over whose turn it was to choose the radio station, Delaney exercised her driver's rights and chose it herself. All three kids had howled in misery when she cranked up the classical music. So she turned it up louder. Then Sarah started in, yelling over Beethoven.

"Aunt Dee, Mom said you and Jake the Dreamy are *kind of* going steady. Is that true?"

"Do you have homework tonight?" Delaney said.

"Is it true, Aunt Dee?" Luke said.

"Are they giving homework in kindergarten these days?"

"Stop it, Aunt Dee," Luke said. "I'm not in kindergarten any more. You know that."

She turned the music up even louder, and saw Sarah and Luke exchange very adult eye rolls.

Since Jake had abandoned her at The Sand Witch, Delaney thoughts had centered around who could possibly have called him. He hadn't seemed upset, so she doubted he'd gotten bad news. In fact, he had seemed excited. So why hadn't he explained his hasty exit?

As she approached the intersection where she'd first laid eyes on Jake Rhoades, she scanned the traffic behind her to see if he was there now. Then she did a mental head slap. Of course he wasn't.

During the remainder of the drive, Delaney compiled a list of reasons Jake had ditched her at lunch: an old, totally hot flame (Brittany?) had invited him over for a quickie; someone he'd had his eye on from Find-Love.com had finally called and asked him to meet up right away; his wife was having a baby – triplets, actually.

Delaney pulled into Summer's driveway and rubbed her hands over her face. Now she was getting carried away. It was unlikely that Jake was married. But the other options were wide open.

What did her intuition say? It was coming up dry, too.

It said he was telling the truth about his gallery. He was passionate about his work and wanted to make a living at it. The timing for a new, hot-and-heavy relationship wasn't stellar. But the louder, meaner voice (the one that insisted on a "fail-proof" backup system for dating) told her not to get her hopes up.

Of course, Sarah took advantage of the sudden silence that rang out when Delaney turned off the van in the Grays' driveway.

"So. Are you?" she said.

"Am I what?" Delaney said.

"In love?"

Delaney rolled her eyes.

Giggling, the boys clambered out of the van while Sarah held the door open, her eyes never leaving Delaney's.

"Why won't anyone leave me alone?" Delaney said.

"Geez. You sound like Nate when Mom wants him to take a bath." Sarah said.

"Shut up."

They both closed their doors and as they came around the front of the van to walk into the house, Sarah said, "You can't say that to me. I'm just a kid."

"Whatever," Delaney said.

"I get grounded for saying 'Whatever.'"

"Ground me," Delaney said, putting an arm around Sarah's shoulders and giving her a squeeze. "See who picks you up from school next week, you snotty little brat."

"Aunt Dee!"

Just as she'd been doing since Sarah was born, Delaney kissed her on the head. "Love you. Here's the keys. Tell your mom I said to stop talking smack."

"Fat chance."

CHAPTER THIRTY-FOUR

Neither Josie nor Summer were at their table when Delaney walked into Rowdy's on Thursday night. She slid onto a stool and waited. Unfortunately, being alone gave her more time to fret about Jake.

She *still* hadn't heard from him since he took off halfway through their lunch date.

Patsy Cline's "I Fall to Pieces" played, and Delaney wondered if it was a sign: *You want me to act like we've never kissed. You want me to forget, pretend we've never met. And I've tried and I've tried, but I haven't yet. You walk by and I fall to pieces.*

She knew she was being ridiculous. He'd invited her to lunch. And nothing had gone wrong. Had it? Again, Delaney dissected every word they'd spoken to one another before he got that phone call.

She *had* run into the glass door when she first showed up. Then, had she made too many stupid jokes? Made that weird face Summer and Josie said she always made when she drank soda out of a straw? Maybe she had sprouts stuck in her teeth the entire time and Jake was too grossed out to see her again. Had she talked with her mouth full? Although she'd never gone so far as to tell herself Jake was The One, she had felt something special between them.

He wouldn't take a phone call from another woman while we were together. And he certainly wouldn't run off to another woman mid-date. Would he?

If Jake wanted to end things, it meant the failure of The Dating Intervention. Not only that, it meant she simply wasn't dateable. It made sense that she couldn't choose men that were a good match for her, but if she couldn't make it work with even *this* man, the man Fate kept throwing in her path, the man her friends (and the algorithms on a dating website) chose for her, Delaney faced a spinster life. When she had imagined that before, she'd always done so from a place of humor. Like it couldn't happen in reality.

But maybe it could. Maybe she could end up alone and lonely … forever. She pictured herself sitting in a rocking chair, Pixie curled on her lap and a herd of cats perched all over the house—the couch, the windowsill, the kitchen counter. For a moment, Delaney found herself struggling to breathe.

"I'm So Lonesome I Could Cry" came over the speakers: *I've never seen a night so long, when time goes crawling by. The moon just went behind the clouds to hide its face and cry. Did you ever see a robin weep, when leaves begin to die, that means he's lost his will to live, I'm so lonesome I could cry.*

Yes, Delaney thought, *I'm so lonesome I could cry*. Tears threatened as she imagined going to sleep alone every night, for the rest of her life.

She had never been more grateful to hear Josie's voice, even if it sounded a little grumbly at the moment.

It was like a soothing balm: "I can't take the stress of this interview tomorrow. Do I have to do it?"

Benjamin hurried over to their table, his tray laden with drinks.

Delaney sipped her beer and with a gargantuan effort, mentally switched gears. "Do you want to practice interview questions?" she asked Josie.

"When Summer gets here."

They sat in silence for six entire minutes, and of course Delaney's mind went straight back to Jake Rhoades. What could that call possibly have been? If Summer were here, she'd say something about turning off the mental chatter. She'd say of course the call was about something other than romance. His art gallery, maybe? A piece he was trying to sell? Or maybe it was a family emergency.

But, even though she knew it was juvenile, Delaney continued to analyze. Maybe she hadn't acted grateful enough when he brought coffee to her at work. Maybe she hadn't thanked him in a big enough way when he sent her flowers. She drummed her fingers on the tabletop. She jiggled her leg. What if it wasn't something she'd done recently? What if he was just coming to terms with the fact that she was in her mid-thirties and she still partied like a twenty-something at The Teeter Totter? The list of possibilities was long.

Finally, Summer rushed in, distracting Delaney from her own endless loop.

For the next half-hour, Summer and Delaney hammered Josie with all the questions they could think of: Why do you want to be principal?

Why this school? What are your plans for the staff and students? How do you feel about sleeping with your staff members? What are your short- and long-term goals for the school? What is your stance on nylons? How do you feel about training for teachers and staff? How will you fund extracurricular activities?

"You mean, like the sewing club?" Josie hissed at the last one.

The girls laughed at that.

"I think you sound great, Josie," Delaney said. "I think you're ready."

Summer nodded. "You're going to kill it."

Josie inhaled deeply, through her nose, then let out the breath through pursed lips, psyching herself up. "I can do this."

"What time's your interview?" Summer asked, her tone so innocent Delaney knew she was onto something else.

"Well, since it's an in-service day, it's at ten. So I'll go in at eight, like usual, go to our first training and then go to the interview."

"Great," Delaney said. "Sounds perfect."

Under the table, Summer had grabbed her knee and squeezed it in a vise grip. It was everything Delaney could do to keep from crying out in pain.

"Has Jake texted you today?" Summer asked, her eyes boring so hard into Delaney's that Delaney thought she might combust.

"Um, I don't know," Delaney said.

"You *so* know," Josie said, her eyes twinkling with their usual mischief. "You're probably checking your phone twenty times a day."

Delaney shrugged one shoulder, embarrassed Josie had guessed the truth so easily. "So what?"

"Check," Summer said.

Oh. Delaney pulled her phone out of her purse and saw Summer's text: *You need to clear your schedule tomorrow morning. We have to be at Josie's school to keep her from chickening out last-minute.*

Quickly, before Josie could look over her shoulder and see the message, Delaney clicked out of it. When she did, she saw that Jake had, in fact, texted her. Her heart rate increased. Her hands shook. Which was ridiculous. She opened the message: *Sorry about the other day. I'll explain later.*

Well, he wasn't ending things. Yet. That was good news, right? Or was it? He said he'd explain later, which meant he planned on speaking to her again. So that was good. Unless his explanation was actually him dumping her. Why had it taken him so long to apologize?

Still shaking, and with more questions than answers, Delaney slipped her phone into her purse. Summer gave an exaggerated shrug, which reminded Delaney that she should have responded to Summer's text. She fished her phone back out.

"Actually, he did text me," she said. "Apologizing for running out on our lunch date. I should respond real quick."

Her fingers flew across the phone's keyboard as she responded, first to Summer—*I'll be there*—and then to Jake—*No prob*.

Although she actually felt like there was a problem, and she'd prefer to text straight to the bottom of the Jakes Rhodes mystery all night, he and his strange behavior would have to wait.

For now she had to play coach to Josie, who'd undoubtedly need all the coaching she could get.

CHAPTER THIRTY-FIVE

Delaney's phone chirped at six-thirty a.m. She didn't have to look to know it was Summer: *I'll meet you at 9:30. That's what time Josie's first training gets out. Park in the back, by that big Dumpster.*

Delaney: *Perfect. See you then.*

Since Doctor Kat had made a recent habit out of laying all the cards out on the table, Delaney asked her straight out if she could have the morning off so she could ride herd on Josie. Naturally, Doctor Kat agreed it was a great plan. Armed with double her typical caffeine intake and a huge dose of nerves, Delaney felt a pretty decent buzz when she met Summer at nine-thirty.

Summer, too, seemed more energized than usual as she practically leapt from her car behind the Dumpster in Josie's school parking lot.

"So I was thinking," she said without preamble. "We should just go look through her window and see if she does this on her own. If she does, we wait out here until it's over to see how she's acting after. If not, we charge, get her into the office and blockade the door so she can't leave 'til it's over."

"Sounds good," Delaney said. "But isn't her room on the third floor?"

Summer nodded, shrugged.

Delaney drew a deep breath, rolled her shoulders. "Let's do this."

American Traditional School was a one-hundred-year-old old brick building with an original external fire escape. Spying on Josie through her window, then, meant climbing a small rickety ladder and then three flights of ancient, narrow metal stairs.

"Are you sure you should be doing this?" Delaney asked as Summer hiked up her long magenta skirt and put a flip-flopped foot on the first rung of the ladder.

"I'm pregnant, not on my deathbed," Summer growled, hoisting herself up. "Come on."

The metal creaked as they made slow progress upward.

"We should have done this one at a time," Delaney said when they finally reached the third-floor landing, panting.

"She's not there," Summer said.

"Shit," they said at the same time. Together, they bent down to look through the open window at the empty classroom.

"What time is it?" Summer asked.

"It's nine thirty-four," Delaney said. "Could she have left already?"

"Her door's open. She's probably in the bathroom."

"What should we do?"

Summer's lips pressed together. "Climb in."

"You first," Delaney said to Summer, who nodded, brushed her hair out of her face, then hiked up her skirt again and lifted her leg over the windowsill.

At that very moment, Josie walked back into her classroom. She froze when she saw Summer, half-in, half-out of the window.

"What are you *doing* out there? You're going to kill yourself. *And Baby Number Five.*"

She marched over to the window and took Summer's hand to help her inside, muttering, "Delaney, I can't believe you let her climb the fire escape. You guys are crazy."

"She's pregnant, not on her deathbed," Delaney said. Then she regained her senses and said, "Why aren't you heading to the interview?"

"I was." Her eyes darted around the room. "I was just peeing first. And anyway, it's not for another half-hour."

"You're lying," Delaney said, jabbing a finger at Josie from her spot on the fire escape landing.

Without answering, Josie slammed the window, forcing Delaney to withdraw her arm. *She just shut me out here!* Delaney stared at Josie from the fire escape outside. Her mouth dropped open in surprise. She closed it. It dropped open again. Like a fish.

"Open this window, Josie," she yelled. "Open it right now!"

Josie gave her an evil glare, then stalked out of the classroom, Summer bustling along in her wake. A minute later, Delaney heard them emerge into the parking lot below.

"You have to do this, Josie. Get back in there."

"You can't make me."

"Seriously? You sound like one of my boys."

"I'm not one of your boys, Summer. I'm a grown woman. And I've decided not to apply for this position."

At this, Delaney sensed danger. She clambered down the fire escape as fast as she could to a cacophony of clanks, bangs and groans from the metal. She hoped it didn't collapse.

Josie continued, "I'm perfectly fine without your interference."

"No you're not," Delaney said, rushing up to them. "You're not fine. Get in there, now. Do the damned interview and get it over with. We'll be waiting outside."

She grabbed Josie's arm and marched her toward the front of the building, between the carved stone pillars that had seen a hundred years' worth of principals come and go.

"Stop giving up on yourself. Get in there."

"Fine!" Josie said, jerking her arm loose and then smoothing her suit. "Fine."

She stalked into the building, the heels of her expensive alligator leather shoes clicking loudly on the original wood floors.

"That was close," Summer said from behind Delaney.

"Really close," Delaney said.

Summer held up a hand for a high-five. "Success," she breathed.

"Success," Delaney echoed, slapping Summer's hand. "We did it."

"Do you think we should blockade the doors?" Summer said. Delaney smiled.

CHAPTER THIRTY-SIX

The first time the romance of the rodeo dance stole Delaney's heart, she was sixteen. She'd heard the music from the Mack's Grocery parking lot when she stopped to buy milk on her way home from a babysitting job. Curiosity got the better of her, and she was standing outside the fence in a matter of seconds, leaving the milk to sweat on the roof of her car.

On the high school football field, cowboys in Wranglers twirled their skirt-clad, cowboy-booted women on the temporary dance floor, which was surrounded by bales of hay and covered by a red-and-white-striped awning. String lights illuminated the entire space and a band played from a stage up front.

Now, almost twenty years later, she'd attended the dance every year, without fail. This year, The Sweets' appearance delivered a new, special shiver of excitement. Summer and The Sweets were setting up and Josie and Delaney stood in line at the beer counter behind a group of scantily clad young women out looking for horsemen.

"So the interview went well?" Delaney lifted her cowboy hat to smooth her hair.

"It went okay," Josie said. "But I'm sure it was a formality. Scott Smith has the hots for Blair Upton and I'm sure he's going to give her the job."

"Witch," Delaney said, earning a small smile from Josie before she turned away and made a big show of watching Summer assemble her microphone stand.

They were at the front of the line now.

"I'll get two beers," Delaney told the server, who had leather for skin and corn kernels for teeth.

Beer slopped over the sides of the plastic cups as the woman slid them across the counter and Delaney and Josie each took one, sipping foam as they made their way to a vacant hay bale and sat down.

"Jake coming tonight?" Josie said.

"I don't know. I haven't talked to him in a few days." Delaney heard the edge in her voice and took a deep breath to smooth it out.

"Hmm," Josie said.

"What does that mean?"

"Nothing."

"It means something," Delaney said.

"I just said, 'Hmm,'" Josie said. "Let it go."

While Summer did a sound check, Delaney sipped her beer. Josie sipped hers. The line to get into the dance grew longer, which meant the rodeo performance, in the arena a few blocks over, had ended. A sea of cowboy hats in every color and material – black, tan, brown, pink and white in felt, leather, straw, and sequins – filled the space under the tent.

Finally, The Sweets started to play, leading off with a fast, beat-heavy dancing song that made Delaney wish even harder that Jake would show up and dance with her. She forced herself to leave her phone in her pocket. She didn't want Josie to know she'd even noticed Jake hadn't yet materialized.

Couples and groups of women flocked to the dance floor, spinning and jumping wildly to the beat.

"They sound good," Delaney yelled to Josie.

Josie nodded. "Want to dance?"

She had that gleam in her eye, and Delaney remembered the first time she'd joined Josie on a dance floor. Homecoming, freshman year. Delaney had still been awkward, shy, pimply. And Josie had been exotic, smooth and filled with women's wisdom, even at the age of fifteen. She dragged Delaney onto the floor and patiently taught her some choreographed routine that had Delaney shaking her hips and stomping her feet. It had been so much fun, and for the first time, Delaney felt somewhat confident in the dark, sultry confines of the school gym.

Of course, Josie still had it. They danced, holding hands, song after song. They moved close to the stage whenever they could, to give Summer a thumbs-up. When The Sweets finally took a break, Delaney and Josie ran up to the stage.

"So? How do we sound?" Summer asked as they embraced.

"How do you think you sound? Look at these people!"

Hundreds of people were still hanging out on the dance floor, waiting for the band to start up again. A group of girls chatted nearby. A couple continued to dance, singing the chorus of The Sweets' last song. Summer looked around, took it all in.

Someone found a CD to fill the silence and blasted old-fashioned, twangy country music into the crowd. People covered their ears and scooted off the floor. In the melee, a crowd of rowdy guys jostled each other and one of them spilled his beer on Delaney. She looked down at her feet to see if it had gotten on her boots and bent down to wipe it off as best as she could.

When she glanced up at Josie and Summer, she noticed something in their body language had changed. They were looking toward the beer counter. Their heads were close together as if they were whispering. She turned around, hoping to see whatever they were looking at, but the crowd shifted, obscuring her vision.

"What?" she mouthed at the girls, lifting her hands.

Both Summer and Josie looked startled. Summer attempted to cover up her surprise by plastering a maniacal smile on her face and Josie shook her head, raising her eyebrows as if to say, "It's nothing."

Delaney knew something was up. Without waiting for an explanation, she turned around again and powered her way through the crowd and up to the beer counter.

She immediately wished she hadn't.

There, ordering a drink, was Jake Rhoades. Snug-fitting jeans, a t-shirt that showed off the muscles in his back, a look on his face like he'd just won the lottery … and his arm around the shoulders of a tiny, equally-muscled woman, whose long, glossy hair and long, slender legs made her look like a gazelle supermodel in a shampoo ad.

It was the girl from all the FriendZoo pictures, in all her dazzling real-life glory. Brittany. It had to be. There was no other explanation. It took Delaney no more than a half-second to take in the scene and then she fled. She ran back to the dance floor, where Summer and Josie stood perfectly still, a stark contrast to the movement that swirled around them. Rather than revealing the sick feeling churning in her stomach, Delaney grabbed their hands and started dancing.

"It's fine!" she told them. "No big deal!"

Despite that proclamation, she spent the rest of their time at the rodeo dance trying to catch a glimpse of Jake and Ms. Gazelle of the Shiny Hair. At one point she saw them cozied up on a hay bale, both of them cracking up like they'd never heard anything funnier. Later, on her fourth trip to the bathroom in a half hour, she saw Jake tug gently, affectionately, on the end of the girl's hair. There was definitely an intimacy there, she thought, her hands shaking.

She knew it shouldn't bother her. After all, they'd never agreed to be exclusive. They had only been on a few dates. And they were both adults, both with healthy appetites for social ... *interactions*. It was only natural he'd kept dating other people. And he'd known this particular girl before he met Delaney. She had the proof on FriendZoo.

He'd even tried to warn her, hadn't he? Hell, she thought, she'd be dating other people if Summer and Josie hadn't put the kaput on that.

This is why I always have a backup. If I had one right now, I'd be calling him.

A different, cruel voice in the back of her mind sneered: *Yeah, you'd be calling him, heading to his house and regretting it the next morning.*

WHEN DELANEY GOT HOME, she realized she wouldn't be calling anyone. Her phone was missing. As a little girl, she lost things all the time. Her favorite stuffed llama, Salazar, disappeared regularly.

"Where's the last place you saw it?" her mom would say.

Together, they'd walk through what Delaney had done since waking up, coming home, or eating dinner, retracing her steps until they found Salazar. He was usually someplace obvious, like stuffed between the couch cushions or on one of the kitchen bar stools.

Once, though, he'd been in the refrigerator. Delaney had gotten herself a glass of milk and left him on the bottom shelf. When she'd found and rescued him, his huge plastic eyes were cold against her cheeks.

Unfortunately, she thought now, her travels, even during this single evening, had taken her all over town. Most likely, her expensive phone was drowning in an outhouse at the rodeo dance. Distracted after seeing Jake with that Ms. Gazelle of the Shiny Hair, she'd put it in the back pocket of her jeans after checking again to see if he'd sent her a message. And then, the worst folly of all, she'd gone to the bathroom. She couldn't remember whether she'd taken it out of her pocket before entering the outhouse. How many times had she heard of this happening? And now, she couldn't replace it until Monday—nothing in Juniper was open on Sundays.

Weary, she went about her evening chores: making the coffee, feeding Pixie, watering her plants. She noticed the fern Camille had given her was starting to droop. She changed into her pajamas and brushed her teeth. She didn't even bother to stop herself from wondering what Jake was doing right now.

Was he with Ms. Gazelle of the Shiny Hair? Were they just getting back to his place for a nightcap? Were they dancing to quiet jazz music in his living room? Was he kissing her, just as he'd kissed Delaney? Speaking of kissing, why had he made out with her only the one time? Why hadn't he tried harder to get her in bed?

Actually, speaking of that, she was offended. Why *hadn't* he? Maybe this was about Jake, she thought. Maybe he had a fear of commitment. Maybe he was gay. Maybe he liked bartenders but not veterinarians.

In the middle of brushing her bottom molars, she froze. What was happening here? She'd never gone through this kind of torture when her dating system was in place. She always felt confident. She never questioned herself, replayed conversations in her mind, wondering if she'd said the wrong thing. If she had her phone, she would text Summer and Josie, begging them to let her recreate her fail-proof dating system. Okay, so it had failed the one time. But that was only once in seven years. It had taken practically seven minutes for Delaney to start feeling like her nerdy, needy junior-high self where Jake Rhoades was concerned.

On second thought, why did she need their permission? They didn't even have to know. She could log onto her FindLove.com profile right now and start looking for other men in Juniper's sea. But, she thought, Summer and Josie had access to her account and would probably delete the entire thing if she made a move. What if Jake had sent her a message there? She really should log on.

As she debated, Delaney noticed the flecks of toothpaste that spotted the bathroom mirror. Looking up, she saw cobwebs had formed on the light fixture. Big clumps of Pixie's hair had gathered in the corners of the floor.

She sighed, making a decision: in this moment, she would choose to be the new Delaney. She finished brushing her teeth, and then went into the living room and unplugged her computer.

Just like she was cleaning out her dating life, she needed to clean this house. It was symbolic. Tomorrow, she would set everything to rights. She'd scour her house until every surface shone, maybe even plant some flowers. She considered starting an all-night cleaning frenzy, but quickly dismissed it. Her eyes were dry, her legs felt heavy and her brain couldn't take any more. At two a.m., she fell into bed and was asleep within seconds.

CHAPTER THIRTY-SEVEN

 Delaney's mood. Although the spring morning barely registered forty degrees, Delaney flew through the house like a hurricane and threw the windows open.

"Time to freshen up," she muttered to Pixie, who sat on the back of the couch blinking in the bright sunlight, looking as irritable and miserable as Delaney felt.

As she poured her coffee and put a slice of bread in the toaster, she glanced at the computer several times, composing messages to Jake in her mind (*I thought it was love! What the hell were you thinking? You showed me the* hockey *movie*).

Most every Sunday, Delaney sat at her tiny kitchen table drinking coffee and reading the Sunday paper. Not this morning, though. Instead, she set her mug, still steaming, on the counter, put on some Shania Twain and began to clean. Rubber gloves on, hair in a messy ponytail and sweat glistening on her face, Delaney began a deep purge.

Why had she let Jake get to her so much? She set the contents of her fridge on the kitchen counter, separating out moldy leftovers and jars of food that had expired a year (or in some cases, two) ago. She cringed when she saw the sticky residue something had left on one of the refrigerator's shelves. Jake was dreamy, yes. He had nice – no, great – muscles in his back and forearms. He smelled good. He had made her feel, if only for a short time, that monogamy in dating was possible. That was the reason she'd let him get to her.

How had she not noticed the stench from the fridge before this? With her nose buried in the crook of one elbow, she carried the trash out to the trashcan, shuddering as she dropped it in. While she squirted toilet bowl cleaner into the toilets, she remembered dancing with Jake at his new art studio. She could practically feel his calloused hand in hers, her cheek against his chest. She scrubbed the first toilet vigorously, even as her angry tears fell into the bowl.

A couple of times, she'd even imagined him proposing to her. He had turned her into *that* girl: a quivering mess of neediness. She wiped her nose on her sleeve, flushed the toilet and squirted cleaner into the bathtub. It was fine. She'd made mistakes before. But this time, it felt different. It *was* different. She'd been sure Jake liked her. Positive.

Delaney Collins was no dummy, though. She could handle rejection. Heck, she'd been the Queen of the Rejected in middle school, even while Josie reigned in a distant land as the Queen of Courtship. The very same sixth-grade boys with teeth too big for their faces, the boys who had torn up the candygrams Delaney sent them, had brought Josie flowers, offered to carry her bright pink backpack and held doors for her. Oh, yes, if Josie Garcia walked by, these boys – heinous creatures who broke Delaney's pride day after day – practically trembled with nerves induced by some strange middle school hormone.

Delaney Collins could take it. She'd bounced back, right? So what if she still had nightmares about Joe Jansen announcing to their entire pre-algebra class that Dumb Dumb Delaney was a Dumb Dumb Dork and then holding up the note she'd written him, pointing first to her message: *Would you like to go to the movies with me this weekend?* and then to his response: *NO WAY* scrawled heavily across the bottom of the page? So what if the entire class screamed in hilarity, pointing at Delaney?

The adult Delaney realized then that she was about to scrub the porcelain off the bathtub, so she rinsed it before starting on the counter. Kitchen, bedroom, living room, closets … nothing was off-limits to Delaney Collins. She'd scrub every fleck of dust, every smear of grime, right out of this house. "And right out of my life."

Once she was done inside, she moved on to the garden.

Last year, Summer had convinced her to install flowerbeds in front of the house.

"They'll be cheerful," she'd said at the time. "Welcoming."

Standing in front of the shriveled, crispy mass of what, for a week or so last summer, had been a colorful collection of snapdragons and some other flowers whose names Delaney couldn't remember, she doubted very much that Summer would describe the garden as cheerful.

Depressing, maybe. Or terrifying. Or just plain ugly.

Delaney suppressed an evil cackle as she moved toward the flowerbed with her gloved hands outstretched. She couldn't deny a creepy feeling of glee at ripping the parched remains of cheer out of the dirt at the roots.

Ah, yes, it felt good to yank them right out of the ground. Plant after plant. Nothing survived the vengeful attack. Not a twig, not a stem, not a single crumbly leaf. What had Summer been thinking when she talked Delaney into planting a garden? She should have known Delaney wasn't capable of nurturing anything. Anything at all. Not even a relationship guided by the supposed wisdom of her two best friends. What had gone wrong? She'd followed their stupid, sage advice ... for the most part. It should have worked out. It *should* have. By lunchtime, Delaney had pulled all the dead plants, along with a slew of dead weeds, out of the flowerbeds and stuffed them into a garbage bag. Her arms ached, the backs of her legs ached and her fingers hurt.

At least the front of the little bungalow looked somewhat more orderly, she thought as she stepped back to survey the results of her work, but still ... it looked drab in the weak sunlight. Parched, shriveled weeds no longer stood sentry near the front door, but now all that looked back at her was an empty flowerbed. Completely empty.

She felt like crying again, so she yanked off her hat and the gloves and stomped inside to clean her bedroom.

Ten minutes later, the doorbell rang. Delaney, whose entire upper body was lodged under her bed, jumped. She hit her head on the bottom of her box spring, muttered, "Shit!" and slithered her way out, her hands full of rogue hair ties, bits of paper and loose socks.

The tiniest bubble of hope formed, somewhere deep below the surface. Was it Jake, coming to grovel for forgiveness? Heck, she thought, he didn't even have to grovel. At this point, a quick round of begging would do. The little hope bubble grew a tiny bit bigger as it rose toward the surface.

Delaney dumped everything in a pile on the floor, rubbed the bump that was forming on the top of her head and took a quick glance in the mirror on her bedroom door.

Well, if it was Jake and he'd really come to grovel, her appearance would be a test of his undying love. Although she'd pulled her hair into a messy knot on top of her head, shorter blond wisps had fallen down all around her face, framing it in greasy hanks. Last night's makeup (applied with precision so she'd look doe-eyed for Jake) was smeared beneath her eyes and her holey gray sweatpants and blue sweatshirt sagged at the knees and elbows.

She shrugged at her reflection and went to answer the door. The hope bubble, which had doubled in size, burst before reaching the surface.

"Mom," Delaney said.

"Wow. Don't look so happy to see me, honey."

"Sorry. I was just expecting—"

"I hope you weren't expecting company, looking like that," Camille said. She hooted with laughter.

Delaney stepped back to let her in.

"Funny, Mom. What are you doing here?"

Camille didn't answer.

"Sorry. Want some water or something?"

She closed the door, but couldn't stop herself from glancing at the street, first. A few days ago, she probably would have felt all warm and gooey about the glossy new leaves on the trees, but today she only growled at them before turning the lock.

"No, thanks. I just stopped by to see if you wanted to have lunch."

Delaney flopped down on the couch. "Did you think about calling, first?" she said. She immediately regretted it, in part because it sounded so snippy and in part because she remembered she'd lost her phone. "Sorry."

"Actually, I've called and texted several times, but when you didn't answer, I thought I'd stop by." Camille put her hands on the back of the couch and looked down at Delaney. "What's going on, here?"

"Nothing, Mom. I'm just cleaning, okay?"

"Don't get snippy with me, young lady."

"Sorry."

"What's going on, here?"

Delaney jumped off the couch and stalked into the kitchen, where she got herself a glass and filled it with water. "Last night, I went to the rodeo dance with the girls and we saw Jake there."

"Oh, that was nice. Did the two of you dance?"

"*No*, as it happens, we did not dance. Jake was too involved with some other girl to even notice I was there."

She took several gulps of water and slammed the glass down on the counter. Camille looked surprised for an instant, but she quickly regained her composure.

"Let's go to lunch," she said.

"I tell you the guy I'm totally smitten with has spent an entire evening with another girl, and all you can say is, 'Let's go to lunch'?"

"Honey, what do you want me to say? With you in the mood you're in right now, there's nothing I *can* say without you eating me alive. So, let's go to lunch. And have a cocktail."

"Now you're talking."

───────────

"WHAT IS THIS PLACE, the Senior Citizen Hideaway?"

The East-Coast decor inside the Castaway Cafe, all lighthouses and fishing boats and lobsters, did nothing to improve Delaney's mood. Nor did the clientele. Everyone in there, with the exception of the staff, had false teeth and Velcro shoes.

"I'll order you a Bloody Mary," Camille said.

"You get a senior discount here?"

"They have good cocktails."

Delaney stared at the stained white tablecloth, the pink and red carnations in a slim crystal vase. She pinched a petal off a red one, rolled it between her fingers.

"Yep, they're real," she said.

Camille shook her head, reacting in the same way she probably had to Delaney's outbursts at age four. In an obvious attempt to lighten the mood, she said, "So, I noticed you pulled the weeds and plant carcasses out of your flowerbed."

"Yeah, I figured it was bad juju having all those dead plants at my front door."

"Let's replant them," Camille said.

"You've been drinking already, haven't you?"

When the waitress approached, Delaney noticed nothing about her other than the bright blue eye shadow smeared across her eyelids. She stared at it, transfixed, as her mom ordered Bloody Marys.

"Make hers a double," Camille said in an undertone, tilting her head toward Delaney.

The waitress nodded and walked away, and Delaney picked up the conversation where they left off. "Not gonna lie," she said. "I thought about it. But Mom, I kept those last flowers alive for what? A few days? A week, maybe? It's premeditated murder to buy more."

"You need the practice."

"What's that supposed to mean?"

"Just what I said. Planting a garden is like being in love. It takes work. Practice. But with a little nurturing, things blossom."

"Seriously, Mom? That is so cliché my ears are bleeding."

The waitress returned with her blue eye shadow and the drinks. Delaney sipped hers in relative silence, pausing between sips to crunch on the piece of celery. "This is good, Mom," she said. "Good idea. Nice and peppery. Really puts a spring in your step, I'll bet."

"Geez, Delaney," Camille muttered. "You're really on a roll today."

Delaney couldn't help herself. She burst into tears. She buried her face in the crook of her arm and sobbed. Camille reached across the table and laid a hand on Delaney's head.

"Oh, sweetheart. I know you really liked him. He sounded like a really great guy. But maybe he's just not the right one."

"He *is* the right one!" Delaney said without raising her head. "He is. I thought we were, like, an item, you know? I thought he liked me just as much as I liked him. He showed me a hockey movie, for goodness' sake. Where did I go wrong? What did I do? I was actually behaving myself, following Summer and Josie's stupid rules. The stupid Dating Intervention. It's a failure. *I'm* a failure!"

"There's got to be some explanation," Camille said quietly. "He sent you flowers."

"He took me sledding."

"He helped you get that job."

"He brought me breakfast."

"He ate your cooking."

Delaney wailed.

The couple at the table next to theirs gave Delaney a speculative look, still chewing, forks poised over something pink (crab salad, maybe?).

Delaney wondered how long they'd been married. They were old and in everything from their age-spotted, wrinkled hands to their bright pink crab salad to their red cardigans, they looked the same. She wanted to wear red cardigans with Jake fifty years from now.

But she was starting to feel like she'd never wear red cardigans, or get wrinkly hands with anyone, ever. She'd be eating crab salad at the Castaway Cafe, a.k.a. The Senior Citizen Hideaway, alone, no one there to drape her red cardigan over her shoulders or pass the salt and pepper.

The waitress returned with the fish and chips Camille ordered for them.

"You know, honey," Camille said, "I'm almost positive there is more going on there than you know. There has to be an explanation."

"Mom, just because you found true love doesn't mean everyone else is destined for it, too. There is no explanation other than the fact that Jake Rhoades doesn't feel the same way about me as I do about him. I'm destined to be alone forever with a growing number of cats. End of story."

CHAPTER THIRTY-EIGHT

Delaney sat in her front yard, surrounded by flowers. Flowers in little plastic six-packs, flowers in big pots and flowers whose roots were wrapped in plastic. Camille was inside, brewing some iced tea, which Delaney thought she'd probably lace with vodka or bourbon. Delaney looked helplessly around at the cheerful, vibrant purples, pinks, yellows, reds and whites, and she resolved that she wouldn't let them die.

If she was going to be a lifetime singleton, the weird old woman who wore colorful Velcro sneakers with patterned knee socks every day, then she was going to have to learn how to garden. And she was going to have to get more cats.

Pixie glared at her through the front window.

"What are you glaring at?" Delaney said.

Camille breezed through the front door then, a pitcher in one hand and a couple of plastic cups in the other. "There's nothing like gardening on a beautiful spring day to lift the spirits, Delaney," she said.

Delaney accepted the cup and took a big gulp before realizing it was, in fact, laced with something strong. She took an even bigger gulp and set it down.

"Let's get to it, then," she said.

For hours, they worked side by side, on their knees in front of the flowerbed. They turned the old soil, added fresh soil and turned that. They set the plants out, stood back, rearranged them and then began digging holes. It was therapeutic, Delaney thought, but she probably wouldn't go so far as to admit that to her mother. Plunging her hands into the dirt, churning it up, smelling that rich scent. In fact, Delaney thought, she could make gardening her lifelong companion, if she didn't kill all her little charges. Although that's probably what would happen. She would decide she loved gardening and then suffer repeated bouts of heartbreak as each plant withered and died.

"I bought you a special surprise," Camille said as they patted the soil down around a juniper shrub.

"I thought my special surprise was whatever you spiked the iced tea with."

"No, it's even better."

A moment later, she returned from her car with a long roll of hose and small plastic bag.

"A hose?" Delaney said.

"Don't look so disappointed. You'll see. Help me unroll it."

"Wow. It looks pretty impressive," Delaney said a few minutes later. "Thanks for the hose, Mom."

"Delaney. Knock it off. It's an irrigation hose. You bury it in your flowerbed, set this handy timer" – she held up the plastic bag – "and it waters your flowers without you having to think about it."

"Oh. I guess that *is* pretty cool, actually."

As they began burying the hose, winding it between and around plants, Delaney heard a car pull up. She had a vision of stomping down the tiny seedling of hope that sprouted, and then realized that imagery was counterproductive to her new gardening hobby. It wasn't Jake. It was probably someone turning around or going to a neighbor's house or looking for a thinner, longer-haired woman.

Unfortunately, she saw when she looked up that it was Summer's van. Almost unconsciously, she looked for a hiding spot as Summer and Josie climbed out and headed across the grass. Of course, there wasn't one.

"Ooh, great idea, Dee," Summer said. "An irrigation hose. Give 'em a fighting chance."

"Shut up," Delaney mumbled.

"My idea," Camille said. She stood up and gave Summer and Josie each a hug.

"Ooh, testy this morning?" Josie said.

Delaney didn't answer.

"Sorry, Dee," Josie said. She held up a paper bag. "We brought supplies."

"More gardening supplies?"

"No. Heartache supplies. We'll be right back. C'mon, Summer."

When the front door had closed behind them, Camille said, "That's sweet."

It *was* sweet, but Delaney didn't say so.

"We're almost done here, and then I'll leave you girls to your heartache supplies," Camille said. "Just help me bury this line."

As they worked, Camille said in a quiet voice, "You know, honey, I still think there has to be some explanation. You two really hit it off. I wouldn't let it go quite so easily, if I were you."

Delaney's eyes filled, and she wiped them as best she could on her sleeves.

"I'm humiliated, Mom. I thought things were going so well, and then he's just there with another woman. And he knew I was going to be there. Even though I want nothing more than to be with him, I also never want to see him again."

Camille got to her feet and went over to the hose bib to set the timer.

"Oh, honey. I think you do want to see him again."

After a few moments of quiet while Camille adjusted the dials on the timer, Delaney heard the hiss of water running and watched as dark areas appeared in the flower bed. She had to admit, she found this all pretty impressive. Camille turned around, wiping her hands on her jeans.

"All right," she said. "You're all set up. Now, doesn't this look cheerful?"

They stood back and Delaney had to admit: the flowers, bright against the creamy yellow backdrop of her house, did add an air of festivity.

"Yeah, it looks cheerful," she said.

"Could you sound any *less* cheerful?" Camille put an arm around Delaney's waist and squeezed. "This will pass, Delaney. There are plenty of great guys out there. Jake Rhoades isn't the only bull in the pasture, you know."

Despite her grumpy mood, Delaney chuckled.

"All right. I'm going to get out of here and leave you girls to it."

She wrapped Delaney in a tight hug, kissed her cheek and said, "Keep your chin up."

Inside, Summer and Josie had laid out an impressive spread of cheer on the small dining table. Delaney's spirits lifted at sight of the wine, chocolate chip cookies, chocolate bars, pretzels, candy and gossip magazines. Tears sprung to her eyes yet again, and she bit down hard on her lower lip to keep them from flowing freely.

"How did you guys escape your husbands on a weekend?" she asked.

"Paul had an overtime deal he had to do," Josie said, "and I called and begged Derek to let Summer come for just an hour or two."

"He wasn't happy about me skipping out on family day," Summer said. "But I put in a movie and the kids went into zombie mode. That helped a bit."

"Well, thanks for coming over," Delaney said. "Nothing like friends, wine, chocolate and junk food to mend a broken heart."

"We brought a movie, too," Summer said, holding up a copy of "Thelma and Louise."

Delaney couldn't stop it this time: she began crying in earnest. Her body shook with sobs. She sat down at the table, put her head down on her arms and kept on crying. For a full second, no one spoke. Delaney would have found the situation entertaining if she weren't in the midst of a full crying jag. Then Summer and Josie seemed to break out of their collective trance. They rubbed Delaney's back and stroked her hair.

"Men are scum," Josie said.

"Yeah," Summer added. "Total scum."

"He wasn't that great anyway," Josie said. "I mean, he was always wearing a worn-out t-shirt."

"Yeah," Summer said slowly. "And boots. Does he think he's a cowboy, or something?"

Delaney wailed. "That's what made him so sexy!"

She could feel her friends exchanging a glance and a shrug. They changed direction.

"You don't need a man right now, anyway," Summer said. "You need to concentrate on your new job."

"New jobs take a lot of concentration," Josie agreed. Delaney could feel her nodding.

"You're doing that thing," Delaney said. She sniffled as she moved away from them and filled a bowl with popcorn. "You're nodding, which means you don't really believe what you're saying. You're nodding so we'll nod, too, and then maybe what you say will be true."

She wiped her nose. Summer walked into the living room and put the movie in the DVD player. "All right, Dee," she said. "That's enough. We didn't come here to watch you pout, we came here to help you feel better. And the only way that's going to happen is if we eat this junk food, drink the wine and watch the movie."

"But they *die* at the end," Delaney shouted. "They commit *suicide*! That is *so* not healing!"

Josie sniggered, but stopped short when Summer shot daggers at her.

"It's about friendship, Dee," she said. "Now bring your popcorn and come sit. Josie, get the wine flowing."

Delaney and Josie obeyed. As the previews played, the three of them settled onto the couch.

"Don't you guys think I should call Jake?" Delaney asked. "I mean, just to get some closure?"

"Men are scum," Josie said again. "You just need to let him go."

Summer nodded. "I thought he was really great, too, Dee, but we were wrong. Josie and I agreed we need to be much more guarded when it comes to your heart. You looked so happy with him, and he with you, that we thought you could go full-out. Full throttle. Whatever you want to call it. But we realized we jumped the gun."

"But it just doesn't seem right," Delaney said. "I mean, he wouldn't just show up at the rodeo dance with another girl, knowing I was going to be there, if there wasn't some explanation."

"Or, he would," Josie said. "Maybe it was his way of breaking it off because it was getting too serious. He thought he wouldn't have to actually have the conversation with you if you caught him with another woman."

"That stings."

"I repeat: men are scum. How many times do I have to say it?"

"But I have to know *why*," Delaney said. Her voice bordered on whiny, but she didn't care. "There has to be a reason."

Summer put a hand on Delaney's. "People can't always give a reason, Dee. You know I believe everything happens for a reason, but it's usually a reason defined by the Universe."

Josie stifled a giggle. Delaney rolled her eyes.

"Dee, we think the Universe is telling you that you should never talk to him again," Josie said. "And we accept responsibility for selecting a scumbag."

Summer nodded. "The Dating Intervention resumes this Thursday. Take a break for a few days."

She motioned to the table. "Have some wine. Eat some junk food. Watch the movie."

"Wait," Delaney said. "There's something I need to tell you."

"You had sex with him," Josie said, turning toward Delaney, her eyes narrowed.

"No!" Delaney said. "It's not about that."

"You didn't actually lose your phone," Summer said. "And you didn't want to tell us. So you've been sexting with leads you gathered on your FindLove profile page."

"No!" Delaney said again. "It's about my job."

"Your job?" Josie said. "Isn't it going well?"

"It is now," Delaney said. "But it's about something that happened before I left Phoenix."

Summer and Josie looked at each other, and then back at Delaney.

"Does this have something to do with the reason you've worked at Rowdy's for years?" Summer said.

"Yes," Delaney said. "It does."

She was surprised to hear the strength in her own voice as she told them about Howie. She told them the story of their friendship developing, through chats and recipes and books. Her voice wavered a little as she shared with them—finally—the events that led up to her quitting her job at the Desert Veterinary Clinic, and swearing off her career right then and there.

On that last visit, Howie brought Max in because he thought Max was depressed. He was laying around the house all day. He wasn't eating. He wasn't drinking. He didn't want to get in the car to go to chess club. Delaney, believing it was just another visit, delayed going into Max's exam room to stop and talk to the firefighter with the chocolate lab. Then she heard Howie's yells. The frantic tone of his voice. She stood up quickly and ran into exam room five. Max had collapsed. He lay on the floor, his tongue lolling out. Howie lay next to him, sobbing, calling his name over and over.

Delaney and the clinic's owner, Doctor Stanley Wicker, lifted Max onto the exam table and realized it was too late. Max was dead.

Although Delaney tried to comfort Howie, he was inconsolable. She drove him home and heated up some leftover soup he had in the fridge. She'd never been to his house before, and she saw signs of Max—and Howie's love for the dog—everywhere: he had a bed in the living room, the kitchen, and Howie's bedroom. He had a basket of toys next to the fireplace, and more strewn throughout the home. Framed pictures of the dog sat on the mantle, next to photos of Shirley, Shirley and Howie, and their children and grandchildren.

The English bulldog statue Delaney had given Howie sat on the mantle, too.

Howie slurped his soup without speaking, and Delaney, thinking he may need some alone time, left with a promise to check in within a couple of days.

Only, two days later, Howie died.

Sometime that afternoon, Delaney did call, and when he didn't answer, she figured he was busy and would call back.

But he didn't.

And then, the next day, Joe, a member of his chess club called Desert Veterinary Clinic to report that he had died. When he didn't show up for the weekly chess tournament, his friends worried. They called the police, who found Howie dead in his bed.

And Delaney, listening to Joe's gravely voice on the other end of the line, thought, *It's my fault.*

"Wow," Summer said, her voice a near-whisper.

"I had no idea," Josie said. "Why didn't you tell us?"

They'd both come to sit right next to Delaney on the couch, and were holding her hands.

Delaney shook her head. "Because I couldn't. I couldn't forgive myself. And if I couldn't forgive myself, how could you two forgive me? I didn't even go to his funeral because I was afraid his kids would blame me."

"Oh, honey," Summer said, leaning her head against Delaney's. "You couldn't have known the dog was near death. And it was probably Howie's time to go, too. Eighty-four? That's a good, long life."

"I know," Delaney said. "I know it is. Anyway, I just felt like I needed to share that. I haven't told anyone the whole story. Ever."

"Why now?" Summer said.

"You know," Delaney said. "I don't know. I guess, during the time I've worked with Dr. Rick, I've started the process of forgiving myself. I'm a decent veterinarian. I still love animals. And I do still feel some guilt about Howie. I think it may take a little time, but you're right: with his wife passing a few months before, and then Max, it was probably just his time."

Delaney still felt deeply sad about the series of events that led to Howie's death, but she understood now that they weren't her fault. And that understanding, Delaney thought, meant she was an important step closer to becoming the person she was meant to be.

Josie sighed. "You're a good person, Delaney Collins."

"I know," Delaney said. "I really am."

CHAPTER THIRTY-NINE

"How was your weekend, Doc?" Doctor Kat asked, even as she pored over a complicated-looking financial spreadsheet at her desk, using a bright green John Deere ruler to go through the numbers.

"How was *your* weekend?" Delaney asked.

"Real good." She paused and looked up from her spreadsheet. "Real good. How was your weekend, Doc?"

"Seriously?" Delaney said.

A long pause, then Doctor Kat spun her chair around to face Delaney's, and slapped her wide hands on her thighs. "Yep. Seriously."

She leaned forward, looked into Delaney's eyes and repeated each word slowly. "How. Was. Your. Weekend?"

Delaney rolled her eyes. "I don't want to talk about it."

"Yes, you do." She turned back to her desk, picked up the ruler.

"No, I don't. By the way, I need to run out for a bit today to get a new phone. Is that all right?"

Doctor Kat's body froze. "New phone?"

Delaney rolled her eyes again.

"Yep. New phone. I lost mine Saturday night. Store was closed yesterday. Ergo, I need to get a new phone today."

"Rodeo dance?"

This was the second time Delaney's new boss knew something about Delaney's life she didn't have any reason to know. A few weeks ago, she'd known when Delaney and Jake went out … and now she knew Delaney had gone to the rodeo dance.

"How'd you know?"

Doctor Kat turned around again and regarded Delaney over the tops of her reading glasses, eyebrows raised. In a very snooty voice, she answered, "I guess you don't know Jake as well as you thought you did, Doc Collins. But if you're so riled up about him that your weekend was shit, may I strongly suggest you go get that new phone now and call him on it."

"I'm never speaking to him again!" Delaney said. Then, after a pause, she said, "Wait. How do you know this is about Jake? How do you always know what's going on?"

"I repeat: go get yourself a new phone, woman. See you in thirty."

"But I don't *want* to know!" Delaney said, knowing even as she spoke that this wasn't really an appropriate conversation to be having with her boss. But wasn't it Doctor Kat who'd brought up bars and drinking during their first interview? "I don't want to know where I fell short, what I said wrong. I don't want to know if I walked around with a toilet seat cover hanging out the back of my skirt, or, worse, if I was just too boring!"

It was a lie, of course. She did want to know. Desperately.

"Not funny," Delaney said when she saw the humor hovering around her boss's mouth.

"It is, actually, to see you so wound up."

Delaney didn't answer.

"Well, get to it. You have an hour until your first patient. Get out of here. Go get your new phone."

Delaney got up and stomped out of the office. She thought she heard Doctor Kat snicker, but she ignored it.

THE PHONE STORE squatted at the opposite end of town, a low stucco building next to a nail salon. Somebody apparently had a tough time deciding what color to paint the building and decided on a bland non-color that blended in with the dead grass on the hillside behind it.

What did Doctor Kat mean when she said Delaney didn't know Jake as well as she thought she did? Did she know something Delaney didn't know?

The idea of calling Jake horrified her. Mortified, more like. Something in the deep recesses of her mind told her she *should* call him. But what was she supposed to say? It had only been thirty-six hours, but for the past few weeks they hadn't gone more than thirty-six minutes without talking or texting.

Delaney pulled into a narrow parking spot and rubbed her hands over her face, hoping to do something about the blotchiness she'd caused by crying while belting out sappy love songs with the easy listening station. She dragged herself out of the car and into the store, where she blinked as her eyes adjusted to the cavelike darkness.

"Wow. You look like death."

She recognized the voice instantly. Mitchell. Why did he keep popping up everywhere? He was like that stupid gnome that showed up in everybody's vacation pictures. Only not nearly as cute.

"Thanks," Delaney said.

"Are you okay?"

Why hadn't she ever noticed the hair sprouting from his nose? Or maybe he'd trimmed it the few times they'd dated.

"I'm fine," she snapped, then she softened and added, "Thanks."

"What do you need?"

"I didn't know you worked here. I thought you were a waiter."

His eyes darted to the left, then back to meet hers. "Just started."

She glanced at his name tag. *Mitch. Team member for 4 years.*

When she looked at his face again, he shrugged. "Off and on. Just started back up again."

Looking at Mitchell now, she had serious doubts about his claim that he'd finished law school. Not only that, but she also wondered what she'd seen in him. It wasn't that he worked in a cell phone store (that was one thing, but lying about it was a whole different thing). It was his bearing, his aura. He didn't have any of the confidence or charm she'd imagined him having.

And then it hit her: Mitch reflected the person she used to be. She'd seen in him what she wanted to see.

What about Jake, then? He hadn't lied to her. He *was* confident and charming. And maybe there was still hope.

Delaney reminded herself that Summer and Josie said it was over and that she shouldn't call him. Although she didn't blame the girls (they didn't know Jake like she did – or like she thought she did – and he'd definitely been too close for comfort with that girl at the rodeo dance), she wanted closure. Or did she? What if she confronted him and he said something like, "I've been meaning to tell you, Delaney, I'm taking you off the roster." *Or, what if he kisses me senseless and tells me everything's perfectly fine?* She could practically feel his lips, his sexy stubble, his hands on her face.

"Delaney?"

Mitchell.

"Hm. Okay. Well, I need a new phone. I lost mine."

She watched him walk back to the stock room and for the first time noticed the bald spot and comb-over. Why didn't she see it before? It wasn't a deal breaker, but it usually knocked a couple points off the rubric.

Was she having a transformation? Finally? Had The Dating Intervention removed the veritable and apparently semi-permanent beer goggles she'd sported for the past several years? Not that she was drinking all the time. But the concept was the same.

Was she finally seeing things as they really were? Or had she become more critical than ever? Or, *drumroll, please,* was she just finally learning to listen to her intuition? A few minutes later, having noticed Mitchell's clammy hands and his irritating habit of scratching his nose at the end of every sentence, Delaney walked out of the store with her new phone. Mitchell had offered to turn it on and set it up for her, but she'd declined.

"I've got to get back to work."

"Rowdy's opens this early?"

Delaney noticed a flash of disappointment in his eyes when she said, "I got a job as a vet."

Once she got in the car, the internal debate continued. Doctor Kat had given her an hour, and only half of that had passed. She had plenty of time to call Jake. Or maybe she should just stop by. His face would tell the real story.

He'd shown her the *hockey* movie. Didn't that mean something?

She had to know.

She slammed the car into reverse, backed up wildly and hit the light pole between the parking lot and the sidewalk.

"Shit. Shit, shit, shit."

Instead of getting out to survey the damage (it was done, anyway, wasn't it?), she cranked up the radio to blast Shania Twain's "Man! I Feel Like a Woman!" and drove straight downtown, where she parked, tires screeching, along the curb below Jake's apartment building.

MOST OF DOWNTOWN Juniper's shops opened at ten or eleven, so it was still quiet. Nevertheless, a few people craned their necks when they heard Delaney's car pull up at the curb in front of Jake's apartment building. Not to be deterred from her mission, she got out and marched the half-block to the alley. When she began to stomp toward the metal staircase leading up to Jake's front door, though, she stopped mid-stride.

The girl, the lanky, silky, model-pretty girl who'd been giggling so heartily with Jake at the rodeo dance, was coming down the stairs. In pajama bottoms and a sweatshirt. Was it Brittany? In a split-second, Delaney noticed the girl still looked pretty – no, *hot* – even in her pajamas. The girl noticed Delaney, too, and she paused at the bottom of the stairs.

It wasn't a full halt like Delaney's, but a contemplative break in her graceful descent. Like she was comfortable. Confident. Worse, her perfect mouth was spreading into a smirk. One with some classified information behind it.

Delaney measured her options carefully. Should she turn around, get back in her car and drive off a cliff like Thelma and Louise? Should she drive back to work and act like she'd never been here? Should she walk up to the dream girl and confront her? Punch her in the face? Or march right up the stairs and have a word with the man himself, who was probably just now lounging naked in bed waiting for his lover to return from a coffee run?

Before she could decide, the girl spoke. "Delaney, right?"

I could still run.

But then she imagined the girl going back up to the apartment, sliding between the sheets with Jake and murmuring that she'd just seen Delaney outside.

Delaney nodded and noticed her mouth was hanging open.

"Finally! I'm just going for some coffee, want to join me?"

I knew it! A coffee run!

Delaney shook her head, snapped out of it. "No, thank you. I really don't want any coffee."

But now what? Delaney searched her mind frantically for a scathing line about leaving the apartment in pajamas, or sex hair at the coffee shop. But she came up dry.

"Okay, then," the girl said. "Well, Jakey's upstairs. Still in bed. You know how he is. But I'm sure he'd love to see you. Goodness knows he's been talking about you nonstop."

She pulled her hair over one shoulder and began braiding it.

"He has?"

The girl rolled her eyes with what Delaney could tell was mock exasperation. "God, yes. Can't get him to shut up about you, frankly. It's so nice to finally put a face to the name. I mean, usually, he doesn't say anything about the women he's dating."

Delaney felt her jaw drop open again. Before she had the chance to think of anything clever to say (or to ask, like, "Are there lots of other women?") she heard Jake's voice.

"Jenny! Who are you talking to *now*? I need my coffee, woman!"

She couldn't quite see Jake from where she stood, but Delaney could picture him: bare feet, pajama pants and naked, chiseled torso. It took almost every ounce of her self-restraint to keep from pushing past this skinny Jenny girl and running up the stairs to touch his skin. Then she remembered she still hadn't solved the mystery of whom, exactly, this skinny Jenny girl was.

"I'm just chatting with your girlfriend, Jakey," Jenny said in a cheerful voice. "She just stopped by for some – well, what did you stop by for?"

Again, Delaney stared at her, at a loss for words. "I, uh –"

"Say no more," Jenny said.

"She stopped by for some morning nookie, Jakey."

Delaney's eyes met the girl's, which were sparkling with mischief. From his spot at the top of the stairs, Jake laughed. The sound made Delaney weak with desire. Then, Jenny laughed, too, and the pieces started to click into place.

How had she not noticed this girl had the Rhoades eyes? The laugh – a sound like a wind chime – was almost identical.

"You're one of Jake's sisters."

Jenny stopped laughing. Jake laughed louder.

"You mean, he didn't tell you I was his sister?"

Delaney shook her head, speechless. Jenny looked quite amused, and Delaney felt like a complete idiot for not having figured out the connection sooner. Of course. Of *course*! They had the same honey-colored skin, the same straw-colored hair. At the rodeo dance, he acted affectionate, not flirtatious.

Delaney heard Jake making his way down the stairs. The heat rose in her face. Of course it was his sister. Her intuition had been right. He *did* care about her. He *wouldn't* just show up at the rodeo dance with someone else, especially knowing she was going to be there.

Then he was in front of her, exactly as she'd imagined him a few moments earlier, only even more delicious-looking. Bare feet, pajama pants low on his hips and his gorgeous stomach. She felt a little bit of drool at the corner of her mouth, and wiped it off with the back of her hand.

Jenny and Jake stood facing Delaney, side by side. Arms crossed, blue eyes delighted. Jenny elbowed Jake. He winced.

"Delaney, this is my sister, Caboose."

She elbowed him again.

"I mean, Jenny. She's the youngest, so –"

"—So they all insist on calling me Caboose. But seriously, it's really nice to meet you. I caught a glimpse of you at the rodeo dance but then you disappeared. We texted you Sunday morning, but when you didn't answer, Jake said you must be busy. I told him to keep texting but he didn't want to. He said he didn't want to bug you, but I could tell he was getting nervous."

"Was not," Jake said. For the first time, Delaney wondered what Jake must have been thinking, not hearing from her all of Sunday. Even now, his eyes were searching hers, and she had to admit, he looked a bit wary.

"Were too," Jenny said. "But anyway, I'll let you two chat. I'm going to get coffee. Want anything, Delaney?" Delaney shook her head, and Jenny said, "Okay. Back in ten. Nice to meet you, Delaney."

Relief shot through Delaney's veins as Jenny walked away.

"Well, she seems nice," Delaney said into the silence that followed.

"Yeah, if you want to call it that," Jake said.

He ran a hand through his hair. Delaney wanted to run her hands over the skin on his bare torso, so she clasped them behind her back.

"I thought you came to the rodeo dance with someone else," she blurted out.

"I thought you decided you didn't want to see me anymore," Jake said.

"Well, you didn't tell me she was your *sister*!"

"I didn't get a chance," Jake said, his voice rising. "Jenny's like one of those firecrackers. Once you light them, they fly around like crazy until they burn out. She came tearing into town Saturday to surprise us for her twenty-first birthday. She wanted to go to the rodeo dance, and she was even more excited when I told her you'd be there. Before I knew it, it was late, you were gone and you weren't answering my texts."

Delaney cringed. "Lost my phone. Outhouse."

"Really?" Jake said. The mood lightened a bit.

"Really. Just got a new one." She hitched a thumb at her car. "Haven't even turned it on yet."

"So you didn't get any of my messages?"

"Not since Saturday afternoon."

"The ones on Saturday night said stuff like, 'come over here and meet my sister so she can finally stop harassing me about meeting you,' and, 'are you ignoring me?' and stuff like that."

Delaney shifted her weight and scratched her head. "Why didn't you just come over and introduce us?"

"I was nervous."

"Jake Rhoades the Dreamy, breaker of many hearts, nervous?"

"Yes, I was nervous." Jake said. "Saturday morning, I mentioned your name to Jenny – a first, I guess. I didn't realize that, but she apparently keeps careful track of how I talk about the women I date."

He ran a hand over the back of his head and continued. "Anyway, I mentioned your name and she made this huge deal of it, all day. Said she couldn't wait to meet you. So when I saw you at the dance, I pretended you weren't there. I knew she'd say something to embarrass me, and *you*. I didn't want you to leave, thinking I was an idiot. Shot myself in the foot, though, didn't I? Because you thought I was there with someone else! I guess I *am* an idiot."

He'd dropped his hands at his sides. He was still nervous, Delaney realized with some interest. He was nervous because he liked her. He wanted to be with her.

"I'm feeling all warm and fuzzy right now," she said. She felt the smile spreading across her face.

"You are? You don't think I'm an idiot?"

"Well, I do, a little. I mean, of course I'd have wanted to meet your sister, and of course I wouldn't have held her antics against you. I know how siblings can be."

He shrugged. "So, we're okay?"

"We're better than okay," Delaney said, stepping forward and putting her arms around his waist.

He took her face in his hands and tilted it up for a kiss.

"Aw, get a room, you two!"

Jenny's voice echoed down the alley, and Jake deepened the kiss before releasing Delaney, who stood there trembling with the desire to rip his pajama pants off. *Shouldn't be too hard. They're pretty thin.*

As if he could read her mind, Jake retied his waistband.

"Want me to stand in for you at work so you guys can stay here and have it out?" she asked with a wicked gleam in her eyes.

"Ah, no. Thanks. I've got to get back. Doctor Kat's waiting for me."

"Oh, speaking of Doctor Kat, there's something I need to tell you," Jake said.

Jake looked down at the ground and rubbed the back of his neck with one hand.

"Well, that's my cue," Jenny said. She handed Jake his coffee. "It was nice to finally meet you, Delaney. I couldn't have taken the suspense for much longer. Jakey blushes like a teenage girl every time he talks about you. I had to see you for myself."

Jake rolled his eyes as she bounded up the stairs.

"So? What'd you need to tell me?" Delaney asked. Just when she started feeling calm, nerves returned and her heart started racing.

"Doctor Rick, your new boss?"

"She's your wife," Delaney said.

"No!" Jake said.

Delaney started to relax. "She's one of my best friends, though. When you told me you were applying for vet jobs and you mentioned her clinic, I told her she had to hire you."

"What?"

He hung his head, sheepish.

"I thought you had spunk. Kat'd like that. I figured you must be smart. I've seen you work the bar at Rowdy's a hundred times. You were really good. Quick. Great under pressure. Terrific, actually."

"A hundred times?" Delaney was shocked. She felt her head tilting to the side as she searched her Rowdy's memories for visions of Jake. Surely she'd have noticed him. "Why haven't I seen *you* there a hundred times?"

Jake shrugged. "I had a crush on you. So I was shy. I stayed in the back. And you were always flirting with people. I knew you wouldn't take me seriously if I tried to hit on you at the bar, of all places. And then when I stopped after that car accident and saw that it was you, I took a chance."

"Oh, my God." Delaney slapped a hand to her forehead. "This is a comedy of errors."

A sudden realization struck her. "Wait a minute," she said, putting her hands on her hips. "It's all coming together. You saw me with Mitchell at Eddie's, didn't you? Out your window." She pointed up at the window and could have sworn she saw Jenny jump away from it. "And you told Doctor Kat. You told her I had a date with someone else."

Jake grimaced. "Mitchell? He's the puppy-dog-eyed, dopey-faced, frowning guy who looked like all he wanted to do was die, right there at the table?" He slapped his hand to his forehead. "He's the guy you hit it off with? Thank goodness the sparks died out."

Now she was laughing. "Yes! But that's beside the point! You were spying on me. And you didn't even tell me!"

"I wasn't spying, exactly. I just happened to see you. And wonder who that dumpy-looking guy was. That's all."

"And then you told my new boss about it?" She shook her head, incredulous.

"Well, I was thinking of her more as my best friend from high school, to whom I turn for answers to all questions pertaining to the ladies. But yes."

Delaney covered her face with her hands, then dropped them. She said, "Well, since we're having a confessional, I have something to tell you, too."

"You're married with nine kids at home."

"Ha. No. I should have told you this on one of our other dates," Delaney began. "But I was embarrassed. And sworn to secrecy."

"I'm intrigued."

"A few weeks ago, my friends, Summer and Josie, staged an intervention. The Dating Intervention."

"Are you kidding?" he said, his reaction guarded.

"Nope." She winced.

Now his face transformed. "Why? Are you an addict?"

"Well," she said, paused and then plowed ahead. "Remember I told you I'd entitled my own dating life, 'eclectic clearance'?"

"Yeah," he said, drawing the word out.

"So Summer and Josie decided they'd had enough of me finding crappy guys and then sticking with them despite no prospects for a healthy long-term relationship. I think they'd also decided they'd had enough of me dating two or three guys at a time, all the time. Maybe they couldn't keep them all straight, I don't know. In any event, they took control of my love life. I mean, I agreed, but it was their idea. So they created my profile on FindLove.com, and they sent me to a speed dating event where they wired me and gave me instructions as I talked to different people."

"How'd that go?"

"It was a disaster. Instead of coaching me, like they'd promised, they ended up making fun of the people I was talking to, in my ear, the whole time."

"Meddlesome friends," Jake said.

"I know. I know. They do it out of love. In fact, Rule Eight is something like, 'Remember we love you.'"

"So anyway, they selected you for me on FindLove.com without even knowing who you were. I mean, obviously, I wouldn't have known since you used a different name and didn't post a picture. But I wanted you to know. They had me date a couple other people, and they selected you as their Number One Pick."

"I'm honored," he said. "But was I *your* Number One Pick, also?"

"Like I told you, I've been thinking about you since you came to my rescue at Highway Twenty-Three and Pinecone."

"With all those kids."

"Great kids, but not mine," they said at the same time.

"So anyway," she continued, "they've been coaching me all along. They've been telling me what to do. I didn't want to tell you because most of this has been their idea. Actually, I'm pretty sure not telling you was one of the rules. I like you, and you're totally my Number One Pick, but I'm not sure if I'd have acted the same way if they hadn't been looking over my shoulder the whole time."

"What about that message you sent me after The Teeter Totter?"

"They were so pissed about that. That is totally something I would normally do. Stupid, but true."

"So you meant it?"

"Every word."

Jake chuckled. "So if you're normally a two-or-three-at-a-time type of girl, then who else received messages?"

Feeling a little less embarrassed, Delaney related the stories of Jesse the Rancher and Craig the Kindergarten teacher. She even threw in a tiny tidbit about Mitchell.

"Online dating is brutal," Jake said. "I admit, I never expected you to be on FindLove.com. I looked for you on there, actually, right after we met. I even searched FriendZoo, but was too afraid to make a friend request when I found you. So when you messaged me there, I thought it was funny."

"So *that's* why you didn't say anything!"

"Caught."

After a beat, she asked, "So you're not mad? About The Dating Intervention? Summer and Josie know pretty much everything. They're the ones who've been sending you messages."

"Nah," he said. "I have a whole bunch of sisters, remember? So I know how women work. Besides, they weren't actually with us when we were out."

"Well…" Delaney started to pace. "They spied on us. Twice."

"You're kidding."

"Nope."

Seconds ticked by. Neither of them said anything. Delaney continued her pacing at an increased speed. Jake came up behind her and wrapped his arms around her waist. He kissed the back of her neck.

"Meddlesome friends," he said again. "But it's cute. They obviously just want the best for you."

She turned to face him and tilted her head back so she could kiss him.

"Obviously," she said.

"So, are *you* mad? That I told Kathryn to hire you?"

"I don't know," Delaney answered. "Honestly, I thought she'd hired me because I have potential. But regardless, she hired me and I'm grateful for the job. I think I've proven myself, at this point. So I guess I'm not mad."

"Oh, good," Jake said, "because I'd hate to have to earn your forgiveness."

"On second thought, maybe I am mad. But I've got to get back to work. You'll have to earn my forgiveness later. I'm not letting you off the hook."

Jake shrugged, kissed Delaney one more time, then pointed at her phone and walked back up the stairs to his apartment. Grinning, Delaney walked back to her car. As she drove back to work, still smiling, her phone chirped.

Jake: *Want to go steady?*

She was going to be grinning all day.

Delaney: *You bet I do.*

CHAPTER FORTY

"I take it from that stupid smile you've got on your face," Doctor Kat said, "that you talked to Jake."

Delaney nodded, but didn't look up from the chart she was studying. Doctor Kat chuckled and turned to walk away.

"So why didn't you tell me you knew Jake?" Delaney said to her back. "More importantly, why didn't you tell me he was the reason you hired me?"

Doctor Kat froze, then turned around.

"I guess I just didn't want you to know I'd hired you because he told me to," Doctor Kat said. "I mean, I trust his judgment, so I figured you'd work out."

"Would you have hired me if he hadn't told you to?"

Doctor Kat looked paused. "Okay, no. I wouldn't have. I mean, you graduated vet school and you had a little experience. But c'mon, Doc. It's weird you've worked at a bar for so long. Right? Six years or something? Eight?"

"Right," Delaney said.

"Don't get all huffy. I'm serious."

"Well thanks for hiring me, anyway."

"You're welcome," Doctor Kat said. "I get a kick out of you, that's for sure. And it's been fun hassling you about your love life on Jake's account. You know, he must be real interested if he's having me pester you about it."

That was good to hear.

"And you're real interested in him, too. I can tell. You guys make a cute couple. Now stop grinning like the coyote that raided the hen house and get this dog back in the crate."

"Am I grinning?" An embarrassed heat marched its way up Delaney's neck and spread to her face.

Doctor Kat rolled her eyes.

"Are we a couple?" asked Delaney.

"Are you?" When Delaney stared blankly at her, Doctor Kat went on: "I'll just say this, Doc Collins. I saw Jake the other night, after the two of you went sledding all morning. He came over to help my husband with some foaling. He couldn't stop grinning. That same stupid grin you're wearing now. If you're not a couple yet, you should be. And if you don't take that advice, you're missing out. Let's go. We've got a surgery in five."

From her purse, which was stuffed into the cabinet on the wall, Delaney's phone chirped. She put the chart on her desk, dug out her phone and felt a rush of pleasure when she read Josie's text:

I got it. Next year, I'll officially be Principal Garcia. Bow down. Oh, and thanks, ladies. Wouldn't have done it without you Literally.

Summer: *Way to rock it, Josie. We knew you could do it, didn't we, D?*

Quickly, Delaney typed back: *We did. Congrats, Josie. I mean, Principal Garcia. Can I call an emergency Happy Hour tonight?*

Josie: *Everything ok?*

Delaney: *Everything's great. See you at 6?*

Summer: *See you then.*

BENJAMIN GREETED Delaney when she walked into Rowdy's that evening.

"Hey, Dee, which side of the bar are you on tonight?"

For the first time since she'd stopped working at Rowdy's, felt a rush of relief. She really hadn't enjoyed it … but she'd never been brave enough to look forward to doing anything else.

"Emergency Happy Hour with the girls."

"A Guinness, a water and a vodka cranberry," Benjamin said. "Coming up."

Delaney slid onto a stool at the usual table. The place was mostly empty. A man sat at the bar, his elbows up on the counter, his head in his hands, an empty brandy snifter in front of him. *Just a few short weeks ago, I would have ended up taking him home.* She shuddered.

From the doorway, a voice called, "Collins. I want to see you in my office, now. The *Principal's* office."

Delaney giggled, then jumped up to hug Josie. Summer, in her usual fashion, breezed in next and joined them in a group hug.

"So what's this emergency Happy Hour all about?" Summer asked as Benjamin put their drinks on the table.

"Jake and I are going steady," Delaney answered.

Her friends looked at her, stunned.

"But –" Summer said.

"The girl –" Josie said at the same time.

"It was his sister!" Delaney said. "I met her this morning."

She explained everything: how she'd missed Jake's texts when she lost her phone, how she'd wanted – no, needed – closure, and how she'd shown up at his apartment, met his sister and accepted his invitation to go steady.

"The thing is," she finished, "I never would have had the confidence to seek that closure if it weren't for you guys."

"Don't go getting all emotional on me," Josie said. "Please."

Summer wiped a tear from her eye with the corner of her bar napkin.

"Seriously," she said.

CHAPTER FORTY-ONE

Delaney's bedside clock read five a.m. when her phone chirped Friday morning. After an initial bout of panic (was her mom texting to say something had happened to her dad? Was Summer having problems with the pregnancy? Had something happened to one of the kids?) she felt happiness flood her veins as she read Jake's message: *TGIF. I'm getting started early. Want to come over to the gallery after work and help me paint? I promise it'll be romantic.*

Still smiling, she wrote back: *Sure! See you around 5:30. :) PS-how could it not be romantic?*

Jake: *Have a great day. xo*

Delaney: *xo*

She spent the next hour daydreaming about making love to Jake in an empty art gallery, then got up to drink coffee, shower and head to work.

As advertised, Jake made the gallery setting romantic. He draped huge white tarps from the ceiling to cover the windows and placed candles in sturdy copper candlesticks on the floor around the room's perimeter. In the center of the gallery, he set up a little card table. A pizza and a bottle of wine sat on top of it, alongside a red rose in a vase.

"This *is* romantic," Delaney said.

"I figured you're coming to help me," he said, taking her hand and walking with her. "I might as well feed you."

Looking around, she said, "This is going to be a beautiful gallery space. The high ceilings, the tall windows. I can't wait to see your work in here."

"Me, too," Jake said. "Now let's eat. Because I do plan on making you work."

"Don't you have electricity yet?"

"Yeah, why? Oh, the candles. Yes, I just wanted to, you know, set the scene. For romance."

She laughed, and he said, "We'll turn on the lights after we eat."

"Are you sure drinking wine is a good idea?" Delaney asked as Jake put slices of pizza onto paper towels and pushed one toward her.

"Why not?" He shrugged. "I'm an artist, remember?"

She took a sip of the wine he'd poured into a plastic cup. "I'm not, though."

"But you work with your hands." He winked.

Delaney looked around at the gallery space. The shiny concrete floors and visible ductwork gave it utilitarian feel, which would contrast nicely with Jake's nature-inspired work. She looked forward to seeing how it looked during the day, with sunlight pouring in through the floor-to-ceiling windows.

"Ready for the big reveal?" Jake asked a few minutes later, as they gathered their trash into a bag.

"That's what I've been waiting for," Delaney said.

"This is for the back wall," he said, prying the lid off a paint can to reveal a warm, brick red color.

She clapped her hands together. "Love it. It's perfect."

Together, they stretched a tarp out on the floor, then set up their supplies. Jake plugged his phone into his stereo speakers and put on something acoustic and soothing. They began painting, Jake cutting in on the edges with a brush, and Delaney rolling the center.

An hour later, they stood in the middle of the room, checking for streaks and spots where the paint was thin. Jake draped his arm around Delaney's shoulders. She sighed, content. Even though she was exhausted, her body was buzzing with energy. She wasn't going to pretend she didn't know what it was. She wanted Jake Rhoades, in her bed. Naked. Sweaty. On top of her.

"We make a good team," Jake said, halting her fantasy just as it was getting good.

"Oh, yeah. We sure do," Delaney said. She wondered if he could hear her thoughts.

"Thanks for coming with me tonight," he said.

"Thank you for inviting me," she said. "Want to come over for a bit? A night cap?"

"I wouldn't turn down some coffee," he said.

A few moments later, they arrived at Delaney's house. While the coffee brewed, Delaney set mugs, creamer and a sugar bowl on a tray. As she carried the tray into the living room, she noticed Jake had abandoned his boots on the floor in the middle of the walkway. It was nice, she thought, having a man's boots in her living room. She actually enjoyed pushing those boots out of the way with her sock-clad foot, and seeing his jacket hanging over the back of a dining room chair. They were small things, she knew. But they felt comfortable. She realized this was the first time she hadn't felt like a man was preparing to pack up and hit the road at the first possible opportunity.

Jake had stretched out on the couch, and she thought he'd fallen asleep. She set the tray on the coffee table, careful not to make any noise.

"Come here," Jake said.

He pulled her down on top of him, and she propped herself up so she could look at him. He tucked a strand of hair behind her ear. Delaney froze for the briefest second when she realized there was a man on her couch and he was looking at her, staring right into her eyes, like he might stay. Not only on the couch, of course, but in her life, too.

"Thanks again for coming with me today," he said. "It was way more fun with you there."

"It was fun. And you're welcome."

"We should shower," he said.

Delaney moaned in response.

"Don't like that idea?"

"I love it," she said.

For half of a split second, Delaney experienced profound relief that she'd spent an entire morning scrubbing her house clean. When Jake ran his hands down her back, over her butt and back up to her shoulders, her insides quivered and she forgot all about her sponge and spray cleaner and led the way to the bathroom. He followed her. The coffee sat, perched on its pretty tray.

Is this really about to happen?

Delaney Collins was about to have sex with Jake Rhodes. Something inside her told her it was going to be delicious. Beyond delicious, like the fresh-baked rolls at the barbecue restaurant.

Fresh-baked rolls? her inner voice demanded. *More like chocolate cake.*

This was going to be different, and she was going to like it. Not just like it, she corrected herself. She'd waited for it for weeks. She was going to love it.

She turned on the shower and from behind, Jake pulled her sweater over her head. She turned around and he pulled her t-shirt off, then unhooked her bra and cupped her breasts. Her body went weak with desire. He moved with such tenderness that she found herself wanting to take her time, to savor every moment.

Could it be like this all the time? Delaney had waited so long for this. Now that it was finally here, she felt like she wanted to burn each image into her mind. She unfastened his belt, unbuttoned his jeans and began pulling down his pants. He removed them completely. Jake pressed his mouth to hers.

"I think it's hot now," she said against his mouth.

"I assure you, it is," he said.

She giggled and pulled him into the shower, feeling a tremendous amount of anticipation and an unfamiliar level of calm. The hot spray massaged her shoulders, her scalp, her back. She could taste the sweat as the water rinsed it clean. All the while, Jake's hands roamed over her bare skin, leaving tingling trails in their wake.

"Soap?" he said.

She handed him the body wash. He poured some into his palm and began rubbing her shoulders and arms. Her knees nearly buckled from pleasure.

"Your turn."

She turned Jake around and worked the body wash into a rich lather on his back. As her hands made their way down to his waist, she reached around and grasped him. After letting her stroke him for a few seconds, he turned back around and said, "A shower's worthless without a good shampoo."

His hands in her hair sent shivers of desire over her skin. She moaned as he kissed her neck while still working his fingertips over her scalp. He tipped her head back for a rinse and caressed her nipples while her eyes were closed.

Weeks. Her body had begged for this for weeks. And now it was finally here.

Again, she groaned. Her entire being pulsed with the deep wanting she'd begun to feel whenever they were close. She craved, more than anything, that intimate contact. Not just skin on skin, but the feeling that a man was invested. Jake moved closer to her, pressing his wet body against hers. Slick and warm, his mouth roamed over her face, her neck and her collarbone. She felt like she might explode.

Maybe I should cool the water off.

His hands were on her hips and she could feel him pressed against her. She wanted him. One little shift of her hips and he'd be inside her. She could almost feel it now, the slow, rhythmic movement.

Without thinking, she reached back and turned the heat down. She felt his smile against her mouth.

"Too hot?" he said.

"You don't even know."

The forecast had been right: sex with Jake Rhoades was absolutely incredible. Mind-blowing. Toe-curling. Delicious. As she basked in the afterglow, snuggled up to a damp Jake on her bed, she wondered why it had taken her so long to find a guy she really, truly liked – and felt attracted to at the same time. This was bliss.

"So, tell me about your grand opening," she said. "What's the plan?"

For a moment, Jake looked nervous. He shrugged.

"Mingle, show people how we painted the walls. Most importantly, I need a beautiful woman. Arm candy. To take the attention off me. Tell me you'll be there."

"Me? Of course I'll be there. I couldn't stay away."

CHAPTER FORTY-TWO

THE MORNING OF JAKE'S GRAND OPENING, DELANEY SAT DOWN AT HER computer, hands shaking. For a few days, she'd contemplated writing a letter to Howie's children, telling them how great their dad was and expressing her condolences. She was torn. Eight years had passed, and this letter would come out of nowhere for them; yet, she felt like she should let them know he'd meant something to her, as a friend.

A couple of days ago, she found them on FriendZoo—two daughters and a son—and noticed they all had the same bright blue eyes their father had. Still, she didn't write.

Then, this morning, she'd made the decision.

DEAR EMILY, George, and Rebecca,

I WAS a friend of your dad's just before he passed away. I'm the veterinarian who treated Max for that last year of his life. I know quite a bit of time has gone by, but I wanted to write to tell you how much I enjoyed getting to know your dad. He spoke about all three of you with such pride, and it was clear just how much he loved you. He was a kind: he wanted me to learn to cook, so he brought me recipes whenever he came to the clinic. He was fun and funny, and I enjoyed his company immensely. I miss him.

I am so sorry I wasn't able to save Max's life, and I am sorry for the loss of your father. I will always remember them, and will be grateful for crossing paths with them.

· · ·

SINCERELY,

DELANEY COLLINS, DVM

JAKE REQUESTED a pre-Grand Opening Happy Hour date at Rowdy's to relax his nerves. Delaney walked down the sidewalk, admiring the blossoms on the trees and the singing of the birds. In her lovesick daze, she didn't even notice someone was standing on the sidewalk outside Rowdy's until she ran right into her.

"Delaney!"

"Beth!"

They hugged and Beth started to ask, "Have you cooked anything—"

But when she got a good look at Delaney's face, she narrowed her eyes and said: "You're glowing. What's going on?"

Smiling, Delaney said, "What? I'm just going to meet someone for Happy Hour. What are you doing here?"

"I'm meeting Josh. We're having dinner next door." She blushed.

"Ah, I see," Delaney said. "How's that going?"

"Great," Beth said. "I mean, *really* great."

Now Delaney could see the goofy smile everyone had been accusing her of wearing. Beth's face shone with pleasure.

"Have you cooked for him?" Delaney asked.

"Yes! But I totally burnt the roasted chicken."

They burst into giggles.

"Have you cooked for the steamy stalker who was staring at you through the window that night? That guy you're obviously smitten with?" Beth said.

"I did. And I made roasted chicken, too. I didn't burn it. But that's only because I was so nervous I had to call in reinforcements."

Just then, Beth waved to someone behind Delaney. A handsome man with dark, curly hair, dazzling light brown eyes and smooth skin the color of coffee with cream put his arms around her waist and kissed her on the mouth.

When they finally broke apart, Beth said, "Josh, meet Delaney, my cooking partner. Delaney, Josh."

"Ah, so you're the woman who taught Beth how to burn a roasted chicken," he said.

Beth elbowed him. "And you're the man who distracted me, causing me to forget to take it out of the oven before it burnt."

Josh winked. Beth laughed and he grabbed her hand.

"We'd better go," Josh said. "Our reservations are in just a few minutes. It was so nice to meet you, Delaney."

"Yes, and maybe next time we'll meet Mister Steamy Stalker," Beth said.

Beth and Delaney hugged again.

"Actually," Delaney said, "you can meet him tonight. If you guys are done with dinner by seven, you could come to the grand opening of his art gallery. It's in that space off of Main Street, where the glass-blowing studio was."

"We'll stop by," Beth said. "Josh can't distract me at a restaurant."

"But I can try," he said, giving Delaney a lascivious wink.

Delaney shook her head as Beth and Josh walked away.

"Smitten, huh?" Jake's voice came from behind her. She jumped.

"Eavesdropping, were you?"

Delaney's heart was beating so fast and hard she thought she might pass out from extreme embarrassment, even as Jake put his hands on her hips and pulled her closer, then kissed her on the nose.

"Couldn't help it. I came to have a beer, and here you were. Please tell me I'm the guy she's referring to as Mister Steamy Stalker."

He kissed her again, on the lips this time. She wondered if he could feel her blushing. Surely the heat radiated off her skin.

"Came to see me, huh?"

"Well, I actually came to see if I could find a beautiful woman to stand next to at my opening tonight, and I lucked out. I think you'll do."

"Perfect. Let's grab that drink."

JAZZ MUSIC PLAYED, wine glasses clinked and conversation flowed. Delaney kept one hand tucked into the crook of Jake's elbow and the other clamped down on a glass of wine.

"Pretty good party, eh?" Jenny whispered in Delaney's ear an hour in. "Jakey always knows how to throw 'em."

"Yeah," Delaney said. "We even got a few strangers off the street."

"Oh, good. Maybe this will be his big start. I can't believe you thought I was his girlfriend."

Jake overheard her and gave her a playful punch on the arm. "Leave her alone, Caboose."

"It's okay, really," Delaney said. "I plead temporary insanity. I was blinded by jealousy."

Jenny shook her head. "That's so cute. All right. I'll leave you alone. I see a prospect over there."

She sauntered off, tossing her hair back over her shoulder, her gaze locked on a curly-haired man in a fleece jacket, jeans and hiking boots. Jake watched her sidle up to him and rolled his eyes.

Beth and Josh, who'd walked in a few minutes before, were now standing off to one side admiring a glass vase. Beth looked over and gave Delaney a little wave. Summer and Josie stood with another pair of women, admiring one of Jake's tables.

Jake put his arm around Delaney's shoulders.

"I'm so relieved," he said. "I was afraid nobody was going to show up. You're really taking the pressure off."

"All you had to do was ask. I wouldn't have it any other way."

CHAPTER FORTY-THREE

It was Thursday afternoon, and Delaney had suggested that they change up Happy Hour this week. She'd invited Summer and Josie to come over for a home-cooked meal. She was cooking one of Howie's recipes, a lasagna, and the smell of garlic and tomato sauce and melted cheese floated through her house. The girls were set to arrive in about ten minutes, and to pass the time while she waited, Delaney opened the FriendZoo app on her phone. It dinged, indicating she had a message.

MESSAGE FROM EMILY White

HOWIE'S DAUGHTER! Delaney hadn't expected a response from Howie's children. After all, she was a stranger to them. She was almost afraid to read it. What if Emily blamed her for her father's death, just like Delaney had blamed herself for years? Curiosity won, though, and Delaney tapped on the screen to view the message.

DEAR DELANEY,

THANK you so much for your kind words. Dad talked a lot about you that last year. He was so fond of you, and said he felt like you were more of an honorary granddaughter than Max's veterinarian. You were a special part of his final year, and we feel so lucky that he had you as a friend. I spoke with George and Rebecca, and they wanted me to thank you, too. So, from the bottom of our hearts, thank you! Your kindness meant a lot to Dad.

WITH LOVE,

EMILY WHITE

SUMMER AND JOSIE walked through the door a few moments later, and Delaney, blinking through tears, immediately noticed the shine in Josie's eyes.

"I have an announcement to make!" Josie said. "I got it. I got the grant. The Juniper Community Center will open six months from now!"

"That's great, Josie," Summer said, and Delaney said, "What great news!"

Josie pulled an envelope out of her purse. "See? Here it is. In writing."

"Let's see it," Delaney said.

Heads together, Delaney and Summer read the first part of the letter aloud: "Dear Mrs. Garcia, Congratulations! You're the recipient of this year's Stronger Communities Grant. Your passion for helping the children in your community stood out to us, and your plan for the Juniper Community Center was detailed, and thoughtful. Enclosed, please find a check for $100,000."

When they read the check amount, both Delaney and Summer dropped the paper on the table.

"One hundred thousand dollars?" they said.

"You didn't tell us it was for that much," Summer said. "Josie, that's—"

"It's wonderful!" Delaney said. "It's amazing. We're so proud of you."

"Thanks, ladies," Josie said. "I didn't tell you because I was afraid I wouldn't get it. You know."

"Actually," Delaney said. "I do know. In fact, there's something I have to tell you."

"Oh, no," Summer said. "Please don't tell us you're pregnant."

Josie put her head in one hand. "Dios mío."

"You guys!" Delaney said. "It's not that. A couple of days ago, I FriendZoo-stalked Howie's kids. They're adults, obviously. And then I wrote them a note, expressing my condolences about their dad's passing. Just now, I heard back from the youngest one, the professional ballerina."

Her friends exchanged a look, and Delaney took a deep breath.

"She said their dad considered me a friend," she said, her voice cracking. "And they thanked me for being his friend during that last year."

"Oh, Delaney," Summer said. "That's such good news. I'm so happy you reached out."

"Me, too," Delaney said. "Me, too."

"We love you, Delaney," Josie said. "You're better than a strawberry shake."

"Now," Summer said. "What's that cooking? It smells delicious and I'm starving."

As they went into the kitchen to dish up, Josie said, "I can't believe you thought your dating system was fail-proof."

"It *was*. Almost."

"Almost isn't the same as fail-proof," Summer said.

"Hey, remember when this whole thing started and you guys told me I was going to be happier than ever?" Delaney said.

"Yes," Summer said. "And that you'd thank us?"

"And worship us?" Josie said.

"Yes," Delaney said.

"Well?" Josie said.

"You were right," Delaney said. "I am happier than ever. Thank you."

"You're so welcome," the girls said, and Josie added, "But do you worship us?"

"I do," Delaney said. "And, it looks like we're all in a really good spot. "Josie, you've got the new job, Summer, your band is totally rockin' it, and I've got Doctor Kat and Jake. Life is pretty good."

"Life is good," Summer and Josie echoed.

"I want to make a toast," Delaney said. "To friends. You guys are the best in the world."

Summer and Josie leaned toward each other.

"We really are," Josie whispered. Summer nodded.

"To friends," they said. "Best friends."

• • •

THE END

TURN the page for a sneak peek at Book Two in the Intervention Series, The Marriage Intervention.

PREVIEW: THE MARRIAGE INTERVENTION

BOOK 2 IN THE INTERVENTION SERIES

CHAPTER ONE

Sharing a secret can bind people together. Keeping one can tear people apart.

Josie Garcia had kept her own secret folded into the recesses of her memory for the past six years. But things change, and recent developments had forced her to begin unwrapping it, revealing it layer by layer until it stood directly in the spotlight.

Now, she turned her secret over and over in her mind as if it were a precious gem.

Rowdy's Saloon buzzed with activity on this Thursday night. College kids in trendy skinny jeans and beanie caps sipped beers with a practiced nonchalance while basketball games played on a half-dozen TV screens above the bar. The after-work crowd trickled in, and men and women in smart suits drank cocktails and ate pub mix, laughing loudly at jokes too inappropriate for water cooler conversation.

When Josie realized her two best friends, Summer Gray and Delaney Collins, were practically boring holes in her with their eyes from their respective spots at their usual high top table, she tucked that gem safely into the back of her mind and smiled, first at Summer and then at Delaney.

"What?" she said, going for casual.

Delaney picked up her beer, but instead of drinking it, she pointed it at Josie.

"What're you thinking about?"

Her offhand tone contrasted the intensity of her stare. Although Josie was tempted to look away, she gazed back at Delaney.

"Nothing," she answered in a tone she hoped matched her friend's.

"You're a terrible liar, Josie," Summer said.

This time, Josie looked down, into the depths of her vodka cranberry. The half-melted ice cubes shifted, catching the twinkling lights draped along the ceiling at Rowdy's. They reminded her of gems, of the secret she wasn't supposed to be thinking about. She sighed.

"I was thinking about Paul," she lied, knowing they'd believe her.

"What about him?" Summer asked.

"Oh, you know." They didn't, so she added, "Just hoping he stays safe tonight."

That, at least, was the truth. As an undercover cop, Paul's evenings often comprised drug deals and takedowns, shifty, knife-wielding felons and thousands of dollars in cash.

Summer reached across the table and put her hand on Josie's arm.

"You know I'm kind of psychic," she said. "My gut says he'll be fine."

Josie smiled at her, but it was half-hearted.

"This is our weekly Happy Hour," she said. "We should be talking about happy things. I know you quit working here, Delaney, but do you think you could go mix me another drink?"

Delaney laughed. "I'm pretty sure it's still against policy, but I'll go up and order you one."

Summer sighed with contentment as she and Josie watched Delaney approach the bar.

"She's so much happier now," she said. "I am so glad The Dating Intervention worked."

"That was a stroke of genius on our part," Josie said, nodding and raising her empty glass in a toast. "It really was."

Summer clinked her water glass against Delaney's. "We should have taken over her life years ago."

"Definitely," Josie said. "But it's all about timing, too. I don't think she was quite ready for a great job and a great guy before the Intervention."

Delaney returned, Josie's drink in hand. She set the glass on the table and Summer pinned Josie with The Look.

"All right, sister," she said. "You've got your refill. What's going on in that pretty head of yours?"

Josie thought of her secret. She thought of Delaney, still in that new-relationship dream state with Jake Rhoades. She thought of Summer, madly in love with her husband Derek, expecting their fifth child. How could they possibly understand?

"Okay. I'll spill," she said.

Instead of telling the truth, she decided, she would tell *a* truth. It wasn't like she was lying. She was simply keeping a secret. Even as these thoughts rushed through her mind, she chastised herself for finding a loophole. Summer and Delaney had been her best friends for more than twenty years. Since junior high, when they dubbed themselves The Milkshake Sisters. They were thirty-four now. Adults. Surely she could tell them. Again, she sighed. She'd promised to keep a secret, and she always kept her promises.

"It's Paul," she said.

The girls looked at her sympathetically. Summer, who had just popped another green olive into her mouth (she always ate them during pregnancy), nodded. Delaney's forehead crinkled in concern.

"I think we're on the brink of divorce."

It was almost comical the way both of her friends' mouths dropped open in surprise. They glanced quickly at each other, and then looked at Josie again.

"What?" Delaney said. "You're kidding, right?"

"I'm sure you can work it out," Summer said. "Right? I mean, can't you? What's going on?"

"Wait," Delaney said. "How did it get to this point without us knowing about it?"

"Well, admittedly, we've both been a bit distracted," Summer said to Delaney. "You with Jake and the new job, and me with the band and the pregnancy. I feel terrible about this, Josie. Really bad. What's going on?"

"The truth is," Josie began, pausing when she felt the unfamiliar pressure of tears in her throat and behind her eyes. "Things are really, really bad."

When neither Summer nor Delaney spoke, Josie continued. "I never see Paul anymore. I mean, hardly ever. We're never home at the same time, and when we are, he's distracted. Not just watching-basketball-and-eating-chips distracted, but, like, thinking about drug deals and drug dealers and answering calls from informants distracted. And he's so angry. He's angry all the time."

Summer put her hand on Josie's arm again. The gesture was supposed to be soothing, but Josie didn't miss the quick look Summer and Delaney exchanged—again.

Delaney licked her lips in that way she always did when she was nervous. She inhaled quickly, as if she wanted to say something, and then she pressed her lips together as if to hold the words in.

"Spill it, Collins," Josie said, knowing Delaney would cave if she put her on the spot.

Summer's hand slinked back to its own side of the table. She entwined it with the other hand. Josie had no idea what she was looking at. A spot on the table, maybe? A water droplet on her napkin?

"Well?" Josie said to Delaney.

"It's just that, well, you know, Josie, you've been kind of, um, a bit, you know … a little help, here, Summer?"

Summer's eyes met Josie's. "I'll give it to you straight, my sister. You've been pretty angry lately, too."

Well, that was definitely a truth.

Thursday night Happy Hour with Summer and Delaney ended just moments later. Summer's husband called to say one of the kids had stuck a pencil eraser up his nose and couldn't get it out, so the girls quickly packed up their purses.

"This will all turn out fine," Summer whispered to Josie as she wrapped her in a tight hug. Then, still gripping Josie's shoulders, she looked into her eyes with a thoughtful expression. "Hey, I have an idea. Why don't you try really laying on the romance? I mean, how long has it been since you and Paul had sex?"

How long *had* it been?

"I honestly couldn't say," Josie said.

"Well, if you couldn't say, then that means it's been way too long. Go home and set the scene. When Paul comes home, ravish him like he's never been ravished before. It'll be fun. And sex always relieves the tension. Opens the doorway for conversation."

"Now we know the secret to Summer's ever-growing family," Delaney said.

Summer pressed a hand to her belly. "True. But everything I just said is true, too. Try it. Gotta go. As you know, Luke is my difficult child, and you know he won't let his dad get near him with a pair of tweezers."

It was good advice, Josie thought as she perused the meat section at the grocery store a few minutes later. She'd feed Paul a fat steak, a baked potato, and some salad. Add a little wine and music, maybe some candles.

Did they even own candles? Josie checked her watch. It was five-thirty. Paul had gone into work at nine that morning, which meant she had about an hour and a half until he got home. Presumably. Unless something came up, which seemed to happen a lot lately.

"Stay positive," she said to a potato she picked up to examine. "Negativity kills a relationship."

At least, that's what all the "experts" said. If you considered authors of online articles experts. Yes, she'd done a quick Google search in the store parking lot: *how to fix my marriage.*

Was she negative? As she pushed her cart through the store, she thought about some of her recent interactions with Paul. Shame crept in like a spider under a closed door, fast-moving and sneaky.

Just last week, she came home complaining about how the new teachers at her school would be starting at a higher salary than she had during her first year of teaching. The next day when Paul got home, she complained about the terrible driver she got stuck behind on her way to the district office. To her credit, the middle-aged, pot-bellied, mustached woman driver couldn't use a turn signal or go even remotely close to the speed limit to save her life. The next day (the very next day, she thought, wanting to kick herself) she spent some time—a long time, really—complaining about how the school parking lot was closed for resurfacing.

"It's so inconvenient," she said as he took off his gun holster and the bullet proof vest he wore under his T-shirt. "It's like they expect us be sherpas or something! We have to park on the street and carry our supplies all the way to the building!"

Never mind that parking on the street meant walking only a few extra yards.

Yikes. No wonder he wants to work all the time.

Now she was on a roll. She searched the internet for *relationship mistakes*, and found that she was committing quite a few of the "7 Most Common Relationship Mistakes" and "12 Mistakes Couples Make Without Realizing It": taking her partner for granted, complaining about her partner, being passive-aggressive (how many times was she going to "forget" to pick his uniform shirts up from the dry cleaners?), believing her partner should be able to read her mind.

She found some scented candles in the grocery store's home section. Another quick search on her phone turned up an article about the seven best scents to enhance your love life. The top two were cinnamon and vanilla, so she set one of each in her cart.

At home in her kitchen, she laid her purchases out on the counter. To give the candles time to work their magic, she set them on the dining room table and lit them. She popped the potatoes in the oven and went to work on the steaks, rubbing them with olive oil and steak seasoning so they could marinate. As she began chopping vegetables for the salad, inspiration hit and she dug out a love songs CD someone had given to her and Paul for their wedding.

Although she still had another forty minutes before Paul came home, she turned the music on as she finished chopping, just to get her in the mood. By six-thirty, everything was ready, and she figured she had time to take a quick shower.

It had been so long since she prepared for romance that she was giddy with excitement as she soaped up, shaved, and scrubbed her skin to unprecedented levels of softness.

She even found some vanilla-scented lotion in the cabinet under the sink, and rubbed it on, letting the anticipation build. Why had she let so much time pass since they were last intimate? This was going to be fun. And Summer was right. It would give them time to talk when they both had their guards down.

All of her sexy underwear was crammed into the farthest recesses of her underwear drawer. She dug out Paul's favorite pair, lacy white boy shorts he said showed off her perfectly shaped rear end, and slipped into them before pulling on a silky nightgown. The sexual energy could build over dinner, she thought with a little shiver.

She heard it while she was looking in the mirror, smoothing her hair: the sound of a text message coming in.

Paul: *I'll be late. Just got a tip on a meth dealer coming back from Phoenix with at least an ounce. We're hoping to knock him off at Sunset Point. I'll call you when we're done.*

For the second time that day, Josie felt like crying.

When she responded to Paul's text, she left out all the things she wanted to include—a sad-face emoji, something about her plans for the evening, a giant thumbs-down—and she typed: *Okay.*

Then she sent a text to Summer and Delaney: *No romance tonight. Paul is running late. Won't be home for several hours.*

She turned off her phone and changed out of her lacy white boy shorts and silky nightie into granny panties and an old t-shirt Paul brought home from one of his innumerable trainings. Then she downed half a bottle of wine while listening to the romantic music and went to bed, the steaks still marinating on the counter.

Laying there, blinking into the dark, Josie Garcia reminded herself that she didn't believe in romance. For a few minutes, she tried staring at the ceiling, but it spun so quickly she had to shut her eyes. This proved equally dangerous. A kaleidoscope of color swirled behind her eyelids.

Her mother, a stern Mexican immigrant who taught herself English and put herself through accounting school, hammered practicality into Josie's head from the time she was an infant clutching a homemade rattle in her fist. Yes, even her first toy, a rattle made from a baby food jar filled with dried pinto beans, had been practical.

"Don't look for a man who speaks in poetry and brings you flowers, *mija*," Carla Garcia said. "Look for a man who gives you a good life. Stability. Poetry and roses don't put tortillas on the table. They're false currency."

But Josie's mother was gone. She'd died seven years ago of a ruptured brain aneurysm.

Almost in a dreamlike state, Josie let her mind rewind to that moment three days after Mama died … the moment when she met Scott Smith and the universe put her mother's theory to the test.

It made absolutely no sense that Scott's lyrical language and haphazard bouquets of wildflowers had her quivering in her three-inch heels. But they did.

Josie, an orphan at age twenty-seven, sat on a bench downtown, the scorching summer sun making her scalp prickle with sweat.

Standing steadfast in the denial stage, Josie expected her mother to walk around the corner any minute, making *tsk* noises about Josie wearing shorts to work.

"It's summer, Mama," Josie whispered. "I'm just setting up my classroom."

Tears made the scene before her shimmer. The glittering white courthouse, the leaves dancing in the breeze.

It seemed so unfair. Mama dropped dead at her kitchen counter. Why her? She was a good woman. A hard-working woman who raised two children into productive adults, one a teacher and the other a soldier.

She didn't even get to see her grandchildren (not that they were imminent or anything).

There must be some mistake, Josie found herself thinking over and over again when it first happened. Some other woman must have been standing in Mama's kitchen, helping her make tamales or brewing a pot of coffee. Some other woman wearing her ruffled apron, turquoise like the blue bowl she'd brought from Mexico to sit on the kitchen table, full of oranges.

Josie found her lying on the floor, hands covered in masa and a streak of it on her cheek. Her hair was wound in a tight, low bun. Her eyes were open, but Josie could tell she was already gone. A sense of calm came over Josie then, and she remembered the ABCs from her CPR class. Airway, breathing, circulation. Mama didn't seem to have anything in her mouth, and she wasn't breathing. Her skin was cold. She didn't have a pulse.

Still, Josie refused to believe this was permanent. Even when the ambulance came screeching into the driveway, when the paramedics loaded her mother onto a stretcher after performing CPR, or when they told her there was nothing she could have done.

Mama had to be coming back. This was all a terrible nightmare.

She kept picturing herself sitting at her mom's table drinking coffee, tying strings around the tamales after Mama formed them with her strong hands. Three days had passed, and Josie found herself sitting on that bench at the courthouse square, reliving the scene yet again. They were wrong. Her mother wasn't dead. It wasn't true that a blood vessel in Carla Garcia's brain had weakened, widened and then ruptured. Carla Garcia had veins of steel. She was tough.

Summer, of course, helped Josie make the funeral preparations. She put an announcement in the newspaper, chose a dress for Mama to wear and somehow found turquoise flowers for the church. Delaney would drive up from vet school this evening and spend the night with Josie in her childhood bedroom.

All Josie knew how to do to bury the hurt was to work. So she'd holed up in her classroom, scrubbing desks, vacuuming the carpet and color-coding folders for her students. Until today … the day before her mother's funeral. She'd decided to take a break, and walked down to the square in hopes of finding some solace.

Heat waves radiated off the roads in downtown Juniper. The summer sun hung high above the carpet-like lawn. Josie, wearing khaki cargo shorts and a salmon-colored tank top that perfectly matched her pedicured toenails, treated herself to a huge lemonade from the stand on the corner.

That moment, the moment she sought refuge from the worst hurt she'd ever experienced, was the moment Scott Smith walked into her life.

Maybe that's why the romance worked.

Juniper's signature fountain bubbled nearby, and a group of kids sat on the low concrete bench surrounding it, their bare feet in the water. Josie smiled as a little boy splashed his older sister, who responded by filling her empty soda cup and dumping it on his head.

Her own little brother would have done that very thing, if they'd ever gotten to sit around the fountain on a summer day. The truth was, neither of them had had any free time on a summer day since they were old enough to work the fields with Mama. Sometimes, when no one was looking, Juan grabbed a handful of fat red strawberries and shoved them into her mouth. She'd do the same to him, and they'd giggle like fiends trying to swallow the sweet fruit and wipe its traces from their cheeks before their mother caught them and punished them for being silly.

"People watching, huh?" Josie jumped at the voice, which was deep and smooth like a vat of melted chocolate. She loved chocolate.

She looked up, and had to shade her eyes to look at this tall, lanky stranger who interrupted her impromptu break from grief disguised as work. When they made eye contact, the man stepped back.

"Wow," he said. "You're even more beautiful up close."

Despite the unexpected fluttery reaction in her stomach, and the involuntary flush that rose to her face, Josie's internal voice—which was actually her mother's voice—whispered, *Poetry. False currency.*

She smiled coolly. "I was just leaving, actually."

"And your voice," he said, apparently unaffected by what she thought was a clear shutdown. "It's like honey."

When she quirked an eyebrow at him, he lifted his hands in surrender and said, "No, seriously. It is."

"I've got to get back to work," she said. She stood up.

"That's too bad. I'm the new guy in town. I was hoping I'd come down here and meet a friendly face, get some recommendations, on, you know, restaurants, grocery stores, whatever. I never imagined I'd find such a beautiful friendly face."

Josie couldn't help it. She laughed. For the first time since her mama died, the tension her throat and her chest relaxed. "You're good. But I'm afraid you've got me pegged incorrectly. I'm not that friendly."

"Even so," he said, his eyes twinkling with humor and a genuine interest. "Where's the best place to grab lunch around here?"

"The Sand Witch is pretty good," she said, pointing across the street at the deli. "And if you want Chinese, the Red Lantern is just a couple of blocks from here. They have a decent lunch special. Their cashew chicken is to die for."

"If you had to choose one, right now, which would it be?" the stranger asked.

Josie sipped her lemonade and considered, relieved to think about something other than her loneliness and the huge empty spot her mother had left in her life.

"The Sand Witch," she decided after a moment. She took a couple of steps away from him, in the direction of her school, but the stranger didn't take the hint.

Instead, he looked her in the eyes and said, "You know what would really make my day? Lunch with a lovely lady on this lovely afternoon. My treat. Consider it my thanks for your advice."

"I've got to get back to work," she said again. "I'm setting up my classroom."

He stooped and picked a lone yellow dandelion out of the lawn. He held it out to her, and she noticed his eyes were the color of bourbon when sunlight shone through the glass. "Please. Help a guy out. Don't make me eat lunch alone on my first day in a new town."

First poetry, and now a flower. Hear the warning bells, Garcia? Ding ding ding. It wasn't even warning bells, actually. It was a buzzer, the kind they put on emergency exits. For some reason, though—probably because she needed something warm and melty and happy to sink into —she couldn't resist. That's how they ended up eating lunch together that first day ... and spending incalculable time together throughout the remainder of the summer despite the fact they both knew it could never work.

And wasn't that the story of their relationship? She couldn't resist him.

Is it bad juju to daydream about your ex-boyfriend while laying in the bed you share with your husband? Does it still count as daydreaming if you're half-asleep and completely drunk?

Hours had passed since Josie crawled between the sheets in her granny panties.

She'd spent a good deal of that time thinking about the great news she'd received recently: she'd been awarded a huge grant to open a new community center in town.

A few months ago, the idea of opening the center had dawned on her as she watched one of her students, Joshua Morton, struggle in school. He rarely did his homework and often came to school hungry. His parents both worked long hours, and, Josie suspected, held more than one job. So Joshua and his brother were on their own, most of the time. They weren't the only ones. As she talked with other teachers at Juniper Elementary School, she realized a significant number of kids were alone before and after school, and most of them were struggling.

The community center would be a safe, structured place for kids like Joshua to go, to get help with their homework, to hang out with friends, to eat a little something. As soon as the concept developed in her mind, she applied for the grant. She'd been almost positive she wouldn't get it.

But when the envelope came in the mail—a big manila envelope, not one of the small, white ones that always meant rejection—she cried actual tears of joy as she pictured Joshua at the center, fed and happy and getting his homework done. She cried even harder when she pictured him at school, confident and rested. Then, if it were possible, she cried even harder when she imagined the sign that would memorialize her mom: *The Carla M. Garcia Community Center.*

Unfortunately, in addition to thinking about the community center, Josie had also spent hours letting her mind wander to romance. Not romance with her husband of six years, but romance with the stranger from the downtown square, the slightly nerdy guy looking for a restaurant tour.

The conversation flowed so easily during that first meal, that impromptu trip to The Sand Witch.

"Now, because you're a teacher on summer break, I absolutely forbid you from talking about work while we're at lunch," he said as they approached the deli.

Josie wrinkled her nose.

"Then what on earth will we talk about?"

He opened the door for her, and she felt chills where she imagined he touched her lower back to guide her in.

Maybe it's the poetry. You're losing it, Garcia.

In reality, she knew she had fallen into this guy because it gave her the chance to step out of her current situation, to stop picturing the way Mama looked when she died and to stop wishing she'd hop back up and start making tamales again.

After ordering, they sat at a corner table with a window overlooking the square.

"So, let's pretend we're total strangers," he said.

She laughed. "And how shall we pretend we met?"

"Let's pretend I picked you up downtown. At random. Under the guise of being new in town and needing a tour guide. But in reality, wanting a delicious-looking woman with whom to eat lunch."

"And to think I don't even know the name of this man who is lavishing me with compliments."

Blake, the deli's owner, called out their order, and the stranger retrieved the sandwiches from the counter. Josie admired his long legs and his broad shoulders. She admired the way his fingers curved around the plastic baskets their sandwiches were served in.

She knew, at that very moment, that she'd sleep with him. And more importantly, she knew she'd like it.

"Josie," she said, extending her hand when he sat back down at the table.

He chuckled. "Scott."

They shook hands. Suddenly ravenous after not having eaten for three straight days, Josie tore into her turkey and avocado.

"Why don't you play hooky and show me around for the rest of the day?" he said as they finished up. "It's summer. Surely you have a few weeks more to finish up whatever classroom stuff you're working on today."

She needed to prepare for the funeral. She needed to finish hanging the Star Student display and setting up the reading corner. She needed to make up her old trundle bed for Delaney to sleep in.

She needed to mourn her mother.

When she didn't respond right away, he barked out a laugh. "I can practically see the internal debate! You must be a model employee. But come on. Live a little."

"This goes against my grain," she said. "I am a very conscientious person. I have a daily to-do list and I have a compulsion for checking off every item on it."

She never returned to her classroom that day. Instead, grateful for the distraction, she gave Scott a locals' walking tour of downtown Juniper. They went to the famous western history museum, the library with its exquisite sculpture garden, and the little-known bar where Josie had had her first drink with Summer and Delaney.

Probably because she had a specific mission, Josie found herself feeling chatty, and even caught herself saying to Scott, "I'm not normally like this. Trust me. You bring out the friendly in me."

They were sitting on the little brick wall that bordered the rose garden inside the museum, and Josie fanned herself with the brochure she picked up at the entrance.

"I don't believe it for a minute," he said. "You're the nicest person I've met so far in Juniper."

"Didn't you say I was the only person you've met so far in Juniper?"

When they made eye contact, she could practically see little cartoon hearts floating around in the air between them. She still remembered that moment as magical, even now, years later.

The magic lasted about a split second before her inner voice kicked in.

What are you doing? He just likes your curves, that's all. He doesn't even know you.

But Scott was different. He was different from the boys in junior high who faked liking her just so they could get their hands on her breasts or cup her ass while passing her in the hall.

Scott didn't know her, but he wanted to. She could tell. And she liked it. At the time, she relished his attention, bathed in it like a springtime blade of grass bathes in the warm sunlight.

And maybe that was the reason she didn't notice until much later that he had not revealed a single fact about himself over the course of that first afternoon they spent together, or that evening when they made love (actually, scratch that: "when they had frantic sexual intercourse" was a more accurate description) against the side of her car, just steps from Juniper Elementary School.

She asked him questions, but he deflected them like a magician, training her attention on precisely what he wanted her to see, putting the spotlight back on her. Despite spending several hours with him that day, Josie had no idea what he did for a living, why he moved to Juniper, or even what kind of car he drove.

Scott was the first secret-keeper, and because he was a balm to her pain that summer, Josie fell so hard—*too* hard—for him, and became the second.

Keeping secrets is a hard habit to break.

When Scott eventually revealed his secret, Josie realized he was the Romeo to her Juliet. Tragic, lovestruck young people destined to be apart.

He knew from the outset they wouldn't be together. When she casually mentioned teaching at Juniper Elementary School, he should have walked away. But, he said, because he loved the slow curve of her smile, the quick chime of her laugh, he waited until she had fallen for him to tell her, ensuring they'd have at least some time together before school started and their respective career aspirations kept them apart. Suddenly, he said, every moment felt precious, like a diamond hundreds of years in the making, deep underground, only now twinkling in the sunlight.

They saw each other daily. For the first few days, Josie let Scott dictate the direction of their conversations. He steered the vehicle to whichever destinations he chose, never once pulling to a stop in any area of his own life.

Then, curiosity overcame her.

"Scott, you know almost everything about me," she said to him one night while they sat on her porch swing, licking ice cream cones. "But I don't know so much about you. I mean, you said you moved here for your job, but you've never mentioned what that job is. And you're never working."

"Well, I've only been here for a few days," he said, his tone indicating a flicker of offense.

She nodded and laid a hand on his leg. "I know. I was just wondering, that's all. I'd really like to get to know you better."

He sighed then, a big sigh that made his chest rise and fall, and moved the swing so it creaked on its chains. "Josie, there's something I need to tell you."

Uh oh. He's married, with kids. He's a spy and he's not allowed to date people. He's an assassin and I'm his next target. Mission: Kill Josie Garcia.

"I'm the new principal at Juniper Elementary School."

She sat there so long without responding that the ice cream started to melt, running down over her thumb. After a long moment during which the only sound was that of crickets chirping, she cleared her throat. The ice cream dripped onto her leg.

"Wait. So you're, like, my boss?"

He shrugged, nodding. "Well, yeah."

Their relationship could never work. She couldn't date her boss. Imagine what it would do to her reputation. Imagine how it could ruin her career.

Now, she nodded too.

"This can't work," they both said at the same time. Then they laughed.

It was a split-second, knee-jerk decision, and she knew it was the right one. They agreed to date, to enjoy each other's company, for the rest of summer, and not for a moment beyond that.

Chapter Two

The final night of summer break, Scott insisted the two of them do something fun, something, he said, "where we won't even have a chance to notice how sad we are."

That was Scott, always running away from serious topics, always hiding from feelings any deeper than a dirty puddle in the parking lot.

So they went to Orbit Golf. Josie hated that place. She'd gone there junior year on her first-ever date with Alejo Gomez, whom she'd pined after for months. He was the perfect gentleman until they came across some of his friends. It was Hole Twelve, and she was just getting ready to take her first shot. She tossed her hair over her shoulder, hoping Alejo would find the move sexy. Just as she swung her club, she heard the cat calls and teenage snickers. Alejo, embarrassed, insisted very loudly that she meant nothing to him, while her face burned with embarrassment. He told his friends she'd begged him to take her golfing as soon as she found out he got a new car. "Just like a woman," he sneered. His friends laughed. She missed the shot. They finished the golf course and never spoke again.

The grown-up Josie could never share this story with Scott, though. Even now, it made her feel vulnerable, and she was already feeling vulnerable enough knowing tonight was the last night they'd spend together. So she pasted on a smile and went to Orbit Golf to lay their relationship to rest among fluorescent lighting and glow-in-the-dark paintings of misshapen aliens.

Of course, they went back to her place afterwards.

That night and every night thereafter for a few weeks, she cried herself to sleep.

She always wondered, what if? What if they had met under different circumstances? What if one of them worked at a different school? What if she wasn't a teacher?

The answers didn't matter. Josie Garcia and Scott Smith were destined for tragedy.

Once the school year started, they split up. But there was something so painfully satisfying about pining for each other, sneaking kisses in the hallway, casting long looks across the table during staff meetings.

When she and Paul made their relationship official about a month later, though, she told Scott it was over. Really over.

Paul Comstock was exactly the opposite of Scott, and maybe that's why she fell for him so quickly.

They met the second week of that same school year, when she saw him in the classroom next door. He was talking to the second-grade teacher, Susie Lockhart, and Josie snapped a mental photo. Artists dreamed of profiles like Paul's: all clean lines and perfect angles.

He stood with his thumbs hooked into his gun belt and his head cocked a tiny bit to one side as he listened to Susie's questions.

The moment he smiled, Josie knew she was hooked (although she should have known she was hooked the moment she realized she was totally and completely frozen in place, leaning against the doorjamb, her mouth hanging open as she watched him speak).

He had deep, striking crows feet at the corners of his eyes, and rather than making him look old, they made him look fun and kind and down-right sexy.

She imagined him directing that smile at her, then wrapping those big, sculpted superhero arms around her waist right here in the doorway of Susie Lockhart's classroom.

When he did, she would put her arms up around his neck and pull his face to hers. What would he smell like?

Probably leather and cologne, soap and coffee. Don't all cops drink coffee?

Susie Lockhart cleared her throat, and Josie jumped, snapping her mouth closed.

"Did you hear me, Josie? This is Paul Comstock, with the Juniper Police Department. He's coming in next week to give a presentation to my kids."

"Paul," Josie said. "Paul Comstock. Nice to meet you. I'm Josie Garcia."

He took her hand to shake it and looked directly at her. So directly, it almost made her uncomfortable. It should have made her uncomfortable.

Only, it didn't. It made her all fizzy inside, like champagne. Little bubbles kept rising to the surface, bursting gently on her skin and making her shiver.

"Nice to meet you, Josie," Paul said. "Very nice to meet you."

No poetry, just straight talk.

He would later admit he experienced that same fizzy feeling during the handshake and had been rendered idiotic for the rest of the day, misplacing his handcuffs and leaving his gun in the bathroom stall at the police station.

The moment was fleeting though, because Paul's phone vibrated on his belt and he answered it right away in a tone so serious Josie smiled.

Susie wiggled her eyebrows up and down behind his back as he walked into the hallway. Josie shook her head and took that opportunity to slink back to her own classroom, her reason for visiting Susie's forgotten.

The following Thursday, Delaney came up from vet school for a weekend visit. The three girls went to Rowdy's for Happy Hour, and Josie confessed: "I'm not usually one to go for men in uniform, but wowza! I mean, he was hot."

"So did you get his number?" Summer asked.

"I'm working on it. You know, police officers' phone numbers are top secret. Classified."

"Delaney," Summer said. "Look at the way she's grinning right now. When's the last time you saw Josie grin like that? I sense something special about this one."

Delaney nodded sagely. "Yes," she said. "I haven't seen her smile like that since freshman year of high school when Davey Richmond taught her what second base is."

"I'm scandalized," Josie said, but deep down, she knew it was true. She didn't often let guys get to her. Well, not usually.

Scott had gotten to her. And look what had happened there.

"Whoa, that was weird," Summer said. "The grin disappeared. What's up with that?"

"Oh, nothing," Josie said brightly. "Just need a refill, that's all."

The conversation moved on then, to Delaney's final exams at vet school and how Summer's daughter Sarah had started preschool. Even as they laughed at Sarah's insistence on wearing all purple - socks, pants, shirt, a sweater, and boots, Josie felt a tiny bit … nostalgic, maybe? Sad? She couldn't quite put her finger on it.

And worse, she couldn't hash it out with the girls. Because she'd been in the middle of grieving for her mother, Josie hadn't mentioned

Scott when they first met. Then he'd sworn her to secrecy, so solemnly she'd joked they should take a blood oath.

"I can't have anyone knowing we had a relationship," he said to her one night as he stood in her doorway on the way out. "You understand. It just wouldn't be … proper."

Of course, Josie nodded. She understood. She planned to ascend the career ladder, too, and didn't want scandal coloring her resume.

So instead of telling the girls about Scott, she told them she was going through the isolation phase of grief and needed time alone. In reality, she spent every spare moment with Scott. She told the girls she was getting ready for the school year. In reality, she and Scott were having steamy sex on her classroom floor.

It was easy to fool them. Summer was about to give birth to Nate and Delaney was finishing up school. The secret went completely undetected, and it stood sacred, even until present day.

Josie's relationship with Paul erased her feelings for Scott with the efficiency of a chalkboard eraser. The solid lines disappeared, but that fine white dust, made of memories and possibility, always remained.

The following summer, Josie married Paul in a wedding that blended romance and practicality. She carried a bouquet of orchids (romance) and wore her mother's wedding gown (practicality). She and the girls transformed one of Juniper's lakeside parks into a wonderland by draping twinkling lights in the trees and setting potted trees and flowers on almost every flat surface.

As the Comstock-Garcias—she chose to keep her mother's last name —walked back down the aisle after the minister pronounced them husband and wife, Josie felt like she was flying, soaring with happiness. She looked into Paul's eyes and thought nothing could ever take him away from her.

Back in real time, Josie's eyes snapped open when the front door finally clicked open. It was twelve minutes after two in the morning. Although she and Paul both knew she only half-slept when he worked late, Paul tried to be quiet. She could picture him now, pulling his gun and holster out of his waistband and putting them in the safe in the coat closet. He would take off his shoes next, stepping on the heel of one with the toe of the other. He'd set them next to the front door and then go to the kitchen to make himself a drink.

Whiskey on the rocks.

The sounds seemed amplified in the house: the cabinet closing, Paul setting the glass on the counter, opening and closing the freezer and then dropping ice cubes into the glass. *Clink, clink.* Next he'd drop one cube.

It clattered to the floor. "Shit," he muttered. Josie knew he was bending down to pick it up, and then she heard it land in the sink. The liquor cabinet closed next, and she heard the whiskey glugging out of the bottle.

Now he would sit on the couch, feet on the coffee table, and wind down.

And she would pounce. Not in the way she hoped to pounce earlier. She felt her body sway, side to side, as she walked through the bedroom to the living room.

He didn't hear her behind him. With a mix of nostalgia and irritation, she thought about the conversations they had when he couldn't find a specific shoe, or the scissors, or the sharp cheddar.

"The man can find a gram of meth behind the headlight of a nineteen-eighty-five Mustang," she'd say, "but he can't find a pound of sharp cheddar in the fridge."

"I'm off-duty," he'd say, putting both hands up in a "what-can-I-say" gesture.

Now, he sat on the couch exactly as she pictured, reading something on his tablet. As she always did (it had become automatic after all this time), she admired the way the muscles in his shoulders bulged just enough as to be visible underneath his shirt.

"Hi, Paul," she said.

He jumped and the tablet tumbled off his lap and onto the floor. She noticed he managed to keep his drink from spilling.

"Geez, Josie! You startled me! Don't do that!"

"Since when is it a crime to say hello to my husband when he gets home from work?"

He picked up his tablet and set it on the table, then turned around to face her. "I thought you'd be sleeping."

"I was."

"Why is there steak on the counter? Did you forget to put it away? It'll go bad."

She didn't answer, and he said, "I put it in the fridge for you."

"For me? You put it in the fridge for me? Why, thank you, Paul. Thank you so much."

Confusion made his eyebrows draw together and his mouth form a tiny o.

"What are you talking about?" he said.

"God, I feel so stupid!" she said. Then, Josie Garcia did something she had vowed after Scott that she would never do again. She cried. Over a guy. This guy happened to be her husband, but still. The sensation was so unfamiliar she didn't realize it was happening until she felt the moisture on her face.

"Are you crying?"

Again, she refrained from answering.

"Josie. What's wrong?"

He stood up and came around the back of the couch. He lifted his arms as if he wanted to hug her, but he dropped them back at his sides like he was afraid she'd explode at his touch. A small laugh made its way to the surface. Paul had entered full panic mode.

"I feel so stupid," she repeated.

"Is it the steaks? It's okay, I've left meat out before. They'll be fine."

"It's not the steaks," she snapped. "Actually, it kind of *is* the steaks. I've been feeling so, I don't know, so disconnected from you lately, and I thought I'd make a nice meal and, you know, seduce you, and have a romantic evening. I went to the store, bought some steaks. I even looked up which scents are best for romance and bought candles. Candles! I put on those lacy undies you like. I shaved my legs!"

"It does smell really good in here," Paul said. In nervous gesture, he rubbed his nose with the knuckle of his pointer finger.

"But you didn't eat the steak."

"I can eat it now," he said, shrugging.

He was trying, she'd give him that. He didn't like to see her cry.

"You're missing the point," she said.

"Oh. Ah… what is the point?"

"I just told you! Weren't you listening?"

"I *was* listening! You wanted me to eat the steak," he said.

Okay, maybe he wasn't trying as hard as she thought.

"You shaved your legs?" he tried.

Josie sighed, and pressed her fists against her eyelids. When she looked at him again, she saw realization dawning on his face. If it had happened at any other moment, she would have found the transformation comical. His shoulders drooped and he looked down at the floor.

"Now do you get it?"

"You planned a romantic evening, and I ruined it," he said.

"Yes! Yes. Or, your job ruined it. What makes it so bad, to me, is that it's not the first time. Lately, you're barely home. Instead of spending your time with me, you spend it with tweakers and drug dealers. And you know what's really sad? I've come to expect the late nights, the never seeing you, the lack of sex because you're always too tired or too wired or whatever. I've come to expect it. It doesn't even surprise me anymore."

Paul shrugged. Not in a way that signified he didn't care, but in a way that signified he didn't know what to do or what to say. Josie waited.

"It's the nature of the job, Josie," he said. "And I didn't know you were feeling this way."

"That's the problem," she said. "Exactly. If you didn't realize I was feeling this way, and you think this situation is a given, then we have worse problems than I thought."

She spun around and stomped back into the bedroom. She shut the door quietly and leaned against it.

In her imagination, she heard a tongue clucking, and her mother's voice saying, "See, *mija*? You married for practicality and yet you want romance. Romance lets you down. He's a hard-working man, providing for you. Cut him some slack, eh?"

Josie knew she should cut him some slack. But she wanted romance, at least a little. And was there anything wrong with that?

ABOUT THE AUTHOR

Hilary Dartt loves great adventures, whether she's writing, reading, or living them. The author of nine women's fiction novels, Hilary lives in Arizona's high desert with her husband, their three children, her Weimaraner and running partner, Leia, a failed barn cat, and a flock of chickens. She loves camping, exploring in the Jeep, and dance parties with her kids. Learn more at www.hilarydartt.com